MW01273042

Galatians 3:28

TO ANNELIESE

from

Nelle Giesecke

From PRAGUE TO THE PROMISED LAND

A Jewish Family's Odyssey from Czechoslovakia to Israel

ULLA GIESECKE

WestBow
PRESS
A DIVISION OF THOMAS NELSON

Copyright © 2013 Ursula Giesecke.

Cover Image Credit: Serena C. Johnson

All rights reserved. No part of this book may be used or reproduced by any means,
graphic, electronic, or mechanical, including photocopying, recording, taping or by any
information storage retrieval system without the written permission of the publisher
except in the case of brief quotations embodied in critical articles and reviews.

Unless otherwise indicated, Bible quotations are taken from the Revised Standard Version
of the Bible. Copyright ©1946-1952 by Collins' Clear-Type Press, Publishers.

WestBow Press books may be ordered through booksellers or by contacting:

WestBow Press
A Division of Thomas Nelson
1663 Liberty Drive
Bloomington, IN 47403
www.westbowpress.com
1-(866) 928-1240

Because of the dynamic nature of the Internet, any web addresses or links contained in
this book may have changed since publication and may no longer be valid. The views
expressed in this work are solely those of the author and do not necessarily reflect the
views of the publisher, and the publisher hereby disclaims any responsibility for them.

Any people depicted in stock imagery provided by Thinkstock are models,
and such images are being used for illustrative purposes only.

Certain stock imagery © Thinkstock.

ISBN: 978-1-4908-0113-1 (sc)
ISBN: 978-1-4908-0112-4 (hc)
ISBN: 978-1-4908-0114-8 (e)

Library of Congress Control Number: 2013912416

Printed in the United States of America.

WestBow Press rev. date: 9/27/2013

DEDICATION

This book is considered a gift from God!

It is to shed light on Jewish persecution in Europe prior to WWII and the Holocaust. Based on historical facts, the story is fiction. Events that took place between 1933–1940 are highlighted within a fictional frame. *From Prague to the Promised Land* is dedicated to the many brilliant Jewish people who had to flee their homes and professions to avoid annihilation by Hitler's henchmen, leaving a dearth of creativity and excellence in their wake.

PROLOGUE

The year was 1933. The Bartok family lived on an estate surrounded by a park-like area, not far from Prague, the capital of Czechoslovakia. Prague is also known as the Golden City due to the many golden roofs on its old ornate buildings and the golden statues that line the thirteen bridges spanning the Vlatava River.

In order to find the Bartok estate, you have to join me on a drive out of Prague to the northeast. We drive through small villages on the outskirts of the big city before we turn into a country road that meanders through a copse of trees. A sign marked "BARTOK" points us onto a well-kept road to the right. This road is flanked by tall poplar trees. It leads to a massive cast-iron gate which is closed. A tall, black-mustached man emerges from a country cottage connected to the gate by a small door. He inquires about our business, then announces our coming by telephone to the big house. After he opens the gate, we continue on a curved road inside the park, passing a large poultry yard, a tidy orchard, and tall hedges that partially hide a horse stable.

When I saw the Bartok mansion the first time, I was impressed by its size and its architectural beauty. I had come from the railroad station with Francois, the chauffeur. He stopped by the side entrance, explaining that it was easier to unload the luggage there. Both Mr. Bartok and Madame were not at home. Bela the butler, Raika the head cook, and Tirza the maid welcomed me. He also told me that Mr. Bartok was not expected home until the following day as he was away on a business trip. Madame was still at rehearsal where she was preparing for her debut as "Aida" in the Verdi opera of the same name.

After being greeted by Bela, Raika, and Tirza, Francois led me through the spacious veranda which resembled a greenhouse. Hundreds of exotic plants seemed to have found a home here. Some were in bloom, others had vibrant foliage. Adjacent to this gardener's paradise was the music room. Here stood the grand piano. A harp with a golden frame was positioned in the corner. On shelves around the room violas and violins were displayed. I counted at least five. There were also cases that held flutes and recorders. Files for music sheets were arranged along one side of the lovely room. The shiny parquet floor was covered with rugs in the shape of instruments. These rugs were of a lustrous silken quality in a warm golden brown. I made a mental note to ask Cornelia, where she had found such unusual floor coverings.

"Who plays all these instruments?" I asked.

"Mostly Madame, but Mr. Bartok accompanies her on his fiddle, whenever he has an occasion," offered Bela. While continuing into the hall, he added, "I will lead you through the house, Sir. The staircase is being repaired."

Later, I saw the staircase in question; it was a wide, rambling affair leading from the foyer to the upper two stories. It was blocked by drop cloths and tools so we took a small elevator, hidden under its arch, and reached the bedroom floor where the Bartoks, their babies, and their guests spent the night. Bela explained that the top floor held the servants' quarters.

I followed Bela to a spacious room at the end of the upstairs hall. The view from its large windows was spectacular: There were mountain ranges in the hazy distance, the Vlatava River beyond a meadow, and the tree tops of Bartok park directly beneath. Bela, pointing to the distant ranges, offered, "Beyond these mountains lies Germany, our troublesome neighbor."

Placing my luggage on a decorative bench, Bela withdrew, saying, "Feel free to rest, Sir. It will be at least two hours before Madame returns. Refreshments are available in the kitchen. If you care to take a walk in the garden or visit the horses—Madame instructed me to tell you that everything is at your disposal. The children she wants to introduce to you herself. They are napping at this time."

I had come to admire the new babies which were about ten months old, according to my reckoning. Cornelia Kahn Bartok was a dear, long-time friend and colleague. We had worked together for several seasons at the National Theatre of Prague in the opera division. We both had been accepted into the ensemble straight from the music conservatory where we had studied together. We both had been gifted with exceptional voices. I sang basso roles; her voice ranged from lyrical to dramatic soprano.

Cornelia also was an exceptional violinist. In fact, the violin was her first love, she told me once. But one of our professors had discovered her voice, and suggested she pursue developing it, promising her greater success than being one of many violinists in an orchestra pit somewhere.

We had enjoyed a special friendship that later included her beloved Frederic, whom she had married late in her twenties. He was a successful banker who apparently had holdings in other countries as well. Although I accepted a contract with the Vienna State Opera a few years ago, we had remained good friends, and corresponded frequently.

A year ago Cornelia announced that she was pregnant. Later came the happy news that twins had been born in the lovely month of May. With her Hanukkah greeting came the invitation to visit the twins, Romi and Irmi, of whom she and Frederic were very proud. It had taken me a number of months to arrange it, but I was finally here. Theatre schedules made it hard to indulge in one's other interests and obligations.

I must have napped after stretching out on the comfortable bed. A knock on the door awakened me. "Are you decent, Raoul?" Cornelia spoke through the cracked door, and already she was entering the room, her expressive eyes quickly assessing the situation.

"You still like your naps, dear Raoul! Oh, it is so good to see you again." Then she ran into my arms with, "Thank you for coming!" She had hardly changed. Her dark curls bounced as she moved quickly, her black eyes sparkled, and her figure was as slim as I remembered it. Quite an asset, as most of the world's well-known sopranos are oversized. That she had given birth to twin daughters barely a year ago seemed hard to believe.

She kissed me on both cheeks, then pulling me to the door, she said, "Raoul, you just have to see our two darlings while they still sleep. Once they wake up they are a handful." Heading down the hall, she stopped in front of a large door decorated with fairyland figures. Very quietly she opened the door and beckoned me to follow her. We stepped into a large, airy room bathed in sunlight. Each wall was painted with yellow roses that climbed up to the ceiling where a sizeable sun spread his rays into all directions. A little too much yellow for me, but no doubt attractive for a child's room.

Cornelia led me to an oversized crib. It was almost double the usual size. In it rested a dark-haired baby, eyes closed in peaceful slumber. Rosy cheeks contrasted with the yellow sleeper she was encased in.

"This is Romingarde," whispered Cornelia, "but we call her Romi. We consider her the first-born, although she was only eight minutes earlier than Irmingarde." We waved a quick greeting to a pleasant-looking young woman who sat with her embroidery near the window.

"This is Bernie, Raoul. She watches over Romi when I am gone so much during the theatre season." To Bernie she whispered, "This is my friend Raoul. He sings opera too. He is here from Vienna to visit for a few days." Bernie responded with a lovely smile, and nodded in my direction.

Next we stepped across the hall, and entered the other baby's room. Here green vines seemed to grow along the walls, extending up to the ceiling. The curtains were green, and the baby's outfit was green as well. A small reddish-haired girl was lying diagonally in the large crib, guarded by a young woman who sat cribside doing a crossword puzzle.

"Nessie, meet a former colleague of mine from the National Theatre, Raoul, a famous basso who now delights audiences in Vienna," Cornelia introduced me. She had whispered; Nessie however, responded in a normal voice tone, "Madame, Irmi has actually napped long enough. I would rather wake her now, so she will not overstay her regular bedtime."

"Of course, Nessie, you know best. You have been with her all day."

"Madame, are you planning to take the babies out tonight after dinner?" Nessie questioned, to which Cornelia nodded emphatically. Noticing little Irmi stretching and turning, she quickly drew me out of the room, saying, "If I stay now, Irmi will make it very hard for Nessie to change and dress her. We had better go downstairs and have dinner. I know cook has a special treat today. She wants to impress you with gefilte fish, and lamb roast, which she serves with a tasty mint mold."

In the spacious dining-room the table was set for two. Elegant glassware sparkled on a sky-blue tablecloth. Matching gold-rimmed china and gold-plated cutlery set off the table. It was an appropriate setting in this lovely home. Our conversation touched on our present repertoires, the colleagues we worked with, and our future hopes. Overall, I had the impression that Cornelia was content and happy with her life. She mentioned her husband frequently and affectionately, giving me to understand that her marriage was a harmonious one.

We were barely finished when we heard giggles and a faint rumble in the foyer. Then we heard the voices of Bernie and Nessie, who were settling the children. Stepping into the foyer, two bright-eyed babies were sitting in two perambulators, one surrounded by yellow pillows, and the other, by green. Seeing their mama, their little bodies twisted and struggled, their arms reaching up. Cornelia first lifted up Irmi, then Romi, kissing and cuddling them both.

"I think Raoul and I can manage the prams so you can eat your supper and get a little rest," she assured the nursemaids.

"Raoul, do you mind?"

I assured her that meeting the twins was my main reason for coming. I held each one for a moment, as they looked me over with interested eyes. We headed down one of the wide garden paths, pushing the prams. As we approached the stables, both girls clapped their hands, and they showed great delight when a large grey gelding moved towards us. A smaller chestnut mare, apparently Cornelia's horse, nudged against him. Cornelia pulled a treat for the mare out of her pocket while she petted her neck.

She called Petrov, the stable master, who appeared carrying a pitchfork full of hay which he dropped into a nearby trough for the gelding. After she introduced us, he led out two ponies on a long line, bringing them close to the fence. The little girls tried to rise from their prams. They squealed and clapped their little baby hands in great excitement. Cornelia lifted up Irmi, and I held Romi, so that both girls could pat the ponies' heads.

"We are trying to familiarize the girls with the ponies, so that when they are able to ride them, they will not be fearful."

A little while later, we made our way to the poultry yard, where I met Pavel Restok. According to Cornelia, he was not only the gatekeeper and poultry stock manager, but also the man-of-all-trades when it came to repair needed on the large estate.

Pavel accompanied us a short distance to the geese, chicken, peacock, and rabbit pens, of which he had several. There were white angora rabbits, chinchillas, and grey and white bunnies. All a source of great delight to the little ones. Both girls seemed to know Pavel well, and stretched out their little arms to be held by him. Holding Irmi in his right arm and Romi in his left, he carried them around for some time. Then for us it was back to the buggies and on to the homeward stretch.

Back at the house Cornelia handed me the yellow-clad Romi, while she carried the green Irmi. Stepping into the music room, Cornelia brought a large playpen out of a closet, into which she placed Irmi. Taking Romi from me, she brought out a net of stuffed animals and let Romi push it into the other corner of the playpen. Both girls proceeded to pull the toy net back and forth. They soon found the opening, and squealed with joy when teddy bears, bunnies, and monkeys fell out.

Having them thus engaged, Cornelia opened the grand piano and improvised the well-known march from *Aida.*

"Raoul, are you up to it? Will you share a little music with me?" Then pointing her head to the shelves with the instruments, she added, "Just choose your own fiddle."

Finding a viola to my liking, I soon had it tuned, and like in the old days, when we used to meet with other musicians within our circle of friends, we played for sheer enjoyment. Cornelia leading on the grand piano, we jumped from opera to operetta, then to our favorite, Schubert Lieder, and so on. Sometimes only humming, other times singing with full voice. Oh, what fun! It wasn't long until Tirza the maid looked around the corner and asked whether the household staff might sit in the background and listen in. Permission granted, they trooped in and became our respectful audience "in the wings."

Knowing Cornelia's velvety soprano voice, I wondered whether she had further developed it, since I had last heard her. I suggested that I take over the grand, and accompany her. Did I have a surprise coming! Not only had she mastered most of the roles of a prima donna's repertoire, but she had also greatly improved in tone and range. It was a pleasure to hear her sing and interpret arias from *Madame Butterfly, La Boheme*, and *La Traviata*. Next, we joined in a few duets. Still the little ones played contentedly, and the staff enjoyed their private concert. Later, the babies became impatient and needed attention, which signaled bedtime for everyone.

CHAPTER ONE

THREATENING CLOUDS

The next day was Saturday, a rehearsal-free day for Cornelia. We enjoyed a leisurely breakfast, after which she invited me to join her on a drive to town to surprise Frederic. He was expected to return by express train later that morning.

"We might combine this with a short sightseeing trip to the National Theatre and the bank," she suggested. "You never know whether we might run into somebody who remembers you. Perhaps you will want to dress up a little more." I had come down to breakfast in shorts and sport shirt, prepared to spend time with the babies. When I mentioned that, she said, "Starting this evening, both nursemaids are off until Monday morning. That means I'll be the main caregiver. Even with Frederic's help, my time with you will not be undisturbed. So we had better use these few hours of free time to our best advantage."

Asking me to be ready in thirty minutes, she disappeared and I heard her moving about in the babies' rooms as I shaved and changed. Exactly thirty minutes later I caught the elevator down, arriving in the elegantly furnished foyer before Cornelia. This room was an especially fine feature of this home. A red and light green Persian rug covered most of the brightly polished hardwood floor. A massive, round mahogany table stood in the center, surrounded by substantial leather armchairs. Sunlight flooded the room through the open front door, reflecting rainbow patterns onto the wall, caused by the chandelier's glass pendulums hanging above the table.

A short while later, Cornelia joined me in the back of the fashionable limousine. Gesturing with small gloved hands, she entertained me with vivid accounts of her husband's frequent trips to foreign countries. I took note of her stylish attire. She wore a tight-fitting cordovan tweed skirt, with matching cape. A green silk blouse peeked out around the slender neck that housed the vocal chords of a human nightingale. Her black curls were held back by a reddish-brown headband.

Following our animated conversation, Francois turned, asking, "Madame, do you want us to await Mr. Bartok's arrival here?" We were surprised to be already in front of Prague's major railroad terminal.

"Why don't you two wait here while I inquire," Cornelia was out of the car before I knew it. She returned a few minutes later with the news, "The express from Paris is expected to be half an hour late. Why don't we walk over to the National Theatre, Raoul, and see what's going on there this morning?" and to Francois, "Would you mind waiting for us, Francois?"

On our short walk we reminisced. It was a lovely early spring day; the old linden trees along the boulevard ablaze with green buds.

"Do you remember the *Carmen* performance when Carel arrived late, and walked nonchalantly across the open stage, carrying his lunch bag?" Cornelia giggled, remembering an event that cost Carel a tidy sum and the teasing of his colleagues.

Then I reminded her how she herself had paid a stiff fine, for forgetting to take off her engagement ring in *Gypsy Baron*. "Oh yes," she confessed, "that was a budget-breaker for me. I truly learned my lesson." Now we could laugh about it together.

Reaching the stage entrance, Wladislav, the long-time security guard, greeted us with a friendly smile. He still remembered me, "Monsieur Raoul, welcome! I will never forget the rainy day when you left in tuxedo and top hat, in full make-up, to make the train to the Salzburg Festival."

"You met my need that night, Wladislav," I replied. He had supplied his worn raincoat and a big handkerchief, with which I could remove the make-up in the taxi on the way to the station.

"Those were the good old days," he said. "Now there is hardly a soul who would accept such a favor from me. Everyone has become rather arrogant."

"Is anybody rehearsing today?" Cornelia asked, and then added, "I would love to show Raoul around."

"No, they are all at the company picnic," Wladislav replied. "They probably wonder why Madame is not showing up."

"You know, I completely forgot," Cornelia admitted. "With the *Aida* rehearsals yesterday and Raoul's coming . . ."

"You most likely did the better thing," said Wladislav. "All they do is gossip, talk shop, and eat food too rich for them." Laying an arm around Cornelia's shoulder, he added jovially, "You can do without that, dear girl." To which Cornelia agreed, rewarding him with a friendly peck on the cheek. Afterward, we made our way back to the station, reaching it the same moment the international express roared in.

Frederic Bartok emerged from the first-class compartment looking exactly as I remembered him from his frequent visits to the theatre five years ago. He still had the same athletic built, dark handsome features, and strong eyebrows that met over the bridge of his nose. He wore an elegant grey suit, tailored in the latest fashion. He removed a soft hat and kissed his wife, then turned to me, shaking my hand.

His first words to me were, "We are so glad, Raoul, that you finally made time to visit us! May we hope that you can stay a while?" I told him that I only had a five-day break before having to sing *Falstaff* in Vienna.

"Oh, you theatre people," Frederic exclaimed, "You lead such structured lives, just like the military. One can never plan anything. You are more than bond slaves to the establishment."

With that he turned to his wife, smiling, who replied, "True right! True right!" I sensed that this was a bone of contention between them. But they played over it with charm.

We boarded the limousine, and Francois whisked us across Wenceslas Square to the large bank building which Frederic owned. Security guards welcomed us politely, opening a side door through which we reached Frederic's office by elevator. After locking his briefcase in a safe, he offered us a glass of port and invited us to sit down.

The view from this spacious office revealed a wide avenue that led away from Wenceslas Square. In the distance we could see the statue of St. Wenceslas and the National Museum. We sat around a marble topped table while superficial conversation flowed about Frederic's trip to Amsterdam, Brussels and Paris.

Folding his hands, and avoiding eye contact with us, he stated, "It is not an easy matter which I want to bring to your attention, but I consider it my duty to not let you remain in the dark about the ominous events that seem to be heading our way."

As we looked at him with somber expectation, Frederic continued, "This is truly bad news I bear." Then looking first to Cornelia, and next to me, he said, "You understand, of course, that in the country north of us, grim developments are taking place. Since the new chancellor Adolf Hitler came to power he usurps more and more control over Germany. He is not an ordinary politician. I believe he will be a dictator unparalleled in our time. Besides, he has surrounded himself with a clique of henchmen who are unscrupulous and brutal. He has already a clever propaganda machine in place that puts out slogans such as, 'A Job for every German!' 'A solid German Currency!' and 'Equal opportunities for all Citizens!' The truth behind the scenes is quite different."

After a short pause, he continued, "Plans are being made to establish so-called concentration camps, where enemies of the Reich will be held against their will. He wants to bring a pure Aryan state into existence. All persons of Jewish descent are considered enemies that must be eliminated. And that means us!" He had raised his voice, but realizing the futility of it, continued, "The heritage of Jewish culture, religion and property is threatened not only in Germany, but also in Poland, Austria, and in our own Czechoslovakia. He wants to reclaim the Rhineland and other western lands that were lost to Germany after WWI and the Treaty of Versailles."

"I had heard of these plans by the new chancellor of Germany, but I ignored them, believing them to be the pipe dreams of a little man who didn't have any political experience," I said.

"I have read his book, *Mein Kampf*, (My Struggle) in which he declares the goals of the National Socialist Workers Party. I am convinced," Frederic told us, "that this Hitler is a modern version of Haman."

"You mean the hater of Jews from the book of Esther (or Hadassah) in the Jewish scriptures?" Cornelia asked.

"Yes, my Dearest. And I am afraid this Austrian—for he was born in Linz—will be more successful than Haman, who was stopped by God because Mordecai, Esther, and their Jewish community fasted and prayed."

While we considered the enormity of what Frederic had just shared, he continued. "You may think, oh, we live in Czechoslovakia and Austria, nothing can touch us. But I warn you, I have heard of plans already on the books in Germany that call for annexation of both of our countries to the 'Great German Reich.'" Looking out onto Wenceslas Square, he added, "I foresee a mass exodus of Jews from our countries—or many Jewish lives will be lost."

"Where did you hear all this, my dear husband?" Cornelia asked. "It sounds like the proclamations of a doomsday prophet! If I didn't know and trust you, I would reject all this as unfounded rumors!"

"I wished that was the case," Frederic replied. "My sources are well informed and have nothing to gain by revealing the new dictator's agenda. The challenging truth remains that Germany, our northern neighbor, is changing into a highly-controlled police state, whose main goal is to destroy all Jewish people."

"But couldn't you see that other nations, for instance Great Britain and France, might object to hostilities against the Jewish people?" I asked.

"As of now, these nations try to shine up to the German Fuehrer by offers of appeasement. An outcome of people of peaceful coexistence seems to be not on that dictator's wish list," Frederic replied. "The fact is, we are all of Jewish heritage: Cornelia and I are full-blooded Jews, as are our twins, of course." Then looking at me, Frederic added, "I seem to remember, that you too, Raoul, are Jewish from your mother's side, am I right?"

I nodded in agreement. And Frederic continued, "We all would be on their lists to be eliminated. Two alternatives remain to us, going into exile, or produce faked genealogical information. The latter is against my beliefs!" And turning to me, Frederic added, "If I were you, I would stretch out my feelers. With a voice such as yours, you can probably find a position anywhere in an opera house in the western world. You may have to learn a new language, but that is not as bad as losing your life."

Shifting his attention to Cornelia, he said, "My Dearest, nothing of what I shared here can be discussed at home. Our household staff is dear, but I am not sure that they can be trusted with this information. That is why I chose to bring you here to inform you where no one can overhear us.

We left a little while later, riding in silence, and arrived at the Bartok estate in the early afternoon. It was hard for me to imagine that this country manor with its tasteful design and well-trained staff might only be temporary in the lives of my friends. Knowing Frederic, however, I had no doubt that this warning of danger was real. So I decided to keep my eyes open and pay more attention to the political scene. Working within the confines of the theatre, it is easy to disregard the development in the geo-political area.

We had a lovely weekend with the babies, as they determined very much what we adults could or could not do. I even took them on an extended outing in an oversized pram myself. This allowed Frederic and Cornelia to enjoy two hours of horseback-riding together. I admired their horsemanship, and how they handled their spirited steeds.

Our time together passed quickly. The evening before my departure, we joined together once more to make music. The household staff came again to listen. We, that is Cornelia and I, sang duets from the operas we knew, while Frederic accompanied us expertly on his violin. We concluded by playing a number of favorites as a trio: Cornelia on the harp, Frederic changing to the viola, and me accompanying both on the grand piano.

I asked her later, "Is the harp now your favorite instrument, Cornelia?"

She smiled and said, "All credit goes to my dear Frederic! He encouraged me to take lessons. Then, when he saw how I enjoyed the instrument, he bought me this one, and paid for more instruction. I could never have afforded such extravagance while I was single."

The next day Francois drove me back to the railroad terminal. This happened five years ago . . .

CHAPTER TWO

THUNDER FROM THE NORTH

When spring came to Czechoslovakia in 1938, there were not only hopes for warmer days and flowers after a severe winter, but also fears of what their neighbor in the north was about to undertake. In fact, it was in the lovely month of May, with the fruit trees all in bloom, that President Benes ordered partial mobilization of the military forces of their small country.

It was rumored that an attack from Germany could be expected. Only two months before, Austria to their south had ceased to be independent. German dictator Adolf Hitler had ordered his troops to occupy and annex Austria to the German Reich. Since then, Czechoslovakia lay between two arms of a vise. German greed for land and power controlled the giant arms of this vise. Although not known by most, a secret directive would be signed May 30 by Hitler that decreed the "smashing of Czechoslovakia" by military action as soon as October 1, 1938.

The Bartok family, meanwhile, was preparing a birthday party for the twins' sixth birthday. They were not aware of these evil intentions for their beloved country, although Frederic and Cornelia knew that changes were coming. In spite of this, they wanted to celebrate the twins' special day with their friends.

For this gala event, Romi and Irmi had each invited six of their young friends from the private school they attended. Mommy Cornelia, Bernie, and the twins had planned this special event for weeks. This birthday party was to be the best one ever! There were to be games outside, including pony rides. The food would be served inside.

When the sun rose on their birthday, Pavel was already on his way with a wheelbarrow loaded with white and blue flags. His goal was to attach flags of alternate colors to every other tree. By the time he returned, he had attached thirty flags to the stately poplars lining the avenue. No one would miss the way to the Bartok gate.

Right after breakfast, Romi and Irmi ran to the horse enclosure. Petrov stood ready to help with the currying of the ponies. "Do you know, Petrov, that we will even have a pony race when our guests are here?" asked Romi.

"And you know, Mommy even has a prize for the two who come in first and second, but she won't tell us what prizes they are," added Irmi.

"I suppose, she wants to keep you on your guessing toes," Petrov chuckled. "For what surprise is there, if you know the outcome beforehand?"

The twins were called to the house a little while later to help set the table under Bernie's supervision. Fancy party hats sat at each place, and colorful streamers hanging from the chandelier added to the festive setting.

"Can you bring each six candles from the box in the dining room?" asked Mommy. After handing them to Cornelia, both girls watched with great interest as their mother poked them carefully into the two triple-tiered cakes that Raika, the cook, had baked for them. There was one with a creamy chocolate frosting which was decorated with Romi's name and big "6" in pink on its top, and there was another one with a delicate pink frosting that had Irmi's name and a big "6" in chocolate frosting on its top.

Raika, who had seen the little girls grow up, knew all about their likes and dislikes.

"Raika, I am so glad you remembered how much I love chocolate," said Romi. "Can I taste the frosting by licking just a little at the side of this scrumptious cake?" as she approached with her small forefinger poised to swipe a lick. Instead, Raika beckoned her into the kitchen where she showed her the frosting bowl with lots of chocolate still clinging to its sides.

"Happy Birthday!" said Raika. Knowing Romi, she had kept the bowl especially for her." "Of course," she continued with raised voice, "as usual Irmi has no time to lick, so her bowl has to go a-wasting!"

But already Irmi came running, and putting her little arms around Raika's ample waist, she begged, "Oh, dear Raika, you can't forget me! Don't you remember that Dr. Sisla said I am supposed to eat extra much to keep up with Romi?" So both girls gleefully licked up the rich frosting, which clung to their noses, lips, and fingers.

Raika heaved a secret sigh of relief when Bernie came to pick up the twins for clean up. She and her two helpers needed all the kitchen space to prepare the dinner courses for the guests. Gravies had to be stirred for the roasted lamb and the baked beef. Casseroles containing vegetables and homemade noodles were being prepared. Tirza, special maid to Cornelia, had been recruited to make jellied fruit salads. She also washed and pared all the vegetables.

Meanwhile, upstairs Romi and Irmi were scrubbed and combed before donning their fancy party dresses. Romi's was red, and sported a white bow; Irmi's was white and had a red sash. Romi, her hair in a pageboy haircut, only needed a red hair band to complete her party outfit, but Irmi's hair, as usual, presented a problem. Crying, she continued to struggle as Bernie tried to untangle her unruly curls. Beloved Bernie became her enemy during these hair sessions. Bernie patiently continued until even the black curly top of little Irmi was rid of its tangles.

Bernie quietly observed the personalities of her two charges: Romi was easy-going and steadfast, whereas her sister was like quicksilver, with varied interests, always looking for new challenges. When help with chores was needed, either picking up eggs with Pavel, or currying ponies with Petrov, it was usually Romi who volunteered and did a responsible job. Irmi would rather practice her violin, or plink on the piano, of which she had already quite an amazing mastery for her age, self-taught.

Although born within a few minutes of each other, like many other fraternal twins, there was hardly any physical resemblance between them. Romi was at least two inches taller than dainty Irmi, who checked in six pounds lighter on the bathroom scale. But in spite of their differences and preferences, both girls got along famously and often spent many hours in happy play.

When Irmi's last curl was in place and her feet slipped into patent leather slippers, both girls skipped down the staircase to the foyer, where they found thirteen chairs lined up in preparation for a game of "musical chairs" later on. Stepping outside, on the expansive green lawn a barrel had been placed, around which a circle of garden chairs were grouped.

While they were wondering what this was all about, the first car arrived, bringing Benny and Bobby, their only twin friends. They were the sons of the Redgraves who were British citizens from London, England. These blond-haired, blue-eyed boys also attended the private school to which the girls travelled daily, chauffeured by Francois.

Mr. Redgrave was a business friend of Frederic's, who held several accounts in the Bartok bank. He had lived and worked in Prague for many years. In fact, both of his boys had been born in the Golden City.

"Will there be a chance to speak with you privately?" Mr. Redgrave asked, while shaking hands with Frederic.

Frederic nodded, suggesting, "After the children have a go at the games, there should be a chance, or we'll make it." Mr. Redgrave, not missing a beat, bent down to the girls and wished them a happy birthday as his sons each pressed a small package into Romi's and Irmi's hands, respectively. More excited children began to arrive, swarming around, handing out presents, hugging the twins, and expressing their delight at being at the party.

Suddenly, from around the corner of the house, a tall, jolly-faced clown appeared, dancing a little jig and singing a song in a high falsetto voice. He immediately attracted everybody's attention. After bowing, he announced he would assist with party games, and invited the children to find a seat around the barrel.

Romi whispered to Irmi, "Have you ever seen him before? Where does he come from?"

Irmi shrugging her shoulders, whispered back, "Perhaps Bernie knows; I'm wondering myself."

Before Bernie could be located, the clown led the children to the barrel and asked them to sit down, while he pulled the chairs away before they could sit. They quickly caught on, snatching a chair before he could get to them. He was a remarkable sight! His bright red hair stuck out in a fringe around a bald top, on which sat the tiniest top hat. Baggy pants with lots of patches covered his long legs, and a green jacket, which was much too large, billowed around his wiry frame. His feet were encased in enormously large shoes, which were tied with purple laces that frequently came undone, causing him to stumble. At which time, he would bend down and laboriously retie the awkward things, causing laughter all around.

When the children were finally seated, he asked them to guess his name, promising a prize to the one who could guess it first.

"Is your name Benji?"

"Or Topsy?"

"Or Bobo?"

"Or Papok?"

"Or, perhaps, Karel?"

He shook his head so hard his long ears flopped around like a puppy's, while the children continued,

"Is it Liliput?"

"Or Pootsey?"

"Or Flopsy?"

"Or Archy?" and so on.

Irmi, easily frustrated, called out, "You funny clown, you tire me. We've tried all the names we know!" then she asked, "Perhaps your name is "Rumpelstiltskin?"

Everyone watched as he made a broad bow, reached deep into one of his pants pockets, and pulled out a small recorder. He handed it to Irmi with another bow and a jump, then pretended he lost balance, and sat down.

"Rumpelstiltskin! Rumpelstiltskin!" the children chorused, "what do you want us to do next?"

Rapping himself behind his clown ears, he said, "I quite forgot, I have to collect two items from each of you, and they have to go into the barrel."

As the children gave him sashes, rings, bow ties, socks and more, he placed them all into the barrel. He then instructed the children to suggest a song or an activity. Little Maria stood to her feet, saying, "We'd like to hear a song." The clown plucked a bracelet from the barrel and told Romi that it was her turn to sing.

"I will sing our Czech national anthem—I know that best." There was applause from all the adults who were gathered around. Modestly she said, "We sing that in school each day. We all know it."

Next was Bobby, who announced with a loud voice, "The person whose item Rumpelstiltskin picks next, must go to the house, and find a paper napkin inside for us all to see." He astounded everybody with his clear directions. One of the men said, "He will be a leader when he grows up!"

There were chuckles from the adults. Poems, cartwheels, and dances followed, until the clown held up the last item, and Romi proclaimed, "The next person has to play a song on the half-violin we have in the music room."

"Oh, Romi, you planned that, didn't you?" Irmi blushed. But she went and brought the small violin back and proceeded to play a lullaby from the children's opera *Haensel and Gretel*. She played with great skill to a round of clapping from the parents.

There was a refreshment break, when Cornelia and Bernie brought trays with creamy strawberry drinks. All the little guests eagerly reached for the colorful straws that came with them. The adults were served fruit punch in crystal goblets.

Having finished their drinks, the clown lined up the children by twos, and led them down the garden path to the horses' pen. He explained that each would get some practice so that they could participate in the pony race after supper. Four ponies stood ready for this purpose, and the children were eager to begin. They were assisted by Pavel and Petrov. Frederic had rented two extra ponies for this occasion. They were in the middle of being shown knee and hand positions when the bell for supper sounded from the house. Since they were not finished, it was decided that the parents of the children would have their meal first.

After each child had practiced on a pony, Rumpelstiltskin led the lively group back to the house. Coming from the twilight into the brightly lit foyer, the little ones "ah-ed" and oh-ed" when they saw the large, festively decorated dinner table. After washing their hands, everyone located their name plate. Then Raika and Tirza appeared bearing bowls of delectable food.

There was a lot of talk at first about what everybody liked and disliked, but at last all the plates were served, and for a while only the clattering of spoons and forks was heard. When the boys became restless, little Maria started the Czech birthday song, and all but the twins chimed in. Even the adults who sat at small tables on the veranda and in the music room came into the foyer and sang.

Barely finished, the door to the foyer opened, and Pavel, Petrov, Raika, and Tirza appeared with beautiful lanterns, shaped like the sun, moon and stars.

"Can we have a lantern parade through the garden?"

"Oh, let's!"

"It's getting dark outside!"

"I'm afraid of the dark!"

Such were the comments from the little guests, but finally the parade got under way, escorted by the staff. Music from a hidden gramophone wafted on the night air as the children made their way through the darkening garden paths, carrying their lanterns.

As they walked towards the horse enclosure, John Redgrave sidled up to Frederic asking, "Could you spare a few minutes my dear friend?"

"Sure, we can stay behind while Cornelia and Bernie supervise. You have my ear, John!"

The Englishman cleared his throat, then whispered, "You must know, Frederic, that I was recalled to London this morning. I have not even told my wife yet. The reason is top secret!" As they made their way towards the corral, his voice grew louder. "Next week I will have to close my accounts at your bank, and by June 7, I am to take up work in London."

After a short pause, he said, "I must warn you, Jewish holdings will not be safe here after July 1. I am quoting reliable sources." Stopping, he turned to Frederic, "My advice to you: Do not remain here longer than prudence dictates. I know how hard you have worked to build up a reliable business, but the dictator from the north is no respecter of persons, especially Jewish persons. Banks and estates can be replaced, but your family cannot. They are precious; take them out of here before it is too late."

Patting Frederic on the back, and putting an arm around him, they walked toward the others. Before joining the group, Frederic said, "I knew it was coming, but I thought I still had until summer. Many thanks, John! I appreciate your warning."

The two dads rejoined the others, cheering on the last two riders, relieved that they had not been missed. The winners of the pony races were congratulated as they received two giant, stuffed clowns. By now the young party guests were getting noticeably tired, but everybody perked up when Cornelia invited them to the house for birthday cake.

Seeing the triple-tiered, luscious cakes, sitting like two towers in chocolate and creamy pink on the dining table, revived even the most tired of the little people. Bernie sliced carefully into cook's tasty creations.

"Chocolate, please!" or "Pink for me!" could be heard, until all were served. Before the last crumb had disappeared, Romi and Irmi each brought a large basket with gaily wrapped gifts to the table. Going from child to child, they offered one to each of their friends as farewell gifts.

As limousines pulled up, and while thank yous and yawns abounded, two little girls hugged their Daddy and their Mommy until the last taillight disappeared around the bend of the road. It was not long afterwards that Romi cuddled against her Daddy, as he carried her up the broad staircase, with Mommy Cornelia following, holding Irmi in her arms. It didn't take long before the two six-year-old party girls were tugged into their cozy beds, and sleepy-eyed, kissed their parents good night.

CHAPTER THREE

LATE NIGHT DIALOGUE

The household staff was busily putting the downstairs rooms back in order, while Frederic sat for a time at the desk in his study. Cornelia, after laying out the children's clothes for the next day, dropped onto the piano bench and improvised some of the melodies that were foremost in her thoughts. She then changed to the arias that she would have to sing during the next days. This was her customary routine before retiring.

When Frederic beckoned her through the open door, she closed the piano. Humming her last tune, she followed her husband upstairs. They both looked in on their girls. A gentle breeze was billowing the curtains. Cornelia bent over each little head and pressed a gentle kiss on disheveled hair. Then they went into their own bedroom.

After closing the door carefully, he drew her to the small sofa at the foot of their cherry wood four-poster. Sitting beside her, he pulled her closer, and said, "What I have to say cannot wait, regardless of how tired we are."

Cornelia, taking note of his determined chin and strained expression, snuggled up to him, waiting. He continued in a low, nearly-whispered voice, "I received upsetting news three days ago and again tonight."

"Was John Redgrave the bearer of these news?" Cornelia whispered back.

"I saw you stay behind with him, and I wondered what was going on."

"My Dearest, it seems events are shaping up much faster than we expected. Redgrave shared with me that he is leaving Prague in just a few days, ordered back to London by his company's management. He will close all three accounts that he established with us when he first settled here."

"You mean that they are leaving before school ends in three weeks?"

"Yes," Frederic replied, "it seems so very soon, doesn't it?" After a short pause he asked, "When are your last performances, my Love?"

"Just yesterday I counted," Cornelia answered, "there are still three performances of *Aida*, one of *Gypsy Baron*, and two of *Bartered Bride*. Unless there is a program change, my last performance this season is scheduled for June 12. Then vacation . . ." her voice trailed off.

"What would you say if I made reservations for you, Bernie, and the girls on June 14?"

Cornelia's face turned ashen. She sat straight up and looking into his eyes, said, "Do you really have to send us away? And to where?" And as tears stole down her face from under lowered lids, "Is trouble coming so much sooner than we thought?"

He nodded gravely, taking her small hand and kissing it, said, "It was not Redgrave alone; I had another warning three days ago. My usual source called me from the Netherlands and said a prearranged word which we had agreed to use only in emergencies. He also added that a vacation would be good for you and the children, since you had such a trying season at the National Theatre, with so many performances. He suggested our families could meet in Geneva for our annual vacation on the 14th of June."

"But why Geneva? Doesn't everybody always go to Geneva?" inquired Cornelia.

"I agree with you, Dearest, Geneva would not be my first choice either, but we can use it as a transit point. What would you think if we contacted Madame Perrot in Evian? She provided such a restful break for us when you were expecting the twins six and a half years ago."

"I certainly remember. Madame was a fine hostess; her meals, her beds, and the countryside could not be equaled."

"Would that be acceptable as a temporary residence?"

"Oh, yes," she nodded, remembering the peaceful hikes near the pleasant pension on the southern shore of Lake Geneva, the morning views across the shimmering lake, and the alpenglow of the French Alps before night fell. "I couldn't think of a more delightful place." Then after a pause she said, "But to leave our home, knowing that we will never be able to return—that is hard to accept!"

"You realize, Dearest, that we will have to be playacting, besides," Frederic reminded her. "No one must suspect that we are leaving for good. All preparations must appear to be only for a month-long vacation. We can only take the most necessary items, nothing else."

"Frederic, where will you be during all this?" Cornelia looked at her husband with great concern. "My dear Husband, you have worked so hard to keep and even increase what your father bequeathed to you when he died. Now it seems it is out of our hands. Our future is in the hand of the King of the Universe, who made us and allowed us all these things."

She kissed him then with loving compassion, and said, "How good that we are not married to these things, but to each other. We need one another now more than at any other time. So, please, don't endanger yourself by staying much longer after we are gone." He held her in a close embrace as tears coursed down her pale face.

Whispering close to his ear, she continued, "You must let nothing deter you from finishing up your affairs here as soon as you are able. You have trustworthy employees; give them full authority, and plan a 'business trip,' even if you are never going to take it. You know we all need you!"

"Dearest, we can't make final decisions tonight. I simply wanted to let you know where we stand. Once you and the children are in a safe place, I will have a free hand to arrange affairs at the bank and settle everything that pertains to our home."

Then he cautioned her again, "Please let utmost caution guide your every decision. Nobody must know that our departure is for good, that we don't intend to return. You can't cancel your contract at the National Theatre. The children have to remain on the rolls at school, and all of our friends in town must expect us to return." After a short pause he mused, "How glad I am that both your sisters are settled in New York with your mom so that we don't have to fear that they might become targets after we leave."

"What about dear Bernie?" Cornelia wanted to know.

"We can't even let Bernie know that this is not just a vacation. Once we are in Evian she can make up her own mind whether she wants to stay with us or return to her home. Since she is not a Jewess she can return, if she so desires."

They sat for a while, quietly thinking, holding on to one another for comfort. Then Cornelia slipped down beside the sofa, beckoning Frederic to join her. "Let us pray to Almighty God together. He alone can show us the way and keep us safe." With bent knees and closed eyes, their hands joined together in prayer, they committed their family's lives to the mighty hand of the Shepherd of Israel.

An hour later with moonlight filtering through the half-opened curtains, Cornelia was sleeping evenly, while Frederic lay with his eyes wide open considering their options. Before too long he also fell into a deep and dreamless slumber provided by their loving God.

CHAPTER FOUR

VACATION

The next day at breakfast, Frederic mentioned casually that it was time to prepare for their upcoming vacation. He said, "I'm really concerned about your well-being, Dearest. This theatre season has been so much more demanding than previous ones." Pausing momentarily, he added, "I have thought about it for some time, and I have decided to send Mama, Bernie, Romi, and Irmi to a nice place at Lake Geneva. There one can always count on a comfortable climate during the summer months."

He did not mention which country the place was in to which he would send them, aware that many ears were listening. "You can get your suitcases out and start packing a little each day. Then by the time Mama has finished her last performances and Romi and Irmi get through their last quarter of Madame Klotskly's school the packing is mostly done."

Turning to Bernie, he said, "Dear Bernie, see to it that the children pack no unnecessary items, only what they will need for the vacation."

"Certainly, Sir," her reply came quickly, "I remember last year when we started early as well."

"We hear you, Papa," cut in Irmi, "but I wish to take my violin and the recorder that Rumpelstiltskin gave me for guessing his name. By the way, how did that clown disappear right after the party?" And turning to Romi, "Sis, did you ever find out who he really was?"

"I don't know, but I'm sure Mama does, right?"

Here Cornelia smiled brightly at her children, glad to have a change of subject. Looking at Frederic, she asked, "I wonder whether Papa minds, if we ask our young man to come in for a minute?"

"No objection," Frederic replied.

Cornelia then turned to Bernie, and asked, "Bernie, could you ask our friend to come in for a moment?"

A few minutes later, Francois in his chauffeur's uniform entered, asking, "Did anybody want to talk with me?" He bowed from the waist, and spoke in his high-pitched clown voice.

"O Francois, you really tricked us!" Romi exclaimed. "You were a super clown!"

"Did you ever take clown lessons?" said Irmi.

"Will you do it again for our next birthday?" Romi asked.

"I never make long-range plans because in a clown's life things sometimes change altogether."

He spoke again in a high-pitched voice, but Irmi stopped him, "You shouldn't strain your voice so much. Don't you remember how Mama always has to pay attention to her singing voice?"

Here Francois bowed again, and waving at the girls, did a little jump, and left.

"You both can talk to Francois some more when he drives you to school tomorrow," Cornelia stated. But only Romi went with Francois to town the next day. Irmi had developed a fever overnight and suffered from chills all day. Dr. Sisla, their trusted pediatrician, made a house call.

After carefully examining Irmi, he said, "This young friend of mine has a classic case of chicken pox—I see the eruptions breaking out all over." Showing them to Cornelia and Bernie, he said, "What puzzles me is this, that Romi doesn't show any signs of it. Usually twins come down with these contagious childhood diseases at the same time."

"What is breaking out all over?" Irmi whined, blinking tears out of her eyes. "Will I feel bad for a long time?"

"You will feel much better once these pox stop itching. Until then, Mommy and Bernie will give you baking soda baths when you itch and will bring you cool apple juice and all the food you like."

Then taking her dainty hand in his, he said, "Irmi, I know you are a brave little girl. You will take naps when you are tired and Bernie will read you fairy tales, and time will pass quickly." Promising he would be back in a few days unless things got worse, he closed up his black doctor's bag and left.

The next ten days flew by, and finally Irmi was ready to go back to school. "Just for a week," their Mama said. The same day Romi complained of a headache, and sure enough, she had a fever and red spots began appearing on her back and on her legs. Her face, strangely, remained clear. But she did have a hard time of it. Three times a day she had to sit in her large bathtub, soaking in baking soda water just to keep herself from scratching. Meanwhile Irmi, who had lost weight and was pale, went back to school.

During their days at home, Bernie first helped Irmi, then Romi, to fill the large wickerwork trunk that Cornelia had set out with things they wanted to take on their vacation. They would send this trunk ahead, Cornelia had said. "Then on our flight to Geneva, we will only each need a small satchel that is easy to carry."

"Mama, do we really get to fly?" asked Romi.

Irmi added, "We've never flown before."

"Actually, we took you once to Paris by plane. That was four years ago. You were toddlers then, and both Nessie and Bernie came along, because I had to sing at a benefit."

"What is a benefit?" Irmi asked.

"It means, you do something for a cause that you believe in," explained Cornelia.

"What was the good cause you believed in?" questioned Romi.

"At that time the Jewish Agency was collecting funds to build a new hospital in Jerusalem. Jerusalem is a special, holy city for us Jewish people," Cornelia explained.

"What does 'holy' mean, Mama?" Irmi asked next.

"It is something set aside for the use of God," replied Cornelia.

Remembering their flight to Paris, Cornelia continued, "By the way, on that flight to Paris four years ago, we could see the countryside below us so clearly; it was a lovely, sunny day, and then on our left, the Parade of Giants! Do you remember the glistening mountain tops,

Bernie?" she asked the governess who had been straightening out clothes that were to be packed.

"It was a sight I will never forget!" Bernie exclaimed. "The mountains I had only read about, like the Jungfrau, Monte Rosa, and the Matterhorn, so awe-inspiring and majestic, yet they appeared as if we could have touched them."

"You mean, all these high mountains stand in a row, and you can see them?" Irmi asked.

"Are they higher than the German mountains we can see from our bedrooms on a clear day?" said Romi.

"Yes, Romi," from Cornelia. "Because they are much higher, you can see snow that never melts on the tops of these Swiss mountains!"

"Will you have to sing this time, too?" Romi wanted to know.

"No, I don't plan to. Papa thinks, and he is right, that I badly need to rest my voice."

"How many more days until we leave?" queried Irmi.

"Counting today it will be four days," Cornelia answered. "I still have to sing the *Gypsy Baron* tomorrow, and on Monday *The Bartered Bride*. The children were familiar with her performances. Bernie had taken them, on occasion, and they had learned to sit quietly during the long operatic acts. They also knew that these operas were hard for Mama to sing, and she was often tired the next day.

"Will Papa go with us on vacation?" Romi wanted to know next.

"When we leave, Francois will take us to the airfield, because Papa has to be in Paris that day," responded Cornelia.

"Oh, I miss Papa already! Can't he at least say goodbye to us?" Romi asked.

"But we will miss our school party," Irmi sobbed. "Benny told me that Mrs. Klotsky always plans a big surprise for the day after school is out."

"Please, Irmi, don't be sad," comforted Romi, "You know, I couldn't come anyway while I am still trying to get rid of these chicken pox that you gave me." Turning to her Mama, she added, "I hope they let me on the airplane!"

"By then all your pustules will have healed nicely," Bernie said, "and since you have none on your face no one will know anyway, unless you tell them."

When Irmi returned from school on Monday, she said, "Madame said our class will have an outdoor picnic, and then the school will close for five weeks. I told her that Romi and I would be back for first grade. Is that right, Mama?"

Cornelia was bent over her own suitcase trying to put a safety lock on so that she could send it ahead with the girls' trunk and Bernie's luggage. Francois stood ready to take her to her last performance. Irmi's question hung in the air and remained unanswered, as Mama bent down to kiss her girls, saying, "Darlings, mind Bernie! Pray for me. This is my last show this season."

Cornelia made it, somehow, through this last performance. She was in tears when the final curtain fell. Knowing that this was her last show in her beloved National Theatre, a wave of unexplainable grief came over her. Here she had experienced her greatest success as an artist; but now a new emphasis must take hold in her life. She must concentrate on being a helpmeet to her husband, a good mother to her children, and a responsible neighbor to those she came in contact with.

Her colleagues were milling about, discussing their vacation plans. She controlled her emotions as she reflected how just three weeks ago a chilling hint of her changing status had surfaced. Thinking on that incident would make it easier to part with them. She had overheard some of her associates mention that members of the Czech Nazi Party had come to the personnel department.

"What for?" Cornelia's friend, and well-known alto, Elsa, had asked.

"They were inquiring who is Jewish among our performing artists," the choir spokesman replied. When he noticed that Cornelia had overheard his remark, he added, "Sorry, Madame. That's what they told me." Suddenly, there was an ominous silence on the set, as one by one her colleagues disappeared. Only Elsa, who stood next to Cornelia, remained. Elsa placed an arm around Cornelia and led her away, assuring her of her friendship.

Last week another event had occurred. Their stage manager, known for his sympathy with Nazi ideology, slammed the stage door in her face as he was leaving the building ahead of Cornelia. Wladislav, the door guard, whispered, "Don't take that to heart, Cornelia. He is an oaf, and you and I know it!" Then he opened the door and looked around for Francois and the car. Waving, he accompanied her to the car, opening the door for her, and checking that she was safely inside before leaving her.

Cornelia, who had been highly esteemed, who had always been courteous even to the lowliest stage hand, was not used to being a victim. But she became one as the poisonous anti-Semitic ideology permeated even the tolerant world of the theatre.

Now with the last show of the season behind her, Cornelia removed her make-up and changed into her street clothes. She kissed her wardrobe mistress good-bye, leaving her an envelope with a gift of money, as she usually did before theatre vacations. This dear lady was like a mother to her, having seen to her every costume change, always aware, for instance, which wig went with each outfit throughout her career. She had taken care of Cornelia's personal needs as well. Now Cornelia could not even bid the woman an honest farewell; she just hugged her with tears in her eyes, then left through the back door where Francois was waiting.

She slid into the back seat of the limousine. Her tears could flow freely here. She knew that she had passed a milestone. An important part of her life had ended tonight. She allowed herself a time of mourning as scenes of her eventful life flashed by.

She remembered the joyful day when she graduated from the Conservatory of Music with a great number of her friends around her, Raoul among them. Both Raoul and she had been star graduates that day, and agents had promising contracts for them. She had been in conflict, because a fine contract was offered her by the Bavarian State Opera in Munich. The Budapest Opera Company had offered a similar contract to her, but her hometown opera house had won out! Her beloved daddy had suffered a stroke and needed special care. How could she have left her family at this critical time?

Besides, her older sister had met and married an American businessman who took her to live in New York City in America. Her parents would not have been able to let another daughter go. But in staying she had been blessed. In the following season, the musical director had discovered Cornelia's potential. She not only had a fine voice caliber and exceptional stage presence, but she had also picked up roles as an understudy that a lesser singer could not have mastered.

By the following season, she was considered first soprano of the National Theatre. She remembered how her rendition of *Madame Butterfly* had opened up her career; she had become a world class singer. Soon thereafter, she had been given the roles of *La Traviata*, *Carmen*, and *La Boheme*. On principle, she never complained when the rehearsal schedule was tight, and when she had to stay extra hours. The directors appreciated that.

In those days, her younger sister Miriam had been her strong supporter. She had patiently waited for her after late shows. Miriam made sure that Cornelia could relax when she was at home and had taken care of their ailing dad without grumbling. But then, Miriam, too, found the love of her life in a teacher of the local Yeshiva and eventually also settled in America.

About that time, Frederic Bartok appeared on the scene. After having seen Cornelia in the *Gypsy Baron*, he sent flowers and waited for her in his car at the stage door. He courted her patiently, understanding her obligations to her family and to her demanding job. Soon he proposed marriage to Cornelia.

Observing the physical and emotional strain the Kahn family was under to provide adequate care to their ailing father; Frederic suggested a care center of good reputation for the gentleman. Believing it to be his duty and privilege as a son-in-law, he paid expenses for Cornelia's father to reside at the facility. For nearly two years her father had enjoyed a lovely setting and excellent care. While his family visited often, they were able to pursue their own lives to a large degree. Cornelia's dad, surrounded by loved ones, left this life during Hanukkah the year before the twins were born.

They had moved into their present home at the end of her pregnancy. She still remembered this life-changing event! Her mother had lived with them then. She had assisted Cornelia in running the household until an urgent call came from New York: Grandma was needed there to help care for her sisters' children. Both of her daughters and their husbands needed to work to make ends meet. So when Grandma departed for the United States, two nursemaids, Bernie and Nessie, were hired. With Nessie's and Bernie's help, the household continued to run smoothly, aided by Raika the cook, Tirza the maid, and Bela the butler.

Cornelia acknowledged with gratitude that her mother and her sisters and their families were comparatively safe in a country where Nazism was not a threat. She sobbed as she realized that she could not even mention to them her upcoming, drastic move. Just then Francois pulled into their driveway. He had observed her tears and her struggle in his rearview mirror. Yet he never said a word, considering that she had a good reason to cry. Respectfully, he opened the car door and Cornelia slipped by him, unable to speak.

After she slipped in the side door, passing her plants, she stepped into the music room. She allowed her fingers to pass over the grand piano and the harp. Then sitting down and opening the keyboard, she struck a few chords, but was unable to continue, realizing the finality of it all. She knew she could not allow herself to indulge in self-pity. She had to pull herself together. She headed upstairs, went into the children's room, tousled their hair gently, and breathed a prayer for their well-being.

She was grateful for the quiet in the house. The household staff and Bernie were asleep. A little while later, she allowed the warm spray of the shower to drain away her fatigue and strain. She focused her thinking on God's goodness. He had always cared for and provided for them. He would not let them down now. Dressed in a fresh linen shift and a comfortable magenta robe, she sat down at her spotless kitchen table with a sandwich and a glass of cider, sorely missing her husband. She concentrated on making a list of what all had to be done in the morning.

Before lying down in her four-poster bed, she knelt at her bedside and said prayers of thanksgiving to Almighty God. Apprehension and anxiety gradually left her, and a mantle of peace enveloped her. She snuggled under the light quilt as sleep came softly to her weary body.

CHAPTER FIVE

ENEMY AT THE DOOR

T he next morning Cornelia awakened when her bedside phone rang. Hearing her husband's voice comforted her, even though he spoke guardedly. Both of them knew their conversation could be overheard.

"My Dearest, I was with you in thoughts and prayers," he assured her. "How was the last performance of the season?"

"I'm so glad it is over for a while. Everybody has plans for summer vacation. All I hope is that you will return soon, dear Husband!"

"Business has been demanding, and I will try my best to be back in Prague by the week's end. You, my Dearest, go ahead with your vacation plans; don't be deterred. I love you, and I hope to see you soon!" With that he signed off.

Cornelia quickly arose and put on a practical house dress. She had much to do in preparation for their trip. She looked in on her children, both of whom were still in their beds, breathing evenly. She decided to finish some of her personal packing, and was sitting on her suitcase in order to lock it, when Romi came running into her room. In the background Irmi's screams could be heard; Bernie was untangling her curls.

"Mama, there is a black limousine out front, and some men are coming to visit!" were Romi's alarming words

"Why wouldn't Pavel have let us know?" Cornelia, jumping up, replied. Looking from behind the curtains down onto the front steps leading up to the house, she saw two men emerging from a black car, heading towards the front door. Cornelia quickly stepped into the children's room, leading Romi to Bernie, saying, "We have an issue to deal with. Please keep the girls with you. They must not come down. I hope to handle this without interruption. Thank you, Bernie."

Cornelia was descending the stairway when Bela ushered the two men into the foyer. They wore black boots, black leather coats, and carried uniform caps under their arms. One of them stepped forward with an affected grin on his face that didn't reach his eyes. His dark hair was slicked back, revealing an ugly scar from his right eyebrow to his hairline.

Cornelia, summoning up a charmingly confident stage persona, asked, "What brings you gentlemen here so early in the day?"

"Inspector Gavek," the scarred man said, introducing himself and clicking his heels together. "We have been asked to make a survey of the country estates in the area. For reasons of defense we have to know how many people live here, how many rooms you have, and what acreage your property covers."

"Inspector Gavek, we appreciate your interest in defending our country; however, I am a woman whose husband is away on a business trip, and I really cannot comply with your request. When he is back, you can make an appointment to see him, and he will consider your requests. He will answer your questions as he deems fit." Then she asked, "How did you get through our gate? Our man Pavel has instructions to announce all arrivals."

Gavek flashed an identification badge in front of her face too quickly for her to read and said, "He opened it right away after seeing this." He didn't mention that he had threatened the surprised man with force if he didn't open the gate immediately.

"Is Pavel in your organization?" she asked next.

"No, but he knows better than to resist us!" came Gavek's impudent reply. The other man stepped forward then and whispered into Gavek's ear, who then asked, "Are you the opera singer Cornelia Kahn?"

Nodding her head, she replied, "Do you enjoy music? Have you been to the National Theatre to see one of our productions?"

This seemed to take the wind out of his sails. His next question came a bit more respectfully, "Do you live here alone with your husband?"

"We have several employees who assist us in running the estate, since both my husband and I are gone frequently." Eager to be rid of them, she added, "God willing, my husband will be back on Friday. Please make an appointment with him then. Without him, I really cannot help you." Turning to Bela, who had stood respectfully to her left throughout this interchange, she said, "Please show these gentlemen out!"

Her words had a commanding finality about them, and Bela opened the door, bowing as he usually did, while the men left without further ado. Cornelia noticed how they settled themselves comfortably into the large, black car before swerving around the circular drive. Picking up speed, they left the estate, trailing a cloud of dust behind them.

"Bela, what do you make of that?" Cornelia asked, ashen-faced and fighting a trembling that had come upon her.

Bela closed the massive door quietly, then turning to her, he said, "Mr. Bartok would be proud of you Madame; you acted exactly as you should have. You handled the situation with strength and charm." After a short pause he continued, "Pavel must know more about them, or wouldn't have let them pass without announcement. We must warn Mr. Bartok, Madame, so that he'll be prepared for their next visit."

"Give them a few minutes to clear the gate, then please call Pavel to the house. I want to speak with him," Cornelia said. Just before Bela reached the intercom, she added, "I would prefer that we do not speak to Pavel about our departure. He will find out soon enough."

It was an exceptionally beautiful morning. Birdsong drifted through the open windows, and a bouquet of spring flowers graced the breakfast table. It promised to be a good day for planning an excursion, more specifically, a journey on an airplane.

Pavel arrived on his bike fifteen minutes later. He appeared nervous when Cornelia asked how these men in the black car could have entered the grounds without his usual announcement.

"Oh, M-Madame," he stuttered, "when I stopped them and asked what their business was the scar-faced man jumped out of the car, telling me he was on official business. He threatened me, and said that I'd better not make trouble. He showed me a badge. It was a badge of the so-called defense forces, but my brother tells me, the people who carry those badges are really in cahoots with the Nazis."

Pavel seemed to be very upset. Then looking directly at Cornelia, he asserted, "These people are no good; they are traitors to our country. They expect the Germans to take over soon. My brother's friends told him that they are Nazi collaborators." Crushing his cap in his work-worn hands, he continued, "I could tell they had no good in mind. The scarred man pushed by me, opening the gate before I could react. I am truly sorry that this happened, Madame; I am sorry that I didn't warn you. Please forgive me!"

Pavel stood contritely before her. Cornelia was reassured that he had no connection to this traitorous group. She thanked him for his report and sent him away. Bernie, who had heard their exchange, turned to Cornelia and stated, "I can't imagine the temerity of those men, pushing past Pavel like they did. I would lay my hand in the fire for such a sincere man. He seems to be a person without guile."

Later, as they sat down to breakfast, the girls asked many questions regarding their early-morning visitors. Romi said, "Mama, Pavel always helps Bernie and me when we come for eggs in the morning. He never says a bad word."

"And he collects beautiful feathers for us," added Irmi, "and he tells the best animal stories. I really like him!"

"I'm quite convinced myself that Pavel has nothing to do with these men. I'm sure that your Papa will know how to deal with them."

With this Cornelia turned her attention to Romi, "My dear little Chicken-pox Lady, do you think you would like to go to school today? This will be your last day of class for the year in Mrs. Klotsky's school, or do you prefer to stay home."

"If my legs were clear, I would like to go to school, but look," she lifted her knee to show her Mama, "See these red splotches . . . I wouldn't like it if everybody asked me where I got them."

"You know, Mama, today at school we will only be packing up all our belongings, like the paint shirts and the modeling clay. Then we will go outside to play. I would rather do that at home. Would you mind if I don't go to school either, "Irmi pleaded. "I would like to keep Romi company and pack the rest of my things for tomorrow. Please say that you'll let me!"

It didn't take Cornelia long to make that decision. Knowing that today was their last day on their own land and in their own house, she gave permission for Romi and Irmi to stay home. The girls rode their ponies and helped to curry them. They laughed and played together. They read their picture books with Bernie, putting away those which had to stay behind. They had a very good time. Finally, they packed away the dolls and the other toys that they were not taking on the trip, to prevent them getting dusty while they were gone.

Altogether, it seemed that the day passed far too quickly. Before bedtime Romi and Irmi soaked in a full, sudsy bubble bath. Mama and Bernie kissed and hugged the girls and then turned out the lights. The clear June night settled over the big house. The stars seemed to twinkle more brightly, while a half-moon bathed the grounds in mellow light. Cornelia stood for some time at her bedroom window, surveying the peaceful scene, before lying down on her four-poster for the last time . . .

CHAPTER SIX

OFF TO FREEDOM

The next morning involved a little more scurrying and excitement than usual. Breakfast was a hurried affair, eaten in the kitchen and followed by farewells from their beloved staff. Meanwhile, Francois had stacked all the suitcases and travel bags in the large trunk of the car. Ready at last, his passengers climbed into their seats, waving to Bela, Raika, and Tirza as they had done every year before when leaving on vacation.

As they drove, Cornelia kept her emotions under firm control so that she would not sob; fully realizing that she was leaving her cherished home and her hometown for good. When they arrived at the airfield they were surprised by the throngs crowding the airport entrance.

"Are all these people taking vacation even before school gets out?" asked Irmi.

Cornelia, who was not surprised by the vast numbers of people, said, "They must have their reasons for travelling by airplane today." Although she could guess why, she did not elaborate, keeping her anxious thoughts to herself.

Francois approached a luggage attendant, asking where he could best unload their bags. The man shrugged his shoulders and said, "This is unheard of. We are overwhelmed; we don't usually see such crowds around here. Perhaps they have heard about the menace coming from the north." Scratching his head, he added, "I'll bet, most of these people are Jewish, and they fear for their skin." He turned and pushed his handcart, loaded with suitcases, to the baggage area.

Romi, tugging at her Mama's sleeve piped up, "Mommy, we are Jewish too, aren't we? The man said the Jewish people fear for their skin. We don't, do we?"

Francois inched the limousine towards a side entrance of the building, wanting to park for a short time to unload their things. Cornelia, understanding his plan, smiled and handed him a bank note saying, "Perhaps you can entice somebody to help us with this." Francois lost no time. He quickly entered the hangar through the side door. They saw him talking to a Green Cap. The man came with him and helped unload their luggage onto his cart. Then he stood by while Cornelia, Bernie, and the girls emerged from the car.

"Madame, I shall accompany you to the departure point," Francois said, while locking the car doors. "I promised Mr. Bartok that I would get you safely to the airplane, and we hadn't expected anything like this!"

Taking Cornelia's elbow, he led her through the side entrance, beckoning Bernie and the girls to follow them. Immediately, they were surrounded by jostling men, women, and children all hurrying in different directions.

"Please let us stay together," Cornelia turning, admonished her small entourage. "Follow directly behind us. We'll play tugboat with Francois leading us to the right plane." They approached an elevated platform on which stood a uniformed official.

"Form queues to the right and the left of this platform!" the man addressed the crowds with a bullhorn. When he stopped for a moment, Cornelia asked him to point them to the plane leaving for Geneva. When the man saw her, his expression changed and he jumped down, bowing from the waist, and asked, "Madame, would you by any chance be Cornelia Kahn, the famous opera singer?" When Cornelia nodded, he excitedly exclaimed, "I have seen you at the National Theatre many times. I see you every Thursday night; I have season tickets. Never did I think I would meet you in person and here you are!"

Then he remembered what she had asked, and inquired, "You want to fly to Geneva now that you have theatre holidays?"

33

Here Francois interrupted, asking, "Can we make the plane in time?"

"There is absolutely no hurry," the opera enthusiast replied. "We have just been informed that the plane from Vienna for Geneva will not be here for another two hours. In fact, if it were here now, you would have to wait because we have to get the planes off to Paris and London first." With that he pointed to four long queues of frustrated passengers lined up behind signs that indicated flights to Paris and London. He continued, "We are sending two extra airplanes to those destinations in order to get these people out of here. Most of them were scheduled to depart over two hours ago!"

He smiled at Cornelia and bowed to Francois, saying, "It would be a great honor to lead you to your departure queue." Taking her arm, he steered her to the opposite wall, where two shorter lines had formed. At the front of one of the lines a young woman clad in a blue uniform and wearing a jaunty flight cap was examining papers and travelling passes.

"Josephine, this is the lady I have been telling you about," he introduced Cornelia. "She is the leading star of the Prague Opera Company, Cornelia Kahn. She will be flying to Geneva with her family. Look after her for me, will you?" Then stepping back, with a smile and a bow, he hurried away through the surging sea of humanity.

The young lady responded by offering Cornelia, Bernie, and the twins places at the head of the line. Cornelia declined, saying, "Thank you, we don't want special privileges. We just hope to get away to Geneva along with these other passengers today."

"Madame, we are sorry for the delay," the young stewardess explained, "it will be at least two hours before we can board and take-off. The airplane is not even here yet." One could tell that she'd made similar statements many times already on this day. She led Cornelia and her party to the end of the line, and added, "The passengers for Paris and London need to leave first."

They took their places behind a young blonde woman who held a pink-clad baby in her arms. A little boy was clutching her skirt, whimpering. The blonde woman spoke to them apologetically, "We came from Carlsbad early this morning. Little Louis is only four years old, and he has been hungry for over an hour now. The food I brought

34

with me is gone. We had no idea there would be such a long delay before we could leave. Do you think they will offer a meal on the airplane?"

"It does not seem likely now;" Cornelia said, "if there will be a meal it might not be until evening." Turning to Bernie, she asked, "Did Raika send something along for the girls?" Bernie nodded, taking a white bag out of her satchel and handed it to Cornelia.

"This might be something we could share," Cornelia stated, while taking out two delicately wrapped sandwiches, two apples, and two cookies. Meanwhile Louis had stopped crying and looked longingly at the things in Cornelia's hands. "Perhaps this will tide your young son over," she said, offering the sandwiches and the apples to the young mother.

A grateful smile was her reply as she accepted the food. Then the woman said, "Could you add another blessing to your gift and hold my baby for a moment?" Bernie reached out for the little bundle while the young mother turned over her suitcase to make a seat for her son. Then she unwrapped one of the sandwiches for him. Francois, who had watched the proceedings, offered his pocketknife to cut the apple. Here amidst the turbulent comings and goings was a small island of goodwill and peace: A little boy was happily chewing his sandwich while his mother sliced the apple for him.

"Seeing him eat makes me hungry, too, Mama. Do you have another sandwich for Irmi and me?" Romi asked.

"Perhaps I can make a quick dash home?" suggested Francois. "I will take a shortcut and have Raika prepare more sandwiches, fruit, and drinks, if that's alright with you, Madame. I could be back in an hour, I think." He looked expectantly at Cornelia, then at Bernie. Both ladies, considering their present circumstances, nodded approval.

"Francois, that is a very good suggestion, if you don't mind making the trip a second time. As it appears now, we might be stuck here for awhile, don't you think Bernie?"

"So it appears, Madame," Bernie replied. "And even if the impossible might happen, that the plane would take off before you return, Francois, it looks like there are hundreds of people here who would like some nourishment besides us. You would have no trouble giving it away."

"Just don't break any speed records, Francois," Cornelia admonished. "It seems we will be here a long time." With that Francois took his leave, and a short time later, disappeared into the flood of humanity surrounding them.

Cornelia and Bernie handed out the remaining sandwiches to the girls, sharing another with the young woman, to whom they gave some of the milk as well.

The little baby girl began to cry. The young woman laid her next to her brother on the suitcase and changed her diaper The twins followed this process with great interest. The baby still fussed so the young mother nursed her. While the woman fed her child, Bernie took first Romi, and a few minutes later Irmi, on trips to the rest room.

At Bernie's suggestion, the girls taught Louis the game, "I see something that you can't see." About that time, the stewardess came around, announcing that the flight to Geneva would depart within an hour. Concurrently, Francois reappeared, carrying a large box from which he produced two thermos bottles filled with hot cocoa, and sandwiches for the adults. Besides this, there were strawberries in small bowls and delicious cookies wrapped in cellophane for everyone.

Francois blushed when Cornelia rewarded him with a kiss on the cheek. Romi and Irmi hugged him tightly. He embraced Bernie, and said to everyone, "*Bon voyage*! I hope to welcome you back soon." Cornelia thought about what a faithful employee he was and how they would probably never see him again. Just then, two stewardesses walked past the line of waiting passengers, announcing preparations to depart.

Instead of boarding a plane, however, they were hustled into several buses that slowly crossed the airfield. They stopped at the far end of the tarmac. Only a few moments later, a plane taxied toward them. Once it came to a stop, steps were rolled against the passenger door, and they were helped aboard the "big bird."

The young woman with two children who they'd met earlier ended up seated directly in front of them They heard that another plane was expected to carry the rest of the passengers to Geneva. For Romi and Irmi, who sat with Cornelia and Bernie, respectively, this had turned out to be like a big family outing. Louis, his baby sister, and their young mother had increased the girls' family circle, which made all of them feel more secure.

The stewardesses gave the order to fasten seat belts. As the plane sped down the runway, Cornelia couldn't help the tears that coursed down her face. Saying good-bye for good to her beloved homeland was hitting her hard. Romi, seeing her tears, asked, "Mama, what is the matter? Are you sad that we are going on vacation?"

Cornelia shook her head in denial, then said, "Sometimes one can be both happy and sad. That's what I am feeling right now."

CHAPTER SEVEN

EXILE

The plane took off and headed south-southwest; by the time it crossed Austrian airspace and was heading into Switzerland, both girls' heads were leaning against their seatmates. They were napping soundly. The long wait, the excitement of boarding, then seeing their country disappear, had worn out everybody. The sleeping twins missed the Parade of Giants, the snow-capped peaks of the Alps to the south, aglow in the evening sun on this clear day.

Cornelia considered it prudent not to wake the girls, as they still had to last through a boat ride across Lake Geneva. When at last the plane banked to the right for its approach to the Geneva airfield, both Romi and Irmi awakened, and at first had a hard time remembering where they were.

Then Irmi shared, "I had a dream . . . Petrov told me to canter behind him through the orchard to the fields. He said, 'we had to speed so that Papa wouldn't have to wait too long for us.'"

Romi hearing this, asked, "Don't you wish Papa could be here with us? I really miss him!" Her face was sad, as if she knew their lives were going to be drastically changed. Bernie handed out chewing gum for the descent, and told them to swallow several times as well, to equalize the air pressure in their ears. As the stewardess checked their seat belts, the plane dipped lower on its approach for landing. Everybody's attention was diverted. Before long the twins were startled by the bumps of the plane's wheels making contact with the runway.

After they taxied to the gate, mobile steps were again placed against their exit door, and they followed their new friends down the steps. As their suitcases and satchels were loaded onto a truck, they bid good-bye to the young woman and her two children.

There were long lines inside the terminal again. However, here the accommodations were more modern and spacious than the ones in Prague. Some customs officials checked their luggage while others checked their passports and stamped them for transit to France. They asked Cornelia and Bernie where they were headed, how long they wanted to stay, and what they wanted to do in France.

"We are looking forward to spending our summer vacation in Evian," Cornelia replied. "We have been there before, and we need a break very badly."

To which Bernie added, "Besides the milder climate will do the two little ones good; they have just been through a bout with the chicken pox."

As they left the terminal, they found themselves on a beautiful, tree-lined boulevard. Cornelia hailed a taxi that carried them straight-away to the harbor. There were a number of piers along which boats were moored. The taxi driver dropped them off at a ramp that led upward to an elegant, white steamship, the *Evian Star*. White-clad sailors greeted them and led them to the promenade deck. From here they could see the expanse of the lake in the falling dusk.

The girls had many questions: Why couldn't they stay in Geneva, and see the city? Would they be able to climb the mountains to the south? When was their Papa coming to be with them? Bernie had some of the same questions, but she held her tongue, knowing that Cornelia had enough on her plate right now.

"You see, my dears, Papa and I spent a very pleasant time in Evian, while we were waiting for you to be born. We loved the Pension Perrot in Evian, and we know the proprietor to be a charming woman and a fine hostess. As tired as I am now, I need rest more than I need to visit this busy city or to climb any mountains. Once Papa gets here, we'll do some sightseeing, but he is very busy in Paris right now and will join us as soon as he is finished with his work there."

While Cornelia gave this explanation, they leaned on the railing, and Bernie observed, "This lake actually has three names: The French call it Lac Leman, the people who live here say, Genfer See, and the visitors from England and the United States call it Lake Geneva."

"What should we call it?" Irmi asked.

"Considering that we will live on French soil for some time, we should probably stick with Lac Leman. But perhaps you should check with your mama on that one."

"Your solution suits me, Bernie," Cornelia responded. "We had all better work on learning French so that we can converse with our hosts."

It had grown dark, and the temperature had dropped. Romi and Irmi willingly put on their sweaters. Cornelia suggested they all have soup and dessert in the ship's dining room.

They joined other people heading to the gleaming gold and white eatery upstairs. A friendly waitress seated them by the window, and as they watched the sailors wind up the anchor, the motor roared into action,

Cornelia asked Bernie, "My dear friend, how are you holding out on this trip?"

"Madame, I can't tell you how glad I am to be out of Czechoslovakia with you and the children! I have been praying for a long time that you and Mr. Bartok would see the warning signs."

"But Bernie, why didn't you ever say anything about your concerns to us?" Cornelia asked.

"I have learned to lay things before the Lord, and then I wait for His guidance. When I heard about the vacation plans, I supposed you both had been warned. And when things went so smoothly, I concluded, it is always better to pray than to talk."

During this conversation, the girls had been looking out onto the lake, watching the glittering lights of the shoreline disappear. The waitress came to apply small guard rails around their table.

"What are these for?" Irmi asked. Since she had asked in Czech, she got no reply, only a questioning smile from the young waitress. Bernie translated her question into French, and then she translated the waitress's reply back into Czech,

"She says, 'there often come sudden squalls on the lake, and when that happens, all the dishes would slide off the table if it weren't for the rails.'"

"What is a squall, Mama?" this time from Romi.

"It is a brief, violent storm that comes mostly unannounced," explained Cornelia.

The waitress brought steaming bowls of soup and fresh rolls. The aroma tempted them to partake of this fine meal, which was topped off with a dessert of coconut pudding, served in tall glasses with dollops of whipping cream. Both little girls clapped their hands and said, "Thank you!" to which the waitress replied: "*S'il vous plait!*"

"She understood that you thanked her, and replied in her language, "You are welcome!" Bernie explained.

"How is it that you speak French so well?" Cornelia asked.

Bernie rejoined, "French was a favorite subject of mine in school, and since Francois and I have worked in your home together the last six years, I often begged him to speak French with me just to stay in practice, as you know, he is a French citizen."

"What does that mean, to be a French citizen?" Romi asked.

"It means that he was born in France, he has a French passport, and he was just visiting in our country," their Mama responded.

"Perhaps he traveled a lot, being a clown in a circus. That's probably how he came to Czechoslovakia in the first place," Bernie said.

"I had no idea, you two had this in common," Cornelia observed.

"Please don't think we have a relationship or anything like that," Bernie blushed. "We are just fellow employees, who occasionally shared what was important to both of us.

"There is nothing to be embarrassed about, Bernie. Being absent as much as I was because of the theatre, I had 'tunnel vision,' and was not aware of what was going on around me. I am really pleased that you can help us out now with this language difficulty."

When the boat docked in Lausanne, they left the hospitable dining room and joined some other passengers on the mid-deck. They sat down next to a French family with three children, perhaps three, six, and eight years old, who looked curiously at them. The twins tried to speak with them, but got no reply until Bernie stepped in again to translate, and to explain that they had just arrived from Prague and didn't speak the language yet.

They heard a band playing in the park near the pier.

"What kind of music is that?" Irmi asked.

Romi chimed in, "We have never heard anything like that before, have we?"

"It must be a marimba band from the Caribbean Islands," Cornelia explained, and added, "It is a most melodious sound, isn't it?" Then the motors of their vessel roared back into action, and the sweet rhythms of the band faded away as the boat made its way back onto the lake.

"Mama, I am worried that we won't find any playmates in Evian," Irmi piped up

"Why would you think that?" Cornelia asked.

Romi joined in, "I think, Irmi is right; we won't have friends because we can't understand anybody in France. We are going to France right now, aren't we?"

Her little face was all puckered up. Bernie, who had come to her side, put an arm around her, saying, "That will give us a good reason to study French really hard so we can understand and speak it well. You and Irmi have an added advantage, because both your Mama and I know, that children have special gifts in picking up a new language quickly, especially if they live in a place where it is spoken by everyone.

The ship backed into the dock at Ville d'Evian now. That's what the mother of the French children explained to Bernie, who passed on the information. They gathered their belongings and went down the long gangplank to disembark. They found themselves on a brightly-lit pier, looking for somebody to assist with their luggage. Then they noticed two horse-drawn carriages alongside the dock. Cornelia waved, and one driver responded while Bernie explained their desire to be taken to Pension Perrot. The man had a special trailer attached to his carriage where he stowed their belongings. Then the twins, followed by Cornelia and Bernie, climbed into the comfortable conveyance. The driver assured them he knew the Pension Perrot well.

"I drive out there almost daily," he said. "Madame Perrot and I have known each other a long time." They clip-clopped along at a steady pace. They turned a corner at a sign pointing to Tholon and were soon on a country road. In the darkness they could see blooming trees and impressive chalets on their left. On the lake side, outlines of animals came into sight. The man continued to guide his horses with encouraging "clucks." It was not much later that he took a sharp turn up a sloping driveway.

A large chalet appeared at the end of the driveway. He stopped in front of the entrance door, and started to unload, saying, "Madame will be right out. She greets all her guests personally, day or night." And he was right, Bernie and Cornelia had just climbed down from the carriage when the front door opened, and a slender, white-haired lady emerged, greeting them with a friendly, "*Bon soir!*" But realizing who her new guests were, she quickly changed to the more familiar English, and exclaimed, "Welcome to the Bartok party! Am I right, you are Madame Bartok, Bernie, and the precious children?"

Shaking her hand, Cornelia replied, "The last time we met, Madame Perrot, these two little ones had not been born yet, and Bernie did not join our household until after their arrival. We are so glad you allowed us to come!" with that she introduced Bernie and the twins.

Hugging Cornelia, Madame Perrot said, "I remember you well, you sweet nightingale from Czechoslovakia, and how your songs brightened our evenings."

Leading them inside, she asked a, handsome young man to carry the satchels, suitcases and bags upstairs. She introduced him as Pierre, and said to Cornelia, "Pierre has taken his grandfather's place; he helps me with the upkeep of the Pension."

While leading them upstairs, she said, "At first, we expected you in the afternoon, but then we heard on the wireless about the crowds at the airports, and the stampede of refugees leaving their eastern homelands. Fear of Nazi oppression is overwhelming everyone. So we thought that you might also be caught in this exodus, and wouldn't arrive until tomorrow."

"Somehow, by God's grace we made it," Cornelia admitted." But it was a very long day for all four of us. Especially for the two little ones who need a bed to stretch out on."

"Yes, Madame, all is ready and waiting for you on the third floor. Your husband requested the same suite that you had last time, and we obliged. He advised us that you would prefer the greater privacy the upstairs provides. He said that you might stay here at least four weeks."

Reaching the third floor landing, she opened the first door on the right. They entered a spacious room that featured a large bed covered with a colorful quilt embroidered with alpine wildflowers. A round table stood in the middle of the room, surrounded by four upholstered chairs that looked inviting and promised to be comfortable for playing games or doing crafts. A large chest-of-drawers, on which stood a beautiful bouquet of peonies, was next to a door to the balcony.

"Would this room be suitable for Mademoiselle Bernie?" she asked.

Passing through a connecting door, there was a bathroom to the left with double sinks, a comfortable tub, and a toilet. The room they now entered was attractive, with two small beds lined up along opposite walls. At the foot of each bed stood a large chest-of-drawers painted with a sunflower motif. Two small desks were placed under the windows that faced the lake. Each desk was equipped with a writing pad and a collection of crayons and pencils in a vase-like container. The curtains were decorated with trees, mountains, and flowers in colorful profusion. At this time they were drawn, but a slight breeze caused them to undulate gracefully.

Romi, taking in everything with a glance, threw herself on the nearest bed, pleading, "Mama, can I stay here and sleep without undressing? I am more than tired, and this is a lovely room right for Irmi and me!" Her eyes were already closed. Bernie dropped everything and busied herself removing Romi's shoes, socks, and her outer clothing. She washed Romi's face and her hands and dressed her in a nightie, then tucked her in.

Irmi followed her mother and Madame Perrot into the largest of the three rooms. It occupied a corner with windows and a door leading to the wide veranda surrounding this floor. An upright piano stood along the wall opposite two large beds. There were comfortable love seats, stuffed chairs, and benches arranged around the pleasant room. Irmi discovered a door to the left of the beds that led to another spacious bathroom with a shower and tub.

"This must be Papa's and Mama's place!" Irmi stated.

"It is exactly as I remembered it," Cornelia admitted. She longed for a refreshing bath after this exhausting and emotionally taxing day. Turning to Madame Perrot, who was pulling back the cover on one of the beds, Cornelia said, "It is a little like coming home. Thank you, Madame; we will be very comfortable here. Tomorrow we'll talk about necessary things. For tonight, could we just have some juice, bread, and cheese in case somebody gets hungry in the middle of the night?"

Meanwhile, Pierre hauled all of their luggage upstairs. After Cornelia thanked him and gave him a tip, he returned with a tray of delicate cheeses, small bottles of juice, and some rolls. Then they were left to themselves. It wasn't long afterwards that Irmi too, went through her bedtime routine with Bernie, and joined her sleeping sister in the darkened room. Having hugged her Mama repeatedly, Irmi was content to have the doors closed on either side of their room, knowing that Bernie would be in a room on one side of them, and her mother on the other side.

After a refreshing bath, Bernie put on a light robe, which was a present from Cornelia, and stepped out onto the balcony to look at the stars reflected in the glittering lake. She was surprised to hear Cornelia's voice in the dark, "Bernie, I am thinking about our day, and thanking the Almighty for getting us here safely." Then she asked, "Would you mind if we talked for a few minutes?"

Bernie, finding a comfortable chair, sat down across from Cornelia, who she could now vaguely see. "I am rather overwhelmed myself, Madame. This morning we had breakfast in Czechoslovakia, and tonight we are sitting here, as if we belonged, on a balcony overlooking this magnificent lake in France. I agree with you, we have every reason to thank the mighty Lord of the Universe!"

Cornelia mentioned their unfinished conversation from the boat, and asked, "Tell me, why you wanted us to leave our homeland, and how did you find out that we were planning to leave for good?"

"Oh, that wasn't so hard, Madame. Every weekend, on my days off with my family, my dad mentioned what a hard time was coming for the Jews should our country be annexed to Germany, just as Austria has been for some time. My dad even suggested that I should invite you all

45

to come to our farm. He said we could hide you there for a while until you could make plans."

She looked at Cornelia in the dark and continued, "We have been praying for quite a while that you would receive God's guidance. Whenever I left after a weekend at home, Dad told me, 'Bernie, remember to pray for your employers daily!'"

"What a dear man your dad is! But didn't he encourage you to think about your own future, and what you should do once we left?"

"Oh yes," Bernie admitted, "he said that I should have a plan, but asked me to lay it before the Lord Jesus first, and that is what I did. Everything seemed to work out: the end of the opera season, the children's school year finished, and Mr. Bartok arranging for a vacation. Nobody suspected that this might be a permanent departure."

"So you knew that we would not be able to return, did you?" Cornelia asked and Bernie nodded. "Mr. Bartok and I understand your position, Bernie. Should you want to return to your homeland after a few weeks here with us, you know that you are free to leave, don't you?"

Cornelia rose and moved to the railing, leaning against it, while continuing, "Bernie, in no way do we want you to feel that you must stay with us in exile. You are not Jewish; you will have no difficulties because of your race. So I trust you will make the decision your Lord leads you to. Of course, the girls have bonded with you, and a separation would affect both of them deeply. So for now, our main job is to carry on as if this truly were only a vacation. We leave the future in God's mighty hand, if that is alright with you?"

"You are very kind to me. As I see it, for the time being, I am supposed to stay with you. The children have become so dear to me that I really cannot see myself in another role. I would love to stay with your family until you don't need me anymore!"

After these words Cornelia came over, bent down, and hugged Bernie, saying, "You are a precious faithful one. You know we need you and cannot do without you. Thank you!"

CHAPTER EIGHT

VITAL DECISIONS

Back in Prague, Frederic Bartok waited in line for the customs officer to stamp his passport. He reflected on the happenings of the past few days. His family had arrived safely in Evian. He had been able to make arrangements with his friend and business partner in Paris to remodel two stories of his patrician home in the north part of town. Davide Cohen and his twenty year old daughter Rachel had heartily invited him and his family to join them.

Before he could leave, however, he wanted to set his affairs in order. His sources had informed him that plans for the occupation of Czechoslovakia were in place. The government of the Third Reich, under its dictator Hitler, stood poised to annex his dear homeland, just as it had taken over their smaller neighbor Austria a few months before. Frederic had heard of the massing of troops along the borders Czechoslovakia shared with Austria and Germany.

The four-million strong Czech army had been mobilized to defend these borders. So far, no border had been able to withstand the German war machine. Frederic secretly feared that the takeover of his homeland would become reality before his departure. There were decisions to be made rather quickly concerning his home and the bank.

After he received his stamp for reentry from the customs official, he quickly made his way towards the waiting taxis. Before he could hail one, his own limousine crept up beside him with Francois beckoning him to jump in. Seating himself quickly, he turned to his faithful chauffeur with, "How did you know I would arrive on this particular plane, Francois?"

"That was not so difficult to figure out, Mr. Bartok. A quick call to your bank in Paris connected me to the gentleman who drove you to the airfield. He gave me the information."

"I forgot that you speak French, my dear Friend. So there is no language barrier for you. You talked with Leon Legout and he gave you my itinerary, good! I hope you will always be on my side. I wouldn't want you for my enemy." Frederic concluded, smiling.

"Speaking of enemies, Madame wanted me to mention the unexpected visitors that came to the house the day before her departure. Two men from the so-called defense force showed up. They forced their way past Pavel and didn't allow him to announce them. They wanted information about the estate; its size, the house, and who all lived there. Before I left, Bela mentioned that they intend to return tomorrow morning at eight o'clock."

While winding his way through the heavy afternoon traffic, Francois waited a minute before continuing, "We know that these people are in league with the Nazi Party here in Czechoslovakia. They hope for big rewards once the Nazis take over, which is probably only a matter of time." Frederic did not know that this personal threat to his property was already in the making. He was quietly weighing his options, when Francois said, "Mr. Bartok, may I mention something else of concern right now?"

"Of course, Francois. If it is something we should discuss, you might want to turn into Wenceslas Square. We could park here a moment, before I head for the bank." Looking around for a good parking spot, Frederic pointed to the right, and said, "It may be an unnecessary caution, but I am very conscious of this big limousine, now that the family is no longer here . . ."

Francois cut in, "That is exactly what I wanted to mention to you, Sir! Driving this attention-getting car seems not a wise thing to do. I wanted to suggest that I take the limo to the Citroen garage for an overhaul and leave it there. Meanwhile I could ask for a small Skoda for a rental, if you approve, Sir."

"Exactly my thinking," Frederic agreed. "Perhaps you can get this arranged while I am at the bank this afternoon. I might have to work longer tonight. Pick me up around eight. Please let cook know that we plan to make it for dinner by half past eight." After thanking Francois, he quickly made his way across the busy square to his bank.

When Frederic emerged from the bank building promptly at eight, he couldn't spot Francois until a small two-door Skoda, Czechoslovakia's own economy car, pulled up beside him, and he saw his chauffeur smiling at him from behind the wheel. This inconspicuous car was much more suitable for the necessary business trips that had to be taken during the coming days.

He complimented Francois, who reported that a lost part of the limo could not be found in Prague. Procuring it from France, where the manufacturer was located, would delay the overhaul. He held up a small part which he had removed. Frederic smiled as they made their way home in slow traffic.

"I need to bring something else to your attention, Sir," said Francois.

"You needn't be so formal," replied Frederic. "As long as we are by ourselves, you can speak freely." Francois was visibly moved by his employer's kind words.

"Maybe you are not aware of this, Mr. Bartok, but I too am part Jewish. On my mother's side I am of Jewish lineage. We just haven't lived the orthodox way. We rarely kept the Sabbath or visited the synagogue."

Frederic nodded, and said, "And you are not alone, Francois. As you might have noticed, we hardly visit the synagogue. Our excuse is our working schedules, but we have tried to observe the Sabbath by not working." Pausing a moment, he continued, "But actually, since we moved into the country, we have truly neglected our worship, especially as I increasingly realize that everything we have is a gift from the King of the Universe." Here Francois cleared his throat, and Frederic finished by saying, "Forgive me, Francois, I interrupted you to do a little confessing. Go ahead, now I will listen."

"Actually, by sharing this, Mr. Bartok, I must burden you with yet another thing," Francois said, while leaving behind the last houses of the Golden City and heading with added speed for the Bartok estate.

"I perceive that you will have to leave this country if you want to save your family and yourself. In fact, my family has already left. When Hitler took over Austria with no interference from other nations, they understood that our country might be next. They reached a quick decision to leave. They packed their bags, took only the most necessary things, and departed as if for a vacation. We have cousins in Portugal who have done well and agreed to help us. My father and my sister's husband found jobs right away."

Then glancing at Frederic for a moment, while navigating the smaller country roads, he continued, "I want to offer you my services if you could see to include me in your staff in France. I would work for you without salary, for just room and board, if you can use me. I hope you don't think me too presumptuous; I thought my being fluent in the language might be of help to you."

"As I made my preparations with the greatest of care I always presumed that nobody would guess what I planned to do—but you, Francois, seem to have everything figured out," Frederic exclaimed. "I just hope my other employees are not aware of my intentions!"

"I can assure you, Sir, that I have discussed nothing of this nature with anyone. I have only followed the news broadcasts and the newspapers. Then, when I noted your frequent trips abroad, mostly to Paris, it made sense to me that you might want to leave, just as my family did." He paused for a short while as he turned into the long, poplar alley leading to the Bartok gate, then he added, "I must admit, I have enjoyed working for you and Madame. I also know that starting all over in France will not be easy for you and your family, so please consider my offer."

Frederic asked Francois to pull over to the side of the road before they could be seen by Pavel in the gatehouse. He was aware that his trusted chauffeur was Jewish, as the mother's lineage determines the ethnic ties according to Jewish law. He also appreciated Francois' linguistic skills, and considered them to be an asset to any person in his household.

To assure himself of Francois' intentions, he asked him, "Francois, have you considered the ramifications of leaving this country? My assessment of the situation is that my family and I will not be able to return to Czechoslovakia. The Nazi takeover is definitely coming. If this is clear to you, and you desire to stay with us, however unstable our circumstance is, you are surely welcome. But one thing must be clear; we cannot let our plans be known to anyone. Therefore we cannot talk about our scheme where we can be overheard. We also cannot leave together when the time comes. You understand that?"

"Of course," Francois agreed, "that makes sense, and I will abide by it."

"We'll continue with business as usual, alright?" from Frederic. "When we have more definite plans we can discuss them while you drive me, nowhere else, understood?"

With that Frederic gave the go-ahead, and shortly thereafter Francois pulled up to the gate. Pavel approached asking what their business was. He had not recognized Frederic Bartok or Francois in the small Skoda. He bent down and saw Francois's smiling face behind the wheel with Frederic beside him; they explained that the limousine was in the garage for repair, and that's why they were in the Skoda.

"You can drive around to the back and park as usual," Frederic said. Before leaving the car he quickly shook Francois' hand, thanked him, and smiled, then hurried up the back steps, where Bela opened the door for him.

After a fine but lonely meal, during which Frederic checked his mail, the phone rang. The call was from Cornelia in Ville d' Evian. She wanted to know whether he had reached home safely. Assuring her that his plans were proceeding as hoped was not easy. They were aware that phone calls from foreign countries were being monitored. Therefore, they used prearranged code words to communicate particular things, such as musical terms that they were familiar with.

Next, the girls wanted to talk with their Papa. Romi asked, "Are you coming soon to visit us? We want to take you on a boat trip, Papa."

Then he heard Irmi's voice, "Papa, we have been to Ville d'Evian (she pronounced it with correct French pronunciation) twice already. We also take French lessons every day. We have a lady tutor. Even Bernie shares our lessons."

Then it was Romi's turn again, "Papa, next week we start swimming lessons, Mama promised. Then we might meet some other children."

He was about to say goodbye to his wife when the operator cut him off, informing him that they had exceeded the ten-minute call privilege. Frederic was disgruntled by this abrupt closure, but was pleased to hear that the twins appeared to be adjusting to their new environment. He so hoped that they would remain upbeat and be free from homesickness.

Early the next morning three leather-coated, black-booted men appeared at Frederic's door. He stepped outside, not allowing them to set foot in his house. Knowing their authority was limited, he gave them only minimal information. He asked for their official papers, which they could not produce, and advised them to return when they had such papers. He counted on the government of President Benes to still protect its citizens from unwanted intruders.

Later that morning Francois drove Frederic Bartok to town. They visited a large Catholic orphanage. Frederic had met the administrator of this institution before when he brought gifts for the five orphaned Jewish children who resided there. Madame Hradek had run the orphanage efficiently and lovingly for many years. She appeared to be a kind and trustworthy woman.

Hoping to keep his estate out of the hands of the evil people from the north, he had decided to bequeath the title of his property, and, of course, his beautiful home to the orphanage. This would relieve the crowded conditions in the children's home, and he would have the satisfaction of knowing that needy orphans would benefit from his property rather than the usurpers from Germany.

He hoped that this generous gift would make a difference in many lives. In Francois' presence he shared his plan with Madame Hradek. Her expression changed from one of stunned disbelief to understanding compassion. She realized full well what this well-known banker was entrusting to her. She also knew that this gift of land and buildings would greatly benefit her overcrowded orphanage.

They agreed that this transaction would only take place after Mr. Bartok had safely left the country. Frederic explained that the title and legal documents of his bequest would remain with his attorney, a trusted family friend, who would proceed with the actual takeover as soon as Frederic had reported from France.

CHAPTER NINE

ANXIETIES OF ANOTHER KIND

ornelia sat on the balcony in the afternoon sun overlooking the shimmering waves of Lake Geneva. She told herself she ought to be grateful and content, having arrived safely, and being surrounded by so much beauty. Her children were in the back with Bernie, where a brook and a beautiful meadow were home to a small herd of sheep that belonged to Madame Perrot. There was also an enclosure for chickens that provided fresh eggs for their breakfast table each day. For Romi and Irmi, it was a small recompense for their animals at home.

Cornelia was pondering a phone call she had received that morning which left her strangely disquieted. The director for cultural affairs, a Monsieur Ridreaux, had been on the line. He explained that a musical soiree was planned for Saturday of next week. As soon as he had found out that she was in town (she wondered how he could have found out), he had decided that she, too, must participate in this first-class event.

He told her that he had seen her perform in Prague two years ago and considered her to be a stellar singer. Was she aware that diplomats from many different nations were coming to town? It was a conference called by the president of the United States of America.

Although the director's call appeared to be cordial, Cornelia had the uneasy feeling that she was being ordered to a command performance. Her desire was to decline this invitation to perform, especially since it was scheduled for a Saturday. In all the years she had worked in Prague, her request to not work on the Sabbath had been honored. Not even once did she have to perform on a Saturday. Now, when she looked forward to a few weeks of voice rest, this unexpected event! She had no idea what this conference was all about, and did not really care. Why had the director's voice sounded so ominous?

She heard Bernie and the children, back from the outing, in their room with their French tutor. She noted that Irmi had a knack for French inflection, whereas Romi could not easily overcome her native tongue. But both were eager to learn French as they hoped to make new friends they could play with.

What else had the man said? She remembered that he wanted her to come to a rehearsal this coming Friday. She hoped to stall him, wanting to talk with her husband about this situation. But to consult Frederic at this time of great pressure for him about such a banal concern as this, seemed not the right thing to do. Maybe, if she obliged and performed as requested, this threat to her tranquility could be averted. She decided to run it by Bernie, and ask her for her thoughts in this matter.

When the French lesson broke up, both the tutor and Bernie stepped out on the balcony to greet her. Cornelia inquired, "Did you two ladies hear anything about the conference that is to start here in Evian this coming week?"

"I only know that there are preparations for it everywhere," Bernie replied. "They are planting new flowers, redecorating shop windows, and are giving the town a major facelift, it seems."

"Oh, yes, Madame, my boyfriend told me that this will be a gathering of the representatives of the League of Nations. I believe, he said thirty-two nations are involved. They are sending diplomats and their assistants by the hundreds. They are to decide what to do with the Jewish refugees that are pouring out of Germany and the Eastern countries . . ." With that she bid them *adieu* and descended the stairs, not aware of the reaction that her words had caused in Cornelia's heart.

"For the first time, I comprehend what kind of international crisis we are involved in. We are caught up in a very real, monstrous calamity which has befallen the people of my race, and I am being asked to sing!" she exclaimed. "Doesn't that sound like Psalm 137 revisited?"

"I don't know what that says," said Bernie, "could you help me to understand?"

A sudden wind was disturbing the waters of the lake. Looking over the blue-green waves, Cornelia recited, "For there they that carried us captive required of us a song; and they that wasted us required of us mirth." Tears were welling up and coursing down her pale face. "Bernie, I have not told you, but they want me to participate in a soiree to entertain those diplomats who are to decide the fate of my people. I would rather not, but I need advice—Oh, I wish I could ask what Frederic would have me do?"

"Madame, as we don't know when Mr. Bartok will arrive, let us put our concerns before the Lord. He alone can give us wise counsel." So the governess and the well-known prima donna bowed their heads before the Lord of the Universe and offered up a petition for His guidance.

When Friday came around, Cornelia walked to town at the appointed hour, holding both Romi and Irmi by their hands. She believed that bringing her children to this appointment would make it clear that she was on a family vacation and had responsibilities. She wore a flowered sundress and a wide-brimmed straw hat. The children were decked out in similar attire.

Entering the "theatre" that was located on the east side of the Casino, Romi asked, "Mama, have you ever sung here before?"

And Irmi observed, "The Prague National Theatre is quite a bit bigger than this, isn't it, Mama?"

Turning to Romi, Cornelia said, "No, I have never sung here before," and to Irmi, "You are right, Little One, the National Theatre in Prague is quite a bit more spacious."

A corpulent, short man approached them at this moment, saying, "We don't admit visitors at this time. A rehearsal is in progress."

Romi, perceiving that the man did not want them to enter, said, "We are not visitors, Monsieur. My mama was asked to sing here."

"And who might your mama be?" the man asked, wondering whether the lady leading the children by their hands was their governess. Cornelia looked young, pretty, and informal in her summer dress with the hat covering her dark curls. It seemed to dawn on the man that he had misjudged appearances, and then he asked deferentially, "Madame, with whom do I have the honor to speak?"

"Mr. Ridreaux asked me to come and rehearse this morning," Cornelia replied without giving away her identity. "He indicated that he was planning a musical soiree a week from tomorrow. However, if you already have an adequate number of performers, I would be glad to be excused as my first responsibility is to my children."

"Madame, please follow me," the little man said. Then the brightly lit stage was before them. They saw a group of men and women around a grand piano. A few steps up, and the stage lights engulfed them. A tall, black-haired man who had been addressing the group turned, and seeing Cornelia, exclaimed, "*Bon jour*, Madame, I am glad you found us!" and to the group, "Here comes Cornelia Kahn, straight from Prague. I remember hearing her sing *Madame Butterfly* a few seasons back. She was superb!"

A white-haired, distinguished-looking man rose from the piano chair, and heading for Cornelia, enveloped her in a hearty embrace, saying, "My dear Nightingale from Prague!" Then he kissed her on both cheeks. Noticing the twins clinging to her skirt on each side, he bent down, asking, "Do you two sing, too?"

Irmi spoke first, "We do not sing like Mama, but we can play the violin."

Bending down, Cornelia whispered, "Andre, what a wonderful surprise to find you here. What is going on? Can I refuse, or do I have to go through with this?"

Meanwhile, the black-haired director had turned back to the performers and was no longer paying attention to the small group on the side of the stage. The pianist straightened up, and spoke in a hushed voice, "It looks as if we should comply and get it over with, *mon chou*. Maybe your singing and my playing will make the players in this international game more inclined to give our people a chance. Let's hope for that!" He then placed his expressive hands on the girls' heads as in a blessing. He returned to the piano, and the rehearsal officially got under way.

First, a polished master-of-ceremonies addressed an imaginary audience, both in French and in English. A lovely ballerina followed with a solo *on pointe* to an air of Debussy. A violin concerto was played by an able musician. Duets for alto and tenor followed, and a chamber quartet performed. And still Cornelia and her children were waiting.

At first the little girls had paid attention, but now they were walking around and wanted to climb up to the balcony. Cornelia admonished them to stay close by, but was losing her patience. During the next break, she walked up to her friend Andre, saying, "Dear, I have to take my little girls home. We are here on vacation, not for me to perform. We are staying at Pension Perrot, if you need to reach me."

She had taken her twins' hands and was about to withdraw through a stage exit when the director noticed her leaving. He stopped the proceedings, running after her, demanding, "And where do you think you are going, Madame Kahn?"

Cornelia, who usually was not one to display her anger, was fatigued and hurt by the disrespect shown her. She replied, "Monsieur, I don't remember having signed a contract or being under obligation to perform for your soiree. My children and I have waited longer than an hour. We are on a vacation, and I deem it fit to take them home." After a moment in which she tried to regain her composure, "Remember, I did not apply for this chance to sing, in fact, I need voice rest more than anything after a very trying season at home. *Au revoir!*"

With that she drew both her girls out the back door and left the man standing, glaring after her. When the next horse-drawn carriage passed them, Cornelia hailed it, and with one girl on each side, headed back to the pleasant Pension. The horses clip-clopped steadily, and soon her tired children went to sleep. They leaned against their mother, napping, while Cornelia replayed the ugly scene in her mind until they arrived home.

After reimbursing the driver, Cornelia eased Romi onto the seat, and carried Irmi up the front steps and through the front door of the Pension, where she positioned her on a pillow on one of the chaise lounges in the foyer. Running back to the carriage, Bernie intercepted her and carried Romi into the house and up the steps to their rooms. Cornelia followed with Irmi.

When both girls were settled on their beds for a needed nap, Cornelia beckoned to Bernie, and told her what had happened. "In retrospect, I am not happy with myself. I realize that this is not the National Theatre where everybody, aside from the stage manager, knows me and shows me respect. But I simply ran out of good will, and, I know, I will have to make up for that one day. Right now, I am emotionally drained; I feel like collapsing right here. I can't go down for a meal!" Looking pleadingly at Bernie, she continued, "Bernie, would you be able to entertain the girls alone this evening?"

As Bernie nodded her consent, she asked, "Should anyone connected to this performance show up and wish to speak to you, Madame, what should I say?"

"I cannot face anyone from that outfit again today. But should a white—haired, slender man by the name of Andre Girardeau show up, don't turn him back. I will see him."

Cornelia changed into a comfortable shift. Bernie offered a back and neck rub which she gratefully accepted. Soon thereafter, she joined her daughters in a needed rest. She slept through Bernie and the children getting ready for supper. She didn't hear them play in the backyard afterward either.

Pierre, the young handyman of the Pension, joined Bernie and the girls and was whittling small reed pipes for them. He was in his late teens and had taken an interest in them. Secretly, he admired Bernie, who with her crown of blond hair, her sparkling blue eyes, and her attractive figure, seemed to him, a dark-haired Frenchman, a true beauty.

He was a rather shy young man whom Madame had accepted into her household when his grandfather, with whom he had been living, had to enter a nursing home. Pierre had assumed all the duties of a man around the house. He took care of the team of horses, the sheep, and the chickens. He lived right on the premises. Therefore, he was called to carry luggage, serve trays to rooms, and run errands for the guests. When any kind of repair work was needed, he would help out as well.

There was hardly ever a word of complaint from him as he performed his versatile duties. The other staff, the kitchen helpers and the chambermaids, all liked him. This particular evening Pierre had brought his whittling knife, and after selecting some suitable willow switches, he whittled two small reed pipes for the girls.

Irmi who was taken in by patient, kind Pierre, smiled at him, saying, "You did a fine job whittling a singing pipe," then she played two notes which emerged clear and precise. Next she said, "Romi and I brought our violins and a recorder with us. With those we can make real music."

And Romi added, "Would you like to visit us upstairs someday so we can play for you?" Throughout their conversation with Pierre, Bernie had to translate for them.

"*Oui*," he replied, and kept on whittling, making a third pipe for Bernie. "Aren't you too little to hold a violin and really play it," Pierre asked the girls. But Bernie assured him, the girls were quite competent. So he agreed to visit them one of these next days and have them show him their talents.

When they came upstairs, their Mama was sitting at the piano, improvising melodies and folk tunes they knew from their beloved Czechoslovakia. She was her usual cheerful self and asked what they had done after supper. They blew their little pipes for her and told her about Pierre's forthcoming visit. "Did you thank Pierre for being a good friend and whittling you such precious pipes?" Cornelia asked.

"Bernie had to translate most of what we told him, and at first, he wouldn't believe we could make real music. And, yes, Mama, we thanked him right good," said Irmi.

"It seems to me, Mama, if he wants us to play for him, we first have to find our violins and the recorder." Romi said.

"And right you are, Romi!" Cornelia agreed. "They are still buried in the wicker hamper. I suggest, after your baths, we have a search, and perhaps check who can still play?" Baths never went by so quickly; afterwards, they had a special time for the girls to reacquaint themselves with their instruments.

That led to an hour of music-making with their mommy who patiently helped with the fingering on the small violins. Together they were able to play several short trios. Then came a duet for violin and recorder by Romi and Irmi. Meanwhile, Bernie sat outside on the balcony in the twilight, giving thanks to the Lord for His gift of restoration to her mistress.

CHAPTER TEN

FRIENDSHIP RESTORED

The slender man wearing a Panama hat made his way slowly up the road from Evian. It was past nine o'clock. Bernie noticed him first. He appeared to be fatigued, but he was clearly aiming for Pension Perrot. She heard him inquire at the door whether Madame Kahn and her children were staying here. He said he was an old friend, and wanted to speak with her. By then, Bernie had made her way downstairs. She asked him what his errand was.

He introduced himself with a courteous half-bow, "My name is Andre Girardeau. I am a former colleague of Madame Kahn." Bernie offered him a seat in the foyer and went upstairs, while he mulled over the conversation he had had with the irate director, Monsieur Ridreaux. The same had been livid after Cornelia's departure from the rehearsal.

"If she knows what is good for her and her family," he had sputtered, "she had better do her part in this performance!" He had continued for all to hear, possibly to impress upon the others the importance of this occasion. "She may have been the adulated and successful diva in Prague, but times are changing rapidly. She probably has left her homeland for good, fearing the measures of the German government against her and the Jewish people."

Then he had turned to Andre as if he was responsible, "If she intends to work for another opera company, she'd better learn to make concessions! I can make her life unpleasant if she is unwilling to participate in our soiree next Saturday. You'd better convey this message to her!"

Andre knew the man as one not to be fooled with. He offered the excuse that the presence of her children had prevented Cornelia from being at ease. Ridreaux shot right back, "Can't she get help with those Jewish brats? That is not our concern!"

So Andre had come to Cornelia with a heavy heart. He had known Cornelia for many years. He had been her rehearsal pianist and conductor for several seasons in Prague. He knew her extraordinary gifting in music. She was not only an outstanding soprano, but also an instrumentalist of rare talent. As he recalled, she played both the piano and the violin with the best.

When he heard a light step on the stairs, he looked up, and there she was.

Kneeling down beside him and taking his hand in both of her own, she said, "Dear old Friend, did the enemy send you after me?" As Andre nodded, she pulled him out of the chair, leading him upstairs to her suite.

Out on the balcony, with the night getting darker, Cornelia asked, "Dear Andre, don't spare me. I know I crossed him, but he had me wait and wait, and the children were tired. They are my first concern."

As Andre accepted a cool drink, he smiled sadly, crossed his legs, and said, "Let me start with something unrelated, but which gains in importance in these dark days. I gather nobody can hear us here?"

"Unless they speak Czech, and that is highly unlikely," Cornelia spoke.

"Let me go back in time a little, Cornelia, perhaps then you will understand what we are caught up in. Remember when I left Prague for Vienna? It was for career reasons. I had hoped I would be successful, with greater responsibilities, and a higher salary. I hoped for an easy acceptance by my new colleagues. Instead, both my wife and I realized, we were outsiders, and the easy camaraderie we had taken for granted in Prague, we would never experience again."

He looked into the distance, as if better to remember the past. "The fact is, I was often in despair, remembering what I left behind. My wife's depression and subsequent suicide were the result of this rejection. They treated us like aliens, even Raoul noticed that. He didn't have that same struggle. He was accepted as a basso, highly acclaimed and needed. After Lydia's death, I applied to the Paris Opera and received an offer. At that time Raoul had a guest engagement in London and was offered a contract. So we both left Vienna the same summer."

Looking at Cornelia, he clasped his hands around his knee, and continued as she listened attentively, "But, you see, in Paris it is not much different. I have a job accompanying rehearsals, and working with individual singers, but conducting? No way. There are untold numbers ahead of me. Ridreaux, the director in charge of the soiree, is one of many directors at the Paris Opera. He has strong fascist leanings and foresees that France will have to bow to Nazi force eventually. He doesn't like Jewish people, but occasionally he gives me an extra job, because he needs me, and because he knows that I have no family and, therefore, am less tied down."

"But he is fully aware that you and I are of the 'Chosen', and therefore have to be endured, continued Andre. "He insists that you perform. He expects you back for rehearsal tomorrow morning at 10 a.m." Looking at her with compassion, he asked, "Do you have somebody for the children?" Then, after her affirmative nod, he added, "I believe, if you can leave the little ones here, you would be less stressed, and we could decide which numbers would be right for the occasion."

"You know, Andre," Cornelia replied, "daily I understand better what we are up against. We are the hunted and the persecuted. We have no rights. And it appears that we have to dance to the fiddle of the conquerors already, right? Of course, right!"

Andre had watched her with compassion. He still felt the closeness between them that he had felt during the years of their collaboration. He had never had the joy of having children, but Cornelia had been the closest to a daughter that a man like him could have had. Sitting opposite him right now, he took note that she was still the kind, loving, humble person he had known so many years ago.

Looking at him with her nearly black eyes, she explained, "You must believe me, dear Friend, that I am truly sorry for not having kept up our correspondence. I heard about your dear wife and your leaving Vienna for Paris, but at that time Claire Votek gave up her unfinished contract, and the powers that be at the National Theatre asked me to step in and take over her roles.

This was a time of great challenge and stress for me, but also of unprecedented career advancement. The roles I had studied for years, I suddenly had to make my own. It was truly a dizzying time. While singing *Madame Butterfly* or *La Traviata,* I would think of my new babies and have such a longing for them. Frederic was very understanding, but I could not ignore him either. Something had to give . . ." She looked down, then asked contritely, "Andre, can you forgive me?"

"My dear Cornelia," he assured her, "you have always been a little like a daughter to me, and parents understand when life's pressures are troubling their children." Taking her small hands in his, he added, "Let's not beat ourselves up over nothing. We are being commanded to perform and, with God's help, that we will do! How are you at handling Puccini or Verdi? If you are up to it, we could run through a few arias tonight?"

As she nodded approval, he sat down on the piano stool and intoned the first aria. It was as if time had never passed. He accompanied her with the same sensitivity as he had in the past. They spent a good hour reviewing suitable music. Passers-by stopped, listening to the superb soprano and her pianist.

It was already close to eleven, when Andre rose, saying, "Let us be thankful that we can face together the forces of opposition tomorrow. Nobody can reach your stature on a professional level. What I just heard is first-class, and I thank you for letting me accompany you!" They hugged in farewell. Then Cornelia arranged for Pierre to drive Andre home with the Pension's own horse-drawn carriage.

As requested, Cornelia arrived at the Theatre at 10 o'clock the next morning. Her heart was elated. Her husband had called her close to midnight the night before. Just to hear his voice was comfort to her soul. He told her that he would play his violin for friends on Tuesday. She had wished him success, knowing that this was his way of telling her when he might arrive in Evian.

Afterwards, they had shared news about the children's activities, and he reported that he had been in London and had talked with Raoul. Then again the operator cut in, and there was no occasion to even say a proper good-bye. But she had new hope and prayed that Frederic would be given God's protection for his intended departure from his home country,

Even Monsieur Ridreaux's brash manner could not disturb her now. She followed orders, sang her two arias, and was about to leave, when he called her back and asked for another number. He said the audience would include statesmen from many countries that were not familiar with operatic music. Could she perhaps add a more popular song or folk-tune for their benefit? Something on the lighter side?

As she looked at Andre, she hummed a few notes from "Summertime". He immediately intoned this just recently released song from *Porgy and Bess*, George Gershwin's popular folk opera. The suggestion pleased Monsieur Ridreaux. So it was decided that the program would close with this American song.

The next rehearsal was to take place the following Thursday. Meanwhile, the entire cast had to return to Paris to fulfill their various professional obligations. While Cornelia walked home, she reminisced on the happenings of the past week: Who could have thought, she would be coerced to sing for the diplomats that would decide the fate of her Jewish people?

CHAPTER ELEVEN

GUIDANCE NEEDED

Frederic was hoping to complete his last business transaction Monday. He was eating a quick lunch in his office when the telephone rang and a female voice asked, "Mr. Bartok, may I have a few minutes of your time? I need to explain a necessary business deal to you. Could I meet you in the foyer of your bank in about half an hour to discuss this?"

What a strange request—what might the woman be wanting? Of course, she could not know that this was his last day in the office. "With whom do I have the honor to speak?"

"Mr. Bartok, I will not waste your time or mine. Please allow me to explain when we meet in the foyer. It is urgent business that cannot wait. Thank you!" The phone went silent. Frederic, wondering what that was all about, kept signing his papers. He was planning to leave them in the care of his friend, Joseph Novak, who was an attorney and would handle the transfer of the titles to both his bank and his estate.

Twenty minutes later he was done. He carefully placed all the documents into a large file folder, then headed downstairs. Entering the spacious foyer, he noticed Madame Hradek pacing in front of the glass doors that overlooked Wenceslas Square. She greeted him with an anxious smile, "Mr. Bartok, forgive me for using a friend to make this appointment with you. The lady who called you is Mother Superior of the convent next to the orphanage."

"Do not feel apologetic, Madame Hradek, I know you must have a valid concern or you would not be here. Perhaps we should discuss whatever it is, in my office?"

"I would appreciate that," she whispered, "this matter is not for everybody's ears." With that he steered her up the back steps. When they arrived in his office, Frederic offered her a chair which she declined. Just then his secretary entered, asking whether he could spare her for ten minutes so that she could run a personal errand. Waving her on, he turned his attention back to Madame who excitedly proceeded to tell him about a startling and unexpected visit by two leather-coated, black-booted men.

Her attendants and the children, who were gathered around their tables for breakfast, had been more than a little bit upset when these men entered unannounced. One of the two men asked whether she still had five Jewish children among her charges. When she replied affirmatively, he asked especially about the children of Rabbi Englestein. He wanted to know how old they were and how long they had been in the institution. Then he informed her that new accommodations had to be found for all Jewish children, all five of them. He would be back as soon as things were arranged.

Right after that a call came for Madame from Mother Superior next door. She requested Madame Hradek see her immediately. When she had calmed her employees, and the children were again eating their breakfast, she had hurried to the convent next door, where Mother Superior explained that these men had come to her first, apparently by mistake. "Madame Hradek," she had implored, "you and I must take immediate action before these evil men can come to collect the Jewish children. They are Czech Nazis with a goal to destroy Jewish lives!"

They had prayed and asked the Lord for guidance. "That's when I remembered that you were leaving the country. You had told me, you were leaving for Geneva. We know of a Benedictine orphanage near that city, and we will try to arrange for the two Englesteins, their names are Hannah and Max, to be transferred to this place. The problem is the transportation, which must be set up as soon as possible. We can't wait another day."

"Our request: Mr. Bartok, could you see yourself taking these two along? Hannah is eight and Max is five. You might remember that their parents were murdered in Poland about a year ago when they tried to arrange for Jews to leave that country. The other three Jewish children have already been placed. We are mainly concerned about the two Englesteins as their father was so well known. And they have travel documents—arranged by their father when he left with his wife on that last trip."

Frederic understood that these two youngsters were in grave danger. He remembered the report that the late Rabbi Englestein had been involved in anti-Nazi activities. The death of both the Rabbi and his wife had been attributed to Nazi countermeasures.

Not considering his own safety, he replied, "There is no doubt, these children must be removed from here. I suggest you get them ready immediately; pack only the most essential items into a small satchel or a knapsack. My chauffeur will purchase two extra tickets for my flight tomorrow morning. Then he can pick them up before supper and take them to my friend's home across the street from here. There they can be sheltered for the night. I have one request besides, please pray for us. God has to intervene for this to work on such short notice. My hope is that there will be no backlash for you, Madame, when they ask where the five children disappeared to."

"We have already appealed to the child placement agency who are Christian people. They have promised to cover for us."

"There is another factor to be considered," Frederic said. "Do you think the children will understand that they must go with Francois and me, so that there will be no scenes in public? Perhaps you can explain to them that we want to help them, and that they must act as if they have known us a long time."

Madame nodded in agreement, saying, "I don't think there will be a problem. They are both well-behaved children. Hannah, who is the spokesperson for the two, is mature beyond her years. Max is a little shy, but will do what his sister tells him." She shook Frederic's hand gratefully, and added, "We will do as you suggested. They will be ready and waiting in the backyard of the convent in about one hour. The other children under my care must not be involved."

With a quick good-bye she headed down the steps, while Frederic followed a few minutes later, carrying the legal papers to his friend's office across the street. Joseph Novak had been his attorney for many years. During the process of time and of many interactions, he had also become a dear friend.

When Frederic entered, Joseph greeted him cordially and led him into his private office. He received the signed deeds and contracts and locked them into his safe immediately. They had determined these transactions some time ago and nothing needed to be said. At this time, Frederic informed Joseph of the danger the two Jewish children were in at the local orphanage.

"Would you and Irene be able and willing to shelter these two for one night?" he asked next. "They are Rabbi Englestein's children, and I intend to take them with me to Geneva tomorrow. There another orphanage is to receive them," he added. "You understand, this is a very delicate situation, and nobody else must hear about this."

"We will be looking out for them, "Joseph assured him. "Today the office closes at three. They can come upstairs, and remain in our apartment until you pick them up in the morning." With that and a friendly hug, Joseph opened the door to an alley beside his house, and Frederick quickly left to return to his office. Meanwhile, Francois was already on his way, purchasing the children's flight tickets.

Night was falling when Francois drove his employer home. They were discussing the unusual turn of events. Francois reported that when he arrived at the convent's backyard, both children were waiting hand-in-hand, Madame Hradek beside them. There was no discussion. She simply opened the back door of the Skoda, hustled the children inside, and closing the door, waved them on.

Once on the inside, Hannah had said, "Monsieur Francois, Madame recommends you highly, she says you and another gentleman will take us away so we will be safe." After that, both children sat quietly in the backseat until they reached the Novak home.

"Madame Irene was ready for them," said Francois. "She received them warmly and led them upstairs to their living quarters. I told her that I would be back in the early morning. She promised to have them ready. That is all that transpired, Sir." Then as Francois turned into the alley leading to the estate, he added, "Mr. Bartok, you will be charmed by these two; I felt privileged to transport them. I hope that somebody will give them a good new home someday."

Just then they passed the gate, and Pavel, not knowing that this might be his master's last homecoming, waved them through as usual.

Later, as Frederic was sitting in his spacious dining room enjoying a tasty dinner especially prepared by Raika, who knew his likes and dislikes so well, he went through his mental check list, praying that God would keep him on track. He must remember all of the necessary steps in accomplishing his plan.

He fully intended to set his house in order and leave his responsibilities in able hands. He had seen to it that all his employees would receive their last two months salary. He had written personal letters to all, thanking them for their faithful service. He had explained his family's dangerous situation and asked them for forgiveness for leaving without good-byes. He also wished them God's blessings for their future. These letters would not reach his employees until he was gone a week.

Special privileges had been granted to Petrov and Pavel. Both had served under his parents already. Title and ownership of the cottages would go to them. Frederic had long known that Petrov and Tirza were planning a married life together. His gift of home and land was to help them in their common future. He was assured too, that Pavel would be a wise steward with what had been entrusted to him.

After dinner Frederic packed a few things. Most of his wardrobe had been sent to the cleaners, who would be asked later to forward his garments to Paris. Some portable items had already been shipped to Evian. In the morning, he planned to leave with just his usual briefcase and his satchel for toiletries. It was to be business as usual.

CHAPTER TWELVE

FAREWELL

A t that time, on the top floor of the Bartok mansion, Francois had opened a map of Europe, and was busy plotting a travel route. He had decided he would drive the fancy French limousine to the west. Frederic had given him both registration and title to the car, encouraging him to sell the limo to make some extra income for himself. Realizing, however, the major losses Frederic had to deal with, Francois had made it his goal to drive the car to freedom, thereby preserving one item of his employer's property.

He had a plan of his own. He had written a friend who had left Czechoslovakia a year ago for Berne, Switzerland. Both Louis and his wife Beate worked in a well-known restaurant there. In order to help out Francois, Louis had agreed to purchase the limo simply as an agreement on paper. The "contract" to have the car delivered to its new "owner" by July 1, was already in Francois' possession.

Considering the difficult decisions his boss had had to make, Francois simply had not mentioned his plan yet; besides, who knew whether he would be successful? He counted on his dual citizenship papers to make it across both the German and Swiss borders.

His parents had moved their family from France to Czechoslovakia roughly fifteen years ago due to great unemployment in France. Then, Francois had still been in high school. He had a hard time of it in his classes, due primarily to missing language skills. But by the end of his senior year he had made acceptable grades and was even recommended for entrance to the university. His family had no means to support him for years of study there. So, instead, he had hired on with an internationally known circus, where he first served as handyman, and later as clown.

For the first several years he had enjoyed the traveling from country to country. He had spent time in Norway, Sweden, Finland, even in Russia. Later, he went to Poland, Germany, and the country of his birth, France. He had learned to put up with many hardships, living in modified railroad cars, tents, or makeshift housing.

His father had encouraged him to leave his nomad existence and had even arranged for an interview with Mr. Bartok at the time. Frederic Bartok, who personally interviewed him, was favorably impressed by this clean-cut, energetic, young man who seemed both intelligent, and experienced in various languages. He had hired him on the spot.

Francois was employed on a security detail at the bank at first, but when an all-around efficient chauffeur, valet and grocery-procurer was needed at the estate, Frederic offered the job to Francois, who had filled it longer than the twins were old. He had faithfully served this multi-faceted household, putting always his personal comfort behind the needs of others.

Now it seemed that their comfortable and familiar daily routine was coming to an end as the threat of a Nazi takeover of their beloved country loomed over them. Francois, who had grown very attached to his employer's family, and secretly to Bernie as well (though he would not admit that to himself), had now one goal: he wanted to rescue his employer's car.

His intention was to share his plan with Frederic on the way to the airfield. Meanwhile, it had gotten late, and Francois was bone-tired. He had helped with all the preparations for his employer's speedy and safe departure. The moment his head touched the pillow, he surrendered to a deep and dreamless sleep. When his alarm clock chimed at 5 a.m., he had only 30 minutes to get ready.

Francois was waiting in front of the main entrance at 5:30 when Frederic emerged, just carrying his briefcase and a small satchel. The household staff was not in appearance as Frederic preferred to leave for his frequent business trips without fanfare. No mention was made of their leaving for good.

Francois drove at the top speed allowed. The early morning traffic was sparse. No unnecessary words were spoken. Both men were emotionally drained. Picking up the two children from the Novaks proved to be a welcome distraction. Frederic was prevented from dwelling on his exceedingly great losses, and Francois was left to his own thoughts.

The children stood dressed and ready between Mr. and Mrs. Novak in the upstairs hallway. They recognized Francois and greeted him, looking at Frederic with shy glances.

"I have two little girls who are a little younger than Hannah, and a little older than Max," Frederic said, kneeling down to be at eye-level with the children. "I hope we will get along together!" Then he smiled, and asked, "Have you ever seen a stage play?"

Max nodded, and Hannah replied, "Yes, our mama took us to the theatre twice. I remember that."

"We will all have to be good actors, as if we are on a trip together and have known each other a long time." Looking first at Hannah, then Max, he added, "It would be good, if you called me Uncle Frederic. Do you think you can remember that?"

"We have been told that you are helping us to get away, Uncle Frederic. We thank you! We don't want to be killed like our parents were," Hannah said. "Max and I have been asking the Ruler of the Universe to let us be with a family again. Perhaps we can find one in Switzerland."

Frederic pulled them close into a hug, and trying to hide the tears in his eyes, he said, "Francois and I will surely pray with you about that, won't we Francois?"

After that it was farewell to the Novaks and a quick transfer to the car; then they were on the way to the airfield. Twenty minutes later, Francois pulled into a small parking space and accompanied the threesome to the queue for the plane departing for Geneva. Remembering the huge crowds at Madame's, Bernie's and the children's departure, Francois said that the wait looked considerably shorter. To an outsider, Frederic and the children appeared to be a family group heading to Geneva for a short vacation.

When their travel passes were checked by a customs official, he asked Frederic when he would return, reminding him that his visa was for a one week stay only. He wanted to know, "Are you accompanying the children to a new place of residence?" Frederic nodded, and the official went on to other passengers. A few minutes later they were directed to the bus that shuttled them across the airfield to the waiting plane. Only when they were out of sight did Francois remember that he had not mentioned any of his plans to Frederic Bartok.

Being suddenly without obligations or definite directions, Francois decided to stop at the garage to find out the status of the limousine. Seeing the elegant car standing ready for inspection, he took it on a spin around the block. The engine purred and obeyed his every touch. He felt led not to return to the Bartok estate. Instead he decided to leave immediately, while he still had the courage to do it. This would save him a day of waiting. According to Frederic Bartok's instructions, he put the repair charges on the business account of the Bartok bank. Then he wound his way through the early morning traffic and left Prague for points west without regrets.

Sitting in his chauffeur's uniform behind the wheel of the Citroen, a casual observer might conclude, he was on an assignment to pick up an important personage. He was on his way to Pilsen (Plzen), when he ended up behind a long convoy heading west to the border of Germany. A heavy rain was closing in over the dreary landscape. Francois felt led to take a more northern route to a border crossing point. His new goal brought him through Karlsbad (Carlovy Vara), the well-known spa, to which he had taken Madame, Bernie, and the children a number of times.

He was now driving through intermittent thunder and lightning, and the traffic had thinned out. Most travelers apparently chose to wait out the storm, but he saw his advantage in this weather condition. The closer he came to the border, however, the traffic picked up. Approaching Cheb, his intended crossing point, he pulled over to fill up the gas tank, using the ration stamps he had collected. Due to the heightened alert of the Czech military, all civilian gasoline consumption had been limited. He had saved a book of gasoline stamps for this very purpose while using the small, economical Skoda.

When he reached the border, he presented his French passport, and pretending his French was better than his Czech, the border guards bought his story of having to deliver the car to its new owner in Switzerland. The Germans, looking for smuggled goods, made a big show of opening the trunk, looking under the car, taking out the seats, and making a very thorough inspection. Seeing his small traveling case, containing only personal items and clothing, they checked his passport, stamped it, and allowed him to pass.

Thanks to the newly-built *Autobahn* (four-lane superhighway) from Hof to Nuremberg, Francois made very good time. His goal was Ulm, the historic town on the Danube River, known for its medieval cathedral whose steeple is the highest in all of Europe. He hoped to cross into Switzerland near there, thinking that his French car would not attract unnecessary attention in this southwestern corner of Germany. At the outskirts of Ulm Francois found an inn that was serving supper already. In the small parking lot he found a space for the car under an old linden tree.

When he entered the smoke-filled *Wirtsstube* (dining room of an inn), he noticed nearly all tables were occupied. The red-cheeked, buxom waitress led him to a small table in the back where a uniformed *Wehrmacht* (German army) officer was eating his meal. Francois suddenly realized how hungry he was, not having tasted any food since early morning. Studying the menu, and wondering what the German dishes might be, the officer came to his help by pointing to an entry, marked, *Rouladen mit Rotkohl und Bratkartoffeln.* He told him, in passable French, that this was the specialty of the inn.

While Francois waited, the German officer asked him where he came from, and where he was going. Francois explained how he was to deliver this French car to a client in Berne. They then discussed weather and traffic, while Frederic hoped to hear about the best border crossing into Switzerland. When his food arrived, Francois enjoyed the tasty beef roll-ups, served with red cabbage and fried potatoes. He was grateful to the man for suggesting this dish and told him so.

The officer left shortly thereafter. Francois noted through the window that he was driving an official German staff car, a black Mercedes Benz. After using the restroom and checking his map, Francois chose to use the same country road he had seen the German officer disappear on. It was dark now. The small German villages he passed seemed to be devoid of life. Coming around a bend of the road, Francois stopped when he saw a car with smoke billowing out from under its hood. Looking for the driver, his table companion from the inn stepped out of the shadows.

"Hello, my Friend," he said, then went on to explain, "the smoke began to obstruct my vision the same moment I noticed the heating gauge had jumped to its highest reading. I am no mechanic; I am at a loss about what to do." The officer was anxiously puffing on a cigarette. Francois indicated he would look at the damage then he moved the Citroen out of the way of possible danger.

When he returned with his repair kit, the officer told him, "This car was in the shop last week, but they were exceedingly busy and put me off. They told me to come back next week. Meanwhile, I received orders to make this trip into Switzerland, and now this!" He kept puffing on his cigarette until Francois admonished him to put it out, reminding him of the danger of being near a gasoline-filled vehicle.

After the billows of smoke dispersed, Francois carefully opened the hood. The officer supplied light with a strong beam from an army flashlight. After some probing, he found a faulty wire and a frayed timing belt. Francois replaced both and the officer thanked him, offering to lead him to the nearest border crossing, which, he said, was five miles away.

This time with the Mercedes Benz in front of him, and the officer gesturing to the guards to wave him through, there was not much of a delay. They simply checked the undercarriage and the interior surfaces. Then Francois shook the German officer's hand and bid him "*Adieu.*" He got the go-ahead from the guards, and resuming the driver's seat of the Citroen, he was soon on a well-groomed Swiss highway, heading for Berne.

Although it was late, he hoped to find his friend Louis and his wife Beate still up. He had not announced when he might arrive for the simple reason that his plans had been dependent on the safe departure of his employer and his family. It was nearly midnight when he pulled into the parking lot of the large apartment building where Louis and his wife lived. Their small apartment was on the first floor. Before he rang the bell, he assured himself that his "baby" would be visible from their windows.

Louis and Beate were overjoyed to see their good friend Francois, and laughed when he stated, "I finally brought you the vehicle you ordered!" After Francois refreshed himself, Beate asked the two men to join her for *Breakfast at Midnight*. This was actually the title of a German play, which was well-known at the time. While eating a light meal of fruit, soup, cheese, and fresh rolls, they shared their stories. Louis and Beate were very interested in the most recent developments in Czechoslovakia and listened eagerly to Francois as he told them about the growing Nazi threat, the rationing of gasoline, and what he had seen of the troop buildup at the border.

Later, after Beate had prepared a comfortable bed for him on their living room sofa, Francois knelt for a moment in grateful prayer. He realized it was not by his own skill and strength that he had made it out of the ever-tightening net around the beleaguered land he had called his home for over ten years.

CHAPTER THIRTEEN

FOUR-LEAVED CLOVER

When Frederic Bartok and his small charges walked into the Geneva Customs Bureau, they had a surprise coming, and not exactly a happy one! There was standing-room only, wall-to-wall crowds. Long queues of men, women, and children were lined up in front of five customs agents who sat in small glass-enclosed offices on the far wall. Everyone in this group had heavy pieces of luggage. Snatches of conversations in many different languages bombarded their ears.

Seeing their small satchels, and Frederic's briefcase, an overseer waved them on to another part of the building. Here they lined up behind distinguished-looking gentlemen accompanied by eager assistants and secretaries. There were also military *attaches* in colorful uniforms.

"Where are all these people going?" asked Hannah, while Max held anxiously onto Frederic's hand. Both children had been quiet and subdued during their flight from Prague to Geneva. They had sat on either side of Frederic in wide-eyed wonder. Nothing escaped their notice as they overflew farmlands and cities and gazed at the snow-capped mountains in the distance.

Frederic remembered that he had promised to make a phone call to Evian upon arrival in Switzerland. However, with impenetrable crowds and no phone booths in sight, he saw this promise evaporate. When he inquired about the Benedictine orphanage, nobody seemed to have heard of it. Finally, a young porter told him *"L'Ecole de Benedictine"* was located to the west of the city of Geneva, reachable only by streetcar or taxi.

Once they had been processed and their passports checked, Frederic asked for a taxi and was directed to a fancy hotel. Here a phone was available, and he could finally place a call to Pension Perrot. The receptionist who assisted him bade him wait in the foyer until she could make the connection. "Sometimes these calls to France are lengthy waiting games," she said.

"While we wait, could Max and I have a drink of water?" Hannah asked.

"Of course," Frederic acknowledged, guilt-stricken. In his previous experiences with children there had always been Cornelia or Bernie with him, and they had cared for the children's needs. So he quickly made amends, "Let's visit the restroom first, and then we'll order apple juice and sandwiches." Hannah and Max cheered up once their needs were met, and although there was more waiting, they walked around hand-in-hand looking at displays in the hotel lobby, then settled down next to Frederic until the call came in.

At first, he could hear his wife clearly, but the connection deteriorated as he tried to explain that she should not expect him just yet, because he first had to accommodate his two travelling companions. Next, Cornelia tried to tell him what had happened in Evian, but she was rudely interrupted by the international operator, "One minute to cut-off time!"

The last words Cornelia said were, "Frederic, I am so glad you made it to Switzerland! Come when you can and bring anybody you want." Then the line went silent. He pondered what she meant by her last statement . . . had she understood that two precious young lives were entrusted to him?

Hailing a taxi now was no problem, as most of the travelers had dispersed. When he inquired at the hotel about the many foreign visitors, besides the refugees, the answer he received couldn't have startled him more: The very Evian that he had sent his family to, had been chosen by the President of the United States of America to be the seat of a conference that would decide what to do with the Jewish refugees streaming out of Eastern European countries. And that included his own family, too!

Inwardly he was berating himself for sending his loved ones into the very eye of the hurricane, so to speak. How could he have known what the President of the United States would do when he had decided on the Pension Perrot for a safe haven for his own family? Frederic remembered a Proverb of Solomon: "Man's mind plans his way, but the Lord directs his steps. (Prov.16:9)" This was an assurance from the King of the Universe that He ultimately was in sovereign control of where His children were going. These thoughts were flitting through his head while the taxi was making its way through the outskirts of Geneva.

"Mr. Bartok," Max asked, "do you think this orphanage will be as nice as Madame Hradeks's in Prague?"

"But Max, how can Mr. Bartok know; he has never been here before either," his sister countered.

"That's right, I have never been in the countryside around Geneva before," replied Frederic. "Whenever I visited this city before, Francois would drive me around from one place of business to another. But don't you think that everything looks pretty nice and cared for here?"

Just then the taxi driver turned into a cobblestone street that led to a high iron gate. Behind it, they could see crowds of children jumping, running, and paying no attention to an old man who was standing by a fountain in the middle of the courtyard, trying to direct this traffic. Two sisters wearing habits of the Benedictine order stood near the gate, apparently agitated and unable to control the pandemonium in progress.

"This must be their afternoon break," observed Hannah. Then the gate was opened by the nuns; Frederic paid the driver, and as they were ushered in, the gate clanged shut behind them. When they asked for Madame Guignon, the head mistress, they were directed into a building, down a long hallway, and up a number of steps to a small office, where a friendly-looking Benedictine mother was stacking charts into piles all over the floor.

"What gives me the honor of your company?" she asked, then registering that this man and the two children must have come on an errand, she inquired further, "Would you be the party from Prague that Madame Hradek called me about yesterday?"

She extended her hand first to Frederic, then to Hannah and Max, and explained, "We received that long-distance call at a very trying time and were disconnected before I could tell Madame that we have absolutely no room left for additional children. In fact, we are understaffed, and have not even the beds necessary for the twelve children that were sent to us from Austria. We had to turn away five young ones that came from Breslau in Poland." She looked up to Frederic, pleading for understanding, "I feel absolutely helpless, Monsieur. Although I would like to be of assistance, I cannot help you."

It became clear to Frederic that this was not the place he could leave the precious children entrusted to his care. He shuddered inwardly, envisioning his twin daughters in a place like this with no personal care, little supervision, and no hope. While he considered his options, Hannah and Max, who could not understand the conversation stood next to him. Reassuringly he pulled them closer as he whispered, in Czech, "We tried, but I think we'll find another way."

At this time, they heard somewhat of a stampede, as the children from the courtyard rushed inside. There were yells, shouts, and shrieks, while Madame shrugged her shoulders, saying, "It is supper time, and they must be hungry!" She then led them back the way they had come. When they reached the entrance hall, they found a chaotic scene. Girls and boys in all sizes, disheveled and excited, were trying to line up in front of three sinks, where they apparently were making an effort to wash up before their meal. They saw boys shoving, girls spitting, and general turmoil. Madame Guignon smiled apologetically, saying, "We have seen better times around here!"

Frederic nodded to the lady, grabbed Hannah with his right hand and Max with his left and pulled them energetically towards the door, his only desire to get them out of this ear-shattering noise. Once outside, with the door shut behind them, he heaved a big sigh; then he noted Hannah wiping her eyes and Max looking downcast and pale.

The little boy spoke up next, "This lady sounded nice, but she had no room for us, did she, Mr. Bartok?"

"Yes, Max, I guess all three of us could tell that without her saying anything," he replied.

"I had hoped so much that this place would be just a little bit like Madame Hradek's orphanage in Prague," sobbed Hannah. "But this was worse than anything I could imagine." With that she stepped over to Max and held him tightly.

"Perhaps we should get ourselves together and step over to the street. I have hopes that a taxi will come our way to carry us back to Geneva, children." Seeing the hopelessness of the situation, Frederic had decided to take the two orphans back to Evian with him. He also remembered his wife's words from their last communication, "bring anybody you want."

It was twenty minutes later that the three were making their way slowly back to Geneva on foot. Frederic was holding Hannah's hand and was carrying Max piggy-back, when a shiny touring car pulled up alongside them. The window rolled down, and a female voice inquired, "Might you be in need of a ride?"

"Actually, I was hoping for a taxi to come along, because we need to go all the way back to Geneva," replied Frederic.

"I can see the children are tired, and so are you, Sir. Why don't you let us drive you where you need to go?" the lady offered. "My chauffeur and I were just taking an idle drive. We might just as well help you out, if you'll let us." Frederic nodded his assent. With that the car door was opened by the chauffeur, and first the children, then Frederic slipped in to sit opposite the gracious lady.

"And where might we take you to this evening?" the woman asked.

"First let me introduce myself, Madame. My name is Frederic Bartok, and we've just arrived in your beautiful city from Prague. The children are Hannah and Max Englestein, daughter and son of the late Rabbi Englestein and his wife. We became aware of a Nazi plot to collect all Jewish children, so we decided to remove them from danger as quickly as possible."

"Oh, my Dears!" the lady exclaimed. "I thought you were a family. Are you trying to find a new home for these two precious ones?"

"I was given directions to drop Hannah and Max at the "*Ecole de Benedictine*," but decided that this was not the place where they could be housed and taken care of."

"So what are your plans now?" the lady questioned. "By the way, Claude and I were just told that impossible conditions exist at this orphanage. The city of Geneva has to bring relief we understand. But what have you decided to do?"

"We are three weary travelers who need shelter for the night and a light supper," Frederic said. "Tomorrow, God willing, we'll try to make it to Evian, where my family is vacationing," Frederic replied.

"Did you hear this, Claude?" the lady said. "Should we try Mademoiselle Lebere?"

"Good idea, Madame! I can have you there in about ten minutes."

"Let me explain what we are trying to do," the lady offered. "We are heading for a very pleasant small pension which Claude and I have known for a long time. I often let my guests stay there, because my home is not adequate for more than a single visitor. Mademoiselle Lebere is friendly, and runs a decent lodging house. Let's hope she has a vacancy tonight."

Here little Max spoke up, "Mr. Bartok, my head hurts, my stomach, too."

"I think Max is hungry, Monsieur," was Hannah's response.

"My dear children, I could understand that much," the kind lady said in broken Czech. "You must have had a long and difficult day. But look, here we are already. Let me talk with Mademoiselle." And already she opened the door, and headed for a bell at the side of a bright sign that read "Pension Lebere."

Claude, the chauffeur, who had watched the proceedings in the back, said, "Sir, you will like it here, if Madame can arrange to get a room." Everything went quickly after that. Madame reappeared and led them into the foyer of the pension. Here a smiling, middle-aged Mademoiselle Lebere beckoned them to follow her. She showed them two small rooms with a connecting bathroom between them. There was a double bed in one, and twin beds in the other.

"Seemed to me, this arrangement might suit you," said the lady from the car.

"Dear Ladies, this is what I was hoping for!" agreed Frederic. The three of them said grateful good-byes to the kind lady from the car before the children went in to refresh themselves and Frederic ordered a supper.

They met their gracious hostess a few minutes later in the dining room. The children looked at the prettily set tables. Each table was covered with a white tablecloth, upon which sat dainty vases with fresh flowers in them. The tables sported butter and jelly dishes in silver containers. Already, Mademoiselle appeared with bowls of vegetable soup, baskets of rolls, and a platter of cheeses and tiny sausages. Hannah and Max had not seen anything this appetizing for a long time.

When they just stared and didn't help themselves to the food, Mademoiselle said teasingly, "Perhaps, this is not good enough for my young guests? Should I bring something else?"

As Frederic translated, Hannah said, "It is really too good to be true! Our Abba would say, "Let's thank the Lord of the Universe." And that's what they did and then ate heartily. Even Frederic couldn't remember when he had enjoyed a meal as much as this, considering the despair they had experienced in the afternoon.

When they returned to their rooms, Hannah asked, "Would it be alright for Max to take a bath, and when he is done, for me to take a shower? We don't need any help." Frederic would use this private time to call Evian and talk to Cornelia.

Half an hour later, when Frederic got ready for bed, he heard Hannah's clear voice reciting the Shema, then the 121st Psalm. Looking in on them, he saw Hannah bending over Max as she kissed him goodnight. When he asked whether they needed anything, Hannah tiptoed across the room to him, and whispered, "Mr. Bartok, would it be alright to keep the door to your room just a little bit open? Then we wouldn't be afraid—everything is so new."

"Of course, my dear little girl, you adjust the door just as you like it." Then touching her cheek affectionately, Frederic withdrew to his own bed, but he couldn't sleep for the longest time, contemplating how he could get Hannah and Max across the French border.

CHAPTER FOURTEEN

REUNION IN FRANCE

"I t seems Papa has found two travel companions!" Cornelia shared with Bernie and the twins.

"Where did Papa find these travel companions?" Romi asked.

And Irmi wanted to know, "Did he say whether they were grown-ups or children?"

"You know, it didn't even occur to me to ask. I presumed they were adults," responded their mommy.

"They must be helpless people, or Mr. Bartok wouldn't need to find a place for them, don't you think?" said Bernie.

"You might be right about that, Bernie," Cornelia said, "so all we can do, is be patient and speculate."

They were hoping for another call and stayed near the telephone. Finally, it was bedtime for the girls. While Bernie was reading a bedtime story to them, Cornelia was called to the phone. Cornelia noted that her husband sounded less frustrated than before, and asked, "Whom do you have with you, Frederic?"

"We will probably be cut off before I can tell you this long tale, my Dearest. Can I ask you to make room for two more little people? I'm bringing Rabbi Englestein's children with me tomorrow, God willing."

"You mean, you brought them with you from Prague?"

"Yes, my Beloved, they were about to be picked up by Czech Nazis. Therefore, Madame Hradek, the head mistress of the orphanage,

84

contacted me. She knew I was leaving, and that the children, if left there, were in grave danger."

"But how did this lady know you were leaving?" Cornelia queried.

"My Dearest, that is another story which has to wait until we can talk with one another face-to-face," Frederic replied. "Would it be possible to arrange with Madame Perrot for one more room to accommodate 8-year-old Hannah and 5-year-old Max? Both are very sweet and undemanding."

"That shouldn't be too hard. I will arrange it with Madame as soon as we hang up, but . . ." realizing the difficulties at the border, Cornelia added, "how will you make it through Swiss and French customs tomorrow?"

"I must confess that I have no idea. You must understand that this was not the original plan. I was simply to accompany them to a Benedictine orphanage here in Geneva, which we found to be overcrowded and impossible! While observing the turmoil there, I had a vision of Romi and Irmi in similar circumstances, and I shuddered. I then remembered your words, 'Bring anybody you wish.' That helped me make up my mind. Also, the Catholic nuns in Prague promised to pray for us. I believe God has a plan in all this."

"It would seem . . ." Cornelia began, but was cut off by the operator. No time for good-byes again, but Frederic was relieved that his wife was not opposed to having the two children join their family in exile.

When Francois awakened that Wednesday morning, a sparkling summer day greeted him. He looked out over the parking lot to check on his "responsibility." The bright morning sun reflected from the Citroen's windshield. It stood stately and unchanged from where he had left it last night. The sweet fragrance of freshly baked rolls and aromatic coffee drifted in from the kitchen.

Sometime later, having showered, shaved, and changed back into his chauffeur's uniform, Francois joined Louis and Beate around the festively set breakfast table. While the sun shimmered through the open kitchen window, a white tablecloth topped with fresh flowers in a small vase and shiny silverware set the background for delicately browned croissants, puffy omelets, and a fresh fruit salad.

It was good to be with friends, Francois had to admit. But when Louis inquired how long he could stay with them, Francois said, "It would be great fun for me to stay a week with you, my friends, but I have the strong conviction that I must press on and make it to Geneva as soon as possible. Somehow, I believe that my employer has need of me."

When both Louis and Beate looked at him questioningly, he explained, "I have driven Mr. Bartok for a long time and have come to know his way of operating. Often I have had intuitive hunches of what he needed. Anyway, please understand the seriousness of our situation. We are refugees, have neither home, nor jobs, nor addresses; besides, there maybe two young orphans depending on us." He then proceeded to tell them about the Englestein children whom they had rescued out of the clutches of Nazi oppression.

He helped himself to Beate's home-baked croissants, tasty omelet, and fresh fruit while drinking her strong coffee, and assured them that when he once again had a home and a steady job, he would love to spend more than a night with them.

Not much later, the sleek Citroen was purring its way to Lausanne where the decision would be required whether to head southeast to Vevey and Montreux, in order to reach Evian from the east, or to head for Geneva, which would mean a southwestern turn around the lake. After considerable thought, and listening to the news reports about the international conference beginning in Evian, Francois decided to drive to Geneva. He hoped he could blend into the general hubbub that would surround the arrival of many refugees as well as their international controllers.

Francois proceeded with the glittering lake on his left. It wasn't long before he could see the spire of the Cathedral of St. Pierre to the south, topping the hill of the "old city." Today he would not waste time in the old part of town, which was the historical, well-preserved Geneva. Instead he headed for the steamer docks. While inching along in the crowded city streets, he was on the lookout for his employer. He had the definite hunch that Mr. Bartok's plans had changed, and he was in need of assistance.

Francois was aware of Geneva's division into left and right banks, meaning the shores of the River Rhone. Eight bridges spanned the river, connecting these banks. He tried to maneuver his car into one of the smaller side streets in order to locate a parking spot. While braking for a truck that blocked his vision, he suddenly heard a familiar drumming on the trunk of the limo.

In the rearview mirror his employer was smiling at him while making a hand motion to open the back door for him on the sidewalk side of the car. Then Francois noticed Hannah and Max, who were literally clinging to Frederic's coattails. There was no time for explanations. While creeping at his slowest speed, Francois pressed the door opener, and first Hannah, then Max, and lastly, Frederic boarded the welcome transportation.

"You deserve highest praise, Francois!" said Frederic.

"Monsieur Francois, you will not believe how thankful we are to have found you, or did you find us?" Hannah exclaimed.

Max chimed in, "Monsieur Francois, you rescued us in Prague, and now again. Thank you!"

All these praises were embarrassing to Francois, then Frederic added, "I second that, because I really imagined you had sold this car and were planning to join the family by train or plane. How in the world did you get the limo out of Czechoslovakia?"

"Perhaps I share about this at a more opportune time," Francois replied, "because we have to decide right now which route we should take, if we want to make it to Evian today." Taking a sharp turn away from the docks, he asked, "How do everybody's passports and travel documents match up?"

"We just spent two hours at the passport and visa department, after obtaining a statement by the headmistress of the *"Ecole d'Benedictine"* that neither Hannah nor Max can be admitted there due to overcrowding. On this basis, we obtained exit visas for them. Perhaps the Swiss authorities thought that it would be one less problem for their country."

"This is good news for our intended purpose, to enter France still today," Francois acknowledged while peering through the windshield for the road signs to the border crossing.

Frederic saw it first, "If I remember correctly, we have to head for Carouge in order to make the crossing at Annemasse. Note the sign on your right, which points us to take a left turn for Carouge. Can you see it, Francois?"

"That seems to be what we need," replied Francois. He was following a big truck, leading in the desired direction. "I remember vaguely that we crossed into France this way before. Then it should be a straight shot along the southern shore of the lake to Evian."

"The traffic appears more congested here, but that could be advantageous for us—the attention of the border guards may be less intense," Frederic said.

"I hope you are right, Sir!" Francois conceded, heading into the southbound traffic. A fantastic view of the Alps to the south opened up before them as they crossed one of the bridges. They joined a long queue of slow-moving vehicles, heading away from the lake toward the small town of Carouge, and on to Annemasse.

Frederic offered a prayer, "Master of the Universe, have mercy on us. We thank You for bringing us so far. If You have no better plan, allow us to make it to Evian and be united with my family."

Hannah and Max had folded their hands and were praying too, while Francois agreed, and silently added, "and with Bernie!"

A few minutes later, a Swiss border guard was sticking his head through the open window, asking why they were leaving Switzerland. Frederic explained the situation, and he waved them on. At the French crossing point, they all had to leave the car, which was checked in front, under the chassis, and in the trunk. All seats were removed. The border police then used small hammers to check for secret compartments. After their small satchels and valises had been opened and searched, the officer asked, "How long are you intending to visit our country?"

To which Frederic replied, "We are on the way to join my family who is vacationing in Evian."

"We have heightened security due to the influx of many foreign diplomats," the man volunteered. "But I suppose you are not involved with the conference."

"True, true," offered Frederic, not aware that his own wife had been recruited to entertain these foreigners. Finally, their passports were stamped; they were allowed to get back into their car, and they were now rolling east to Evian on French soil.

"Monsieur Bartok, could we perhaps stop soon for Max and me to use the restroom?" Hannah asked.

"Of course, you patient little passengers, let's appeal to Francois to stop at the next petrol station." They didn't have to wait long. While Frederic paid for the limo to be serviced, the children disappeared for a short time to use the facilities. Frederic then produced the delicate sandwiches provided by Mademoiselle Lebere.

"What about you, Francois?" Frederic asked. "You have done your share of driving today. Not even to mention the anxiety of the border crossing. Perhaps we should all have a short rest and repast here." So a short while later, all four of them sat under a shady tree, munching on the tasty treats their friendly hostess of the night before had sent along.

"It seems to me," Francois said, "that we left Prague a few weeks ago. So many experiences have been packed into the last thirty hours." Then he shared some of his adventures of the previous day. The children hung on every one of his words. In fact, Frederic noted, little Max had arranged to sit real close to Francois; not as before, clinging to his sister.

CHAPTER FIFTEEN

HOPE IN TROUBLED TIMES

I f you turn right at the top of the steps in Pension Perrot, you come to the Bartok Suite. To the left, however, is the favorite room of the children, the Sun Room. Here one can find board games and puzzles. Besides, there are four square tables for doing crafts and art projects. Several comfortable chairs invite one to sit and enjoy the scenery. The view is to the south. In the distance one can see the French Alps, and on a clear day one can even spot Mont Blanc, Europe's highest mountain.

Passing the Sun Room and on the opposite side of the hallway, there is another guest room that has twin beds, a small bath, and a spectacular view of the lake. This room has been readied for the two "travel companions." It seemed logical that the Englestein children would have their own room.

When Romi and Irmi were told about the arrival of two children from Czechoslovakia, they were very excited. Romi asked, "Mama, do they really speak Czech?"

And Irmi concluded, "Then we can play with them and tell stories, and we don't have to worry about learning French!" Their only contacts with outsiders had been their French tutor and Pierre. For this reason Cornelia and Bernie had tried very hard to provide creative and productive activities for the twins.

That morning after their French lesson, Cornelia, Bernie, and the children went to inspect the room for the newcomers. They also joined in prayer, asking God to bring their Papa, as well as Hannah and Max, safely to them in Pension Perrot. Then they waited . . .

They had the hardest time sitting down to eat their lunch. They told Madame Perrot several times that two more children were expected. The other guests knew by now as well.

"Couldn't we go down to the pier and wait for them there?" asked Irmi.

Cornelia explained that their papa had not been able to tell her which way they might arrive. They agreed, considering the many different approaches to Evian, that waiting at the Pension would be the wisest idea. When Pierre invited the girls to go fishing with him, Cornelia didn't hesitate; she helped them change into shorts and sun hats and sent them off. Anything was better than to have them ask every few minutes about their Papa's arrival time. Shortly thereafter, they headed, with Pierre in the lead, through the meadow and along the little brook that meandered peacefully behind the Pension to the lake.

Cornelia, meanwhile, practiced the arias for the soiree while Bernie folded clothes and straightened the girls' room. Through the open windows they heard the motor of a car coming to a stop, which was a frequent occurrence when new guests arrived at the Pension. Madame called out a greeting. When they distinguished Frederic's voice in reply, both Cornelia and Bernie flew down the steps.

There was a joyful reunion! Frederic drew Cornelia into his arms, then presented Hannah and Max, who had stood back, hiding behind Francois, who was already unloading their belongings. Cornelia bent down, exclaiming, "Welcome to Evian," stretching her arms wide to enclose both Hannah and Max. Bernie stepped closer and greeted first Francois, then the children, with a warm handshake.

"Dear faithful friend, you must have worked a miracle, with God's help, to get the limo out of enemy territory!" Cornelia said, as she approached Francois.

The tall, young man smiled and said, "It was all in a day's work, Madame. And actually it was an interesting adventure, now that I look back on it. But I think Mr. Bartok had even more excitement getting Hannah and Max here."

"Both of you have to tell us your experiences soon," said Cornelia, while she led the newcomers into the welcoming door of Pension Perrot. In the foyer she stopped, taking Hannah and Max by their hands and addressing Madame Perrot, she said, "Here come two playmates for Romi and Irmi straight from our country. These are Hannah and Max Englestein for whom you prepared the extra room, but . . ." she added, "we have another visitor!" introducing Francois, who had followed them, loaded with luggage.

Madame Perrot was surprised when Francois addressed her in his precise French, "*Bon jour, Madame. Comment allez-vous?*"

"Monsieur, you sound like a native. Are you French?" Madame Perrot queried.

Oui, Madame," was Francois answer. "But for a number of years I have lived abroad for employment reasons."

"When we made the arrangements for the Englestein children, we had no inkling that Francois would be able to join us, Madame," said Cornelia. "Now we have to figure out how best to accommodate all of our large family." It delighted Francois to hear himself regarded as family.

"There is always the room next to Pierre's, just let me know what you need," Madame replied, then she was called off to the kitchen.

They were making their way up the steps when Bernie said, "There might be a way for Francois to stay on our floor with us, without renting another room. If Hannah would be willing to join Romi and Irmi, which I know would delight them, then we could check with Francois to see if he wouldn't mind rooming with Max."

"What a splendid idea, Bernie!" Cornelia agreed. Then to Frederic, "Dearest, can you think of a better solution?"

"Perhaps we are a bit hasty with all these logistical decisions," said Frederic. "Let's wait a while and talk it over with the rest of our people. Francois, Hannah, and Max have never been here and need a short time of acclimatization, don't you think?" then turning to Bernie, he asked, "What about my twin daughters? I had hoped to greet them, and wanted to introduce Hannah and Max to them."

"Dearest," Cornelia interrupted, "We sent Romi and Irmi fishing so that they would stop asking about your arrival. You must all come in first and make yourself comfortable, then we get them back from the creek."

Concerned, Frederic asked, "They wouldn't be alone by the creek, would they?"

"No, Monsieur Bartok," replied Bernie. "They have made one good friend here; his name is Pierre, Madame Perrot's handyman. He invited them to go fishing about an hour ago."

"Oh, yes, Frederic, this young man can be trusted. He has the nicest way with children." Turning to Hannah, Cornelia asked, "Hannah, could you see yourself sharing a room with two six-year-olds? Romi and Irmi, our twins, would love to have you for an older sister."

"Perhaps we should ask them first, Madame," Hannah replied with a shy smile. "Then, if they agree, and you still want me to, I'd be delighted to stay here. Long ago when our parents were alive, we each had our own room. But in the orphanage we slept in bunk beds. There were sixteen bunks in each hall. The setup here is very beautiful." She had spoken more in the last five minutes than she had during the entire trip. Then she asked, "Would Max have a nice room like this, too?"

"This we have to discuss," Cornelia said. "We need to ask both Francois and Max whether rooming together might work for them."

"Are you suggesting that Max and I might be roommates?" Francois asked, as he passed by with his last load of paraphernalia from the car. "My response would be, am I worthy of such honor? Here is a little prince, and I am only a lowly chauffeur and a former clown."

"Monsieur Francois, don't make fun of me!" Max piped up. "You know I'm no prince; I come from the orphanage. Being in the same room with you at bedtime would be so nice. I like you because you remind me of my Abba." He said this while looking sincerely at Francois with his big, dark-brown eyes.

"Max is right," confirmed Hannah. "Monsieur Francois looks a little like our father." Both Cornelia and Bernie grasped the significance of the moment.

Just then Frederic appeared, and said, "Why not show these two young men the room you are talking about." So they all went into the room with the twin beds and the lake view.

"Perhaps you two can give it a try for a day or two." Frederic suggested, addressing Francois and Max. "This is not a bad place, in fact, it has a magnificent view and a private bath."

"This is a beautiful room for a refugee," Francois confirmed, while tousling Max's hair, he added, "and to share it with this well-behaved, young man will be an honor for me." His reward was a bright smile from the frail, little boy. "I'll even let you choose the bed you like best."

"You really mean that, Monsieur Francois?" And when Francois nodded emphatically, Max went over to the bed with the green bedspread, touched it gently with his small hand, and said, "The pattern on this one reminds me of a puzzle I did with my Abba long ago."

"You are a very observant young boy," noted Frederic.

"If Madame and Mr. Bartok agree," Bernie suggested, "I could take Hannah and Max with me now to pick up Romi and Irmi."

"I think this is good timing," said Cornelia. "The twins had enough time to fish, and it would give my husband a little break."

As the children willingly and expectantly left with Bernie to meet Romi and Irmi, Cornelia hugged her husband, trying to hide her tears, but he noticed, asking, "My Beloved, has it been so hard to be here as an exile?"

"Dear Husband, I'm just so very happy that you and the others showed up!

I finally comprehend the perilous times we live in." She led him towards their room, saying, "You must have something to drink, change perhaps, and refresh yourself, before we go to see the girls. Once they see you, there will not be much leisure for you, my dear One."

"I perceive that you are troubled about something, Cornelia. Do you think the Englestein children are too much for us to care for?"

"Oh, my Dearest, absolutely not!" was Cornelia's reply. "In fact, I consider their arrival a sign from heaven. Romi and Irmi need playmates, and these two precious ones seem to need some parenting as well. You can rest assured, I'm very glad you brought these two with you."

A moment later, she added, "But you are right, something is troubling me; it is the conference that is being held here. And the part you don't know yet, is that I have been more or less coerced to participate in entertaining the conferees." Then the whole story poured out of her.

"I can't believe, Cornelia, that I sent you with our children to this place! But who could have known that!" He drew her into his arms assuring her that together they would cope with this situation. There was a knock at the door, and the twins raced in, hugging their Papa, and taking turns telling him how much they loved having Hannah and Max.

"They are waiting in the Sun Room with Francois and Bernie," said Irmi.

"They are speaking Czech and don't know much French yet." Romi stated. "But Francois wants to teach all of us."

The next morning the Bartok party enjoyed their first meal together. They had gathered around the largest round table in the breakfast room. Through the open windows the glittering lake beckoned; the curtains were moved by a warm breeze.

Around the table sat Frederic, with Cornelia at his side. Romi, Hannah, and Irmi had joined them next, with Francois and Max right at their heels. Bernie came last and closed the circle. For the first time the children were lined up next to each other—quite an eye-opener for the adults. Hannah, still wearing her bleached dress from the orphanage, appeared emaciated and small next to the well-cared for, rosy-cheeked twins. Max, wearing clothes rather too large for him, looked smaller than his five years. But his face shone this morning as he looked at his sister from across the table.

Romi and Irmi, overlooking externals, took turns saying, "Having Hannah and Max here is such fun!"

"It's like getting a ready-made brother and sister!"

"Now Mommy and Bernie can let us four play all kinds of games," said Romi, "and they get some rest."

Cornelia and Bernie smiled when they heard this. Then Hannah interjected, "Where Max and I come from there was not much time for playing." Looking first at Romi, then Irmi, she said shyly, "You'll have to teach us to play."

"When Papa called Mama and told her he had two travelling companions, we thought, you were two old ladies!" Romi said. That broke the ice and they all laughed together.

"You are much better than old ladies," said Irmi, and reached for one of the sweet rolls in front of her.

Frederic cleared his throat, saying, "Looking at my family which has swelled to eight members, I think we owe a word of thanks to the Master of the Universe." And that's what they did before helping themselves to the luscious treats on the table. There was fresh fruit: bananas, oranges, and strawberries in bowls, beside platters with different cheeses and sliced lunch meats. And then there were the rolls, which the twins liked best, although their mama encouraged them to take the slices of country rye bread.

"That's healthier than these rolls!" she urged. There was also butter shaped as lambs and chicken, and small bowls with honey and different kinds of jams.

"I have never seen so many treats on one table in all my life," little Max said with awe. That made the adults realize how deprived the two Englesteins had been.

While a young woman poured juice and milk for the children, Madame Perrot herself came with two carafes of aromatic French coffee, saying, "I hope everybody had a bed and slept well! Especially our newcomers?"

"Your beds are the best, Madame. We are so thankful, you could accommodate us all!" Frederic replied. "At least, I hope I am speaking for all of us." He looked at Francois, asking, "How did our young men make out in their quarters?"

"I have to report that my roommate did not snore and allowed me a needed rest." Looking at Max, Francois added, "Thank you, Master Max!"

Here Hannah inserted, "May the Ruler of the Universe reward the Bartok family for allowing us to be here."

"Just being together is a true gift from God!" Cornelia said. Then the phone rang, and Pierre appeared, addressing Cornelia, "For you personally, Madame!"

In Cornelia's absence, Bernie asked, "Would this be a good time to ask Francois how he smuggled the car out of Czechoslovakia?"

"But Bernie, why did he have to smuggle the car out?" Romi interrupted. "Don't we have to go back in a few days?"

"Yes, we will need the car again in Prague when our vacation is over, won't we?" Irmi asked.

"We will explain that when Mama returns," replied Frederic, while the others kept their thoughts to themselves.

"Andre was on the phone from Paris," said Cornelia, as she slipped back into her chair. "He said that I was expected for rehearsal this afternoon at four o'clock. Presently, he is still at a sing-through at the Opera. They intend to come by plane to Geneva. He also said that dress rehearsal is tomorrow at two, and I can bring anybody who wants to see the entire program. Perhaps you all will want to come, even Madame and Pierre?"

"Would it be understandable for the children?" asked Frederic.

"Mama, the last time you took us it was so long and boring," whined Irmi.

"You did not get the right impression that day," explained Cornelia. "Then everybody had to learn the program, therefore, we had to wait so long. After today's rehearsal, all the rough spots will be eliminated, and the numbers will be done in quick succession. You probably remember that dress rehearsals are like the real performance; you attended a number of those with Papa and Bernie in Prague."

"Remember, too, this always was a special occasion to dress up," said Bernie. When Hannah heard this, her little pale face became more pinched-looking, and tears formed under her heavy black lashes.

"You are sad, Hannah, what is the matter?" Romi asked, having noticed the older girl's reaction. And trying to persuade her, she added, "You will probably like this show. There are ballerinas, and musicians, and Mama will sing."

Hannah whispered in reply, "Max and I haven't been to a theatre for a long time. We'd better not go. We wouldn't have the right clothes to wear anyhow." Looking at Cornelia, she added, "Madame, it would be a great honor to see you on stage, but Max and I wouldn't mind waiting here in the Pension."

Cornelia realized how thoughtless she had been, to invite everybody to a dress-up affair.

Before she could reply, Frederic suggested, "I know the perfect solution to this problem, Hannah. This afternoon, when Romi's and Irmi's mama has to go to the theatre to rehearse, we will go with Bernie to town and do some shopping. What do you think, my Dearest?" he said to Cornelia.

"If Bernie is willing, this would be a good idea. We had noticed that the twins are rapidly outgrowing their clothes."

"You know what?" Romi interrupted, "We still haven't heard why Francois had to smuggle the car out of our country. Aren't we going back to Prague pretty soon?"

There was a moment of silence as the adults were trying to think of how to tell the twins the inevitable. That's when Hannah spoke up, "May I tell Romi and Irmi what is going on in our homeland?"

"Go ahead, Hannah! Tell what happened to you and Max," Frederic urged.

"Only three days ago, Max and I were very afraid. While we were eating breakfast in the orphanage, two mean-looking men in leather coats and black boots entered—they did not knock or use the doorbell. They told Madame Hradek, they were looking for five Jewish children. They said they had heard that Rabbi Englestein's children were in the orphanage.

One of the men asked, "Is this right, Madame?" When she nodded her head, they said that they had found a new place for us and would pick us up that very evening. After they left, Madame told us she would not allow these men to take us away."

Max who had listened very attentively, spoke up, "We had to stop eating and pack up our things right away. Then we went to the nice Mother next door, where we had to wait until Madame found someone who would take us away."

"Yes," Hannah continued, "Mother Superior of the convent next door let us wait in her office. She told us that Jewish people all over Czechoslovakia were being picked up and taken to places called concentration camps, and she didn't want us to go there."

"Is this why you left too, Papa?" Irmi asked, her dark eyes probing her father's face.

"Yes, Irmi," Frederic said. "In fact, on the night of your birthday party, Mr. Redgrave, Bobby's and Benny's dad, warned me about it. He said we should all leave as soon as we could. He was ordered by his company to return to London with his family."

"This was hard work for your Papa," Cornelia explained. "He couldn't just leave the house; there was Petrov and the horses; Pavel and the chickens and the rabbits; and besides that, Bela, Raika, Tirza and all the people at the bank depending on your Papa."

"What did you do with the house, with Raika, Tirza, and Bela, and the animals?" Irmi asked.

"What about the ponies, and Petrov, and Pavel at the gate, and the chickens?" Romi wanted to know.

As everybody looked at Frederic, he explained, "When I understood that we couldn't take the house, or the bank, or all our dear helpers with us, I asked the King of the Universe for guidance."

"Did He tell you what to do?" asked Romi.

"Actually it was more like getting an idea that I had not thought of before," said Frederic.

"Tell us what happened," Irmi urged him.

"First I heard of friends who had a large house in Austria. The German army took away that house, and told the owners to leave. Then they trashed that house."

"Does that mean the house was broken?" asked Romi.

"Yes, broken all over, and I didn't think we wanted that. Then I remembered Madame Hradek who never has enough room for her orphans. I also liked the idea of children living in our house. They could have the garden and the animals to work with. Anyway, I called Madame, and arranged for a meeting with her. Francois came along, right, dear friend?"

Francois nodded, and Frederic had the full attention from everyone around the table, as he continued, "Madame understood that I had to leave secretly and that nobody could know about my departure before I was out of the country. So we shook hands on that, and I promised her the necessary papers and the title to the land and house, to be transferred by my friend Novak a week after my leaving Czechoslovakia."

"Now I understand how Madame Hradek knew of your plans, so that she could send Hannah and Max with you," said Cornelia.

"Yes, Dearest, it was a plan only God could have designed! That very same afternoon Francois was able to pick up Hannah and Max, and carry them to the Novaks. The other three Jewish children were sent to other locations."

"Yes," Hannah said, "Max and I saw them leave before us. But nobody was supposed to know where they or we went!"

"Does that mean we can never go back, or never see Petrov, Pavel, or Raika again?" As this reality dawned on the twins, they both began to cry. Irmi ran to her mother, putting her face in her lap, while Romi headed for her Papa, sobbing.

"Romi and Irmi, you still have your papa and your mama, also Francois and Bernie, but Max and I . . ." here Hannah went to Max, and held him tightly. Then these two cried with silent tears as well, grieving their losses.

CHAPTER SIXTEEN

COMMAND PERFORMANCE

Finally, Saturday and the soiree arrived. At seven o'clock Francois appeared. He wore his chauffeur's uniform. The car was cleaned and polished. Bernie had assisted Cornelia, whose gowns needed pressing. Now she was standing on the steps with the children.

Frederic looked stunning in cutaway and top hat as he helped his wife to the car. Cornelia was gowned in a lavender dream of tulle over satin in a tightly-cut creation accentuated by a silver sash around her waist. She wore silver slippers and elbow-length silver gloves. A small tiara, featuring the Star of David in precious stones, sat on her black curls, and a necklace of the same stones graced her slender neck.

Romi and Irmi, who often had seen their parents in evening attire, were not overly impressed, but Hannah and Max stood with big eyes, not able to comprehend the change in the lovely lady who had hugged them and made them feel welcome earlier.

When they saw her in the matinee, Cornelia wore a red, full-skirted dress and a wide-brimmed straw hat. She had looked pretty stunning, they thought. They watched the ballerinas dance, heard the musicians play, and watched Cornelia perform. The high point had been when she circled the stage singing "Summertime" from the American musical *Porgy and Bess*.

Hannah and Max, too, were able to dress up as Frederic had sponsored their visit to the children's dress shop in downtown Evian. Max now owned a suit, and Hannah a lovely pink dress. Besides that, they had new

101

play clothes, the same as the twins. There were new outfits for school, which would start later this summer, and new underwear and night clothes. The girls now owned dirndl dresses too. These puffed-sleeve dresses in bright colors featured full skirts and small white aprons that tied around the waist. Bernie advised them to get different colors. The twins had chosen green and red dirndls while Hannah had chosen a blue one.

"That way they can tell us apart," stated Romi.

After waving to Frederic, Cornelia, and Francois as they drove off to the theatre, Bernie said, "There are two surprises waiting for us in the sun room. If we tiptoe upstairs without making any noise, you can find out about both." Of course, everybody wanted to find out what these surprises were; therefore, nobody made even the slightest sound as they made their way upstairs.

They found a big sign on the door, saying, "Only people who have taken their baths can enter. Night gowns and pajamas permitted."

So they scrambled to get these necessary chores out of the way. In the end, it was Max who was done first, waiting at the door respectfully. Inside was Pierre, ready with a lovely repast of Madame Perrot's cherry tarts and special creamy drinks.

"Did you set up these games, Pierre?" asked Irmi, looking over the three play tables ready for board games.

"I'm only responsible for the one over here," Pierre pointed to the small table in the corner.

"Do you know how to play chess?" Hannah asked.

"Actually, my grandpa was one of the local champions in chess," Pierre explained. At last, when he could not go out anymore, his only joy was for me to play with him." And he added, "When Bernie told me to bring board games, I thought, perhaps, these smart children could learn and enjoy chess."

"First let's gather over here," Bernie announced. "The treats have been sitting out a while and need our attention. Then we'll decide what we will play tonight." She had them all fold their hands and give thanks for the food. Then she said, "How would it be, if each of us gets a chance to tell something about ourselves that the others may not know?" Her intent was to allow especially the two Englesteins and Pierre to share without being drowned out by the less-inhibited twins. "This means, that we all eat our treats while we listen to one person who gets our undivided attention, do we all understand this?"

As they all nodded their agreement, Romi asked, "May I start, because I just remembered something not even Bernie or Irmi know about." Her large brown eyes sparkled, as she began: "When Irmi and I started to go to school in Prague, Mama said we had to be in different classrooms, to get used to be separated sometimes."

"I remember that!" Irmi cut in, then saw Bernie motion with her finger in front of her mouth the signal for being quiet, so Irmi stopped at once.

"My sister just broke the rule, I think," and everyone smiled, as Romi continued: "Anyway, here I was in this class with boys and girls I had never seen before, and I started to cry. I was sent to the principal. She asked me why I cried, and I told her I was lonely for my sister. So she took me on her lap and told me she understood. The next day I was permitted to be in Irmi's class. That is my story."

"Thank you, Romi, for sharing something personal," Bernie encouraged. "Would you care to be next, Pierre?"

"My story is about fishing with my grandpa. One day he invited me to go with him, and I knew he left very early, before daybreak,. I had pestered him many times to take me, but he always said, 'You need your sleep and I leave before the birds wake up.'" This was translated by Bernie from French into Czech. "So that particular day, I decided I would stay up and wait, so that I wouldn't be sleepy when he picked me up."

"How old were you?" asked Max, and saw Bernie's finger go up.

He blushed, then Pierre continued, "I must have been eight, I think. The trouble was, I was ready to go when Grandpa picked me up, but I fell asleep in the boat and didn't wake up until I was back in my bed. Grandpa thought I was sick, until I confessed what I did."

"Thank you, Romi and Pierre, for sharing your stories! We seem to have finished our snacks. So we will give everybody else a chance to tell their unknown adventures tomorrow night, would that be alright with you?" Bernie asked. "Are we all ready to play one of our favorite board games now?"

"Oh, yes, dear Bernie. I like 'Girlfriends,' how about you?" asked Irmi, looking at Hannah and Romi.

"You always pick that one," said Romi, "but Hannah probably has never played it, have you?"

Hannah shook her head, saying, "Any game is fine with me, but I think if that is a girls' game, Max should probably find something else to do with Pierre."

"I think it has already happened," said Bernie, pointing to Pierre and Max, who were bending over the chessboard, completely absorbed."

Little Max seemed to have an innate understanding of the game. Although Pierre explained the capabilities of each chess piece to Max in French, the five-year-old immediately comprehended and remembered. It was amazing to Pierre that someone so small could be an able chess partner in so short a time.

Francois, meanwhile, had driven Frederic and Cornelia to the *"Theatre of Ville d'Evian."* In the back seat of the car, Frederic held his wife and wished her well before Francois dropped her off at the backstage entrance. When Cornelia appeared backstage, her colleagues, admiring her lovely outfit, gave her a round of applause. What happened next, though hard to understand, showed the mindset of people poisoned by anti-Semitism.

Monsieur Ridreaux had noticed immediately the Star of David in Cornelia's tiara. He angrily insisted that she remove the offensive piece of jewelry. While her colleagues remonstrated with the shouting man, he yelled, "We won't have our performance tainted by Jewish symbols!"

Frederic was ordered to come backstage and receive the tiara, which the angry director had personally removed from Cornelia's black curls. A compassionate wardrobe assistant produced a small silver veil over an ornamental comb that provided a similar effect. Then finally, the show got under way.

While Francois parked the limo, many foreign diplomats and their consorts, as well as military attachés, flocked into the festively decorated theatre. The dress uniforms were colorful, and the ladies gowns sparkled with sequins and rhinestones; many feather boas completed the picture.

As Francois left his car for a short stroll, another chauffeur approached him. He wore a black uniform, was tall and muscular, and appeared to be in his early thirties. After mutual introductions, they walked together around the theatre. The young man, whose name was Maurice Cheveaux, had driven the French delegation to the conference. They found a number of common interests to discuss. They both agreed that the Jewish people were being unjustly persecuted.

"Oh yes, there is no doubt," Maurice said. "And I feel we young people ought to do something about it!"

"To be open with you," Francois responded, "my employer's family and I left Czechoslovakia barely a week ago, fearing for our lives. We are Jewish, and we saw no hope for our future there. We heard threats that all Jewish people would be disowned and sent to so-called concentration camps."

"Have you heard of the French Underground?" Maurice asked; and, of course, Francois had to deny that. "Some of the people here in France fear that Hitler and his war machine will not be satisfied with annexing Austria, and in the near future, Czechoslovakia. We are convinced he'll stop at nothing. Here in France we have a weak government and an unprepared army. Nothing will hinder Hitler from overrunning our country, just as he did the others."

"And you think Jews will be persecuted even here?" asked Francois.

"No doubt," Maurice replied, "if Hitler and his henchmen make it to France, anti-Semitism will be practiced big time. You already now and then get glimpses of it."

"And you think an underground organization could stop that?" asked Francois.

"If not stop it, at least we could prevent some things and interfere with the rest. I personally have thought about it a good deal, and I am ready to join." Turning to Francois, he said, "Give it some thought; and perhaps you, too, might want to help. My reasoning is this: if we, the young, do nothing, then we will become victims." He handed Frederic a card with his name and address, and added, "Should you be interested and want to know more about this you can contact me anytime."

Pondering what he had just heard, Francois explained, "I have spent more than ten years away in Czechoslovakia and other countries; I have no understanding of the political climate here. I will have to acclimatize again, and see where my place should be.

105

As of now, I am obligated to serve my employer and his family, as I have no family of my own in danger. In fact, we were just quietly moving to Paris, where my boss owns part of a bank, when this unforeseen conference interfered with the family's plan. They corralled Madame, who is a well-known opera singer, to participate in this soiree. It seems somebody has kept track of our move!"

"I wouldn't be surprised," volunteered Maurice. "Knowing the director of this program tonight, I can assure you, he has contacts with leading Nazis both in Germany and here. He is known for his Jew-hating in Paris." He pulled out a cigarette and lighting it, added, "You wouldn't believe how clearly the lines have been drawn already between those who want this dictator Hitler to succeed and those who don't. Count me among the latter."

"You seem to be well informed," observed Francois. "At this point, being actually a refugee and not having an address, I am on the outside, looking in. I wonder whether my boss has a notion what we can expect in Paris. He has not mentioned any concerns about the eight of us starting a new life in France, but he may know more than he lets on."

They had walked around the circumference of the theatre during their conversation, and were near their cars in the main parking lot, when they noticed a small door being opened at the side of the building. A woman was struggling to load several heavy boxes onto a cart. Maurice and Francois offered to assist the woman; this she thankfully accepted, and, in short order, the boxes were stacked on the cart.

Grateful for their timely help, she pointed to a drawn curtain in the foyer. "If you want to see the last part of the show, you can sneak in there and nobody can see you, but you can overlook the stage." The four ballerinas had just finished the "Pas de Quatre" from Tchaikovsky's *Swan Lake* ballet and were curtseying amidst thunderous applause when the master of ceremonies announced a trio of musicians, followed by a special surprise for the final number.

Francois whispered, "This is Madame!" They remained in their hideout while the pianist, accompanied by a saxophone and a trumpet, performed a lively medley of current popular tunes, to which the audience responded with frequent interspersed applause.

It was here that Cornelia entered from behind the big curtain on the right. She wore her red, full-skirted dress with the wide-brimmed straw hat, which gracefully accentuated the rhythm of "Summertime," the popular hit from Gershwin's musical *Porgy and Bess,* as she circled the stage. Her movements were alluring and supple. The musical accompaniment by Andre, at the grand piano, and the saxophonist were just right in their sensitivity. It was an astonishing performance of great artistry. The audience responded with loud shouts and bravos, requesting an encore.

"This truly is a talented lady!" exclaimed Maurice as they both stole through the small door back, into the vestibule, and then outside. On the way back to their cars, they overheard many accolades about the gifted and charming singer Cornelia Kahn, but one shrill voice was heard saying, "All the good singing cannot overcome the fact that she is a Jewess, and we know that Hitler wants to get rid of these people!" Maurice and Francois exchanged glances, and after a quick handshake, made their way to their cars.

While Francois sat in the driver's seat for a few moments, he overheard some French voices behind his car. Again the topic was Cornelia. This is what he heard: "I asked her accompanist about it. He said, at first, that he had no idea where she might find a new job."

"How would he know?" asked the second man.

"They apparently worked together in Prague and remain good friends. When I persisted, he admitted she might try Paris."

"She'd better think of another place! I, for one, will try everything to prevent more Jews from being accepted onto our Paris Opera roster. With the Germans advancing everywhere, we can expect German occupation in the future."

"Where does that leave the French people?" queried the first man.

"We'd better all prepare ourselves and learn German," responded the second.

Francois sat there stunned. What these people had mentioned seemed so possible. Was this what they could expect by moving to Paris? He was not sure whether this information should be shared with Frederic and Cornelia.

Then he heard Cornelia's melodious laughter and Frederic's voice, "Andre, you will have to join us for a light meal at the Pension, for old times' sake."

"Actually, I was going to turn in early tonight because we are scheduled to leave in the morning. But, of course, it would be a privilege to gather for a little while, for old times' sake."

Francois opened the doors for the threesome, and a short while later, they wound their way through heavy traffic until reaching the road to Thollon and Pension Perrot.

Madame Perrot had prepared a tasty soup. The table was set with selections of fine cheeses, rolls and bread, fresh butter, and grapes. For dessert she served petit fours and spicy herb tea.

"Seeing and talking with you two brings back so many memories," said Andre. "But we all know, other realities demand our attention now. We can't plan our tomorrows the way we used to."

"So right you are," Frederic agreed. "But we also know that we belong to a mighty God, who spoke in Proverbs, that 'Man's mind plans his way, but the Lord directs his steps.(Prov.16:9).'"

"My two dear people," Cornelia interjected, "let us remember Abraham and Moses and the odds they faced, yet God was faithful and led them safely through many trials. Considering how He has allowed us to get away in time, how He brought the Englestein children to our household, and how He is providing a new home for us in Paris; it seems to me, we are being well-kept!"

"Right, true right! And *Omayne*," Frederic agreed.

"When do you suppose you will head for Paris?" Andre asked.

"I want to be democratic and call a meeting where all eight of us can decide together." Frederic replied.

"If you ask me, Dearest," said Cornelia. "I am for a move as soon as possible. Mainly, because the children need to be enrolled in school before the summer is over."

Turning to Andre, she continued, "I am looking forward to seeing you in our new home. Promise you'll come, Andre!" Then they kissed good-bye, and they called Francois to give Andre a ride back to his hotel.

CHAPTER SEVENTEEN

ADIEU TO EVIAN

Early Monday morning Francois, in his chauffeur's uniform with the limo polished and shining, drove Frederic to Lyons. There he would catch the express train to Paris.

"I would prefer to take the whole family with me," Frederic shared, "but it seems now that we are eight, we have to prepare larger accommodations for all of us." Francois knew his employer well enough to understand that this was not a complaint, but rather an assessment of the situation at hand.

"My main concern right now is to make the Englestein children officially part of our family. I have my doubts," Frederic continued, "because even declaring Cornelia and the twins as my dependents was a major paperwork battle. I will apply immediately to adopt Hannah and Max, but according to French law these two are refugees, and that makes it harder for them to gain acceptance into this country.

"These are grave concerns," Francois agreed, "but with God's help they, too, will be conquered eventually." He had no idea at this time what role he would play in making the Englestein children citizens of France. They passed wide stretches of farmland as they drove through the French countryside. Cattle were grazing on green pastures, and shepherds knit socks while they watched over large herds of sheep. Everything appeared peaceful.

Francois offered, "I am still marveling at how we all were able to leave Czechoslovakia while the local Nazis tried so hard to prepare for the German occupation by betraying their Jewish compatriots."

"Yes, we experienced God's protection, which allowed us to be informed and plan for our departure," Frederic agreed.

"Mr. Bartok, I want you to know how deeply grateful I am that you allow me to be with you and your family here in France, but I must share some remarks that I overheard in the parking lot during and after the soiree in Evian. They made me realize that even here we cannot expect a permanent haven, should the German onslaught involve France in the future."

"There is great fear in those who are anti-Nazi that German expansionism will extend to all of Europe, and I am aware of this threat," Frederic said, "but at the moment we have to look for a temporary domicile that will allow us to find some sort of normalcy in all this upheaval."

At this point, Francois did not want to repeat the ugly threats he had overheard in Evian. Instead he asked, "Having French citizenship, I shouldn't present an added problem for you, but what about Bernie? Would she be able to obtain a visitor's visa because she is employed by your family?"

"I believe employees do receive temporary visitors' visas which require annual renewal. Once we are settled in our new home in Paris, I will pursue this issue." With this and similar conversations concerning their future, they reached the outskirts of Lyons where the two rivers, the Rhone and the Saone, flow together. They form a peninsula on which picturesque remnants of the medieval city still can be seen. The surrounding hills add to the beauty of the setting.

"It seems only a short time ago that I learned in geography class about the importance of this city," Francois recounted. "We were taught that Lyons is the third largest city of France; that it has its own zoo, many museums, and a fine opera house!"

"You paid attention," said Frederic, "because all you said I've read in the encyclopedia. Do you recall which industries are dominant here?"

"I seem to remember that the metal industry produces electric cables that are world-famous, and that Lyons has sheet metal works and foundries, as well as wire mills."

They had entered the railroad district by then, and Francois asked, while inching the big car through the heavy traffic, "Mr. Bartok, did you choose to be dropped off here because the fastest trains in the world connect Lyons with Paris?"

"Yes, my Friend, this way you won't have to make a needless journey to Paris, but save your energy for the outing to Chamonix, and for the trip to bring the family up to Paris next week." Frederic was referring to a day excursion to Chamonix in order to show the children the highest mountain in Europe, the 15,771 ft Mont Blanc.

Shortly thereafter, Frederic bid Francois good-bye and headed into the main railroad station to catch the Marseilles-to-Paris electric express. He settled into his comfortable seat observing villages and small towns rush by; he had the leisure, for the first time, to consider his and his family's present situation and to wonder what God had planned for their future.

Once in Paris, Frederic hailed a taxi and was at the Cohen's in a few minutes. His business partner's daughter, Rachel, greeted him warmly. They shared a tasty meal which she had prepared. There was delicate beef stroganoff with egg noodles, a spicy bean salad, and a jellied mold, followed by a sumptuous dessert of chocolate torte with whipping cream.

"Dear Rachel, you outdid yourself!" said Frederic thankfully. He noted that his friend and business associate, Davide, appeared somewhat agitated and nervous.

Then Davide shared, "Before we go upstairs and look at the remodeling of your new home, I need to tell you something which may have repercussions in the future." Frederic listened keenly when Davide recounted that he had been approached by people from the United States and Great Britain who wanted their bank to supply funding for important overseas enterprises.

"I have a strange check in my heart when I consider this proposition," Davide said. "In fact, I don't feel right about this. I used the excuse that I would have to consult with you, my business partner, before I would make any decisions. They tried to put pressure on me and urged me to make up my mind in a hurry; then I remembered that the scripture says, 'The believer is not in haste.' That settled it. I strongly believe this funding for 'overseas enterprises' is not for us."

"I am sure glad you didn't jump on this one," Frederic agreed. "Let's first investigate what it is all about." It was later found out that a German-American firm was behind the request for the substantial loan. An English business, too, had been involved by providing a false front to obtain funds that would ultimately serve the German re-armament drive. It was wise and morally right to deny the requested loan at this time, but two years later when the occupation of France by Germany became a reality, this would cause their bank to be classified as "uncooperative."

That same evening, Davide and Rachel led Frederic upstairs. The third and the fourth stories of the stately patrician home had been set aside for the Bartok family. The Cohens would continue to occupy the two lower floors with the kitchen and maid's quarters in the basement or *souterrain*. The first floor held a large living room and Davide's study and library, as well as his and Rachel's bedrooms.

After they climbed the fifteen steps above the first floor, they reached an airy, remodeled kitchen on the second floor. A glass door opened into a comfortable living room, which held the grand piano and Cornelia's harp next to wide windows that looked down on the quiet street below. Across the hall were two spacious bedrooms and a large bathroom with two sinks, a bathtub, and a toilet. This was no longer their lovely estate near Prague, Frederic mused, but he thought in the long run the children would benefit from being conditioned to a more modest lifestyle.

During his last visit to Paris, the fourth floor had not been completed. But Frederic had a surprise coming. As Rachel opened the door to the fourth floor landing, three closed doors were facing them. Upon opening the first door on the left, a good-sized, square room with its windows overlooking the rooftops of Paris, became visible. "Ideal for a bedroom," thought Frederic, but he'd already decided that he would have his wife make the final decision on where everyone would sleep.

When they opened the middle door, a lovely roof-garden opened before them. "Who would have thought this possible here above the roofs of Paris?" exclaimed Frederic.

The first impression was overwhelming. There were beans growing on poles next to tomato plants in large clay pots. An abundance of geraniums and petunias in boxes surrounded raised beds in which spinach and lettuce outdid each other as they strove to catch the abundant sunlight. There was a bench off to the left, and by it were a birdbath and a birdfeeder for small song birds. It looked like a place for leisure and contemplation after a busy day in the overpopulated city.

"How could such a small paradise grow here and be so well-cared for?" asked Frederic. "There isn't even one weed in sight!"

Here Rachel pointed to her dad, as he said, "This had been a pipe dream of mine for some time; when you decided to move in with us, I thought I should give it a try, and it seems God liked the idea too, and gave the growth."

"But, Frederic," he continued, "you have to see what Rachel has prepared for your kids." With that he opened a small door off to the right, and Frederic, stepping from the roof garden over the threshold couldn't believe his eyes.

Here was a playroom complete with an exercise ladder leading up the opposite wall. On the shelves along the other sides of the room were stacks of board games, pots of crayons, pencils, and paper supplies. Two worktables with two chairs each stood under barred windows, and there was an array of children's books spread around, inviting eager little hands to pick them up and read.

"If the children find this place as enchanting as I do, you will have a hard time prying them loose from here," observed Frederic, and he meant it.

Turning to Rachel, he asked, "Was this a favorite place of yours as well?"

"Yes, my brother Nathan and I often brought our friends up here; later it became our favorite reading hide-out, to which we escaped when we didn't want to be disturbed. Now that he has gone to Marseilles to work in the export-import business, I have lost interest, besides, I have so much studying to do, being at the Sorbonne, that I usually end up in Dad's library. Now I have too many heavy textbooks to carry around."

"But we do hope your children will make good use of this place," Davide added. "I know Marie and Rachel spent many hours here last week cleaning away a lot of spider webs, dirt, and dust. Your children should have a good time up here, and they won't disturb their mother if she has to practice. Perhaps you noticed the secure windows and the double fence bordering the roof-garden? We wanted to make sure nobody could fall 'overboard.'"

CHAPTER EIGHTEEN

EUROPE'S HIGHEST MOUNTAIN

The next morning Francois was packing wraps and rucksacks, and boots and provisions into the trunk of the limo. The plan was to leave right after breakfast and visit Chamonix, the French resort at the foot of Mont Blanc. There was a bit of commotion getting all four children ready after breakfast. But since they were all eager to go, they piled into the spacious car without complaint. Max sat on the front seat right next to Francois. He was excited and very observant. He pointed at the rock outcroppings and their fellow travelers along the narrow mountain road.

Francois concentrated as he navigated through the increasingly heavy traffic. He tried to avoid oncoming vehicles, which included slow-moving, horse-drawn carriages.

"Monsieur Francois, is that a mountain goat?" Max pointed his forefinger at the cliffs on the right.

"They are called *chamois* around here, I think," Francois replied in French; because all the adults in the family had agreed to use French exclusively to help familiarize the children with their new language.

"Look, it disappeared; it must be very shy," observed Max. Then pointing ahead, he exclaimed, "Snow in the summer! How can that be?"

"I read that Chamonix is located 3,416 feet above sea level. At such an altitude snow stays longer in the places the sun doesn't reach every day."

"Do we have such high places in Czechoslovakia?" Max inquired.

Hannah interrupted, "Max, you can't distract Monsieur Francois all the time; he has to watch the street to get us safely to the mountains." She was sitting between Romi and Irmi on the middle seat of the touring car, facing Cornelia and Bernie who occupied the back seat. Hannah was grateful that the twins accepted her like an older sister. Her greatest fear was that Max and she would have to return to the orphanage. Her eight-year life experience had taught her that one had to adjust to get along. The adults often marveled how kind and obedient she was in problematic situations.

A short time later they arrived in the mountain resort Chamonix. As they unpacked their gear, Francois saw to it that each of the children carried a small rucksack (backpack); the ladies each a satchel with their provisions, while he shouldered the pack with their boots and heavy coats. They joined a group of hikers who headed for the *Mer de Glace*, the massive glacier stretching down the side of the mountain, from which the river Arve waters the whole valley.

They followed a trail that wound its way upward in a serpentine fashion. Marmots, chipmunks, and agile chamois were visible, and disappeared when their group came too close. The children would run ahead, then, breathlessly sit down and wait until the adults caught up. The views of the mountain massif, with the glacier stretching along its side, were grandiose, incomparable to anything they had ever seen up close. Cornelia and Bernie chose a picnic site among a copse of low evergreens. To their left stretched mountain meadows with a multitude of alpine flowers.

"I would love to pick you a bouquet, Mama," Romi offered, "but I know what you will say."

"Let me guess," Irmi interjected, "Mama would say, "these flowers are much too pretty to be put into a vase, and, besides, they would wilt on our way home."

"Right?" Romi queried.

"True right!" and picking up a rock which glittered with fool's gold, Cornelia suggested, "You could look around for special shapes of these, and we could start our own rock collection. In fact," pulling out some pretty woven bags, "these might be of help in gathering them, but I only have three bags."

"That's good for the girls," Max observed. "The pockets of my *Lederhosen* are pretty big so I can put my rocks into them."

After deciding not to ride the cable car that dangled on a heavy metal coil over the valley and headed upward into low-hanging clouds, the children scampered around finding beautiful rocks of many shapes, until there was a faint cry from behind a huge boulder. Bernie, who was closest, knelt down by Hannah, who had slipped, skinning her shin and knee. At first she whimpered a little, but was brave when Bernie produced her first-aid kit, washed out the wound with alcohol, and covered it with a sizable gauze bandage. After that, Cornelia and Francois walked ahead with the three younger children, and Bernie, holding Hannah's hand, followed.

"This reminds me of walking with my Imma," stated Hannah, still sobbing now and then.

Bernie picked up on the memory, and asked, "What do you remember about your Mama?"

"It's real hard sometimes to remember what she looked like. You know, I don't even have a photo of her." Next she added, "But you, Bernie, are about the same shape. Only you have this wavy, blonde hair. Our Imma had long, black hair which she wound around her head like a crown. She was usually very quiet, and our Abba said often, she was the best helpmeet a man could call his own. You know, our Abba was a Rabbi. Many people came to him, and he talked with them. He was always friendly."

Did he teach you how to talk to God?" Bernie asked. "No, I can't remember that," Hannah replied. "He told me one time, I should become like Hannah the mother of Samuel who was a great prophet. He anointed David to become the second king of Israel." Bernie could not resist asking, "Did he tell you who the first king of Israel was?"

"O yes, his name was Saul, and he was very tall, but he displeased God and didn't obey Him. He died in a battle with the Philistines on the mountains of Gilboa."

"You seem to know stories from the scriptures well. Perhaps you can help me read one to the twins at bedtime. You could help explain them to the girls."

"Could Max listen in too?" Hannah asked. "I know, our Abba would want him to hear these as well. Don't you have a Bible with the Old and the New Testaments?"

"Yes, you are right, I do," answered Bernie.

"They had that kind of Bible in the orphanage, and when we went to chapel, the priest sometimes read from it. But once when I asked Madame Hradek whether I could read from their Bible by myself, she said, 'We don't read the Bible by ourselves.'"

"That's the Catholic way," explained Bernie. "Our pastor wants us to read each day a portion of God's Word, for that's what the Bible is. God gave it to us so that He could guide us. I know a song that explains that." So there on the mountainside, on the trail back to the French village of Chamonix, Bernie sang from the 119th Psalm, "Thy Word is a lamp unto my feet and a light unto my path." She repeated it, and Hannah chimed in. Singing it the third time together, they reached the rest of their group.

"What a lovely song!" Cornelia exclaimed, "It seems to echo back from the mountain. Bernie, you'll have to teach it to all of us."

They reached a tricky part of the trail, where smaller gravel like stones were scattered over a rocky surface, which made their footing treacherous. Coming up the trail, they had not minded, but after Hannah's accident they were trying to make it back to the village during daylight, so they reordered their group.

Cornelia led, holding Max by his hand, and the three girls followed close behind her. Francois reached for Bernie's arm as she lost control of her footing, uttering a short cry for help. She looked up at him, thanking him. As their eyes met, his dark ones meeting her clear blue orbs, she blushed, and he drew her closer for a moment to steady her. There was recognition of a new emotion between them. And although the moment passed, and they continued on their downward trek, both of them were pondering, what they had just experienced.

When they piled back into their car, they carried three bags of selected rocks and the memory of a majestic mountain with its covering by an enormous glacier, the *Mer de Glace*. The first stars were glittering above their long way home through the narrow mountain valley.

It was late when they arrived back at Pension Perrot. Francois carried the sleeping Max up to their room, while the girls tiptoed upstairs in order not to disturb the other guests. Cornelia and Bernie were emptying the car when Madame Perrot appeared with a letter addressed to Cornelia. It was a note from Andre. While reading it, Cornelia couldn't stop tears from rolling down her pale face. This is what it said,

Dear Cornelia, the outcome of the infernal conference is bad beyond description. All your and my hopes have been smashed. Every one of the thirty-two participating nations has decided to refuse immigration to Jewish refugees. Only God can help! I see desperate times ahead. Wished I could share better news. With all my concerns, Andre

Cornelia handed the letter to Bernie, sobbing, "I can't understand such inhuman cruelty." Bernie shook her head, as she perused Andre's writing, and then she reached out to Cornelia who fell into her arms like a helpless child. They stood a moment in despair; then Cornelia righted herself, saying: "Let us keep this information to ourselves for now, Bernie. The others don't need to know this yet."

CHAPTER NINETEEN

PARIS BECKONS

"How is my Dearest today?" Frederic's voice sounded distant and upbeat the next morning, as his call caught them at the breakfast table. He continued, "This will be short, I just wanted to ask you whether you thought it right to close shop in Evian, and head to Paris?"

"Oh, Frederic, that was my very own hope!" Cornelia responded. "I was going to call you and ask you the same thing."

His next question, "How was your outing to Chamonix?"

She answered with, "Seeing Mont Blanc, the scenery, and the wildlife was a treat for all of us, but I have to admit the *Mer de Glace*, this seemingly eternal glacier, revealed to me God's omnipotence and grandeur in a new way. It was as if He revealed to me, 'So far and no further!'"

Here Irmi interjected, "Tell Papa that Hannah had an accident!"

"Yes, Frederic, Irmi reminds me that Hannah got her shin and knee scraped on a rock, but we think she is healing well."

"Can you still hear me?" Frederic asked. "Assure Hannah that God has built into each one of his children His healing power. She will heal just fine."

"We also had a letter from Andre, he reported from Paris about the outcome of the international conference here in Evian."

There was a short pause, and then Frederic said, "My darling, I already talked with Andre. The outcome of this conference is tragic and disgusting, but there is nothing we can do about it. And what is worse, we are part of the refugee problem! If it weren't for Davide Cohen here in Paris, and my holding part ownership in his bank, we, too, would be wandering around, not knowing where to go. As of now Davide and Rachel grant us asylum in their home, but I must admit, this might not be a permanent solution. The signs are not all positive. There are strong anti-Semitic sentiments here. We have to take each day as the Master of the Universe directs."

"I understand, my Heart," Cornelia agreed. She had walked away from the breakfast table and stood in a corner with her back to her family who continued to finish their meal with Bernie and Francois supervising.

"I strongly believe, we should be together at a time like this, don't you?"

"Exactly my understanding," Frederic replied. "I am looking forward to your coming. It may be also God's will that we make a new home for the Englestein children, as well as for Francois and Bernie."

"So true, Frederic!" said Cornelia, and then she added, "Regarding our departure: I will make all arrangements, settle accounts with Madame, and God willing, we'll leave tomorrow right after breakfast."

Frederic's voice became more difficult to understand, but Cornelia heard, "Dearest, be sure to explain to the rest of the party that we have a bunch of empty rooms here. We will have to work together to make this a home for the eight of us. Please tell Francois that we will need his assistance big time!" Then Frederic's voice faded away, and Cornelia hung up.

The next morning, with Bernie and the children tucked into the two back seats of the car in the midst of packages, satchels, suitcases, packages, and provisions generously provided by Madame Perrot, they were on their way to Paris. Cornelia occupied the passenger seat next to Francois. They made good time to Lyons, although they encountered heavy traffic once they entered the Rhone valley.

Bernie had her hands full providing activities and distractions to keep the children from becoming impatient. Occasionally, there would be a shared glance with Francois, or a smile through the rearview mirror that kept them connected. These two trusted employees of the Bartok family had discovered a new closeness, which caused Bernie to ponder. But the demands of the moment kept her from daydreams.

After several hours of travel through the warm July countryside, Bernie and the children experienced the fatigue that accompanies being lulled by a purring motor and a lack of things to do. Francois' call for a break was welcome, and they all wriggled out of their tight places to stretch and look at a big gate right in front of them. The sign over the gate said *"Jardins de Marty-Restaurant."* (Marty's Garden Restaurant).

After a restroom break, Cornelia ordered their meal from Madame Marty. The children ran to a little brook behind the establishment. When they noticed lambs and calves on the meadow nearby, Romi came begging, "O Mama, could Irmi, Hannah, Max, and I go pet the animals in the meadow?"

Hearing the question, Madame Marty, said, "Little Mademoiselle, if you wait for a minute, my husband will come and show you the animals." With that she picked up a long-handled bell, and shook it. You could hear it for a mile away. Soon thereafter, Monsieur Marty appeared. He was dressed in overalls over a short-sleeved checkered shirt and wore a farmer's straw hat. Under it two merry brown eyes sparkled. He was the kind of man you trusted, regardless of how long you had known him.

Monsieur Marty spoke French quickly, in the local dialect, so Francois acted as interpreter. He told them, that Monsieur Marty owned also a string of ponies, besides the lambs and the calves. He would let them ride the ponies, if they would obey instructions. So Bernie and Francois followed the children, who in turn eagerly kept pace with the long-legged Monsieur Marty.

Meanwhile, Cornelia went over to the shady trees along the gurgling brook, removed her socks and shoes and let her feet dangle in the cool water. "It is remarkable how differently the children react towards the animals," Monsieur Marty observed. "Are these children siblings?" So Bernie explained how the Englestein children had spent their last year in an orphanage, but had now become members of the Bartok household who were all refugees from Prague.

"We have heard about your plight," Monsieur Marty nodded. "That conference in Evian was a disaster for all Jewish people." Then he remembered his promise about the ponies, and said, "If you two," meaning Francois and Bernie, "will watch that the animals don't knock over the children, I'll go and get the ponies."

Francois pointed to Max, saying, "Isn't this a very special little guy?" That moment Max put his little arms around a small lamb's head and nuzzled it.

Taking Bernie's hand, Francois asked, "Would I be allowed to hold this lovely lamb at my side one day like that?" Bernie blushed, but looked up to Francois with her loveliest smile.

Monsieur Marty returned, leading six ponies on a long leather holster. Immediately Romi and Irmi came at a run. "Bernie, isn't this one just like my pony at home?" Irmi asked, while hugging a small reddish-brown pony.

Romi picked a black pony, and said, "We didn't have one like that, but it is beautiful, isn't it?"

Hannah and Max joined their group, but didn't dare touch the small horses, "Monsieur Marty, would you allow our four musketeers to try a short ride? They haven't had any animals to handle since we left our home."

"You know, these little horses are in need of exercise. A short ride would be good for all of them," replied Monsieur Marty. Pointing to Romi, he added, "This little girl has the right touch with horses. Could she take the palomino—he is the most spirited of the bunch." There was no problem with Romi. She mounted, and was off to a canter in no time. Then he loosened a white one from the rest, and led it to Hannah. To Francois he said, "She needs a little assistance, I think."

So Francois ended up assisting Hannah, who clung to the gentle pony's mane like a drowning swimmer. Max was assisted by Mr. Marty onto a black pony and seemed to love the challenge. He smiled and patted his steed. He watched Irmi and Romi who took to the unsaddled ponies like long lost friends. They were trotting across the meadow, squealing with delight, while Hannah begged to be taken off the pony. Max, however, seemed to enjoy himself immensely. When Mr. Marty patted his pony on its rear, and it accelerated its pace, Max called out, "I love horsies. It is so much fun!"

Shortly thereafter, the dinner bell sounded and Monsieur said, "That is the sign! Nobody dares to cross Madame Marty. We've got to go and leave the ponies." Quickly he helped the children to dismount, assisted by Francois and Bernie.

A little while later, although the twins complained how short the ride had been, they were heading for the welcoming table under the shady trees, where lunch was being served by Madame and a helper. There were mounds of mashed potatoes, delicate chicken drumsticks, garden peas and beans, and a tureen of the tastiest gravy. Cornelia offered a prayer of thanks. Thereafter, it seemed, the food just evaporated. Fifteen minutes later all serving plates were clean.

But there were more treats! Madame Marty appeared with her young helper again and served cherry cake with whipping cream. While pouring milk for the children and strong French coffee for the adults, she asked, "My curiosity constrains me; may I ask you, where you all are coming from. If I am too forward, forgive me, but I seem to think that you are not my ordinary patrons."

"Perhaps Madame Bartok will permit me to answer?" Francois looked questioningly at Cornelia. He had noted that Cornelia was hesitating with a reply. As she nodded, encouraging him, he said, "We come from Prague in Czechoslovakia. There Madame's husband is a banker, and Madame a well-known opera singer. All of us, except Mademoiselle Bernie, here he touched Bernie's shoulder gently, are Jewish. We are proud of our heritage, but because of the mad dictator in Germany, our lives are threatened, and we aim to relocate in Paris where Madame's husband co-owns another bank."

"Thank you, Francois, this was well said," Cornelia stated.

Madame Marty had listened with great interest. Now with excitement, she looked at Cornelia, asking, "Madame, my husband and I are opera fans. Whenever we can take a few days off, we visit our daughter Laurette in Lyons. There we always make time to see an opera. Would you mind telling me which roles you have sung?"

Bernie knew how uncomfortable this questioning must be for Cornelia, so she explained, "Madame is known as Cornelia Kahn internationally. She has sung major roles in *La Traviata*, *Rigoletto*, *La Boheme*, *Carmen*, and recently *Aida*.

Here Romi called out, don't forget *The Bartered Bride*, and *Madame Butterfly.*

Cornelia smiled as her dear ones enumerated her roles, then she added, "Sometimes I even do light-hearted parts like *Gypsy Baron* and *Die Fledermaus.*

Madame Marty, who had listened with enraptured attention, now couldn't contain herself any longer. She called her husband, wanting him to hear about their illustrious visitor. As he approached, she shared all she had heard.

"Did you tell them what we do, when we visit Laurette?" he replied. "Oh, yes! I mentioned that we love opera."

As Monsieur Marty sat down with them, he asked, "Are you intending to sing with the Paris Opera, Madame?"

Her reply was cautious, "Monsieur, that depends on many factors. Perhaps their roster of singers is complete, or they won't need someone with my voice range."

"Listen to me, Madame! We try to stay informed concerning what goes on with the leading singers in our country. What we hear about the Paris Opera is not the best. There is a lot of cliquishness and party spirit that interferes with quality performance. And you probably won't believe me, but we hear from guest performers to the Lyons Opera House that they rather perform here than in Paris."

"Marty speaks the truth, Madame," but as the lady was about to continue there was a scream from the nearby brook and all the adults rushed there, finding a dripping Irmi.

"Oh Mama, I liked the cool water so much! But then I fell over a rock and couldn't keep my balance. Please don't be mad with me!" So Bernie headed for the car to bring dry clothes for Irmi, while Cornelia took her into the large kitchen of the establishment, stripped off her clothes, and wrapped her in a large towel Madame Marty provided.

In spite of the warmth of the day, little Irmi shivered, "That really cooled me off, Mama." Then turning to Madame Marty, Irmi said, "Merci beaucoup, Madame!"

Then it was time to depart. Other guests arrived, and there was no further talk as Francois saw to the seating of his six charges. They entered the outskirts of Paris in darkness. Francois had studied the map and found their new home near the *Gare du Nord* without difficulty. As he pulled up in front of the house owned by Davide Cohen, it took a moment to rouse his sleepy passengers.

They all sat up and, one-by-one, tumbled out of the car when Rachel Cohen and her daddy came running to welcome them. It was only seconds later that Frederic Bartok appeared and first enclosed his travel-weary wife, then one child after the other, into a loving embrace. He introduced Bernie and Francois, and soon the noisy party entered the hospitable, old, four-storied house.

The children marveled at the many steps leading to the third floor. There a spacious, modern kitchen greeted them, the table set under bright lights. All kinds of goodies were waiting, along with glasses of lemonade. The children scrambled to the bathroom and after everybody had washed hands, Frederic asked, "Shall we eat first or see our new living quarters?"

Cornelia, taking her husband's arm, spoke for all, "You'd better do us the honors and show us around or else we won't even be able to find our way to the bathroom at night, right?" The food and drink were forgotten as they all pressed around to explore their new domicile. Frederic led the way, from the kitchen through a wide door, into the sizable living-room. Here a grand piano stood against the wide windows, and a harp was positioned in the opposite corner.

"My Dearest has been at work here," Cornelia stated with tears in her eyes, touching the keys of the grand. The tour continued across the hall through two large bedrooms, and a bath which accommodated an old-fashioned bathtub, a shower, and three sinks.

"Where do these steps go to?" asked Romi. She was already three steps up when her Papa firmly took her by the hand and led her upward, with everyone else following behind. After climbing another fifteen steps they found themselves on a landing from which three closed doors led to the "unknown."

"This reminds me of a story our Abba used to tell," Hannah said with wonder in her voice.

"Yes," Max agreed, "it's like Jacob's ladder when he saw the angels going up and down on it."

"But we are only on the fourth floor, not in heaven!" Romi corrected.

"I'm really curious where these three doors lead to." Irmi added.

Frederic stepped back, saying, "Let the littlest one have the first try."

So Max stepped forward, looking up to Cornelia, and when she nodded, he opened the first door, the middle one. Although it was dark outside, the canopy of stars overhead, and the fragrance of the flowers were a special surprise to all.

"This is a real roof garden," Cornelia exclaimed while they all stepped out, looking up to the sky and standing in awe of God's wonder world. Now they saw the bench, the beans climbing on the beanstalks and the raised beds full of petunias, geraniums, and zinnias. Far below them they could see the traffic faintly; the many lights reminding them that they were in a large city.

"It's high time we had our late supper," Frederic said next.

"What about the other two doors in the hall?" asked Romi.

"You are so observant, Romi!" her daddy said. "Let's take a quick look, and then it is downstairs for our late-night-meal." With that he opened the door to the left which was a large, mostly empty room. "We still don't have furniture, but this could be a nice bedroom for somebody." Then opening the third door, he said,

"This is your gift from Mademoiselle Rachel. She has worked here nearly a week to clean it up for you—it is really the nicest room."

The four children came forward and stood for a moment looking, then went around and touched the ladder on the wall for exercise, next the shelves with the board games, which were so attractive to the twins. Hannah discovered the table tops with the crayons and pencils in special containers, and Max found the big chest. When Max looked around, Frederic encouraged, "Look inside! Open it!" The little boy's face lit up as he held up stuffed animal after stuffed animal, showing them around. There was a white teddy bear, a giraffe, two bunnies, and even a little red horse. All the children came close to see.

"This is like a birthday and Hanukkah rolled into one," declared Francois, "isn't it?"

"There will be plenty of time to explore tomorrow," observed Cornelia. "Let's go down now and eat the treats Papa has prepared for us."

A few minutes later, they were seated around the long table, with Frederic at one end and Cornelia at the other. They asked Bernie to give thanks, before they savored a cool fruit soup, French bread with butter, and small quarters of cheese. The lemonade was gone in no time, together with the rich cookies that served as dessert. All along the children tried to tell Frederic the adventures of their trip to Mont Blanc, and today's visit to the *Jardins de Marty.*

CHAPTER TWENTY

NEW BEGINNINGS

Max awakened first the next morning. He tiptoed upstairs, remembering that Francois had volunteered to sleep on one of the bunk beds in the playroom. When he peeked in after opening the door, he saw Francois still asleep on the upper bunk in the corner. The chest he had opened last night drew him like a magnet, because he remembered seeing many other things under the stuffed animals. As he carefully lifted the lid, he whispered, "What a pity, so many toys and nobody to play with!"

Francois had heard the door open but had feigned sleep; he watched Max, wondering what he was up to. 'This little one is a model of self-control," Francois said to himself. Then there was a knock on the door, and Cornelia stuck her head in, informing them that breakfast was being served downstairs. Francois stretched and yawned, pretending to wake up. He saw Max close the lid of the chest carefully—not having touched anything.

After jumping down from the bunk, Francois took Max by the hand and led him to the bathroom. As they passed the bedroom on the upper level, Francois judged from the mattress and the ruffled bedclothes on the floor that most likely Frederic and Cornelia had chosen this rooftop room for themselves. What a far cry from their elegant bedroom in the Bartok mansion in Prague!

Francois helped Max with his morning routine, then showered and shaved himself. When he returned to the playroom, Max was sitting at one of the little desks drawing on paper a tall structure which resembled the Eiffel Tower.

"That looks like a big building," Francois remarked while changing into fresh clothes.

"I was trying to draw the lighted tower we passed on the way here last night," Max replied.

"Now I see, this is the famous Eiffel Tower! We will try to climb it one of the next few days. From there, one has the best view of our new hometown. But Max, I think they are waiting for us downstairs. Shall we go and see?"

Max left his unfinished drawing and followed Francois obediently to the kitchen, where the rest of the family was already gathered. Frederic was just bidding his family goodbye. When Francois offered to drive him, he said, "My dear Friend, you are needed here today. Besides, Davide and I have discovered a convenient bus ride to town. This particular bus stops only a block from the bank. Cornelia will tell you, she needs you to find the necessary beds and household items, and then transport them here."

To his wife Frederic said, "Dearest, you and Francois have to do the shopping and hauling by yourselves. This will be a big relief for me, because things are buzzing at the bank and need to be put in order."

Turning to Bernie he said, "Dear Governess, your job is cut out for you, as you can see. I hope you will consider staying with us a long time and will keep these four youngsters productively occupied. I have great hopes that practicing French is a daily item on the agenda." With that, he waved and was already down the stairs, where they could see Davide Cohen waiting for him.

"How did everybody sleep?" asked Cornelia while dishing out portions of thick porridge, mixed with raisins and nuts. Bernie handed around a pitcher of cream and then poured coffee for the adults and orange juice for the children.

"Actually, Mama," said Irmi, while looking at the other three children, "we really liked sleeping on the floor and pretending we were camping out. We don't think we need fancy beds at all. Isn't that right?"

"When I woke up, I felt so happy," Hannah agreed. "I really like to pretend we are on a campground. It was comfortable. What do you think, Max?"

"Opening my eyes, I thought it was too early to wake anybody. So I tiptoed upstairs to see where Monsieur Francois was sleeping. He had said that he wouldn't mind sleeping on the bunk in the playroom. He really has the best place. I would like to be on the lower bunk bed, if he wouldn't mind."

It was then that Hannah asked, while looking thoughtfully into her porridge and stirring it, "When do Max and I have to leave?"

Francois who first caught on, said, "I don't think anybody wants you to leave at this time, am I right?"

"Have we treated you badly, Hannah, that you want to leave us?" asked Cornelia in return.

"Oh, no, you all have been very good to us," Hannah replied, "but Madame Hradek had told Max and me that we would only be with your family while we travelled. Then she expected us to be back in an orphanage."

"Have you been worried about this all along?" asked Bernie.

Hannah, nodding while two big tears coursed down her pale little face said, "Yes. You already have two children, and Max and I on top of that make a lot more."

Max listened to what his sister said and added, "You know, we are orphans with Abba and Imma gone; that makes us sort of leftovers."

Cornelia was considering what reply she should give. She had not imagined that these precious two expected to be sent away again. She needed to assure them that they were wanted by Frederic and her. Before she could speak though, Romi ran around the table, and Irmi followed her, both lovingly embracing their playmates and whispering soft words to them.

So, Cornelia, following her daughters' examples, bent down and hugged Hannah with one arm and Max with the other, saying "You two dear Ones, don't you know that we want to keep you forever? In fact, Romi and Irmi's papa is trying to adopt you as our own if the authorities will allow us to do that. We believe it is like Mordecai so long ago, who said to Queen Esther, "Who knows whether you have come to the kingdom for such a time as this?"

Then smiling one of her radiant smiles, she continued, "Of course, our family is not a kingdom, but we want you with us, and that includes Francois and Bernie, right? We all are thankful that God sent you to us. He will make a way for it to happen!"

Hannah's eyes overflowed as she looked up to Cornelia and said, "Madame, Max and I are very thankful for what you and the twins have just said. It is like having a family again!"

Right then they heard a knock at their kitchen door, and when Francois opened it, Rachel Cohen stood there with a newspaper in hand, saying, "I brought you this because sometimes you can find bargains in the estate ads, if your timing is right." They invited her in to have breakfast with them, but she declined with, "I already ate, thank you! I am about to leave for my classes at the Sorbonne."

"What are you studying at that famous institution?" asked Cornelia.

"I hope to become a teacher, so right now I take mostly education classes," replied Rachel.

"When you are finished studying, you can be our special teacher," suggested Romi.

"How long will it take until you are done?" asked Irmi.

"Most likely, Mademoiselle Rachel will want to teach in a public or private school, right?" asked Cornelia.

"Actually, I have to complete a 'practicum,' which means I have to practice teaching," Rachel explained. "I could probably teach these four little people and call it my practicum, if you wanted me to; that is, if you wanted to start school in late August with the rest of the children in France."

"We actually had no idea when the school year begins in these parts," Bernie offered, and looking at Cornelia, added, "We will really have to make a big effort to reach entrance levels for Hannah to the third grade, the twins to the first, and Max to kindergarten."

"We'd better hire Mademoiselle Rachel on the spot!" Cornelia decided. "And we all will help by speaking French most of the time." Turning to Francois and Bernie, she begged, "Please speak nothing but French with the little ones, so they won't fail when school starts for them."

"But, Mama," Irmi pleaded, "we have to speak Czech at least during one meal a day."

"And we need a bedtime story in our own language," added Romi, "or we will forget it altogether!"

"My dear little Ones you are so right!" Brushing back her black curls, she said, "So it is with all things, if one doesn't practice them, one easily forgets, and that applies to my singing too!"

Chapter Twenty-One

The Covenant

Every Shabbat morning, Neveh Shalom was the meeting and worship place for the Jews in the north of Paris. Davide Cohen and his daughter Rachel belonged to this congregation for several years. The synagogue was small. Located on *Rue de Victoire*, it was only a short walk from the Cohen house. A young rabbi by the name of Eli Baron was the teacher and spiritual leader of this congregation, to which many prominent business men and their families belonged. For a few Shabbats, the Bartok family, including Francois and Bernie, had joined the Cohens for Shabbat services.

On this particular Saturday morning, Rabbi Eli pronounced the Shema: "Hear, O Israel, the Lord our God is one Lord: And you shalt love the Lord thy God with all thine heart, and with all thy soul and with all thy might. And these words which I command thee this day shall be in thine heart." 5. Mose 6:4-6.

Turning to the congregation, he said, "I wanted to continue with our reading of Esther-Hadassah today, but then another portion of the Tanach seemed to come to my mind repeatedly this week, and I wonder whether our mighty God had a reason to remind me of it. So I will share it with you. Perhaps it means something to someone here." With that he opened a drape that hid his collection of scrolls.

Reaching for one, he said, "This word comes from the fourth chapter of the book of Ecclesiastes, starting with the ninth verse: 'Two are better than one; because they have a good reward for their labor. For if they fall, the one will lift up his fellow; but woe to him that is alone when he falleth, for he hath not another to help him up. Again, if two lie together, then they have heat: but how can one be warm alone? And if one prevails against him, two shall withstand him; and a three-fold cord is not quickly broken.'"

Both Francois and Bernie seemed to hear this with a special awareness. Francois reached for Bernie's hand. Bending to her ear, he whispered, "This is for us, Bernie!" She, too, was convinced that this scripture was exactly what they needed to hear. The Lord in His kindness had spoken to them through Rabbi Eli.

Walking back from the synagogue behind the others, Francois asked Bernie, "Weren't the verses from Ecclesiastes that the rabbi shared meant for us? I had prayed to God that He would make His will known to us." Taking her hand, he continued, "Didn't you feel a conviction too, that this was God's answer for us?" When she raised her blue eyes to his and nodded, he continued, "The only thing I didn't understand was the three-fold cord that could not be broken."

"The way I understand it, coming from my way of faith, the three-fold cord in a marriage covenant is the Lord Jesus Christ, the Messiah of Israel, entering into the marriage agreement with the couple. He must be in our lives, or the words of the marriage covenant are meaningless."

Here she stopped, raising her face up to Francois, she explained, "My father is a very insightful man, besides being a devout Christian. He has always told me, 'Never make the mistake, Bernie, of marrying a man who does not believe in the Messiah of Israel!' And being so far removed from my homeland and my parents' house, you can't meet my father so that he could ask you this question himself. Therefore, I have to ask you, Francois, does the Savior, the Lord Jesus Christ, mean anything to you?"

Francois stopped, and taking both her hands in his, he looked down into her lovely face, saying, "I have heard, of course, claims about Jesus of Nazareth being the Messiah of Israel, but all my Jewish relatives have refused to believe in Him."

"Dear Francois, I didn't ask about your relatives. I wanted to know whether you personally had ever thought about what the Messiah of Israel means to you."

"Bernie, I don't know what to say!" his handsome features were downcast as he looked with compassion into her eyes. "Why have you not shared your concerns with me before?"

"We simply have not had time alone together, Francois. But before we enter into a marriage with one another, this important issue has to be settled."

Cornelia, who had Irmi and Max on either hand, was aware of a discussion going on behind them. She turned at this moment, and said, "Bernie, don't hurry home. We have decided to take the children out. Give yourselves some time. You both deserve to have an afternoon off." With that she hurried after Frederic, Hannah, and Romi.

"Should we go back and talk with Rabbi Eli?" asked Francois. "If you don't mind, Bernie, he might be able to shed some light onto our particular situation, if you now have second thoughts about our engagement." With this they turned around, and were back at the synagogue in a short time. They caught the rabbi on his way out.

"Are you in a great hurry, Rabbi Eli? If so, we could come back at another more convenient time," offered Bernie.

"My dear people, I would rather talk with you than sit down to a lonely Sabbath meal with my cat." He beckoned them to follow him to his office.

"What brings you back?" he asked, after he asked them to sit down. "Were you the ones our Almighty God wanted to reach with His Word from Ecclesiastes?" Noticing Bernie's blushing and Francois' nodding, he asked, "If you have heard from God, what help could a mere man offer?"

Francois, searching for the right words replied, "We have reached an agreement to marry each other. We have both been employed by the Bartok family for a number of years and have gotten to know and trust one another. When the takeover of our home country by the Nazis appeared to be imminent, we agreed to flee with our employers. We are attracted to one another, but now there is an issue with Bernie being a Christian. She believes that Jesus of the New Testament is the Messiah of Israel."

"And I agree strongly with her," interjected the rabbi.

136

Startled, Francois looked at him, and asked, "But you head a Jewish congregation, how can that be?"

The rabbi, folding his hands, looked down and said matter-of-factly, "There is no doubt, if one studies the Jewish scriptures, that the coming of the Messiah is foretold in numerous places." First looking at Francois, and then at Bernie, he continued, "Nobody in the entire world has fulfilled these prophecies, except the great Nazarene, Jesus the Christ, or as we say in Hebrew, *Yeshua ha'machiach*."

"Does this mean that you, a Jewish rabbi, really believe in Him?" asked Bernie.

Nodding, Rabbi Eli replied, "I consider myself a Messianic Jew to whom God has revealed His Son, and I have asked the Risen Christ to be my Savior." Then addressing Francois, he inquired, "What about you, my friend? Have you ever considered who Jesus is?"

Francois, seriously pondering this question, sat up straighter; after a pause, he said, "Nobody has ever challenged me with a question like this. But hearing that you, Rabbi, are a follower of this Man and call Him Savior, and Bernie saying she does not feel right about marrying me if I don't believe in Jesus . . . It makes me wonder. I respect the Bartoks, and I have never heard them talk about Jesus the Nazarene."

After saying this, Francois experienced the strangest conflict within himself. He later confessed that two voices seemed to oppose each other in his mind. One kept repeating, "This is a lot of fantasy and make-believe. You can't trust that!" The other voice, full of conviction, said, "Francois, trust my two witnesses."

Bernie interrupted at this moment, asking, "Rabbi Eli, would you care to share with us how it came about that you started to believe in Jesus as the Jewish Messiah?"

"I'd love to tell you about that," the Rabbi replied. "In fact, if someone from the congregation here at the synagogue asked, I would give the same testimony."

He cleared his throat, and began, "I grew up in a small town south of here. My family belonged to a congregation of orthodox Jews. We stayed separate from the rest of the people, practiced our kosher lifestyle, wore traditional garb, and, in some cases, even wore earlocks. My mother always kept two sets of dishes; one set for meat, the other for dairy products—we followed the whole kosher system."

"When I went to seminary, I carried the heavy burden of these traditions with me. During my third year, I suffered from severe burnout. Too many nights staying up late, inadequate nutrition, and bearing a load of guilt. At that time, a fellow seminarian asked if I'd like to accompany him to an evangelistic meeting in another town. He said to me, 'We have to know what the other side believes.' So, I went with him."

"Listening to the evangelist, an older man who spoke kindly and objectively, I was astounded. That man knew the Hebrew scriptures as well as the New Testament. He listed many of the Hebrew prophecies and then showed how Jesus fulfilled each one of them."

"The Holy Spirit convicted me that his claims were true, and I went forward when an altar call was given. As I prayed the sinner's prayer, repenting of my unbelief, my rebellion, and my sins, the King of Kings came into my heart by invitation, and I have never been the same. Yet, I am still Jewish and love our Jewish traditions, but I know now who my Messiah is; that He came once and that He will return."

Not one word of this personal testimony escaped Francois. After the rabbi finished, he said, "Could I ask for prayer. I understand that you had this special experience, Rabbi Eli. I should read the Jewish scriptures and the prophecies you were referring to, in order to believe for myself. Would you and Bernie please pray for me that I, too, could believe?"

The rabbi then reached out his right hand to Francois and his left to Bernie and offered a simple prayer, "Lord God of the Universe, You sent your own Son, the living, loving Lord Jesus to die for our sins. Please make Him real to Francois, and let us all live to follow Him for the rest of our days. Amen."

Before they left, the Rabbi went to a shelf, took from it a small black book, and handed it to Francois, saying, "This is both the Old and the New Testament in one book. If you read it daily, asking God to show you His plan of salvation, you will find the Truth yourself." Then he hugged them both and sent them on their way.

CHAPTER TWENTY-TWO

THE RECITAL

An unexpected event brought changes to the Bartok and Cohen households. Three weeks after the arrival of the Bartok family, the bank co-owned by Davide Cohen and Frederic Bartok was burglarized. "Nothing like that ever happened before!" Davide stated angrily.

"We must have more visible and well-trained security guards," Frederic suggested.

Both owners made an appointment with the *Prefet of Police*, who promised to assist them with training a more efficient and effective security detail for their bank. Davide and Frederic agreed that Francois should be entrusted with the hiring and managing of such a detail.

Frederic had spoken to Davide about Francois' excellent character, his good language skills, and his versatile gifts; besides, his services as chauffeur were no longer needed. The limo was not of much use in the heavy city traffic. In fact, it was decided to temporarily retire the automobile. There was an open shed in back of the Cohen house. When the garden gate was opened, the limo could be inched through the backyard and into the shed. This way it was sheltered from the weather and the traffic up front.

For Francois, it was like putting a family member into prison. Irmi, who had played dress-up with the other three on the opposite side of the yard, came over and said, "You must feel pretty bad, Francois, hiding our nice limo here in the backyard. But . . ." she added, looking understandingly at him, "here in Paris the streets are much narrower than in Prague, and there are already so many cars." Then, patting the shiny exterior of the car, she suggested, "We really should cover her up and keep her from becoming dusty and dull. Shall I see if Mama can get us a giant cover?"

"That would be a good idea," Francois agreed. "We shall look for one when we go to town the next time."

From that day on, Francois' life changed drastically. He left the house before everybody else got up and stayed late until the whole new security system at the bank was in place. He hired a group of responsible, well-referenced security guards and set up a three-shift schedule, through which the men rotated.

Francois and his security detail also submitted to rigorous physical training involving hand-to hand combat. A police trainer came to the bank for several weeks to train the men and to teach them the use of clubs and leather sticks. Surveillance of the bank's premises was enhanced by new outside lights and door alarms.

While Francois was absent, tending to his new responsibilities, the family got used to public transportation. They used buses and streetcars to travel to town. They visited the *"Bois de Boulogne,"* an extensive, beautiful park where fountains and ponds delighted the eyes. They climbed the Eiffel Tower. This structure, designed by Alexandre Gustave Eiffel, the famous late 19th century bridge-builder, is 1000 feet high, and, on a clear day, provides a fantastic view of Paris.

They also spent a whole day in the Louvre, a world-famous museum, where they saw not only paintings and sculptures, but also displays of trains, toys, and dolls. Meanwhile, the French lessons with Rachel continued, and all four children were challenged to study what their young tutor presented to them. She had a pleasant way of making learning fun. Often she would take them to the roof garden and play games with them, during which, not one word of Czech could be spoken.

One day Andre called. He had arranged for an audition. The directors of the Paris Opera had agreed to hear Cornelia in some of her noted roles. To prepare for the occasion, Andre came daily to the house to rehearse with his good friend for an hour or two. Then he endeared himself to everyone by sharing theatre stories during a shared meal with the family.

When the day of the audition arrived, Cornelia left early. She warmed up with Andre in one of the rehearsal rooms at the opera and then gave a laudable performance that impressed everyone present in her favor. However, the indefatigable Mr. Ridreaux stepped forward at the end of the audition, stating that Madame Bartok was a singer of exceptional talent, but the Paris Opera could not, at this time, have a Jewish prima donna on its roster. Particularly, they could not have one who had fled her homeland to escape the Germans, thereby breaking her contract with the National Theatres of Prague.

A week later, a letter arrived informing her that at this time there was no opening for a soprano of her caliber. If she remained available, they would allow her to substitute on certain occasions. Cornelia had expected something like this would happen and was not badly disturbed, though she felt rejected, of course.

Andre encouraged Cornelia to give a solo recital, knowing what an exceptional musician Cornelia was. She agreed, under the condition that it be a benefit performance. Jewish refugees who needed to establish new homes and roots in other countries were to be the beneficiaries.

A month later, the entire Bartok household was seated in a large auditorium which Andre had rented for the event. There was not one empty seat; in fact, "standing room only" tickets had been issued. Many had heard of the "Nightingale from Prague" and now wanted to hear her for themselves.

Andre acted as both master of ceremonies and accompanist. As the houselights dimmed, he stepped in front of the curtain and gave a short introduction of Cornelia's background, including how she had fled her homeland because she was Jewish. He did not mention, however, that Cornelia, besides being a well-known soprano, also could hold her own as violinist and harpist.

As the curtain opened, the audience saw, to their surprise, a tuxedo-clad Cornelia, her violin poised, joining Andre in a rousing rendition of Anton Dvorak's "Slavonic Dances." Hearing their own Bohemian composer, all Czechs in the audience responded with patriotic fervor.

They stamped in rhythm and clapped deafeningly, while some students jumped up and down shouting "Bravo!"

After a short intermission, the curtain opened on a completely different Cornelia. Dressed in black brocade accentuated with gold highlights, the tiara with the Star of David on her head, she appeared every inch the diva she was known to be. She sang arias from the works of Smetana, another Czech of renown.

A century earlier, this composer had written the opera *The Bartered Bride*, also a more serious work, titled *Libuse*. From both, she had chosen arias which she sang in Czech, to the great delight of her landsmen. She finished this part of the program with a patriotic hymn, "*Die Erben des weissen Berges*," written by Dvorak and later published as Opus 30. This hymn, written in German, she sang in its original language, as Dvorak had grown up in the German-speaking part of Bohemia. The audience responded with a standing ovation.

When the curtain opened next, one could hear gasps of astonishment throughout the audience. Cornelia was seated, the harp before her, on a simulated grassy knoll. She was dressed in a flowing white gown, held together at the waist with a silver girdle. Her black curls hid under a silver scarf. Behind her, veils of different pastel shades were moving, as if in a summer breeze. She began a medley of sacred music. The audience was spellbound, transported into an otherworldly existence.

Even the children were taken in by the beautiful harpist's melodies. Hannah, who sat next to Bernie, reached for her hand while two big tears coursed down her pale little face. Silence prevailed after the harp medley ended. The curtain closed with Cornelia bent over her harp, as if in silent meditation. Then the audience came to life and demanded an encore, which the lovely harpist graciously granted.

What Cornelia didn't know was that two well-known musicians had been invited by Andre. One was Loup de Fallou, the head conductor of the Lyons Symphonic Orchestra, the other, Armande Ballon, the artistic director of the Lyons Opera. Both gentlemen were greatly impressed by Madame Bartok's stage presence and musicianship.

They appeared backstage and literally begged her to repeat this unique recital in the Lyons Opera House. They suggested that she pick a convenient date during the week in September, while their ensemble was doing a number of guest performances in Marseilles. After a while, both Andre and Frederic entered into the discussion, deciding that the guest performance in Lyons could be considered. They would discuss Cornelia's availability, and reach a decision during the coming week.

Another event overshadowed the week ahead, however. A letter from the *Ministry d'Immigration* was received which stated that Monsieur Bartok had been denied the right to adopt the children of the late Rabbi Leo Englestein and his wife Anna. The reason given was their relative short residence in France. It was further stated that unless the children were adopted by a French couple, they were to be extradited to England or the United States of America, in order to be placed with a Jewish family.

"This cannot be the end of our relationship with these precious children!" Frederic exclaimed.

"There must be something we can do!" Cornelia stated, while watching her husband pace around their dining table late that night. He had just shared the contents of the fateful letter with the other adults, and was venting his emotions.

"I wonder whether my citizenship could be of help?" mused Francois. "I have been a French citizen since birth, although I have worked outside my country a number of years."

"What do you mean?" asked Bernie, who sat next to him at the table. "How would a bachelor be eligible to adopt children?"

"Don't you have any imagination?" he asked, looking at her. "Aren't we supposed to get married eventually, anyway?"

"You mean, we might be able to adopt them if we were a couple?" she wanted to know, looking at him with growing understanding.

"Dearest, what do you think of Francois' suggestion?" Cornelia questioned.

"This is an entirely new angle, I would say," Frederic pondered. "Of course, in no way should we influence Francois' and Bernie's decision to tie their bond. They will have to live with this decision for the rest of their lives, but considering all things, this could be a workable solution. I haven't even told you yet about the time limit they gave us!" And perusing the letter again, he said, "They give us an extradition date for

Hannah and Max as October 31, 1938. So consider, tomorrow is August 28—this gives us only two months to work with!"

"I can't even imagine not having the children with us anymore," Bernie stated, putting her elbows on the kitchen table, burying her head in her hands. Francois put his arm around her shoulders reassuringly.

He whispered to her, "With God's help, this will be worked out, Bernie. Don't give up now that we have come so far." Then turning to the Bartoks, he asked, "Do you think I should make a special trip to the Ministry first thing tomorrow morning and ask if Bernie and I would be acceptable parents to adopt children, once we are married?"

"That would only complicate matters," Frederic replied. "The way I see it, this agency is so pressed for solutions right now, because they have hundreds of cases they must solve, that if anyone came up with such a hypothetical case and had no status as a family man yet, they would simply reject you. No hard feelings, Francois! But you two must be in agreement first. Once you have a marriage certificate in your hands, can prove that you are employed, and can support a family, then you have a platform to work from."

"Why don't you two pray about it, talk to someone you trust, and then reach your decision," advised Cornelia.

"Yes, that is my advice too," stated Frederic. "Take a day or two; speak perhaps with Rabbi Eli. Then if you both are sure that you truly care about each other and want a life together, rather than being alone, make a decision. Also . . ." he added, "You must hear from God and know that this step you desire to take is of His will."

"Of course, all things considered, here in our home not much would change. We are all so very dependent on each other, don't you agree?" Cornelia asked.

A little while later they formed a prayer circle, and Francois laid their situation before God. He asked the King of the Universe to make His will known and to show them clearly what to do by giving them His wisdom and direction.

Later, sitting around the kitchen table, Frederic said, "We must be sure of this decision, before we involve the two children. We know how much these two little ones have already endured. Let us not add more conflict to their existence."

CHAPTER TWENTY-THREE

SCHOOL BEGINS

School started all over France only a few days after this conversation. Cornelia and Bernie had registered the children right after their arrival in the French capital. The principal of the grammar school, a Madame Avigne, had welcomed them and had given the children temporary grade assignments. Hannah would go to third grade; Cornelia had requested separate first grade rooms for the twins, and Max would attend kindergarten. After registration, Madame Avigne made it clear that these were simply probationary assignments.

"Please make them understand," she explained, "that if they are not able to keep up with their classmates, we will hold them back a year. This would not mean demotion, but concern for their good." With that the stern lady excused them. Outside, Cornelia and Bernie looked at one another, aware that their assessment of the situation was in agreement. A very authoritative woman was at the helm of this school!

The children had continued their regular lessons with Rachel. They had made trips to the stationary store for copybooks, rulers, pencils, and erasers. Now, on the morning of the real thing, it was difficult to interest the children in eating their breakfast, putting their shoes on, and having their hair combed before going on their way.

Cornelia and Bernie, each holding a child's hand on either side of them, were out of the house by the time the men gathered for breakfast around the Cohen's dining table. It had been decided to have Marie, the Cohen's faithful cook, handle the breakfast for the men during the first week of school. And handle it well she did: Crepe suzettes were on the menu that day. These thinly baked pancakes, powdered with sugar and served with tasty fruit compote, were a very special treat. The coffee, hot and aromatic, stimulated shop talk before the men took off to catch the city bus.

Cornelia, with Romi and Irmi, and Bernie, with Hannah and Max, arrived at the large elementary school along with hundreds of other mothers and children. It took patience and perseverance to break through the pandemonium and find the classrooms of their charges. With Hannah's help, Bernie found Max's kindergarten room. It was in the basement, gaily decorated with balloons and posters of animals. Max was given a place in the front row next to a little blond boy, who greeted him with *"Bon Jour!"* and a shy little smile.

Bernie promised to pick Max up after the morning session, and he was content to stay and find out what kindergarten was all about. He was an amazing little boy; dark-haired, ready to laugh, obedient to his elders, and very devoted to Francois. He waved to Bernie and his sister, and they felt sure that he would be able to manage.

To find Hannah's room on the third floor, they had to use the back steps because the big stairway in front was blocked, from the street in. When they arrived in the airy, high-ceilinged room, there were only five boys present. The teacher, Madame Souvrier, a rather stout, jolly, lady in her fifties, explained that everybody else was stuck in the crowds on the way up. She appointed Hannah a place on the side and told her that a girl by the name of Marie would be her desk-mate. She then dismissed Bernie, telling her that the children had to get acquainted and not remain overly dependent on their family.

Not bad, thought Bernie, though she regretted she had not explained to Madame Souvrier that Hannah was not her own child, but an orphan she was taking care of. On second thought, she knew, eventually, Hannah would share about her parents, but the first day of school was probably not the right time to do that. A few minutes later she met Cornelia, who was still looking for Irmi's classroom on the second floor.

"If I had known I would be so far away from Romi, I would have begged you to let me stay with her, Mommy!" Irmi whined.

Cornelia's and Bernie's eyes met, confirming that they had to stick this out and meet Irmi's complaints with a united front. Finally, they found her room. When Irmi saw 20 pairs of eyes on her and her classmates already in their seats, she quickly curtsied for the teacher and sat down in her appointed seat.

Mademoiselle Fleury seemed to be friendly enough. She appeared to be about thirty years-old and had bright red hair, which she wore in a chignon covered by a black net. Both women assessed her as having a good command of the class, and after promising to be back in the afternoon, left Irmi to her fate.

As they stepped into the clear morning air, Cornelia heaved a sigh, and said, "How about a stroll through the neighborhood, to clear our heads after all this commotion?" This suggestion was met with Bernie's approval, and, for the next half hour, they walked along the streets of the neighborhood, finally ending up in a small park, where they sat down on a bench.

"Have you thought any more about your decision?" Cornelia inquired, after making small talk for a little while.

"It is really on my mind a lot," Bernie admitted, "and it occurred to me that I would love to call my parents and hear their advice on this matter."

"Why haven't we thought of that before? Of course, you must call your parents. Perhaps, after you receive a confirmation, Francois, too, should talk to them and express his honorable intentions."

"Yes, I have talked to him about my plan, and he agreed that this would be the right action to take. In fact, he has made an appointment with Rabbi Eli for tomorrow. He is still struggling with his understanding of Jesus being the Messiah of Israel."

"You know, Bernie, I have given this a lot of thought myself, since you brought to our attention the importance of knowing Yeshua as the Savior of mankind." She looked down upon her folded hands, and continued, "Not until we met Rabbi Eli, did we ever hear of Messianic Jews.

In 'shul,' as we grew up, we all were taught that the Messiah would come someday, but nobody would know the day or the hour of His appearing. And now, we hear that Yeshua, the carpenter of Nazareth, did come to be the Messiah, was crucified for us, was resurrected from the dead, and lives forever—seated at the right hand of the Master of the Universe." Shaking her head silently, and looking at Bernie, she asked, "How can we be sure that is so?"

Bernie replied, "Rabbi Eli said, in order to comprehend, one must read the Word of God and ask Him to make it real. I can attest to that, as He has done so for me countless times."

"It seems the more I desire to find out about this Jesus, all sorts of distractions and doubts come, and I stop thinking of Him."

"I understand that, and if you can believe it, Madame, this thinking is from the Lord's archenemy, who projects hindrances of all kinds into our minds when we want to listen or pray to our Lord Jesus."

"Who are you talking about?" asked Cornelia.

"It's Lucifer, also known as Satan, who is the enemy of our souls. In fact, when Francois was confronted by Rabbi Eli, he had a typical experience. He told me that he heard two distinct voices within himself. One voice was urging him not to listen to these fairytales and legends, while the other spoke comfortingly, encouraging him to listen to the two witnesses, which, at the time, were the Rabbi and I."

"Thank you, for sharing this with me, Bernie! Both Frederic and I need a closer faith walk. I believe, we ought to make an appointment with Rabbi Eli too. Perhaps he can help us understand what it takes to follow this Jesus." The two women rose then and headed home, both in thought about what they had shared.

Cornelia broke the silence, "Bernie, please feel free to use the phone any time to make your important call home. I can imagine your parents would love to hear your voice. I know, you have been writing, but a conversation always beats a letter. Just be careful not to mention anything that the operators may hold against your parents."

Since the children were at school, the men at work, and Cornelia was practicing in the living room, Bernie took the opportunity to call Czechoslovakia. She prayed, first, that the Lord Jesus would be in full authority over this call, and then, that she would be able to reach at least one of her parents. When the phone kept ringing with no one responding, she was ready to give up. Then there was her father's out-of-breath, familiar Czech greeting.

Bernie asked, "Am I calling at a bad time, Daddy? This is Bernie."

And from then on, they communicated as if they were calling in the same town. He told her that he had been out in the chicken house making repairs, while her mama had gone to the neighbor to borrow some yeast. He seemed overjoyed to talk with his beloved daughter and assured her that she was daily in his prayers, as were her employers and their four children, as he put it. Then Bernie explained that the French government had refused the adoption of the Englestein children by the Bartoks, and how Francois and she wanted to help out and were praying about their marriage.

"Daughter, is he a man Mama and I would welcome into the family?" He asked next, "Does he have a good character? Is he loyal?" As she had only good things to report, he next asked about Francois' faith. "How does he stand in relationship to our Savior Jesus Christ?"

"I knew you would ask me that, dear Father, but I have to say, he is seeking. He is of Jewish descent and has no role model in his family of anyone following our Lord, but we have a precious rabbi in the local synagogue here who is a Messianic Jew. He has talked to us and confirmed his belief that Jesus is the Messiah of Israel. So Francois is reading the Bible, and he has asked us to pray for him."

"It seems that he is open to our Lord, and the scriptures will convict him," her dad perceived. When she mentioned the plight they found themselves in, of keeping the Englestein children with them, yet the Bartoks having no governmental approval to adopt them, he offered, "By marrying him, you might be instrumental in saving two of God's Chosen, am I right?"

Then there was a short pause, as her mother, apparently, had just returned home. She heard her dad say, "This is Bernie—long distance."

She heard her mother's voice, saying, "Tell her that we think of her daily and love her."

Then again her dad's deep basso voice, "Listen, Bernie, you don't have to decide today. You were taught from childhood that the believer need not act in haste, right?"

"Perhaps your intended can give us a call tomorrow, possibly in the evening. Then we can get to know a little about him, if he is willing to speak to us. He has to assure us that his intentions are honorable, and that he is able to look after you; besides, being willing to take on two children with a new wife is not an easy deal. But the times are trying and more uncertain than ever; therefore, we must pray more and learn to rely on our able Lord for all things."

Here the operator cut in, with, "Other international calls are waiting."

All Bernie could say quickly was, "I love you, Papa!" then the connection was severed.

That same evening, when Francois returned from his meeting with Rabbi Eli, they all could tell that he had experienced a life-changing event. His face glowed, and he seemed to walk with a spring in his step. When he joined them at the supper table, he said, "I feel like dancing and singing. A deep new joy has entered my innermost being!" Then he sat down next to Bernie and put an arm around her, saying, "Bernie, I want to thank you with all my heart, for it was you who first made me aware of my lost condition."

"Francois, you really were not lost!" chirped up Romi. "We saw you leave this morning, and now you are back."

Francois looked at her, and replied, "My little friend, I was not speaking of having lost my way around town, but of being without the certainty of knowing who the Messiah of Israel really is."

"I went to Rabbi Eli, and he walked me through the Word of God. He showed me from the Torah scrolls (which he brings out every Saturday during the Sabbath service) that many hundreds of years ago, The Master of the Universe spoke to the prophets and gave them knowledge of things that were to take place. They clearly announced the coming of the Messiah, who did not come by His own will, but who was sent by God the Father after an angel announced Him to Mary. She was even given His name. Just imagine, before his mother knew He was growing in her she was given His name by the angel Gabriel!"

Everybody stopped eating and was listening to Francois. Both Frederic and Cornelia realized their lack of knowledge of these wondrous happenings. Bernie beamed with the conviction that God had heard her many prayers for her employers and her fiancé, who could not have been a better witness in his newly found salvation.

Before the next Sabbath came around, both Frederic and Cornelia had been to Rabbi Eli, who was thrilled to share the good news with these new members of his congregation. He was convinced that in these days of upheaval God was calling more of His Chosen to become followers of Yeshua, the Messiah of Israel. And true followers they became, sharing with their children and the two Englesteins the vital importance of belonging to the One who had died for their sins and was now seated on the right of the Majesty on High, listening to the prayers of His own.

In the midst of this spiritual awakening, which involved even the Cohens, a letter arrived for Madame Cornelia Bartok. It contained a contract signed by Messieurs de Fallou and Ballon on behalf of the Lyons Opera Theatre. Madame was to perform the recital given in Paris, in two identical performances at the Lyons Opera House, during the fourth week of September, while the regular ensemble was touring the southern parts of France. An adequate honorarium for her and her accompanist, as well as the transportation of her instruments and props, was guaranteed.

After Frederic and Cornelia shared this news with the rest of their household, there was a lively discussion about the pros and cons of such an undertaking. Frederic suggested laying the need for guidance before their mighty God, which they all immediately heeded, by bowing their heads and personally imploring His direction from their newfound Master. Afterwards, Frederic asked, "What does my Dearest have to say of such a major effort requested of her? Please share your thoughts, my dear Wife."

"Of course, I am flattered by this opportunity to sing again, and in a well-known Opera House, at that. If I consult with Andre, he most likely will try to work this into his schedule, just to please me; but it is at least five hours south of here by train, and having to give the show twice that week, I would not be able to return until both performances are given. What would become of everybody here? How could Bernie cope with all four children? Who would help with shopping and food preparation and getting the children to school on time?"

She looked around the circle of her extended family and saw a glint in her husband's eye as he looked at Francois, Bernie, and each of the children. Then he gave a thumbs-up, acknowledging the points she had made, and said, "This would require Francois and me to make some adjustments during the five work days of that week, but as I see it, it is doable, don't you think so, Francois?"

"Of course, Madame, Monsieur Bartok is right. We can manage without you if we start work a little later in the morning, helping Bernie with breakfast, and getting the children off to school first."

"Yes, you are my man, Francois," Frederic agreed. "And then we'll take turns returning early each day to help with supper, homework, etc., and to keep the household rolling along."

Here Hannah raised her hand, asking for permission to speak, "It seems all grown-ups see us children as helpless babies who need to be coddled, while everybody else works doubly hard. If you will allow us to help and give us chores to do, like Max and I used to do in the orphanage, I think we could manage without Madame having to worry about us while she is away for a few days."

Bernie agreed, "Hannah has the right idea. We will be able to manage if we all work on this together. Then Madame will not have to fret and the men might not have to change their schedules so drastically. We would like very much for her to have a chance again to use her God-given talents."

"Yes," said Irmi, "we want Mama to go, and we can help to make it work."

Romi added, "This will be an adventure for all of us, to become more useful, like grown-ups are!"

So it was decided to notify Andre and to make preparations for Cornelia's debut in Lyons.

CHAPTER TWENTY-FOUR

CORNELIA'S DEBUT IN LYONS

The express train to Marseille wound its way through the autumnal French countryside. Cornelia and Andre had bid goodbye to Frederic and Francois after the two had transported all instruments and luggage for the Lyons endeavor to the *Gare du Nord*, the railroad station near their home.

Now settled in their elegant first-class compartment, while Andre was engrossed in the newest edition of *Le Monde,* the Paris paper, Cornelia was finally able to reflect on the happenings of the past several weeks. She had adhered to a strict daily training schedule while the children were at school. Bernie and she had worked out a program by which everyone in their extended family of eight was able to contribute in keeping their ship on course.

She chuckled how her twins had earnestly tried to keep up with being responsible for their own clothes and for cleaning up after meals. Irmi had even promised not to put up a fight over brushing her hair, mornings and evenings. In fact, it had been agreed on that she would do that tedious task by herself from now on. It was astounding that no more yelps and complaints were heard once she was the administrator of her own hair care.

Romi had taken to washing dishes after meals like a fish to the water. She loved to gather cutlery, plates, and empty bowls into the sink. Then standing on a step stool, her sleeves rolled up, she began to scrub and rinse the dishes with delight. Hannah, who had volunteered to dry and put away the dishes, had meaningful conversations with Romi at that time. Bernie usually dealt with the leftovers, watched the children for a short while, and then would go on to other matters.

The train gained momentum, and lovely rural scenes passed by at rapid speeds. As Cornelia alternated between these visual feasts and glancing at the backside of Andre's paper (who was seated across from her) she reflected on the lovely wedding that had taken place under the canopy of congregation Neveh Shalom, only two weeks ago.

Francois and Bernie had made an attractive bridal couple. The bride had worn a calf-length white gown with a veil that covered her curly blonde hair and then fell to her waist. The groom had appeared elegant in a black cutaway, his dark hair slicked back, and his handsome face lean and serious, while Bernie, her blue eyes shining, seemed to express the light of Christ from within. After the celebration at the synagogue, the young couple had boarded a train for the Bay of Biscay, where they spent their short honeymoon in a fishing village that Francois had remembered from his youth.

Meanwhile, Frederic designed, Davide Cohen approved, and two able handymen remodeled the upstairs playroom for Francois and Bernie's use. The children's furniture and play equipment had been moved to the bedroom next to the living room, which Bernie had occupied until then. It seemed that the children actually liked the new location better, although they still went up to the roof-garden on warm days to enjoy the fresh air while playing or studying.

As the express entered the Lyons main station, Cornelia and Andre were overwhelmed by the welcome offered them. Not only were Messieurs de Fallou and Ballon present, but they were flanked by the prop manager and the head wardrobe mistress. After introductions had been made, the property manager, Monsieur Jacques, produced a small electric cart from behind a pillar. This was adequate to carry the boxes of music Andre had brought, all Madame's costumes and paraphernalia, and even the harp.

After assuring their Lyonaise hosts that they were not tired and would love to see the Opera House, they were chauffeured through districts that clearly gave the visitors from Paris a glimpse of the architectural beauty of their host city. They passed the *Place des Terreaux*, an impressive town square, and the *Hotel de Ville,* the city hall. A fountain designed by the 19th century sculptor Bartholdy graced this spot. A short while later, the façade of the Opera House came in sight, as did the *Bourse,* their stock market, and the *Theatre des Celestins*, the drama theatre.

In the Opera House, only a skeleton staff was on duty; the ensemble and all auxiliary staff were on tour. They were shown the main stage, the dressing rooms, and the facilities back stage. Madame Felice, the head wardrobe mistress, introduced Mademoiselle Celeste, who would serve Cornelia explicitly. This experienced *wardrobiere* made an excellent impression on Cornelia, who had a number of faithful ladies serve her in this capacity over the years. Mademoiselle Celeste was approximately forty years-old and wore her hair in a tight bun. She had a warm smile and capable hands. She saw to it that all Cornelia's valuable costumes were promptly hung on appropriate hangers around the spacious dressing room.

It was agreed that rehearsal would start promptly at 10 o'clock the next morning. Until then, it was hoped that Andre and Madame would have a chance to rest up and acquaint themselves with their hotel suite. They were told that both performances had been well-advertised and were sold out already.

"We have a very appreciative music audience in this town," Mademoiselle Celeste offered. "When Messieurs Ballon and de Fallou returned from hearing you in Paris, they wrote under their names a beautiful critique of your performance. Then when tickets went on sale, there were long lines until every seat was sold out."

No one could have asked for a better suite in the first-class hotel which was reserved for Cornelia's and Andre's use by the opera management. They found a sitting room furnished with cherry wood furniture, which was upholstered in a shade of periwinkle that accentuated the beauty of the wood; in addition, a grand piano stood ready for use. To one side of this sitting room, a door led to Cornelia's bedroom with an adjoining bath; on the other side, Andre's suite was similar, but ideal for a male occupant.

Upon entering, Andre, in order to test the tone quality of the grand, sat down and played the grand march from Guiseppe Verdi's *Aida.* Later they shared a meal in the hotel's dining room, thankful that the other patrons were not aware that two celebrities ate among them.

The next two days passed with rehearsals and getting acquainted with stage managers and other backstage personnel. For both Cornelia and Andre it was a comfortable arrangement, as this was a long-established opera theatre with experienced professionals backstage.

The two performances were a total success. There were glowing reviews in the local papers. Madame, with her full-toned soprano, combined with her exceptional stage presence, was praised by all. Andre's sensitive accompaniment and charming introductions were much appreciated as well. Frederic surprised Cornelia and was present for the second performance. He suddenly appeared among the well-wishers after the end of the concert. There were standing ovations for more than fifteen minutes after the conclusion of the harp medley. She also had to give an encore, just as she did in Paris.

Before Cornelia and Andre could board their train for the return trip, she received a telegram. It was sent by the management of the Lyons Opera, and it offered her a contract for the 1938-1939 opera season. She would be required to sing two performances per week. Hers would be the privileges and obligations of the leading soprano. This was an amazing offer, but she had qualms about committing herself, knowing she had responsibilities at home. Frederic, who had pressing engagements in Paris, had already left by plane so she could not ask his advice.

Circumstances beyond her control, however, expedited her and Frederic's decision in this regard. Back in Paris during this very week, five weeks since the school term had begun, Hannah came home to report that she and her classmates had to write about their families and where they had come from. They were required to do research for and draw a family tree. She asked Bernie how she could possibly obtain any information about her father's and her mother's ancestors. Her little face was anxious and pinched as she tried to come up with information she did not have. She asked, if she should make up something.

Bernie, who from childhood on had always been taught to tell the truth, saw no reason to impart contrary principles to her young charges. Since Cornelia was out of town, and the men were at work, she encouraged Hannah to tell the truth about her parents' fate; a decision which, perhaps, she would not have made had she foreseen the consequences of this revelation.

When Madame Souvrier asked everybody to draw their family tree the next day, Hannah raised her hand. When asked what she wanted, Hannah said, "I am sorry to report that I can't do this assignment. Both my parents are dead, and I have no information about my grandparents either. The family I live with wants to adopt my brother and me, should I draw their family tree?"

By then all her classmates' eyes were on her, and Madame Souvrier asked, "How long ago did your parents die?"

"About two years ago, my parents went to Poland to help some Jewish people, but they never came back; we later were told that they were in a serious auto accident."

"What happened to you and your brother then?"

"We were sent to an orphanage in Prague. We were there almost a year before we met the friends who want to adopt us."

Madame Souvrier was not aware that among her class were children of two French Nazi families who had been indoctrinated with poisonous anti-Semitism. So the next day, while Hannah was sitting with her bench mate Marie in the school's backyard eating her lunch, a boy from her class came near, saying, "So, you are a Jew, heh?" He smirked, with an evil gleam in his eyes.

Another bully joined him, asking, "You Jews want to take over the world, don't you? You come to our country and act big, but you will see, and it won't be long. The German fuehrer will get here with his army, and you all will be deported; that's what my dad said." With this he gave his pal a push with his elbow. Then both boys ran off with their soccer ball.

Marie said to Hannah, "He is one of the mean ones in our class. I still remember him from last year. Don't mind him, if he gets worse, we'll tell Madame. With that they joined a group of girls playing marbles. So Hannah didn't bother to tell anyone at home of this incident.

The following day, however, there was another ugly event. When Hannah came out of the school at the end of the day, the same boys were waiting for her; they put a foot out in her path and she stumbled and fell over it. Quickly she rose, brushed off her skirt, and said, "What is the matter with you? Do you want me to report you?"

"You tittle-tattling Jewish pig; you will get it! That's what I say!" With that he kicked her shin and ran away with his friend Pierre.

By now gentle Hannah was sobbing. After finding Max, they walked home together. She held his hand, trembling. They climbed the stairs to their apartment, where Max reported to Bernie immediately, "Hannah has been hurt. She is crying. She won't tell what happened."

Bernie bent down to Hannah, embracing her, and asked, "How have you been hurt, darling girl?"

Hannah just leaned into her and sobbed even harder. Soon, Romi and Irmi arrived and gathered around when they saw their friend in tears. Irmi noticed Hannah's bruised shin and hands and said, "Look, Hannah must have fallen down. How did it happen?"

Hannah rejoined, "Oh, I shouldn't cry like this, because it was not that terrible, but there are two boys in my class who don't like me because I am Jewish. They said ugly things about it, things I don't even want to repeat."

"Does your teacher know about this?" Bernie asked, while drying Hannah's tears with her hanky.

"No, Madame Souvrier didn't see any of this. It started yesterday at recess, and today they waited for me on the sidewalk outside the school gate. They made me trip, called me names, and kicked me in the shin."

Bernie bent down and examined Hannah's bloody shin. She also saw that Hannah's palms were bruised. Romi and Irmi hugged Hannah, telling her how much they loved her. Bernie led her to a chair, brought a washcloth saturated in hydrogen peroxide, and cleaned out her wounds. This process hurt, of course, which made Hannah sob again. Next Bernie applied Band-Aids, and she did need a number of them.

Then Bernie said, "We do have to pray and agree that, first of all, our Lord Jesus will heal these wounds. Then Hannah has to make an effort to forgive these boys. Even though they have been told evil things and have acted badly, God loves them too. If we agree on that, our Lord will see to it that justice will be done." So they bowed their heads and prayed in Yeshua's name.

After that, Hannah could smile again, especially as Bernie provided a fine snack of grapes, cheese, and cream puffs. While sharing these treats, the twins and Max outdid themselves, telling funny stories to distract Hannah. Max reminded Hannah of the time that they had visitors at the orphanage. They had set the tables with plates, forks, and spoons, and lovely paper napkins that somebody had donated.

Then the assistant to Madame Hradek said, "Remember, these napkins are just for show. The guests may use them; we don't, because we might need them another time." So, after the guests had been shown around, they sat down with the children, and the food was served. After they said a prayer at the table, the visiting ladies reached for their napkins.

That's when the littlest orphan, by the name of Vanushka, raised her hand and said, "Don't touch! These napkins are just for show! We need them for another time." She had not heard right; namely, that the guests could use them, but not the children.

At that time Madame Hradek had saved the occasion by explaining, "The children have been told that these fancy napkins were only for guests."

"O Max, do you think little Vanushka and the others, like Hulda, Beria, and Christa are still in Prague? I have not thought about them for the longest time. Thank you for reminding me."

"I enjoyed hearing about life in the orphanage," said Bernie after this. "Max, you told us a funny story. But this being a special day, perhaps we all should go upstairs and play a game or two in the roof garden, before Monsieur Bartok and Francois return."

Just then the telephone rang. Cornelia had promised to call before her evening show. Here she was in Lyons, asking, "How are the guardians of our home? I'm thinking of you. Tell me how your day is going."

Romi, who had answered the phone, broke the news, "Mama, we are all sad with Hannah today. She has been attacked for being Jewish."

"What happened? Perhaps I should talk to Bernie, Romi. Can you put her on?"

159

So all four children gathered around while Bernie explained what had caused Hannah's distress, after which Cornelia asked to speak to Hannah.

"Oh, my dear little Hannah," they heard Cornelia say clearly, "I wish I could take you into my arms and assure you how much we all love you."

To Bernie, Cornelia said, "Considering all things, I suggest, you let Frederic deal with this situation. I know you have already prayed about it. I think that Frederic and Francois should go with the children in the morning and report to the principal what has occurred. The main thing is, we must ask our Messiah to deal with this problem, because He has promised, He will never leave us nor forsake us."

There was a pause, and then she said, "I remember Psalm 144, where He assures us that He is our rock and our fortress, our stronghold and our deliverer, our shield, and He who subdues the people under Him. That means to me that we can trust Him, don't you all agree?" All four little heads nodded in unison.

"We'll wait for Monsieur Bartok and Francois and let them deal with this," Bernie said, then added, "We hope and pray your performance goes well tonight, Madame! Please don't worry about us."

Hannah whispered over the phone, "A good performance is more important than what happened here. I'll pray to the Messiah of Israel about it."

Then they heard Cornelia signing off, "You dear Ones, I love all of you. Tomorrow I will come home."

"Perhaps we should do our homework, after all," suggested Hannah. "Otherwise, we will have to do it later when we are all tired."

So the three girls got out their writing and arithmetic papers, while Max, who had no homework yet, borrowed ruler and pencil from his sister and designed geometric shapes. Bernie was always astounded when she saw what he did. He created triangles, squares and rectangles in various sizes. Nobody had ever shown him how to design such things.

When the men came home, the children were still at the kitchen table finishing their work. They had agreed that both Frederic and Francois needed to eat before Hannah shared what had happened at school. Both men spoke about their day's events and wondered why the children were so quiet. When Frederic asked for the third time how their school day had been, Irmi spoke up, saying, "We had quite a bit of excitement today, but it is Hannah's story—she should tell it."

Francois looked at Bernie who gave him a sad smile and a nod. Then Frederic asked, "Hannah, what is this all about? Are you ready to tell us?"

Looking at the men with her big, brown eyes, she related yesterday's and today's events. Francois could not contain himself, hearing about the plight of his young, soon-to-be daughter. He jumped up, but Bernie put a calming hand on his arm, saying, "Our Messiah teaches us to offer the other cheek, if we have been smitten."

"Yes, but if it happens to one of the little ones—that I cannot stomach," he growled.

"We told Madame Cornelia about it when she called," Hannah said. "She advised that Francois and Monsieur Frederic ought to go with me to school in the morning and see the principal about it."

Frederic was pondering this upsetting news with a heavy heart. He had expected that something of this nature might happen, but not so soon! "It appears, our Lord and Messiah allowed this for a reason, dear little Hannah. May I see how badly you are bruised?" Frederic asked with great concern. While inspecting her shin and looking at the palms of her hands, both red and scraped, he said, "How do you feel about this, dear little girl?"

Hannah looked straight into his eyes, and said, "My Abba told me long ago that we Jews are the Chosen, and God required of us much suffering. He also said if it ever came my way, not to shrink from it, but to face it with courage."

"Your Abba was right," Frederic admitted, "but God spared him from seeing his little daughter abused. Francois and I will go with you to school tomorrow, and see what we can do to stop such trouble."

"If only the adoption papers had come through by now," Francois said, "then we would have something to work with. As it is, Hannah and Max are in this pre-adoption situation where nobody can claim them as their own, other than us in our love for them." Bernie hugged Hannah in a protective way, and Francois, putting his arm around Max,

161

stretched his other arm around Bernie and Hannah. Everyone was moved and concerned about the welfare of these precious children.

Next they bowed their heads in prayer and left the situation in the strong hands of their Messiah. Bernie remembered that Cornelia had proclaimed Psalm 144 over the phone, and she read it now for all of them, "Blessed be the Lord our rock, who trains our hands for war and our fingers for battle . . ." Afterwards, it seemed as if His strength and His confidence were transmitted to them. When bedtime came around, the children settled down without mentioning any fear of tomorrow.

Cornelia finished her role in *La Traviata* the same evening, again to standing ovations. Monsieur Ballon, the artistic director, and Monsieur de Fallou had been in the audience and both congratulated her warmly. When she finally came to her dressing room, it was filled with bouquets from admirers, which she would have to leave in Lyons, as there was no way to transport them to Paris on the train.

Finally, she could think about what had happened to Hannah in school. It grieved her to think that this precious child had become a target of anti-Semitic hatred. To her, Lyons seemed to be a much more pleasing and accepting town. But, of course, she was an adulated prima donna, and her family lived on another level. While she was preoccupied with such thoughts, she was helped by Mademoiselle Celeste to remove both her costume and her wig. It was only natural that they discussed next week's schedule and demands, especially which outfits were to be worn for *Carmen*, and that the *Traviata* costume had to go to the cleaners before it could be worn again.

It was then that Cornelia asked, "Mademoiselle, do you ever hear of any houses for rent here in Lyons? Going to the hotel after each performance is very depressing to me. It may be luxurious, but I lack for privacy."

"Let me think a little about that one," Mademoiselle Celeste replied. "Perhaps, by next week, I'll have an answer for you." After she heard about Hannah's plight, she added, "Madame, you have to consider that there is only a small percentage of people whose minds have been poisoned by anti-Semitism. You'll have to observe whether this will be the only incident against your loved ones. I can understand, however, if such things should continue and your family is no longer safe in Paris, then you might have to move away from there."

The next morning, after a refreshing rest, Cornelia boarded the Paris Express. She was more hopeful, as Frederic had already reported to her about his and Francois' visit to Madame Souvrier's class. They had met the two culprits who had caused Hannah's injuries. Both had confessed and promised to leave her alone. And Hannah, like the good and courageous girl she was, had consented to go back to her class and forgive them. Madame Souvrier had assured both men of her watchfulness. "There won't be any repeat performance of such meanness," she had assured them. At that time Cornelia had, of course, no idea what would befall her own dear twins.

CHAPTER TWENTY-FIVE

ANOTHER MOVE

On Monday of the following week, the day before Cornelia had to head back to Lyons, a letter was announced by the *Bureau de Poste* both *par expres et recommandee*. "This means it's a letter sent special delivery and registered," Bernie observed.

"Would you please pick it up, Bernie," requested Cornelia. She was packing her suitcase for next day's trip. She added, "Perhaps, it is good news for a change."

It took Bernie only a minute to get her jacket, put on her hat, and head for the post office. She joined a line of waiting people. A heavy letter was handed her, addressed to Monsieur and Madame Francois Leclerq. As it was from the *Department d'Interieur*, she chose to wait and have her husband open it when he came home from work that evening.

When Bernie showed it to Cornelia, they speculated whether it was finally the needed adoption papers—then they went about their business. They had planned a shopping trip after school because all four children had outgrown their shoes. This overshadowed even the important letter. Cornelia had promised to take them, including Bernie, of course, to one of the large department stores downtown. All three girls were looking forward to the occasion, which usually included a stop at a nice café. Max had been invited by a classmate to play after school. Therefore, it had been decided that Francois would take him separately to purchase shoes, as Max needed play time with a young boy. At home he was always surrounded by young ladies.

The girls rushed in promptly after school let out. They washed up, and after combing their hair, were on the way with Cornelia and Bernie. It was a cool and windy October day. They had the wind at their backs as they headed for the bus station. There were several groups of people waiting already. When the bus arrived, it was crowded. A number of young people who had waited at the curb before them brushed by rather impolitely. Cornelia and the twins had to stand in the aisle, while Bernie and Hannah found places when a couple left their seats for them.

Cornelia, whose hearing was extremely sensitive, was aware of whispers behind them. When she turned, she noticed the group of young people gathered by the back exit, casting angry glances their way. They became louder, and what she heard was, "Jews . . . Jewish Shiksa with her brats!" followed by raucous laughter. Suddenly a hard object flew by her, hitting Romi, and another, Irmi. The twins ducked, held their heads, and started crying, both from pain and from shock. People screamed and the bus stopped, then the back door opened, and the perpetrators left in a hurry. Derisive laughter was heard before the door slammed shut.

Both Romi and Irmi stood crying, holding their heads, tears rolling down their ashen faces. Bernie was immediately at their side, comforting Romi, while Cornelia held Irmi, then she looked down and saw two rocks wrapped in newspaper at their feet. She picked them up, and exclaimed, "Look at these rocks! They were thrown at my children!" with that she pushed through the passengers toward the driver, imploring, "Can you call the police?"

"Lady," the bus driver replied, "I only drive the bus. I have no control over what the people in the bus are doing!" His face was red and angry when he asked with a raised voice, "Did anyone else see this happen?"

A number of people raised their hands, and a man said, "I heard those fools say anti-Semitic curses before they did it. What has our country come to?"

Another said, "One can't even be safe in a place of public transportation. These rocks could have knocked out somebody's eyes!"

"You had better get these children to a doctor!" said a lady with a large shopping bag. Now everybody could see blood was dripping from Romi's ear, and Irmi held her head where the rock had grazed her.

The driver said, "I suggest, Madame, that you file a report with the police, because I have to finish my run. Afterwards, I can file a report of what happened with my superiors."

Bernie lifted up Romi, and Cornelia took Irmi, while most people in the bus expressed their sympathies. They clambered down the front steps, and Cornelia hailed a taxi, ordering it to take them to the closest physician's office. She pressed her hanky against Romi's ear after ascertaining that Irmi's injury was not bleeding. Apparently, her curly hair had acted as a protective shield.

The physician was Dr. Rosenbaum, clearly one of the Chosen. When he heard the report, he quickly disinfected Romi's ear, then explained that he had to put in at least three stitches to close the wound. While he worked, he asked what had happened. Then he put a bandage on and advised Cornelia to come back in the morning for a dressing change. Meanwhile, Irmi had developed a sizeable bump on her scalp. He strapped an ice bag to her, which looked like a little chic hat, and encouraged them to keep it in place until bedtime.

"The way you describe it, Madame, these hoodlums expressed anti-Semitic sentiments before they acted. This is the typical tendency now. With this madman Hitler and his anti-Jewish proclamations, more and more uninformed people have become incensed against us Jews because they don't have facts. They act and respond to the hate propaganda coming out of the German Reich."

Looking at Cornelia, he asked, "Haven't I seen your face before, Madame?" After pausing a moment, he remembered, "I went to an extraordinary recital not so long ago. A well-known opera star from Prague, a Cornelia Kahn, performed not only singing arias, but also showed that she was an outstanding violinist and harpist. Could this have been you, Madame?"

Romi answered for Cornelia, "Yes, Monsieur, that was my Mama."

And Irmi added, "Although she can sing very well, the Paris Opera did not take her, so she has to sing in Lyons instead."

"Is this a fact, Madame?" the doctor asked.

Cornelia smilingly offered, "You see, my public relations people may be injured, but they are not out of action. So, they must not be too badly hurt?"

Whereupon, the good doctor said, "Their guardian angels were on duty! They could have been hurt much worse." He nodded, as if to approve of his own statement, and then he opened the door to the waiting room, where nearly every chair was filled with waiting patients, among them, Bernie and Hannah. The latter was still sobbing for fear that her little friends had been seriously hurt.

Once outside, Cornelia made a quick decision. She knew she had to leave on the noon express for Lyons the following day. The performances could not be cancelled on such short notice. She also realized her daughters had experienced shock and injury to their young bodies. She concluded that they needed distraction and nutrition. So they hailed a taxi again, which took them to a small restaurant where they had stopped once before.

Most tables were taken by an early-dinner crowd, but the friendly waitress showed them to a small side room where there were three tables ready for customers. Soon they had mugs of hot chocolate and some delectable almond pastries in front of them.

"It is probably not a good idea to still buy shoes, is it, Mama?" asked Irmi.

"But my toes hurt every time I wear these old ones," complained Romi.

"What do you think, Bernie; should we still venture to the shoe store even though it is getting pretty late?"

Their waitress, who had overheard Cornelia's words, spoke up, "Did you know there is a children's shoe store right around the corner?" After explaining how close it was, she said, "I sometimes take my children there. They have a good selection of shoes, and they have toys to play with while you wait."

So, twenty minutes later, the saleslady at the shoe store kept her place open especially for Madame Bartok, Bernie, and the children.

While one of them was being fitted, the other two looked at fairy tale books and put puzzles together. They ended up with each having two new pairs of shoes. When the saleslady heard their tale of being attacked on the bus, she gave them a healthy discount on the second pair of shoes.

When they arrived home with their new purchases, Frederic and Francois had already picked up Max and were waiting to have dinner with them. What a shock it was for them to see Romi all bandaged up and Irmi with an icepack strapped to her head!

After recalling the whole event, Bernie remembered the envelope which had arrived by registered mail. "This had better be something to cheer us up after the sad happenings of this day," Frederic said.

While Francois opened the letter, all eyes were on him. His face lit up, and he said, "Finally, here is the good news for which we all hoped and prayed."

"Bernie," he said, taking her by the hand and leading her to Hannah and Max, "here are your new children! And Hannah and Max, we are your very own parents, if you will have us."

He held out the official letter to show Frederic and Cornelia, who had been barred from adopting the two just because they had not been French citizens for the required amount of time. He was so overjoyed that he made one of his clown bows and said, "May I introduce to you Mademoiselle Hannah Leclerq and Monsieur Max Leclerq!" And with that everybody clapped so loud that Davide Cohen and his daughter Rachel came rushing upstairs, asking what the good news was.

Then there were congratulations, hugs, and kisses all around. Everybody realized that this was another sign of God's immeasurable love for them, for only four weeks earlier, all signs were pointing to an adoption as being impossible.

"It seems that we have made it before the dreaded extradition of the children could take place," observed Bernie. Hugging Max with her right arm, and Hannah with her left, she added, "Now God has to teach us how to become a family that is pleasing to Him, right, my Husband?" Nodding, Francois smiled, and exchanged a glance of love with his wife.

"This is such wonderful news, and I am deeply grateful that now the Leclerq Family has four members just like ours. Congratulations to you all, dear Friends!" said Cornelia.

"Now here is my personal concern: Before I have to leave tomorrow, I can take Romi to Dr. Rosenbaum for a dressing change. But then I have to catch the noon express to Lyons. I truly hate to leave you with hurt children, and probably fearful ones, after what happened on the bus." Cornelia stopped a moment, looked around, then addressed Frederic," My Dearest, what do you think? Is it alright for the children to continue to go to school and pretend that nothing happened?"

"If you ask me, I don't want to go to school tomorrow," said Romi.

"And me neither," agreed Irmi.

"One could make a point and parade the injuries of the children in front of everybody at the school, but, it seems, the people who hate us will not be swayed by our injuries. Rather they may count these as victories," Frederic offered in reply.

"Paris is becoming very hostile, and I believe we should quietly leave here, in spite of recent renovations, and establish a new domicile in Lyons. What do you all think of this daring scenario?" queried Frederic.

There was silence for a minute, as everybody tried to comprehend what they had heard.

"My Dearest, the same thought came to me already after Hannah's encounters," was Cornelia's first response.

"But what about the Cohens, who have adjusted their whole house because of us?" asked Bernie.

"We wouldn't mind at all," said Davide Cohen. "There will always be other opportunities to use the remodeled spaces."

"The priority must always be the welfare of everyone involved, and the children's welfare has already been threatened. Soon it might be ours, who knows?" Rachel said.

"But wouldn't it be the same in Lyons?" asked Hannah.

Francois, who stood next to her, sat down and laid his arm around her small frame, saying, "I have heard from a friend who has repeatedly asked me to join the "underground resistance," that Lyons is a much friendlier town for Jewish people. He also said there is a strong anti-Nazi sentiment in that area."

"You haven't even shared this with me, dear Husband," said Bernie.

Francois, turning to her, replied, "Why would I want to upset my Love with such news! I'm only mentioning it now, because I think Frederic's idea ought to be considered. We can't risk any more injuries. I heard that in Germany, major anti-Jewish riots are being planned, which easily can encourage the Nazi sympathizers in this country." A moment later he added, "I implore everybody who is present here not to mention this outside this room! Nobody must know what I just told you—to preserve our lives.

Cornelia had been watching her husband. He was deep in thought and prayer. He needed time to decide what to do. Bernie asked everyone to pray for guidance. After the dinner dishes were cleaned up, and the children prepared for bed, Cornelia went to the grand to review her arias for the next days. She was a little apprehensive of the musical score for *Carmen*. She had already studied it thoroughly, but knew concentrating on her work would help overcome the tensions and concerns of the moment.

An hour later, the children already asleep, Francois and Bernie sat again at the kitchen table. Cornelia was still practicing, but Frederic joined them. He had spent some time downstairs conferring with his friend and colleague Davide. He reported, "Davide helped me to put everything into perspective. In short, he encourages us to make plans to move to Lyons, even as soon as this weekend." He sat down beside Bernie, asking, "What do you two think about this?"

Francois stood up, his nervous energy compelling him. He jingled the coins in his pockets, and asked, "Do you mean me to give up the security detail at the bank at this time? Maybe, this is a little premature." Looking at Bernie, then at Frederic, "I could see Bernie joining Cornelia with the children, provided they can find appropriate living accommodations there, and, of course, a suitable school, perhaps even a private one. But the bank business has to continue, doesn't it?"

"Exactly my thoughts," agreed Frederic.

Cornelia, came in from the living room and joined them, asking what the discussion with Davide Cohen had accomplished. They stayed up a long while after that, discussing, praying, and making plans.

Cornelia would leave the next morning, to get ready for the necessary rehearsals and the performance of *Carmen* the following day. All agreed that she needed full concentration for this role. Meanwhile, Bernie would keep the children home. With their help, she would see to it that essential items needed to start anew in Lyons would be packed.

Frederic and Francois would visit the elementary school and request transfers for their children. Francois would then drive Bernie and the children to Lyons, taking the limo out of its retirement. A trusted moving company would be given the job of moving the furniture and boxes that they could not transport with the limo.

Cornelia would hire a private agent to locate a house for rent, saving her unnecessary hassle, and avoiding publicity. With that they prayed and entrusted themselves to a loving, protecting Keeper. Then both couples sought the rest they so desperately needed to face the trying days ahead.

CHAPTER TWENTY-SIX

THE NIGHT OF THE BROKEN GLASS

On November 10, 1938, Cornelia read the headlines in the Lyons paper on her way back from her morning rehearsal. There in bold print it stated that on the previous day a major attack on Jewish houses of worship, Jewish businesses, and Jewish homes had taken place. She read, "On November 9, 1938, the Nazis unleashed a wave of pogroms against Germany's Jews. In the space of a few hours, thousands of synagogues, businesses, and homes owned by Jews were damaged or destroyed." *The Tribune de Lyons,* Lyons' major newspaper, coined this evil event, *"La Nuit de Cristal,"* due to the many German streets littered with broken glass from the Jewish shops and homes.

When Cornelia arrived at the apartment which Frederic and Francois had rented for the family, she found them all huddled around the radio.

"We were listening to our French lesson on the radio when they interrupted with this terrible news," Bernie explained.

"Yes, Mama," Irmi agreed.

Then Romi cut in, "Those bad Nazis have done so much damage all over Germany!"

Anxiously, Hannah asked, "Will they do that here, as well?"

Her little brother continued, "Is there nobody willing to stop these bad men?"

"I just heard about this tragedy myself," said Cornelia. "But to answer Hannah's question, I think that there is less hatred against us Jews here in Lyons. Remember, that was our reason for moving here. Francois shared with us that here in Lyons the people are against Nazi ideology."

"Mama, what is ideology?" asked Irmi.

"It is something certain people believe in, but it is not necessarily true." With that Cornelia took off her hat and her gloves and said, "Perhaps we should turn off these awful news and pray for those persecuted ones in Germany instead."

"Of course, Cornelia," Bernie said. They had agreed some days before that they would go by first names from now on. It had become clear to all of them that God had put them together as a family. Bernie continued, "We must look to our Father in heaven, who allowed all this for a reason that we cannot comprehend."

After they all had joined in prayer for the persecuted Jews in Germany, Cornelia reminded them that they had an appointment with the administrator of a private school, who was going to interview the three girls for possible admission. Max was not eligible because of his age. Bernie had already enrolled him in kindergarten in a public school, only four blocks away. He was to start classes in the following week.

The girls rushed around in order to find acceptable clothes for the important session with Monsieur Germain, the administrator of the private school. They were still getting acquainted with their new apartment. It was actually quite spacious; it had four bedrooms of various sizes, a large sitting room, a parlor, and even a dining room. They remembered with regret the shiny, modern kitchen in their Paris home. This place had an old-fashioned kitchen with a gas stove and a very old sink that showed a lot of wear.

They had found the apartment after consulting with Mademoiselle Celeste, whose brother was a janitor in this respectable, patrician building. There was little time to look around and find something else, so they had taken it without discussion and were settling in nicely. The three girls again shared a room. There were large bedrooms for Frederic and Cornelia, as well as Francois and Bernie, while Max had a small room off his new parents' bedroom.

When they looked out the back of this tall building, they were very disappointed. Not a tree or a blade of grass was in sight. Romi commented, "This has to do for now, but I can't forget about our ponies, and the poultry yard with dear Pavel, who knew so many wonderful animal stories. And then the eggs we could collect . . ." Here her voice trailed off, lost in remembering.

Hannah and Max asked what their home in the suburbs of Prague had been like. Then both Irmi and Romi described Petrov and the ponies, remembering especially the pony races at their last birthday party. And then they took turns describing Bela, Raika, and Tirza, their faithful household servants.

Max asked, "Did you get to ride ponies every day?"

"That really depended on the weather and if Mama had left instructions whether we could ride or not. She and Papa would take out their horses every weekend, but we could only ride when Petrov had time to get them ready for us."

"Is everybody dressed to leave?" asked Cornelia. After Bernie checked hats and gloves, as it was a windy and cold November day, they were on their way. They had to take a streetcar to get to the small private school which had been recommended by one of Cornelia's colleagues. They looked around, still a little apprehensive after their ill-fated bus trip in Paris. But there were only two older ladies dressed in fur coats and a gentleman in a bowler hat, who waited at the curb with them for the streetcar to arrive.

Once seated inside they crossed one of the bridges over the River Rhone. Underneath they saw the broad river that connects with the River Saone, which allows three natural river harbors to flourish in the middle of town. Cornelia told them about the 1 ½ mile long tunnel that connected the two rivers with one another subterraneanly.

"What does 'subterraneanly' mean?" asked Max.

"Anything located underground that you cannot see, is considered subterranean," explained Bernie. By now, the streetcar had been moving uphill for some time.

"We are getting close when we see signs for the *"Tete d'Or*," said Cornelia. She pointed to their left. "That must be it! My colleague

Lorraine said, it is a large park that contains a small zoological garden. It also has a botanical garden and a lake in the midst of it.

"It is very beautiful here," observed Hannah. "The houses here are more elegant than in the older part of the city where we live, right?"

"True right," agreed Cornelia. "This is the wealthier part of Lyons, I was told." Then turning to Hannah, she said, "You are very observant, Hannah."

After descending the steps of the streetcar, they turned right and were now approaching a massive sandstone building sitting behind an iron picket fence. Coming to the gate, they noticed a golden sign stating, "*L'Ecole Germaine.*"

Romi was appointed to ring the bell. A handsome young man answered the door and bid them enter.

"We are expecting Madame Bartok and her children. Is this your party?" he asked.

"We are actually two families hoping to enroll our children." Pointing to Bernie, Cornelia said "Madame Leclerq's family has a daughter and a son. And my family has twin daughters."

Here Bernie picked up, "I understand that my son Max is actually not eligible for your school because he is not old enough yet. But I couldn't leave him at home alone, so he had to come along."

"Quite alright," the young man replied, "Monsieur Germaine will be seeing you shortly. I am only his assistant."

They found themselves in a spacious foyer where photos of students at work and at play were displayed on every wall. There were some benches along the wall and a small table sat in the corner, on which pieces of a large puzzle seemed to lie in complete disarray. There appeared to be more than a hundred pieces of most unusual shapes. While the girls walked around the room looking at the pictures on the wall, Max was attracted to the puzzle pieces

Just then a tall, heavyset gentleman entered the room, greeting them with a booming voice, "Welcome to our school!" Extending his hand to Cornelia, then to Bernie, he said, "You apparently had no problem finding us." Then he greeted the girls, "I am charmed to meet three young ladies of beauty." Noticing Max at the puzzle table, he asked, "Young man, are you good at geometry?"

Max was completely absorbed in what he was doing and hadn't heard Monsieur Germaine address him. When Bernie gave him a little nudge, he turned and bowed from the waist, the way Francois had shown him. He asked, "Monsieur, do you mind if I put this puzzle together while you talk to the girls?"

"Of course, my ambitious young man!" the big voice boomed again. "I just want to warn you, it's not easy. That's why those pieces have been lying there a long time. Nobody has the patience to make a triangle, a rectangle, and a square out of them."

Then he turned back to the ladies and said, "I am George Germaine, I am the headmaster here."

"Thank you for seeing us today, Monsieur! We have brought you three prospective students," said Cornelia. Then turning to Bernie, she said "You introduce Hannah first, Bernie."

"My daughter, Hannah, is eight years-old. She attended third grade in Paris, before we moved here two weeks ago. Her first language is Czech, but she has studied French for the last five months. She is doing rather well with it, as you will see."

"My twin daughters, Romi and Irmi, are six years-old, and have attended first grade in Paris. We also moved here two weeks ago. Both girls have studied with Hannah under French tutors about five months, as well," stated Cornelia.

After the introductions, Monsieur Germaine took both mothers and daughters into his office, offered them chairs to sit on, and then he addressed Hannah, "How old are you, young lady?"

To that she dutifully replied, "I am eight years-old now, but I will be nine next March." Next Monsieur asked her which subjects she enjoyed most in school. She answered in flawless, yet accented French that she loved French and art. When he asked whether she had had any English, she said, "No."

"There will be a need for her to take on this important language," said Monsieur Germaine. "However, we have several new third graders who also have to catch up in that language. Perhaps we can work out some tutoring services for you, after regular school hours." Then he added, "Hannah, I'm impressed. After only five months of studying our language, you have a fine command of French." Then he turned to the twins who stood on either side of their mother's chair.

"You must not be identical twins, because I have no trouble telling you apart," he said.

"You are right, Monsieur!" Romi replied. "I am an inch taller than my sister, and the last time we got weighed, I also weighed six pounds more, but she is smarter and more musical than I am."

"That is quite an admission, young lady!" Monsieur Germaine thundered. "Who has told you about not being as smart as your sister? Because that is something we determine now with our fancy psychological tests." Then he whispered to her, "But I personally think, these tests are not right most of the time."

Then he turned laughingly to Irmi, "I wish my sister would say such nice things about me!"

"I am eight minutes younger than my sister, and I think she just wants to be kind. The one who is really musical in our family is our mama. She sings opera and plays the violin, the harp and the piano."

"But what do you play, or do you sing too?" Monsieur asked.

"I only play the violin a little, and I plink on the piano," she replied.

"I must say, you are a most modest pair of twins. Thank you for answering me so ably."

Here Max spoke up, saying, "Monsieur, I have put together the triangle, the square, and the rectangle, and there are still some pieces left. What shall I do with them?"

Hearing this, Monsieur Germaine slapped his thighs with his hands, jumped up, and went over to Max. He stood over the table where truly one triangle, one square and one rectangle had been formed, with a few pieces lying at the side. Looking at Max, he said, "I can't believe you did this by yourself, young man. Did somebody sneak in here and help you?"

"No, Monsieur," Max answered humbly.

"You know, my child, I have to praise you, because nobody in this school has been able to put these pieces together." Then taking Max by the hand, he brought him into the office. Reaching into his pocket, he brought out a handful of coins, and throwing them onto his desk, he asked, "Do you think you can count them?"

"I'll try," Max said. "My new Abba Francois has shown me the value of the coins we use each day."

While everybody watched, Max counted quietly, then turned to Monsieur Germaine and gave him the correct count: "Two francs and eighty-five centimes."

"Did I say that we couldn't admit a five year-old to our institution?" Monsieur asked. "I revoke that, right now. I will make an exception and count it a privilege to admit this young man Max to our first grade, if you still want to enroll him," with that he looked expectantly at Bernie, who blushed with pride. Hannah seemed pleased too, when her little brother was so openly approved by the headmaster.

Next the headmaster said, "Dear ladies, if you still want to enroll all four children, we will make every effort to teach them the best. I suggest that you enroll them today and start them next Monday. We always begin the week with chapel, have prayer, and then we go to our individual classrooms. The only thing I cannot grant is, to have the twins and Max in separate classrooms because we have only one first grade class and only one first grade teacher. If that isn't a problem, we can start them next Monday at 8:30 a.m. They only need to bring pencils and a notebook. The rest we'll furnish."

Both mothers registered their children, and after that, Monsieur took them on a short tour of the classrooms, the gym, the chapel, and the cafeteria. Then he bid them *"Adieu."*

After they left, the headmaster called his young assistant and showed him what Max had done with the puzzle pieces. "I'll bet not one of the sixth grade boys could do this!" And he was right—Max, a gifted one of God's Chosen, had a brilliant mind, which no one had challenged so far.

After leaving the *"Ecole"*, all six headed for *"Tete d'Or."* The day was still bright. The sun had come out, and the wind had died down. On the way, Bernie said, "Abba Francois will be happy to hear that you were able to fit together those puzzle pieces."

"It really was not hard," said Max. "I love doing such things."

Here Cornelia turned; she had been walking in front of them with the three girls, and she said "This is the mark of true genius, to discover things that are not perceived by the ordinary person, right?"

"True right!" affirmed Bernie.

"We mustn't talk so much about this," Hannah said. "I know Max is gifted, but he is only five years old, and we don't want to turn his head."

"Yes," Max nodded, "but here are the animals. I already see a giraffe sticking its long neck out of that house over there." With that he ran ahead.

Romi said, "He must have eyes like an eagle. Did anybody else notice the giraffe?"

"We didn't," they all agreed.

The children, who had not seen any animals since visiting *"Jardins de Marty"* on their trip to Paris, were all enchanted by the cages with wildcats, bears and wolves. Bernie and Cornelia had to drag them, more or less, into the Aviary where exotic birds abounded. Outside, it was getting cooler, and the warm humid air seemed comfortable. They saw parrots, birds-of-paradise, bluebirds, and cardinals.

"Just imagine, we can go to school only a little way from here. Maybe some weekend, when Papa and Francois come, we can show them this park," Romi observed. They had no idea that both dads would actually join them sooner than expected.

On the way back with the streetcar, Bernie asked the children which of the animals each liked best. "Let's go by ages," she suggested. "Perhaps, we should start with the oldest." They all agreed.

"It's your turn, Hannah," Romi declared.

Hannah blushed as everyone's attention focused on her, but she said, "This is a very hard choice, because each animal is unique. God has made so many different forms of life. But you make me choose, so I would say, the tiny hummingbirds are my favorites. Their tiny wings moved at such an incredible speed. One couldn't even see them."

"Next, we ask Romi; are you ready?" Bernie looked at her little charge that had been under her care the longest.

"My choice is definitely the lion. The zoo lady said, 'the lion is truly the king of the animal kingdom.' So I agree with her. Lions are very special, aren't they?" There was a pause, while everyone thought over this fact.

"May I say my choice now?" Irmi asked.

"Of course, you are next; let's have it," Bernie encouraged.

"If I could be something else, I would love to be a bird. Then I would fly away from all this Nazi trouble." Cornelia and Bernie locked gazes.

Then Cornelia asked, "We saw so many birds. Which would you choose to be?"

"Don't you think the eagle might be strongest and could fly farthest?" Irmi asked.

"Interesting," Bernie observed, "how the twins choose the king of the animals and the king of the birds." Then she spoke to Max, "Our youngest one has waited patiently; he also has had the longest time to think about his choice. What is it, Max?"

"This is not easy, because I do like all the animals. Perhaps someday I can be a zookeeper." He looked dreamily through the window of the streetcar, saying, "I liked the wolves. But I was glad they were behind bars."

They were nearing their streetcar stop; outside it was getting dark, and the streetlamps were coming on. "This was a very eventful afternoon," Cornelia said, "Let us be thankful!"

"Just think, we can all three be in the same classroom, isn't that great?" Irmi observed.

"I am really looking forward to Monday," said Romi.

"For me, the best thing is that Max can go with us," Hannah said quietly, and Bernie heard it with a happy heart. She would need to remember to cancel Max's registration at the public school.

Back in their apartment, Cornelia and Bernie looked over their supplies in the icebox. "How would it be if we made a soup from the leftovers?" Cornelia suggested.

"I agree," said Bernie. "I'll do it."

She used their largest pot, melted a pat of butter in it, and chopped a large onion, which she browned in the butter. She found three potatoes, which she quickly peeled and quartered, adding them to the contents of the pot. She sprinkled three tablespoons of flour, stirring while the mixture got more golden brown. Then she found leftover chicken bouillon and poured it over everything, adding chopped up carrots and celery.

Bernie was in the process of adding eight cups of water, before adding the chopped up chicken, when the doorbell rang. This was a special event, as the doorbell had only rung twice since they had moved in—once when the moving company brought Cornelia's grand piano, the other time, when the greengrocer made a delivery.

So of course, everybody ran to the front door. Bernie advised, "Let the adults open the door." The children obediently stepped back. But the next moment they recognized Rabbi Eli, carrying Torah scrolls, standing in the door, and behind him, a tall, smiling Francois. The latter was loaded down with two suitcases and was carrying a heavy satchel on his back. Before they could make a joyful outcry, Francois motioned for silence by putting his finger in front of his lips, indicating that they had to keep the noise down. The men quickly slipped in and closed the door behind them.

"The first thing we need is a storage place for the Torah scrolls and then a private place for Rabbi Eli," Francois appealed to Cornelia. "Then we will explain what this is all about." To Bernie he said, "This was the only way I could persuade him to come with me." While they were scurrying around showing the Rabbi their storeroom at the end of the corridor, Francois continued, "We bring greetings from Frederic, who, more or less, ordered us to make the trip today." Then he added, "You wouldn't believe what the Nazi hoodlums did to Neveh Shalom."

"Oh, you poor dears," Cornelia exclaimed. "We are so glad you came!"

"Both of you!" Bernie added with a radiant smile.

"Perhaps the girls' room would be suitable for Rabbi Eli? We could always put all four children in the same room," Bernie offered.

"I have a better idea," Cornelia offered. "Of course, the storage room, with its shelves, is ideal for the Torah scrolls; but for Rabbi, we'll just close the sliding door between the living room and the parlor, and *voila*, there is a place of privacy for the rabbi. The sofa in the parlor is suitable for sleeping, I think."

Once the Torah scrolls were in a safe place, the rabbi visibly relaxed. He shook everyone's hands, hugging Cornelia and Bernie, and said, "We have lots to share, Francois and I, but first, let us wash up."

With that Bernie headed back to the soup, and the children set the supper table. A half hour later, they were all gathered around their large dining table, holding hands, while Rabbi Eli gave thanks for the meal they were about to partake and for their safe trip from Paris to Lyons. He also prayed for the safety of Frederic, Rachel, and Davide.

Bernie had used plenty of spices and had produced a savory soup, which was served with French bread, butter, and a lavish platter of cheese slices and cut roast beef. The information that the rabbi and Francois shared was hard to conceive. Apparently, the German anti-Jewish wave of violence had not stopped at the border. The same type of Jew-hating people that the children had encountered in the school and on the bus in Paris, had attacked the synagogue. The windows had been shattered, doors had been kicked in, and Rabbi Eli had received death threats.

A phone call had alerted Frederic, Davide, and Francois, who then hurried to the synagogue. They found a distraught Rabbi gathering his papers and Torah scrolls from the floor and meeting rooms that were in disarray. Immediately, they helped gather all the valuables; then Davide and Frederic persuaded Rabbi Eli to spend the night with them. That morning a *minyan* (ten people of the congregation) had met and decided that Rabbi best leave for Lyons and stay there with the precious scrolls, before more damage occurred.

"I pray I will find a synagogue here in town that will accept the documents and scrolls from Neveh Shalom. I am a Messianic believer; therefore, an orthodox rabbi will not want to have anything to do with me. I will have to leave this with our faithful Lord!" Rabbi Eli concluded.

"Dear Husband, how have you been faring through all this?" asked Bernie. "I hope you don't have to report to the bank in Paris at 8 a.m."

Francois, who had been enjoying the good soup while listening to the rabbi, stated, "Actually, Frederic wants me to stay, in order to see to your safety here, and get Rabbi Eli settled again. That's why I loaded the limo to the top with essentials that both Frederic and I agreed were needed here."

Hearing this news elicited happy responses from everyone. Then Francois added, "After we all eat our fill, there is a big job waiting for everyone. The first rule, however, is that this job will be done in utter silence, so that none of the people in this house or neighborhood find out that two men and a bunch of things have been added to this household."

Turning to Cornelia he said, "I am so glad Madame does not have to sing tonight."

"Remember, Francois, that it is first names only now," Cornelia exhorted, while Francois nodded agreement.

"Coming back to our job," Francois explained, "we'll each probably have to make five trips to empty the car. Then tonight yet, I will take the car to a dealer who offered to buy it back from Frederic, provided that we will buy a small economy car from them tomorrow. We will be able to get around in it, drive to school, and run errands."

Then Francois addressed the children, "When we empty the limo, there must be absolutely no shoving or trying to carry more than I hand you, is that clear?"

"Where do you want everything to be placed?" Bernie asked.

"Perhaps for now, until the ladies decide where everything is to go, we will put all hard objects along the walls of the corridor; soft things like pillows, clothes, and blankets, we will lay on the beds. May we have guidance to find the right bed for each item."

After Romi began washing the dishes, the others formed a quiet column along the banister of the staircase and transported things as in a relay race, from person to person. This was found to be more efficient and quieter than if each person were to make the whole trip to the car and back carrying loads by themselves. This way, lamp shades, blankets, coats, music sheets and books, shoes, baking sheets, and hair dryers, all found their way upstairs. It seemed the limo had never carried such an enormous quantity of goods.

When everything was upstairs and the doors closed, Cornelia said, "Seeing this volume of goods you brought to us, Francois, makes me wonder whether Rabbi Eli had to sit on your lap in order to fit in the car!"

"It wasn't quite that bad, all things considered," Rabbi said, "I simply sat on the back seat, surrounded by a whole array of articles. I was glad I could breathe, and I thanked our King that He allowed us to get out of Paris without further violence."

CHAPTER TWENTY-SEVEN

UNITED IN LYONS

There was a lively discussion around the breakfast table in the morning, while Cornelia and Bernie did their best to keep everyone's plates filled. In honor of the two men present, they decided to serve Swedish pancakes. This meant that two skillets were kept going with the delicious concoction of eggs, flour, and milk. The batter was baked into thin pancake shapes, rolled up, and filled with conserves, then sprinkled with powdered sugar, which melted on the tongue.

"Why did we have to be so quiet last night when we were carrying the things up from the limo?" asked Max.

"I wondered about that too," Romi admitted. "Is it a secret, Francois, that you and Rabbi Eli have joined us here?"

Francois nodded and said, "After what we experienced in Paris, we just don't want to arouse suspicion. Our neighbors here don't need to know that we are coming to stay. We have been told that there are Nazis among the population who report on their neighbors, and that could mean harm for us in the future."

Here Bernie spoke up, "It seems best for all of us to live quietly, and to let Mama Cornelia be the one everybody knows; she can make a good reputation for the family."

"She already does," said Irmi. "She gets lots of flowers every day, and the audience stands up after each of her performances."

"And how would you know this, dear public relations expert?" Cornelia asked, as she served second helpings of pancakes wearing a white apron over a pink dress.

"You know, when Mademoiselle Celeste showed us this apartment, she told us how everybody liked you, Mama!"

"This reminds me," Cornelia said, "today I have to be at rehearsal at 10 o'clock because tonight is *Carmen* again." Putting the last pancake on Rabbi Eli's plate, she asked, "What are the plans for the rest of the family?"

"Would it be a good idea to have a short service after breakfast to get started with our Lord and Master, and have Him show us the way?" the rabbi asked. "We also need to pray for Frederic, Davide, and Rachel. They need the Lord's protection and guidance." He looked around the circle of friends and added, "Eventually Frederic and Davide need to find responsible people to take over their interests at the bank. This is a matter to pray about as well."

Cornelia, shedding her apron, sat down at the grand and played a worship song they all loved. Everyone joined in. Next Rabbi Eli intoned the Shema and read Psalm 25. Then going around in the family circle, each person, from the youngest to the oldest, offered a prayer of thanksgiving along with their personal petitions. They shared close and loving fellowship in Yeshua's name, who alone would be able to shield them from the evil to come.

Afterwards, a taxi was called to carry Cornelia to the opera house, and Francois asked Max whether he might want to accompany him to the car dealer where a smaller car was waiting for them. Bernie appealed to Francois to find a shoe store on the way, so that Max could finally get out of summer sandals and into some sturdy boots.

First, however, a call from Paris interrupted the proceedings. It was Frederic, announcing that he would be unable to join them this weekend because he and Davide had to conclude negotiations. He didn't mention with whom, and they didn't press him because they were aware that the phone was no longer a safe means of communications.

Frederic asked whether the children had been registered at school, and then he talked with each one of them. Hearing that all four would go to "*L'Ecole Germaine,*" he wondered how it was that Max had been accepted. Then hearing about the little boy's geometric feat and the counting of the coins, Frederic heartily congratulated the little fellow. This is how Abba Francois found out, as well, about Max's remarkable performance which earned his acceptance to the private school.

An hour later, Francois was waiting with Max in the spacious display room of the Citroen dealership, in the suburb of Lyons, called Villeurbanne. They looked at a number of smaller models. They both liked the brown, inconspicuous sedan that seated five.

"You are not looking for a big car, Abba Francois?" Max asked. Pointing to a bigger model, he said, "I really like the inside of this one."

"Why is that?" Francois wondered, expecting Max to comment on the soft plush seats.

The little boy, pointing at the dash board, said, "These controls show it must have a fine motor."

Then the salesman appeared, giving Francois a generous trade-in value for the limo he had brought in the night before. Handing him the keys, he said, "We hope you like this smaller car; it is sturdy and powerful. It will not disappoint you."

When they got home, the rabbi was packing. "You don't want to leave us already, Rabbi Eli?" Francois asked. "You haven't seen Lyons yet."

"Yes, and we wanted the rabbi to go with us to '*Tete d'Or*' so we could show him the animals," said Max.

"You had just left, when Rabbi had an international call from Switzerland," Bernie explained. "There is an old synagogue in Geneva where the rabbi recently died. They had been searching everywhere for a replacement. Somebody in Paris told them about their rabbi having to flee with the Torah scrolls. They begged Rabbi Eli to bring the scrolls to safety and to help out until a permanent rabbi could be found."

"Thank you, Bernie, for explaining the situation. I'm still stunned how quickly the Lord is directing my steps. I would have had to search for a home for the scrolls and might have doubted for their safety here in France. I trust our Lord has extended the call. That is why I wish to leave with the afternoon express for Geneva, if you, Francois, could transport me and this suitcase to the station by two o'clock," Rabbi Eli said, while he knelt on the floor, fitting Torah scrolls into a large suitcase.

"But of course, with my utmost devotion," replied Francois. "In fact, now that I have the new Citroen waiting outside, it would not be a problem for me to take you all the way to Geneva. It is, roughly speaking, only an hour and a half driving time away."

"A truly generous offer, Francois, "said the rabbi, "but the people at the other end are so happy that I am willing to come that they have already arranged everything. They bought the ticket, and the Geneva pick-up will be waiting for me at five p.m., so I had better not disappoint them. Tomorrow is Shabbat, you know!"

"Rabbi Eli, we had so hoped you would stay a while and be our rabbi here so that we could have our own worship services and grow in the Lord," Bernie said with regret in her voice.

"My new Imma is right," Hannah said, "When you said the Shema this morning, Rabbi Eli, and when we all joined in prayer, it was a little like it used to be at home with our Abba." She didn't want to hurt Francois and Bernie's feelings, so she added, "Perhaps we can sometimes have private devotions even without Rabbi Eli being here."

"And of course, we hope you will visit here whenever you feel lonely! I know Frederic and Cornelia feel this way too," Bernie said.

Then Bernie served a delicate farewell lunch, packed a sandwich and an apple for the dear man, and Francois whisked him off to the railroad station, bidding him, "Shabbat Shalom!"

Unbeknownst to them, Frederic was flying south just then. His flight plan called for an overnight stop in Tripoli, Libya, with his final destination Tel Aviv-Jaffa tomorrow. He knew that on Shabbat no business would be conducted by Jewish people. But Tel Aviv, being located in the British Mandate, would probably see some business transacted by the non-Jewish population. He planned to get acquainted with the area and looked forward to a well-deserved rest, as his previous weeks had been extremely long and frantic.

His family had no inkling of his trip. Both he and Davide had decided not to involve their families yet. Their plans were tentative at best, but they foresaw without a doubt that France, too, would become a victim of Germany's drive to conquer the whole world. Frederic and Davide's hope was to clear out of Europe before they became the hunted.

CHAPTER TWENTY-EIGHT

ERETZ ISRAEL

Cornelia was taking her last bow in front of the Lyons Opera House curtain, when Frederic stepped on the soil of Israel for the first time. He had just landed by small aircraft shuttle from Tripoli, Libya. Uniformed British soldiers were escorting the few arriving passengers to a small customs station where their passports were checked, and their reason for arrival in the British Mandate was established. The couple in front of Frederic seemed to have trouble with their entry visas so he was led to another office around the corner. Frederic explained his prospective business with one of Tel Aviv's banking houses and provided the paperwork to prove it. He was waved right through.

Frederic, with briefcase in hand, walked toward the downtown area, which appeared to be brightly lit and not too distant. The breeze from the Mediterranean was soft and welcoming. The exercise felt good after sitting for hours in various cramped positions. Within half an hour, he was approaching the business district. He saw tree-lined avenues, bigger buildings, and two or three hotels still open to accommodate late-night gatherings. He knew that Jewish people would be home for Shabbat Eve observations. He concluded that the people in the streets must be English or Arab.

Frederic noticed some slinking, shadowy individuals following him too closely, so he made his way into the first brightly-lit doorway he came to and found himself in a lobby-like entrance hall. A large, black

189

man loomed behind a desk at the end of the hall. This man addressed Frederic in accented English, asking, "Would you want a room for tonight, Sir?"

"If this is a hotel—then, yes!"

To which the black man replied, "We are a guesthouse that caters to British troops and their guests. But I can contact another hotel in town that is still open and ask for accommodations for you there, if you wish?"

"I would appreciate that; I am in Tel Aviv for the first time," Frederic stated. "Besides, I can do without some questionable characters that are out there."

"Yes, this time of night we sometimes have complaints about Arab youths who are roaming around looking for trouble," the man agreed. "It is advisable to have transportation after dark."

In no time, a cab driver was asking for Frederic. After thanking the kind man behind the desk, he was taken to Hotel Excelsior, where a nice, clean room, and a late night snack were made available to him.

Sunday morning it was business as usual in the Jewish sector of Tel Aviv, while the English were attending Sunday services in the Anglican Church on the main boulevard. After a cup of strong coffee, Frederic headed to the building the concierge at the hotel had described to him. The sign over the front entrance said "International Bank of Tel Aviv/Jaffa."

Frederic had been expected. He was promptly admitted to the office of Adam Levi, a man appearing to be in his late fifties or early sixties, who rose and greeted him warmly.

"I am very glad you were willing to see me today," Frederic offered, while shaking the man's hand. "Perhaps we can come to an agreement today so I can head home soon!"

"Don't be in too much of a rush, Monsieur Bartok," Mr. Levi replied. "There is much to discuss if you intend to negotiate with me."

Frederic replied, "I would like to hear what your reasons are for wanting to leave here at this particular time of your life?" Frederic looked at Mr. Levi expectantly.

"I am delighted to oblige this request," Mr. Levi replied, "but may I suggest that we take a little walk." He beckoned to Frederic and led him to a back door hidden in an alcove.

Frederic followed him and found himself in an alley that appeared to run parallel to the main boulevard. After about fifty feet of walking in silence, side by side, Mr. Levi took Frederic's elbow and steered him down a narrow trail to the left. A few steps farther, and they could see the seashore. Stretched before them were the choppy waves of the Mediterranean, reflecting the rays of the morning sun.

"You have to understand, Monsieur Bartok, that here in the Mandate all the walls have ears. I don't want to broadcast my intent to leave before my plans are made, and before we have an agreed date for the takeover of the bank. You want to hear my reasons for leaving? To be straightforward, the major reason is my family. My wife is American, and our only daughter lives in New York." He stopped and pointed into the distance. "Can you see Jaffa, or Yafo, as some people call it, to the south of here?" Frederic nodded, seeing in the morning haze the houses of Jaffa along the shore.

"I grew up there," Mr. Levi continued. "This really is my home. But the problems with the Arabs never end. Then, if they are quiet for a little while, you can be sure that trouble with the English is brewing. You have to be on your toes all of the time! Being diplomatic must be second nature to you, and I am getting older and am tired of this mess."

They walked once more in silence, Frederic trying to understand the other man's motives for wanting to rid himself of the banking house. A bank which had a good reputation, from the references Frederic had been able to obtain.

Then Frederic replied, "What we see in France, and in Europe in general, is a growing unease with the brutal expansionism of the Hitler regime in Germany. What I hear through private sources is very troubling. Therefore, Davide Cohen, my business partner and friend, and I have decided that in order to maintain our assets, we must branch out to this country.

We understand the restrictions placed on businesses by the British Mandate, but that seems to be an easier load to bear than to be subjected to the anti-Semitic Jew-persecutors from Germany. Perhaps you know, I had to leave everything I owned in Czechoslovakia because I wanted to keep my family out of Hitler's concentration camps. Terrible tales come to us about the treatment that Jews receive there."

"I just read a report that was smuggled out of Germany by a Jewish friend whose family was caught by the Nazi's; they lost all their earthly belongings. He fled from Austria, the only survivor of his family!" added Mr. Levi.

"It seems that we are not considered human in the estimation of the Fuehrer of the Great German Reich. The farther away I can take my loved ones, the better it will be," Frederic replied. "Therefore, Davide and I have decided to purchase all your shares in the bank, if you are still willing to go through with this deal. Of course, we must mutually agree on the terms and have help from a lawyer with the technicalities of the transaction. Also, we must conclude our business in a timely manner because we believe France will be occupied by the Germans within a year or so."

They discussed the details of the agreement as they walked back to Mr. Levi's international bank. They agreed that they needed an attorney who could handle the planned takeover honestly and efficiently.

Back in Lyons, Francois stopped in front of the large entrance gate of "*L'Ecole Germaine*," waiting for his four charges, when there was a knock at the driver's window. Inquiringly, he looked at a small man in a short, black overcoat, a beret on his head.

"How can I help?" asked Francois.

"There is a small envelope that needs delivery to Rabbi Eli in Geneva." The man looked questioningly at Francois, "You know the man?"

"He is a friend of the family," Francois replied.

"I knew you were the right person to get it there," the man said. "Your only instructions are: Take it unopened to Rabbi Eli, then turn around and forget about it."

Francois nodded and put the letter in his inside coat pocket. When he looked up, the man was gone. Just then the children arrived, first came Max, who bounced with pent-up energy when he saw his Abba Francois. He greeted him, "*Bon Jour, Abba!*" and asked, "May I sit in the front seat by you?"

Francois nodded, smiling. Max slipped in, put his backpack by his feet, and said, "I really had a good day. We studied Roman numerals, and I know them to one hundred now. I think Romi and Irmi know them too."

"Could you write them down for me at home?" Francois asked. "I might learn a thing or two." Next, Hannah emerged carrying her backpack, which held her books and her gym outfit. She quietly slid into the back seat, while the twins followed behind her.

"I hear that Max had a challenging day and learned all about Roman numerals, how about you three young ladies?" Francois turned and looked at each of the girls, "Do you have anything to report that would encourage me to study also?"

"I think I need help with English," Hannah answered. "My class has studied it since last year, and I came in with no knowledge of it. I can't pronounce it or read it, and the teacher says I must try hard to keep up." Her head hung down, her face pale and sad.

Hannah needed comfort, so Romi reached around her, pulled her close, and said, "Listen, Hannah, we will talk with Papa and Mama about it. Perhaps we can all study English together."

"Somebody in our class said that English was the main language to know in the whole world because more people speak it than any other," Irmi contributed.

"I heard that too, and they explained how children in most countries have to study English first, before any other language," Hannah agreed.

"Irmi, do you remember when we first arrived at Pension Perrot? Mama used to only speak English with Madame because our French was so poor. I believe, Mama would be a good teacher for all of us, if she has the time," said Romi.

Francois was crossing one of the Rhone bridges and had to drive with great care because the traffic was very heavy. Once they were out of the crunch of trucks, delivery vans, and taxis, he visibly relaxed and said, "I wanted to study English for the longest time, even when I still worked in the circus, because we visited England once a year, and I thought it important not to be ignorant of this language. But there was never enough time."

"Abba Francois, I didn't know that you once worked in a circus; you should tell us some of your adventures," suggested Max.

"I thought our subject was English lessons," corrected Francois. "Actually, with all the talk about the English being our allies and neighbors, to know their language would be quite an asset, don't you think?" Meanwhile, he had driven the small car into the narrow alley beside their apartment house. "As for my work as a clown, that will have to wait for a bedtime treat some special day."

Francois saw the children upstairs, kissed his wife, and whispered to her about his Geneva assignment. In the ensuing scramble to the bathroom for washing up, getting homework done, and settling down for an afternoon snack, Francois disappeared without anybody taking notice. When the children finished their snack of grated apples and crackers, Francois was already through Lyons and Villeurbanne, on his way to Geneva.

Courier jobs for the "Underground" were highly secretive. Only Bernie, Cornelia, and Frederic were aware of Francois' involvement. Although Francois had already served a number of times while they still were in Paris, his assignments then had been northward, to Belgium, the Normandy, and the Gulf of Biscay. This was his first trip to Switzerland. The sun was setting behind him when he arrived first at the French, then the Swiss, checkpoints.

When asked by the border guards why Francois wanted to visit Switzerland only for a few hours, he pleaded his need to see his rabbi for counseling. There was no frisking or questions about the legitimacy of his passport. He passed through without a hitch. The problem arose at the rabbi's residence when the rabbi couldn't be found.

"He left this morning for Hebrew shul," said his landlady. A long, winding road later, when Francois arrived at the shul and asked for the rabbi, the caretaker told him that the shul closed at four o'clock. By this time Francois was not only tired and hungry, but disappointed as well. He sat in the car and prayed for guidance. So it was back to the landlady, who informed him that Rabbi Eli had called and said he was at the Hebrew deli. Nothing could have sounded more appealing to Francois at the time.

Francois located the rabbi quickly. He was seated with three young people around a table in the back, eating a kosher meal. Rabbi Eli greeted him cordially, appearing not to be surprised by his presence at the deli. Soon Francois was seated, as well, getting nourishment from cabbage rollups and spiced tea. The young people seemed to be students at the local yeshiva; they discussed their studies of the Torah and eagerly listened to the rabbi's explanations. They said their "Shalom" and left before Francois could finish his meal.

At this point, Francois handed over the letter, which Rabbi Eli immediately put in his inside breast pocket, thanking him. "Do you realize, Francois, that you are saving lives by making these trips for our cause?"

"I do hope I can contribute in some small way, although I am in the dark about what I am doing," admitted Francois.

"You see, this is best," Rabbi Eli replied. "If you were aware of the importance or triviality of these trips, you might suffer more with apprehension. Just be a good courier and know that the cause is being helped."

Then folding his hands on the newly cleaned table, Rabbi Eli asked, "How is your study of the Word of God going? Do you and Bernie find time to read at least a chapter daily and pray together? Even if it is difficult because of your responsibilities, you must, I urge you, not let it slip!" His penetrating gaze held Francois, who admitted that they had not been as diligent as they desired to be. Francois knew that they needed to get back into a routine, now that he did not have to go back to Paris, but was responsible for the household in Lyons.

"I shall pray for you," the rabbi said, "because I know that in our daily lives and the many demands on our time, we forget that 'Man does not live by bread alone, but by each word that proceeds from the mouth of God.' This exhortation, our Lord found fit to mention both in the Torah (in Deuteronomy, the 5. Book of Mosche 8:3) and in the New Testament of our Messiah (in Matthew 4:4). Because of this, we know that it is important to Him that we understand this principle."

Then smiling at Francois, Rabbi Eli concluded, "Now after all my preaching, I must let you depart my dear friend. You still have a considerable way to go before reaching home. You mustn't tell anyone where you have been, except the adults in your apartment." With that he rose, hugged Francois, and clapped him on his back in farewell.

On the way home, Francois lifted his voice in songs of praise to His faithful Lord, who had allowed him to cross the border both ways without trouble. The rabbi's encouraging words had touched his heart, and he determined to begin a daily time of Bible reading and prayer with his beloved wife. He decided if the children happened to be around that they would include them in it as well. In Frederic's absence, it seemed the Lord had placed this charge on Francois' heart.

After parking the car and silently entering the apartment, he found his wife in the kitchen with a flashlight, welcoming him with a warm embrace. They sat quietly for awhile, sharing the events of their respective days. Not wanting to disturb the other members of their household, they tiptoed to their bedroom. Francois placed his hand on little Max's dark-haired head, before withdrawing to the arms of his beloved wife.

CHAPTER TWENTY-NINE

DISTURBANCE IN LYONS

On the surface, looking behind the scenes of the Lyons Opera House, one had the impression of good camaraderie between singers and musicians, support staff, backstage personnel, and administration. But getting to know the truth beneath the surface, in any such institution, takes time.

Cornelia had evolved out of the ranks of the Prague National Theatre and was acquainted with many people. She knew most by name and had good relationships with them. Being in a new, French-speaking institution presented a whole new array of interpersonal challenges.

After awhile, Cornelia found out a number of things. For instance, there was a certain animosity between two female singers. The administration saw to it that these two ladies were not assigned together in any of the productions. It was also commonly known that Loup de Fallou, the head conductor, and the prima ballerina of the *corps de ballet* were considered to be intimate. The two were discrete, but it was common knowledge.

A problem concerning Cornelia developed after she had been working with the ensemble for a few weeks. Her male lead, a handsome, talented tenor who was often cast opposite her, began to admire her, thereby neglecting a young singer who had, until then, been his romantic consort. Cornelia impressed him greatly. He had never encountered such a mature, experienced soprano of Cornelia's stature.

Cornelia's stage experience, her voice quality, and her charm exceeded anything he had experienced in his career.

Additionally, as the days wore on, the entire ensemble became aware of the audiences' great liking of Madame Cornelia Kahn Bartok. The many curtain calls after each performance spoke for themselves. Polite applause would rise to a mighty crescendo when Cornelia appeared to take her turn.

Several experienced ladies and gentlemen among the singers felt ignored by the great acclaim given to their new colleague. A spirit of professional jealousy had begun to poison some relationships. At first Cornelia was unaware of it, but as time went on and more remarks were made, she was enlightened by Celeste, her loyal wardrobe mistress.

What do you think I should do?" Cornelia asked. "I have tried to be friendly with everyone, and I cannot help it that the audience is so selective in its response."

"There really is nothing you can do at the time, Madame," Celeste assured her. "But beware of Mademoiselle Odelle Lucien. She not only has a bad tongue but also a mean temper. Be careful around her!"

It didn't help that Mademoiselle Odelle also sang soprano and still had a crush on the attractive tenor. In the fall of 1938, a new production was planned, and the cast was selected. It was *Madame Butterfly*, and they needed a diminutive singer for the lead role, as she was to portray a small Japanese woman. Naturally, Cornelia, who already had sung the role in Czech, was the choice singer for this part.

Mademoiselle Odelle felt slighted. Although she had the proportions of a *walkyrie*, she felt demeaned when she was not given the lead role, but rather a small supporting one. Her old flame, the tenor, was to play the male lead. Hearing Cornelia excel at the intricacies of the score and seeing her play opposite the man she loved, brought out the worst in Mademoiselle Odelle. Meanwhile, the rehearsals had progressed, and the premiere had been set for January 21, 1939.

The day of the dress rehearsal arrived, the cast was in costume, the orchestra in place, and the performers were waiting at their designated places in the wings. The scene was open, and Cornelia was singing the aria that mourns the departure of the English lieutenant. Suddenly a sharp crack was heard; Cornelia reached for her right side and collapsed onto the stage.

The conductor stopped the proceedings. He noticed the shocked expressed on Cornelia's beautiful face. As the stage manager and other performers rushed to Cornelia's aid, the always present physician called out, "Please don't touch Madame. I have to examine her first." And kneeling at her side, he ran his hand under her colorful kimono until he located the wound from which warm blood spilled.

Listening to her lungs, he stated, "I believe she has been shot into her right lung." Looking around, he said to the stage manager in urgent tones, "She needs emergency evacuation to University Hospital. Tell them a thoracic surgeon must be made available immediately!" Then he saw Mademoiselle Celeste in her white, wardrobe mistress's jacket and declared, "I must confiscate your coat to staunch this blood flow."

By now a veritable puddle had formed next to Cornelia's right side. As Celeste tore off her coat, the physician grabbed it and stuffed it under Cornelia's kimono, ordering everybody off the scene. "Only medical personnel and her wardrobe mistress may remain," he shouted. It was minutes later that the stretcher-bearers entered, loaded Cornelia's still form onto their carrier, and rushed out the backstage door. The ambulance left a minute later with sirens blaring.

When the ambulance arrived at the emergency entrance of University Hospital, the thoracic surgeon was waiting. Cornelia was sent to the operating room immediately. The bullet, which had entered her right lung's middle lobe, was located and removed, and the bleeding was stopped. Within two hours she was admitted to the intensive care unit, and her family was notified.

Francois was next to the phone when the call came in. He forwarded the message to Paris. Davide Cohen received the call in his private office and assured Francois that he would contact Frederic right away, though Frederic was not in the office at the moment.

After talking with Paris, Francois and Bernie offered a fervent prayer for Cornelia. As they were discussing what to do and who should go to the hospital, Frederic called, wanting to know what had transpired. He promised to catch the first available flight to the Bron aerodrome in

Lyons. He asked Francois to go to the hospital immediately. He begged Bernie to stay with the children.

So the moment they hung up, Francois sprinted to the car and was at the hospital in a matter of minutes. He was told he could not get any information about Cornelia's condition because he was not a member of the family. But a gentleman standing by in evening clothes overheard the interchange between Francois and the lady at the reception desk, and he intervened, asking, "Are you a friend of Madame Bartok?"

"Yes! Sir! My wife and I are long-time employees of the Bartok family. In fact, we live together and care for the household and the children while Madame and her husband are at work. We have already notified Monsieur Bartok, who is concluding business in Paris. It will take him several hours to get here. Meanwhile, my wife and I have been given full authority to deal with all emergencies.

After hearing this explanation, the gentleman turned to the receptionist and stated, "This young man represents Madame Bartok's family. He must be given all the information necessary to keep her affairs in order. Her husband will make his way from Paris to here and then will take over."

The nurse then told Francois that Cornelia's right lung was affected; that she was still under anesthesia after the emergency surgery to remove the bullet and stem the bleeding. They were holding her in the recovery room until all her vital signs were stable."

The gentleman in evening attire introduced himself, "I am Monsieur Armande Ballon, the artistic director of the opera house, and I represent her workplace. I was present during the tragic attack"

He continued, "Let me explain what really happened, though I am still too shocked to fully understand what transpired. We were in the midst of general rehearsal for *Madame Butterfly*. All of the performers, costumed and well rehearsed, were standing at various points for their entrance to the stage, when right in the middle of Madame's aria mourning the departure of her beloved English lieutenant, a shot rang out. She grasped her right side and sank to the floor while blood seeped through her kimono."

Leaning in towards Francois, he said, "As far as I know, she had no enemies and maintained courteous relations with other singers and stage personnel."

"Do you think an anti-Semitic plot is behind this attack?" Francois asked.

Monsieur Ballon thought it was not, but stressed, "The police investigation is under way."

They were interrupted when a nurse appeared, saying a phone call for Francois Leclerq was being held at the main desk. It was Frederic, waiting at Le Bourget, the airfield north of Paris, for the departure of his flight. He wanted all the information Francois could provide and asked to be connected with the doctor in charge.

The nurse dutifully called, reaching the assistant, Dr. Vereux, who had been present at the operation with the thoracic surgeon, Dr. Sevignard. He informed Frederic that the bullet, shot from a short distance away, had entered the middle lobe of Cornelia's right lung and had been successfully removed by the operating doctor. She had lost a lot of blood and was weak. She was resting at the present and must not be disturbed.

"Yes," the assistant said, "as soon as you arrive, Sir, you may see your wife for a short while." Then he handed the phone back to Francois, who assured Frederic that he would stay at the hospital in case Cornelia woke up and asked for family members.

Francois also called Bernie, letting her know that he had to stay where he was until Frederic's arrival. He urged her to go to bed and take care of herself, assuring her that nothing could be accomplished by worrying. He asked her not to mention anything to the children. Frederic would have to be the one to tell them.

When Francois returned to the recovery room, Monsieur Ballon was still pacing up and down in front of the swinging door that led to the unit. He said, "They tell me that she is still unconscious, but they expect her to come out of anesthesia within half an hour."

"Sir, why don't you leave me your phone number and go home? I will call and report to you as soon as I see Madame," Francois assured him.

"I am quite concerned about the injury to this lovely and talented woman," the man replied. "We have not had a singer of such high caliber at our opera house for a long time. I have no idea how anyone could be so devilish, wanting to destroy such a special lady!" With that Monsieur Ballon took his leave, and Francois waited for the call to see Cornelia.

About an hour later, the night nurse beckoned to him and led him into the intensive care unit. Cornelia looked at him with her dark, beautiful eyes, whispering, "Dear Francois, I'm sorry you have to lose your sleep because of me! I don't know how this happened. Who would want to shoot me?" She reached out with her small hand; Francois took it, and holding it, assured her that Frederic was on the way.

"Are you able to stand the pain?" Francois asked. "Can you tell me how you are feeling?"

She whispered back, "I have quite a bit of pain in my side, and I am short of breath. But mostly, I need to sleep. I am so tired." She paused to gain her breath and said, "Please Francois, would you pray for me."

So Francois lifted Cornelia's needs before their Father in Heaven. She closed her eyes and went to sleep. The nurse came back into the room and nodded towards the door, clearly indicating that he should leave, and so he did.

The headlines in the morning paper were all on the tragedy at the Opera House; how the talented singer from Czechoslovakia had been brought down by a bullet. Who would have wanted her killed? After reporters interviewed many of Cornelia's colleagues, a theory began to emerge that the attack had come from an individual who envied Cornelia and wanted her out of the way. Photos were spread over several pages of the newspaper, recounting Cornelia's successes in France and in her native country.

When Frederic arrived in the early morning hours, he looked worn with lack of sleep, but still maintained his impeccable appearance. He was led to the intensive care station where Cornelia was sedated. When he saw his wife, who was attached to IVs, propped on her right side, still pale and so fragile-looking, he immediately went to her bedside. He gently touched her curly head and offered a prayer of thanksgiving. When she opened her eyes, smiling at him, he bent down and kissed her on the forehead. Very faintly he heard, "My dear One, how did you get here so fast?"

"My Dearest, I am so thankful for airplanes! En route, I thought about how you really hadn't gotten the voice rest that you needed. Now the Lord is providing you the rest His way, because you and I believe, don't we, that He is in charge of everything we experience? It's just bad for the Lyons Opera House; they will have to rearrange their entire schedule!"

The nurses came in to reposition Cornelia. The one in charge said, "Monsieur Bartok, you may only see your wife for five minutes each hour, and those minutes are now up!"

"Beloved," Cornelia whispered in response, "you would do me the greatest favor, if you would go home, talk to the children, and after Francois takes them to school, would you please take a nap? Please wait until the afternoon to see me again. I am very tired as well."

He nodded in agreement, noting how she was fighting for breath. He took her small hand in his and prayed for her, and then he kissed her hand and promised he would return this afternoon. On his way out, he ran into the pulmonary surgeon who had come for his early rounds with a retinue of interns. When Frederic introduced himself, Dr. Sevignard greeted him, and in his rather brusque way, informed Frederic of his wife's precarious condition.

"She has lost an awful lot of blood," he said, "but she must have had divine protection. That bullet could have gone straight to her heart! She needs rest—no visitors! Mainly, to prevent infection."

"May her children come to see her?"

"Only if they want to see her dead soon. That means, absolutely not! You may come in and then share what she says with them later." With that the efficient surgeon swept by him, three interns in tow, and disappeared behind the swinging door. Frederic walked home. He welcomed the cold morning air. It refreshed his sleep-deprived, troubled mind.

Frederic entered the apartment house through the service entrance in the back, carried up the morning paper and the milk, and arrived at the front door just when the children were bidding Bernie goodbye.

The first to the door was his daughter Irmi, who jumped straight into his arms at the sight of her Papa.

"Papa, how did you get here?" Romi asked.

Followed by Irmi's, "Can you stay a while?"

As he nodded, all four children gathered around him, with Bernie behind them. He exchanged glances with Bernie and asked, "Is this the right time to break the news?"

Here Francois approached, still pale from his short night, saying, "Frederic, before they hear it from strangers; do tell them. If we are a little later than usual, the school authorities will understand."

"Papa, what is it you have to tell us?" asked Romi.

"I believe you all should come into the living room for a moment, because what I have to tell you concerns us all." When they were all inside, he closed the door and asked them to sit down while he and Francois took turns relating the events of the past night. When all four children started to cry, Frederic said in conclusion, "Your Mommy, our dear Cornelia, will not die. She is just badly hurt, and nobody knows yet who shot her or why. So when the children in school want to talk to you about this, it is best to say, "We don't know anything yet. Please pray for her. God alone can heal her."

Then each of them gathered around, allowing the adults to comfort and reassure them. This they did, but Francois, pulling on his gloves, said, "Perhaps it's best to go to school and do something, instead of standing around moaning. Madame Cornelia is helped by our prayers, not by our worries."

Then Frederic said, "Yes, we all have to hold her up faithfully by our prayers. The sooner we do that, the sooner she will again join our family circle."

They thanked the Master of the Universe, the Healer of all, for His faithfulness and for His protection. Frederic prayed, "Thy word says in the Torah, 'You are the God that healeth,' and You, Almighty One, will carry Cornelia through this ordeal. This we pray in the Name of Yeshua, the Messiah of Israel." And they all added their "Amen," which means, "So be it." Minutes later, after bidding Bernie a second goodbye, the children were on the way to school with Francois.

CHAPTER THIRTY

POLICE REPORT

few days later, Frederic received a call from the criminal section of the Lyons Police Department. He was asked to see the department head, Police Inspecteur Rolland. When Frederic arrived, the Inspecteur received him graciously and asked him to sit for awhile with him in his office. He came right to the point, saying, "We have a report here which I wish to share with you before we publish it. Of course, you know, the report is not pleasant. It concerns the person who, without provocation, attacked your wife on the stage of our Lyons Opera House. We are now convinced that the person's motives were not only professional jealousy, but also anti-Semitism."

"Actually, I am not surprised, but had hoped that my wife's professional life and performances were above reproach. So, this has come as a great shock to her, as well as to us, her family," Frederic rejoined.

"We have been informed that her time of recuperation will be prolonged, as the injury was life-threatening, is that correct?"

Frederic nodded and confirmed, "It seems, in spite of the evil intent, she was saved from an early death by divine intervention. The doctors explained, had the bullet gone a fraction further, it would have penetrated her heart. It entered her chest wall and went into her right lung, from which they were able to remove the foreign body within an hour of the attack. But the blood loss was excessive."

"Thank you for sharing with me the extent of the damage done," said the Inspecteur. "My detectives have worked hard to find the reason for this unnecessary bloodshed." Here he cleared his throat and continued. "A fellow soprano by the name of Odelle Lucien has been identified as the attacker. We were not able to arrest the woman. She left our country for Germany. There she is protected by her Nazi cronies, with whom she has some long-standing relations. We have filed for extradition, but have come to a dead-end."

He continued, "But we found out that Odelle Lucien, for several years, has spent considerable time with young men and women who are part of the Nazi leaders' entourage. She apparently had expressed a desire to become a member of a touring group that entertains at Nazi party functions, but was not accepted due to her inadequacy in the German language. Evidently, spending vacations with these German individuals has caused her to absorb their hatred and disregard for all Jewish persons. Perhaps, she hoped that by destroying a Jewish life, she'd find special acceptance by them, who knows?"

"At the Opera, she worked her way up to solo parts and developed a relationship with the lead tenor, who, apparently, had given her hope of landing roles of significance in the future. This tenor, a Monsieur Edvard Bruille, has been cooperative in our investigation. He stated that your wife's professional competence and artistic superiority had aroused envy in Odelle Lucien and others. He said he had overheard remarks against your wife, especially in relation to her amazing success with the audiences. He also mentioned that your wife always treated her co-workers with courtesy and respect. Therefore, he surmised these envious tongues would eventually lose their venom and cease their wagging."

Here Frederic stated, "This seems to be an unfortunate development, of which my wife was not aware. We are not seeking revenge, but would like to know the root cause of this most unfortunate happening."

"Of course," the Inspecteur agreed, "this, too, is the desire of all detectives working for me. Therefore, when we raided Mademoiselle Lucien's apartment, we searched for a weapon, and other evidence which might further explain her motives. What we found has led us to another avenue of investigation, namely, the Vichy Police Department. Vichy was Lucien's hometown, and they have records on her."

"Mademoiselle Lucien, three years ago, was a candidate being trained for a career with their police force. She completed two courses in small arms weaponry before she discovered that she had a voice that would gain her work in our Opera Company here in Lyons." He shuffled through a folder on his desk, from which he now extracted a photo showing a woman pointing a pistol at a mannequin. "This is the woman in question; you can see that she is able to handle a firearm."

As Frederic perused the picture, the Inspecteur looked questioningly at him, and asked, "We have two choices in pursuing this case. As of now, the public is not informed about your wife's ethnic background. Do we want to stress the woman's affiliation with German Nazis and make anti-Semitism a big issue, or do we only want to mention the professional jealousy?"

"To have our Jewishness so widely publicized is not our desire," Frederic said. "My wife's gifting, and her artistry should not be brought into the political realm, I think. We both believe that only the barest facts should be brought before the public at this point."

With this understanding, Frederic left the office of the sympathetic Inspecteur. The next day, he was pleased to read a statement by the police which simply said: "Local Opera Star Recuperating—Madame Cornelia Kahn Bartok is recuperating from a bullet wound to the chest. The attacker was a fellow singer, Mademoiselle Odelle Lucien. Professional and relational jealousies were motives for the crime. The perpetrator has left the country. She now resides in Germany, from which extradition requests have not been responded to."

The report continued: "Madame Bartok had to undergo emergency surgery in the University Hospital following the attack, which occurred during general rehearsal of *Madame Butterfly*. A bullet was removed from her right lung. Due to great blood loss, the beloved singer is weakened and has to spend considerable time away from stage and public appearances to recuperate. It is hoped that Madame Bartok will be able to resume her singing career by the fall of this year."

CHAPTER THIRTY-ONE

TIME OF REFRESHING

It was a week before the children were allowed to see Cornelia. Up until then, Frederic had made the daily trek to the hospital, stayed with his wife, encouraged her to walk, eat, and sleep, and then reported faithfully to the rest of the family. No other visitors had been admitted yet.

After the week of practical isolation, Cornelia had been moved into the VIP suite of the hospital, which was on the top floor. The view from there was panoramic. Lyons, its many hills, the two rivers Rhone and Saone, and its busy harbors, were all visible for many miles. Finally, Romi and Irmi, with Hannah and Max in tow, stepped with Frederic into the elevator, and soon they arrived on the top floor.

It had been agreed that Francois and Bernie would wait to come visit on one of the next few days, in order not to overwhelm Cornelia with too much talk. The children had made a little something to present to her. While Frederic went to see whether Cornelia was presentable, the children giggled and fidgeted as they tried to decide who would go in first. They had also brought the daily collection of mail from Cornelia's fans and admirers, which had begun to ebb a little after the first days of countless cards, letters, and bouquets.

Frederic held the door open as the four slowly stepped in, Romi and Irmi holding hands, with Hannah and Max behind them. Cornelia sat up in bed, wearing a lovely gown of periwinkle with a scarf to match. Her black curls were held back by a headband of the same color, and she was smiling brightly. Her complexion was waxen and deep circles showed under her eyes. The fine features of her heart-shaped face were smaller, or at least they seemed to be.

"Oh, my dear Mama," Romi said, pulling her sister by the hand, "we have been missing you so much!"

"Yes, Mama, we didn't realize how much we love you and can't do without you until we couldn't see you for these many days," added Irmi.

"We were told that we can't even hug you, so we'll only kiss your hands!" This they proceeded to do from either side of the bed.

Then Romi handed Cornelia a little box and said, "Irmi and I made this for you, Mama, but Bernie helped."

"Am I supposed to look at this now?" Cornelia asked, while holding up the little, well-wrapped box.

"Yes, Mama, please do. We thought of you while we made this," said Irmi.

So Cornelia unwrapped and opened the box, which held a hair band decorated with rhinestones and a bracelet to match. She exclaimed, "What a beauty! I didn't know my daughters could do something so professional." She held up the lovely pieces, so Frederic could see as well.

"They spent a lot of time on that and had fun doing it," Hannah said. Then she added, "Madame Cornelia, Max and I wanted to surprise you with a song our Abba taught us long ago. He always said, 'We have to sing the Word of God to fend off the enemy.'"

"I would love to hear it; is it from the Psalms?" Cornelia asked.

"Yes, from the twentieth Psalm!" Hanna confirmed. "Our Abba said, 'the Word of God is not only words, but it has power.'"

Together, they proceeded to sing: "Some trust in chariots, and some in horses, but we trust in the Name of the Lord our God!" They repeated this, and finished with, "They are brought down and fallen: but we are risen and stand upright. To Him all glory be now and forever!" They sang this in harmony, and Cornelia was surprised to hear Max's young voice rise like a bell, clear and able.

Cornelia responded, "Perhaps, we should all sing together a lot so that I learn to sing again, with you all helping me." This appealed to the children, who nodded and stood around the bed talking, while Frederick perused the mail he had picked up from the Opera House before coming.

Frederic came over and handed a letter to Cornelia, saying, "This is postmarked Dijon; do we know anyone from there by the name of Marty?"

She looked at him with her lovely, dark eyes and shook her head, "I can't think of anyone by that name."

But Hannah said, "I think I know who wrote the letter. Remember, Madame, when Francois drove us to Paris and we stopped at the *"Jardins de Marty"*.

"Oh, yes, Mama, remember when I fell into the creek, and you had to take me into the kitchen to dry off?" Irmi remembered.

Then Romi said, "Papa, we told you about that: how we stopped there for awhile and got to ride the ponies and pet the lambs. It was very special for all of us."

"Of course, now I remember!" Cornelia said. "They were so good to us; they fed us and told us how much they loved opera." A moment later, she urged, "Please open the letter and read it to us. We all remember that lovely day."

So Frederic proceeded, "Dear Madame, we still remember you from your visit to us last year. We have been in Lyons a number of times and heard you sing *Carmen* and *La Boheme*. We so admired your performances and felt blessed to know you just a little. We read in the papers about the awful attack on your life, Madame. We also read that you have to convalesce for a long time. Therefore, we have an idea. We own a small house at the other end of our property where visitors hardly ever come to. It sits empty most of the time. It might be a fine retreat for you."

Frederic continued reading, "We wouldn't bother you except to bring you meals, and perhaps, if your family could come on the weekends, we would provide meals for them as well. And we remember your lovely children, who would be welcome to ride the ponies. Because we want to help you, there would be no charge for the use of the little house. The only expense for you would be the food. Please consider it. By the way, there are lovely walking trails in the area. Perhaps the fresh air and the exercise would bring you back to good health sooner. With good wishes for you and yours, Family Marty from *"Jardins de Marty."*

"What a lovely offer!" whispered Cornelia, looking at her husband expectantly. Frederic had secretly wondered how they could afford to send Cornelia to a place of rest and quiet that was not too far from the family residence. Financially, he was more stressed now, as he and Davide were considering acquiring the bank in Tel Aviv while still maintaining their Paris branch. They had to juggle to make ends meet; they had to provide for the salaries of all the employees, the tuition for the children, and the household expenses.

"It seems as if our Heavenly Provider is at work, doesn't it, my Love?" was Frederic's reply. "We'll have to discuss the pros and cons of the situation. Dr. Sevignard said if you are continuing to heal well, he might let you out of here in ten days. That will be the end of February, and the weather will be milder, we hope."

"Papa, perhaps you can check this offer out. I think Mama would like to rest up there." said Romi.

"And remember," Irmi added, "if we visit on weekends, we could be around the animals again. That would be a treat; don't you think so, Hannah and Max?"

It had been a lively hour, and Cornelia was fatigued; one could see her wilting, leaning her head back, trying to find a position that would allow her to breathe more easily. The nurses came in, repositioned her, and brought the breathing tube.

"Papa had better take you home now, although I would like you to hide here in my bedside table and stay until all my treatments are done today. Next they'll come in and make me blow into this tube so that my lung capacity increases. I would rather just take a nap and forget about everything." Cornelia yawned and then kissed each of the children as they carefully came up to her.

Two weeks later, Francois made a trip to *"Jardins de Marty"* with Bernie, Hannah, and Max. Frederic had taken Cornelia and the twins up the day before. She was able to sit in the front seat, and when they arrived, Monsieur Marty had greeted them, saying, "The little house is ready for you, Madame. We are so glad you want to make use of it for a while." Then he jumped on his bicycle and bid them follow. The country road led them around the pony pasture, through a little copse of trees, to the place where the creek fed a small pond. Only a stone's throw away, sat the cutest log cabin.

When the car arrived, Madame Marty stood in the door and welcomed them with open arms. She led the children inside, while Cornelia was being helped out of the car by her husband, and showed them the loft, where beds were made up for them. Downstairs was a spacious living area with a potbellied stove and a cozy bedroom. Madame Marty said, "If Madame is fatigued from the trip, the bed is made up. She can lie down and stretch out. We will take the children with us; they can carry the dinner over here. That will be good for them after the long ride in the car."

And Monsieur Marty added, "We stand by, should you need anything else. Business is not too pressing, and we can help out."

"Let the children freshen up," Cornelia suggested, "then I will be doing what Madame said, I am sorry to still be so weak. Frederic, thank you for bringing us here. This is a beautiful place!" She looked around at the comfortable setting. Outside the first spring flowers showed through the brown earth, the grass was growing, and the trees sprouted little buds.

Romi and Irmi scurried over to try out the ladder to the loft, saying, "Tomorrow Hannah and Max will like this too." Then they walked out with Monsieur and Madame Marty.

Leaning on her beloved's arm, Cornelia took a short walk around the spacious cabin. Everything was spic and span. The bathroom gleamed with shiny fixtures. The small kitchen had a teakettle and one extra burner on a gas stove. And to her delight, she saw an upright piano in an alcove that she had not noticed earlier. "It couldn't be cozier," she said, leaning into her husband with a mixture of gratitude and weakness. "I am, unfortunately, not so strong yet and wonder whether I can keep the children here all by myself. What do you think?"

Frederic held his wife tenderly, and when she started trembling, he knew that they had overdone it a bit. He picked her up and carried her to the bedroom, where he placed her on top of the wide bed, covering her with a soft blanket that had been laid aside for that purpose. She looked very pale as she closed her eyes, already beginning to slumber.

Frederic prayed for guidance. Their plan called for him to drive back to Lyons tonight, while Romi and Irmi were to stay with their mama. Upon arrival, Francois would have to drive Frederic to the overnight express for Paris, so he would not miss another workday. But now, seeing his wife so weak and in need of rest and nurture, he wondered whether he should leave his two lively children with their still-recuperating mother.

Ten minutes later the twins arrived, each carrying a bowl and a handbag with the other dinner components inside. Madame Marty was on their heels, bringing a large container of potato salad. She perceived Frederic's predicament and understood the situation. While Romi and Irmi put out the treats they had carried, Madame Marty asked, "Monsieur, is your wife in bed? I fear the trip and the excitement of being with her family again were a little too much for her." Looking at Frederic, and seeing his concerned face, she continued, "I understand, Monsieur, that you want to return tonight in order to catch the Paris express, and now you wonder whether your wife can handle it alone, am I right?"

Frederic nodded in reply. "I don't think I can leave our two lively children here alone without supervision. My wife nearly collapsed. She is still too weak. At times like this, I have to suppress a real hatred toward the woman that robbed my dear wife of her health and her strength, but my Lord has said to pray for your enemies, and so I stand corrected."

"Monsieur, I understand you have been dealt a heavy blow, but with God's help, you will make the best of it. I suggest, if the children will mind me, that I stay the night here on the sofa in the living room and be available if there are any emergencies. In the morning, they can go with me to feed the animals and gather the eggs. I have things for them to do, and I could help take care of them until their governess and her husband arrive in the afternoon. Would that help?"

Frederic looked at the dear woman and said, "This offer might really work well, if your husband doesn't mind and your business won't suffer. I'm sure our twins would rather cooperate with you than to have to drive back with me tonight." And so it was decided. Madame Marty moved in for the night; she played a board game with the children and put them to bed, while Cornelia rested, and Frederic drove back to Lyons.

When Francois brought his family the next day, he found Cornelia sitting in a deck chair outside, while Romi and Irmi were galloping on the ponies across the pasture. There was a happy reunion between Cornelia and Bernie and the four children. Romi and Irmi left the ponies in their pasture and came quickly to meet up with Hannah and Max. They were eager to show their friends the beautiful loft and the rest of the cabin.

"Madame Marty prepared four special beds for us in the loft up there," Romi pointed to the ladder that they used to access their sleeping quarters.

"Yes, and we can sleep up there at least two nights, can't we, Mama?" Irmi asked through the open door, where Cornelia still remained in her deck chair. "Because this coming Monday is a holiday, and we don't have to go back to school until Tuesday."

"You are right, Irmi. Remember, we were going to do some homework, regardless," said Bernie, after overhearing Irmi's statement.

"Of course, Imma, we will not forget," agreed Hannah. And then all four of them headed up the ladder and decided who would sleep on each of the four cots that Madame Marty had so kindly prepared.

Meanwhile Francois brought in their bags. Then, from the bottom of the ladder he called, "Who will share their cot with Bernie and me? Or are we to sleep here on the living room floor?"

Romi, looking through the small opening above called down, "Madame said, she had a room for you and Bernie at the inn, but we would rather keep you here. We better have a talk about that with Mama, but we don't mind sharing. This cabin is super!"

Then her head disappeared, and Max clambered down, saying, "Abba Francois, it would be better, I think, if we all stayed in this nice house. You can find a place that is good for both of you." And coming close, he beckoned Francois to look upstairs. He was surprised when Francois jumped up, grabbed the sides of the loft window, and pulled himself up without using the ladder. When his head appeared, the girls upstairs shrieked and begged him to come up all the way.

"You must think I'm a Liliputian!" was Francois' reply. "I would have to stay on my knees in prayer up there in order to fit." Then he landed with a soft jump next to Max, who looked at him with clear admiration.

A half hour later, Monsieur Marty appeared with a supper of Beef Stroganoff, fresh vegetables from the garden, soft dinner rolls, and a delicious chocolate cake for dessert. When he found out that Francois and Bernie intended to sleep on the living room floor, he beckoned Francois to come with him. While the women kept the dinner warm and got the drinks ready, the two men disappeared.

Soon Monsieur Marty's truck rolled up and they unloaded a super-sized mattress, sheets, and pillows, and in a matter of minutes, a nice bed was made up in the alcove by the stand-up piano.

After dinner they had a sing-along, led by Cornelia, who said she was feeling stronger. In fact, she sat on the piano bench and played the accompaniment. The children each sang a song of their choice. Francois sang one of his clown songs, which the children wanted him to repeat over and over. Next, Bernie remembered a lullaby that she had learned long ago. It was quiet for a moment, then everybody looked to Cornelia, who hummed "Summertime," then sang it in full voice. Although she feared she would not have appropriate breath control—it sounded beautiful. It was God's grace that her vocal chords had not been hurt, and her energy was returning.

They had a time of thanking the Lord for His goodness, during which everyone in turn prayed to the Master of the Universe, their Messiah Yeshua. When they had finished, Francois offered to tell an adventure or two from his time with the circus, providing all the children were in their beds in ten minutes. Then after bedtime kisses for Cornelia and Bernie, the children scrambled for the bathroom and raced to see who could get washed up and have their teeth brushed the fastest. The two women sat downstairs on the sofa listening attentively to the clown adventures being recounted in the loft.

CHAPTER THIRTY-TWO

CIRCUS LIFE REMEMBERED

W hen it came to storytelling, Francois could not easily be beaten. The following is what he told the children that early spring night in the loft of the cabin at "*Le Jardins de Marty.*" He was lying on the floor between the cots with all four children propped up in bed, listening: "None of you were born yet when I decided to join the circus. Actually, I wanted to go to the university, but my family did not have the money to send me. I needed to find another way to make a living."

"When the circus came through town, I went each night to see the show. I thought it would be challenging to travel from town to town, to tend the animals, to set up the big tent, and to participate in the shows. So I went to the director and told him I was willing to work hard, if he'd give me a job. This gentleman said that he could use a handyman. So I hired on."

"My first job was to clean out the cages of the tigers, the bears, and the elephants. The circus owned two big elephants; they were huge. There was a bull elephant. You would call him a daddy elephant, and there was a mama elephant. The daddy was calm, did his job in the ring, liked to eat his hay, and was obedient, but not so the mama. She had lost a baby, and since then, she had become unpredictable. She sometimes would use her trunk to lift someone high into the air, and then drop them. The trainer warned me, 'Never turn your back to her; stay out of her way!'"

"There was a small man, no taller than Max, who worked as a clown. He did one number where he had to run between the feet of the mama elephant. Because he was very fast, she usually left him alone, but there came a night when she picked him up with her trunk and threw him behind her. He landed on a metal container from which they doled out the elephants' nightly ration of food, and he was badly hurt. They carried him to the doctor's tent, and from there, he was transported to the hospital. He would not able to work for weeks, and they needed a clown. What would a circus be without a clown?"

"This is how I came to be a clown. I volunteered for the job because I had always hoped to make people laugh. I couldn't do the tricks that the little man could do, but I thought of a few others instead. The director said he would give me a chance. So the very night after the accident, I was on. I wore the same suit Romi and Irmi saw me wear on their birthday party."

Here Max interrupted, "Abba Francois, do you still have that suit? Hannah and I never seen you wear it."

"I believe it is still around, probably with all of my old clothes that I sent by package mail to Paris. Most likely they are stored in a room in the basement of the bank. My dear Bernie and I will have to remember to dig them out someday and bring them here."

"Francois, can you please continue with your story!" Irmi pleaded, as she slid out of her bed and sat next to Francois on the floor.

There was a chorus of "Yes, please!" from the others, and he continued: "That first night as a clown was a scary thing because I was making up my own jokes, dancing my own jigs, and singing songs my colleagues had not heard before. Afterwards, I was sitting in my dressing room, when the director came in and said, 'I didn't think you had it in you, Francois! I laughed at what you produced a number of times. You are hired.'"

"So from that day onward, I had a clown's job. Daily I had to prepare better jokes, learn new songs, wiggle my ears, and jump up in the air and catch objects that were fired at me from out of an old cannon. This was accompanied by a very loud 'Bang'. The audience usually shrieked at that moment, and at first, some of the animals reacted, but after a while, they got used to it."

217

"Every day I worked with Mama Elephant as well, trying to get her used to me. We had worked out a trick where she would pick me up, put me on her back, and I would ride out sitting on her. It took awhile, but she became my friend." He paused a moment, then continued "Elephants have a very good memory; they forget nothing, especially if somebody has hurt their feelings. They will remember and pay you back later. There was a young tightrope walker, a pretty, but very willful, young woman. She had once poked Mama Elephant in the back with her balance stick and giggled when the startled, frightened animal kicked up her legs. The young girl had to pay for this with a broken leg. The elephant, weeks later, picked her up and threw her over her back. When she landed in one of the carriages we used to ride in before the show to advertise our circus, her leg was broken in two places. That kept her out of the ring for many weeks."

Cornelia and Bernie, sitting below, felt Francois must be getting worn out telling his stories. So Cornelia called, "We think Francois needs a rest. Aren't you all ready to sleep now?"

"We are having such a good time hearing Francois' adventures," Romi called down.

Then Hannah stuck her head out, saying, "We know so little about Abba Francois and the circus. May we just have one more story?"

Here Bernie asked, "Francois, can you tell us more?"

And he replied, "There is just one more I will tell, and then it is bedtime—absolutely, positively! Everyone agrees?"

They heard all four children beg, "Just one more, please!"

Then they heard his sonorous voice pick up, "There was a special occasion in Belgium one day. We had finished the show; there were many visitors and many calls for more, but we were done, and everybody was worn out, when somebody knocked at my dressing room door. When I opened it, there stood a young man in a military uniform with a white letter in his hand. As it turned out, it was an invitation by the queen of Belgium to entertain at a birthday party for her young son, who was turning seven that year."

"There wasn't much I could say. The director wanted me to do it, and after I talked to the queen's lady-in-waiting, who had come along, I was told to show up two days later and do a routine to entertain eight young gentlemen. And that's what I did. They sent the royal limousine for me; I was dressed in my clowns' outfit, wearing my tiny top hat, and the red-haired wig under it. My jacket was much too big, the pants legs much too long, and my shoes had the longest shoe laces ever."

"Romi and Irmi, you remember, don't you?" The twins nodded, and he went on, "The young prince was much like any other child seven-year old, but in truth, I think Max is smarter. They had never heard of the games I showed them, and it took them some time to learn them. We played the 'musical chair game,' later, 'pin-the-tail-on-the-donkey,' and finally, I had them dress up like knights and taught them how to joust."

"After the games were over, they invited me to sit with them to eat their birthday cake, but I had to leave because the circus had to be in another town the next day. So they took me home in the royal limousine, and that was that. Now I am too tired to speak any more. Good night, my four special children!"

Then Francois' big feet appeared down the ladder, and they heard, "Good night!" and "Thank you!" from all children.

"You know, Francois, you gave Bernie and me a treat by telling of your colorful past. You actually should write down your memoirs; don't you think so, Bernie?" Cornelia said. "Just to think, you lived in our house so many years, and we never knew what all you had experienced!"

Here Francois took Bernie's hand, drew her close, and asked, "Have you shared our secret with Cornelia, my dear wife?"

Bernie blushed and shook her head, "Actually, we didn't have much time alone, did we, Cornelia?"

The latter now alerted, looked at the two with great interest, and said, "Perhaps we should go into my bedroom so that our sleepy people up there can't hear what you will share."

As there was no other separate room, they closed the door, and Cornelia and Bernie sat on the bed while Francois pulled up a nearby chair. Then he looked to Bernie, and said, "This is your turn, my love, I'm all talked out."

Bernie smiled and asked, "Perhaps, you have already guessed our big secret? You asked me the other day whether I wouldn't eat more breakfast, and I told you, I don't feel like eating right now, I seem to have an upset stomach."

She looked questioningly at Cornelia, who suddenly caught on, saying, "Of course, I should have gotten the hint. Do you have a sweet, baby secret?" To which, both nodded with smiles.

"But," Francois said, "we also are concerned that Hannah and Max will think we don't want them anymore because of the new baby. Of course, that isn't' the case, we just consider this the enlarging of our family. And I can take another job to provide for all of us."

"This is absolutely wonderful news!" conceded Cornelia. "And don't you even think of wanting to work somewhere else. We need both of you, just as we have so far, and God will provide for all of us, even if we have to move again." Then she thought a moment, and asked, "When do you want to tell the children?"

"Perhaps it is best that we wait a while with that," said Bernie. "As long as I am not showing yet, it is alright to keep it our secret. Anyway, according to our computation it is still six months before our baby is due." She looked at Cornelia and Francois for affirmation, and as they all considered the fact, they agreed that they would wait for the right moment to tell the children.

Chapter Thirty-Three

Whatever Happened?

At the end of the first week in March, Frederic sat in his office in Paris. He had just concluded a loan with substantial interest for his bank that promised to be of long-range benefit. He was looking through his in-box, when a visitor was announced. To his great surprise, it was his old friend from Prague, Joseph Novak. They hugged and exchanged news of their recent activities. It was time for lunch, so Frederic invited him to eat in one of the small cafés in the neighborhood."

Frederic also invited him to stay overnight, but Joseph declined, saying, "My reservation on the night express to Prague is set, and I don't dare delay because the situation in our country is critical. It seems takeover by the regime from the north is imminent, but I had to make this trip to London and to here before the door closes. Perhaps you are aware, that President Benes has established a provisional Czech government in London?" Looking at Frederic with a serious mien, he continued: "But, as you can imagine, English leadership has enough on their plates and won't give open assistance to the provisional government of a small country, such as ours, as it could impair their international relations."

"May I ask, dear Friend, what your role is in this international game of intrigue?" Frederic asked.

"Frederic, you know that I trust you explicitly, but I am not at liberty to share that information, other than that we are powerless

221

against the giant war machine being prepared this very month to take over Czechoslovakia. I have secret information that Hitler has ordered the destruction of Prague by massive bombing unless the Czech territories are surrendered to the Third Reich immediately. I had to transport important papers out of the country, and I hope to make it back in time to be with my wife when the critical hour arrives."

They reached the small restaurant and sat at a table in the back where they could not be overheard by the rest of the patrons. "But my reason for stopping and visiting you is the important task of bringing you mail that we didn't dare send the regular route; besides, it is good to see you again, my Friend. Nobody dared to write you openly, fearing that the correspondence might be censored, and it might be held against them there, and you here. So Madame Hradek and your employees at the bank and the house have responded to my offer to be a courier. They have sent along the messages they didn't dare to entrust to our mail system."

With that he handed Frederic a stack of letters. Then he asked, "We all heard the tragic news about Cornelia being attacked while performing. How is the she doing?"

"Cornelia is still at a small retreat in the country, where kind people, who are opera fans, have offered their own vacation cabin to us. There we can see her every weekend. It has taken many weeks of recuperation, but now we see clearly that God in His mighty goodness has preserved her, and that she will sing again. Where that will be, is of course still in His hands, and I can't speculate about how soon it might happen."

Knowing that his friend could be questioned about the Bartok's plans and whereabouts, Frederic decided to keep his possible move to Tel Aviv a secret. "But I am really curious to hear what has happened, both the bank and to the estate in the country. Are you free to share about the fate of those two?" Frederic asked next.

They had ordered a meal, and were waiting for it to be served. Joseph seemed to be more relaxed in this more neutral environment, so he answered with candor, "The move of the orphanage is a miracle. You remember how crowded their set-up was and how there were constant appeals for donations and building funds? But since they have resided in your former estate, and that must be already half a year, there are many reports of how the children are thriving, and how the new facilities are helping a large group of children to have the benefit of living in the country at least part of the year. They could not give up the old orphanage; it is being modernized with government funds. However, what will happen when the occupation takes place, and we all fear it will be very soon, nobody can foresee."

Mr. Novak looked down, thoughtful for a moment, and then continued, "My wife and I have said a number of times that when you left you did the right thing, and it seems that God led you to do it at the right time as well." As their lunch was served, Frederic's many other questions were answered about the management of the bank, and he heard Joseph's opinions about what the occupation might bring. Then it was time to part; Joseph had other business in Paris before his departure in the evening.

"You have given me great joy, dear Friend, by looking me up and being a link to our former life," said Frederic with conviction. Then they hugged, and after a warm handshake, Joseph climbed into a waiting taxi.

After Joseph's departure, Frederic looked at the pieces of mail. There was Madame Hradek's letter, one from Pavel, another from Petrov and Tirza, and an official one from his bank manager. He was emotionally stirred that so many dear ones cared to write. He wanted to share his joy with Cornelia, but did not know how to reach her. The little cabin had no telephone, but he tried the Martys' business phone, and he soon had Madame on the line.

When Madame Marty heard his voice she said, "Monsieur Frederic, I have somebody you know sitting right here by me at the counter."

And then there was Cornelia asking him, "Is this my Dearest? I can't believe my good fortune! I just arrived here, after telling myself that I had to walk today all the way to the Martys' to build up my endurance. And here is my reward—hearing your voice."

"I am so glad that I reached you," said Frederic.

"Do you care to tell me the reason for this surprise?" rejoined Cornelia.

"Cornelia, I had our first visitor from Prague, and he brought letters from some of our dear friends and employees."

"Who was this courier of good news?" she asked. When she heard it was Joseph Novak, she said, "He is good friend, to make such a special effort, isn't he? Have you already read the letters?"

"Perhaps I'll keep them until we can read them together. What do you think?"

"I would encourage you to at least read the ones from the bank and from Madame Hradek. You would know best what they are all about. The other ones you can share with all of us this weekend. Would that be alright?"

She then told him that she was eager for him to come and hoped that she could perhaps return to Lyons with him. "It's been now three weeks, and I think that I have had enough rest," she assured him.

"Can I invite Andre to come with me this time?" he asked next. "He has been asking how you are faring. Perhaps Madame would have a room for him at her inn?"

Cornelia inquired of Madame Marty, whose affirmative reply was, "Of course we have a room for another musician. Let him come. We'll be delighted."

A week later, on Wednesday, March 15, 1939, all over the world the headlines declared: "Hitler in Prague—disputed territories of Bohemia and Moravia occupied by German troops. Skoda armament works in German hands." The small print explained that Hitler had summoned two Czech leaders to Berlin on March 14. He gave them an ultimatum, namely, that the city of Prague would be destroyed by German bombs if the leadership of Czechoslovakia would not surrender the Czech territories to the German Reich.

The dreaded event had taken place, and the rest of the world hardly slowed its activities to comment on this new evidence of German expansionism.

Frederic, back in Paris after a relaxing weekend at *"Jardins de Marty"* with his family and Andre, marveled how his friend Joseph Novak had come and gone only one week before the historical surrender of his homeland.

In his private office, Frederic prayed for the people who had written him about their daily lives, who had remembered him and his family with gratitude and compassion. What would become of them now, he wondered? Would the orphanage remain under Madame Hradek's kind management, and would his former home continue to be a source of comfort to many parentless youngsters? Would Petrov and Tirza be able to serve as head caretaker and supply coordinator for such a big operation in the days to come? And would Pavel continue to maintain his poultry yard, supplying eggs and chickens, and be the head mechanic for the estate?

His family had been delighted to hear how everybody had fared after their departure. Would things now drastically change for them all? He hoped God in His great mercy would protect the helpless and the young. He prayed that their caregivers be given wisdom and discernment under the new regime.

Frederic planned at the end of this week to pick up his wife from the retreat in Burgundy near Dijon, where she had been restored to health amidst the beauty of the countryside and the tranquility not found in the big city.

Andre, who had been with them the entire weekend, had commented on the unmatched peace that pervaded the *"Jardins de Marty."* He had played for Cornelia and nudged her to sing, encouraging her to start a challenging practice regimen to regain her voice volume and tone strength.

There had been the sweet interlude when all the children had come in. Ordinarily, they enjoyed helping on the Marty Farm, especially with riding the ponies. But Cornelia, who had worked with them in a playful fashion each weekend, wanted to present to Andre the Bartok-Leclerq *Quartet d'Oiseaux* (bird quartet).

Hannah led the group. She was followed by Romi, ahead of Irmi, and Max. He looked diminutive, and was asked to stand in the front. The children were each to represent birds. Hanna started out in a low voice, being a turtledove, followed by Romi who had the part of a swallow; Irmi played the recorder, trilling her way through by imitating an oriole, and then there was Max, who captivated all by singing, in the clearest soprano, the part of a song sparrow. Andre looked surprised when he heard these lovely children's voices blend together so beautifully. He said admiringly, "The next time we have a recital, these four will have to be in it."

"That's exactly what came to me, dear Andre," Cornelia responded. "I sincerely wish to restart my singing career by giving another recital, this time to the honor of God, with all proceeds, after expenses, to go to my Jewish expatriates. What do you think of this plan?"

Andre countered, "Where would you like this venture to take place, here, or in Paris?"

"I have no desire to go back to Paris, but if we find acceptance by audiences in Lyons, and I think we could have three sold-out performances in the Lyons area, we could even take the show on the road and visit some communities that ordinarily would not have cultural events on a regular basis."

"This is a phenomenal plan!" exclaimed Andre. "The only hindrance is that I am still under contract to the Paris Opera until the end of the theatre season, which occurs around the middle of May. But one could probably work around that; let me think this over and I will make you an offer."

There they had left it, but the plan was germinating in the hearts and minds of all who had a part in it, and the Almighty was being approached for His blessing on this undertaking.

CHAPTER THIRTY-FOUR

RETURN TO NORMAL?

While Czechoslovakia was being oppressed into obedience and German troops and administrators were ordered to take over all government offices of the newly usurped country, the Bartok and Leclerq families had their own problems, and they faced them together in faith. The Friday after the political changeover in their former home country was March 17th. On that day, Francois dropped the children off at the regular hour at *"Ecole de Germaine,"* but instead of heading home as he usually did, he drove on to Dijon and then to *"Jardins de Marty."* Frederic had asked him to pick up Cornelia because he had an urgent business transaction that had to be dealt with in Paris.

It was one of those rare spring days. There were no clouds in the sky, a gentle breeze moved the tops of the greening trees, and spring flowers stood in bloom on the meadows and roadsides. Francois heard the birds singing sweetly, and whistling softly, he turned into the road to the country inn. Monsieur Marty, working on fence-posts, waved him on, as Francois headed for the cabin.

"Dear Francois," Cornelia greeted him, "you are so punctual. I am still finishing my packing."

"That's why I came early, perhaps I can still be of assistance— cleaning the cabin and leaving it as it was when you arrived," Francois said, after greeting Cornelia. "But it looks as if there is nothing for me

227

to do," he observed. "Everything looks orderly and under control. You must have started with the birds this morning."

"You can tell I am excited to be able to go home again and be with the family. I could hardly sleep last night." She was walking through all the rooms making a final inspection. "Perhaps you can make the rounds once more without me, Francois, while I go over to the Martys and check out."

There were hugs and kisses with Madame Marty and her husband before Cornelia finally sat in the car, and they were heading back to Lyons. The Martys had promised to visit the next time they came to see their daughter. They also said that the combined family of the Bartok-Leclerqs could always come back to the cabin if someone needed peace and rest for a while.

"It was a lovely, recuperative time for me with those precious people," Cornelia said. "Perhaps you and Bernie could spend a weekend here before the little one arrives."

"Not a bad idea at all," conceded Francois. "Bernie has had her hands full for the longest time, and then not being able to eat much due to morning sickness, she has lost weight, I'm afraid."

"Give me another month, Francois, and I will have my full energy back. Then we will pick a long weekend when Frederic stays either in Paris or goes to Tel Aviv, so we won't need a car. Let's agree on that right now."

"God willing!" said Francois with emphasis.

They reached the apartment around one o'clock, and Bernie surprised them with a beautifully set table and a prepared lunch. "Welcome home, dear Cornelia!" she had written on a flower-bordered poster. Cornelia's bed was freshly made-up, and everything looked spic and span. Bernie herself looked excited to be seeing her dear friend home again after her long absence. After lunch Francois and Cornelia prevailed upon Bernie to lie down for a nap on account of the baby.

An hour later, as Francois unlocked the car to pick up the children, a woman approached him. She was dressed well and looked about fifty years old. "Would you be Francois?" she whispered. When he nodded, she said, "This little package must go to Vichy still tonight. Could you deliver it by 9 o'clock without making your family aware of your errand?"

"We had a small family reunion planned, so I would at least have to let my wife know. Could it wait until tomorrow morning?"

"Try your best, my Friend," she said. "I think tomorrow might be too late." Then she was gone.

After Francois had settled in the car, he looked at the package more closely. It was addressed to the chief rabbi at the Vichy synagogue. Though he had never been to Vichy, he estimated that the drive would take him at least three hours, roundtrip. But he realized that this was another assignment he could not refuse. It was his fourth mission since he had moved to Lyons.

The children heard that Cornelia was back and were eager to go home. Everyone expressed their delight in seeing their beloved Mama and friend by hugging and kissing her. They had been instructed not to overwhelm her with their attention. Irmi said it best, "Thank you, Messiah Yeshua, for letting our Mama come home. May she be stronger than before and sing better. Above all, keep your guardian angels always around her and us!"

Then a call came from Paris. It was Frederic, asking whether Francois had brought Cornelia safely home and assuring them that he would catch the Marseilles Express this very evening, arriving at midnight. That's when Francois confided in Cornelia and Bernie that he had an assignment to go to Vichy. While the children had their afternoon snack and spread out to do their homework, Francois slipped out. Two hours later he had made contact with the chief Rabbi in Vichy, delivered the package, and was already on his way home.

Everyone had eaten supper and was on their way to bed when Francois returned, just in time for the evening prayers. It was Cornelia's turn to tell the bedtime story, while Bernie fed her husband a late, warmed-up dinner. Afterwards, Francois and Bernie strolled around the block together, leaving Cornelia with the full responsibility of the children.

"You must be fatigued after all the driving you did today, Francois. I wish I could pick up Frederic from the railway station," said Bernie.

"Perhaps you should train both Cornelia and me to use the car so you could have a break now and then, my Beloved."

"You are right," Francois agreed. "Should there ever be an emergency, it would be advantageous to have more than one driver. But I'd better drive tonight, with Cornelia just back, and Frederic coming at midnight. If you don't need me in the next hour, I think I'll take a nap. Traveling 400 miles on country roads today did me in." He pulled her into a close embrace before they sneaked up the back stairs, Francois, to take a much deserved rest, and Bernie, to join Cornelia in the living room.

"What would you think, Cornelia, if Francois taught us how to use the new car?" Bernie asked, as she sat down at the dining table where Cornelia was sorting out music sheets.

"I would be delighted to be able to drive and help out more with the transportation of the children," Cornelia's replied as she looked up.

"For me it would be an excuse to pick up whatever is best for our menus at the outdoor market and not be dependent on Francois having to drive me. Also, he may have more courier runs, so perhaps a second car would be helpful. But, can we afford it? Poor Frederic, he has the whole family depending on him!"

"You are right, my Friend," Cornelia conceded. "I suggest we present it to Frederic after he has rested up, perhaps tomorrow afternoon. What do you think?"

The two women laid out clothes for the children and made the lunches for them, as well as preparing a salad for the family to eat. Then they both put up their feet for a while.

Two hours later, Francois heard the Paris-Marseilles Express roar into the station. As many times before, Frederic emerged from the train, but now from the more moderately priced second class compartment that he had recently started to use. As he joined Francois, he embraced him, patted him on the back, and together they joined a small group of late-night arrivals heading to the exit where Francois had parked.

"How are the Cohens?" asked Francois.

"It seems Davide is inclined to give up the bank as soon as a responsible party can be found to take it over," was Frederic's reply. "Granted that," he continued, "I'm advising him not to make arrangements yet, until we have a firm commitment from Monsieur Levi in Tel Aviv. It is coming, I believe, but one has to pray for the right timing in the matter. Mademoiselle Rachel is her usual cheerful self, bursting with energy."

Back in their apartment, Francois and Bernie withdrew to give the Bartoks some private moments. It had been a long day for all, and soon peace descended upon the Bartok-Leclerq household.

It was still dark when Bernie awakened, feeling strangely uneasy. She experienced pain in her lower back, and then she noticed her abdomen was tight and painful. She got up and walked through the hall and into the living room, trying to overcome what she thought was a strain from the previous day's hard work. She prayed and called upon her heavenly Father, but the pain increased. A short while later Francois drove her to the emergency room, while she quietly whimpered, afraid that she might lose her baby.

They joined a group of troubled people, all waiting to be seen by the emergency room staff. When Bernie was finally admitted to a cubicle, a nurse proceeded to take her vital signs, weigh her, and prepare her for the doctor's exam. Suddenly, they remembered that the children had to go to school. Francois rushed home so the car could be used by Frederic for that purpose. Francois found them all concerned about Bernie. In a matter of minutes, Frederic took Francois back to the hospital and then returned to transport the children to school.

An hour later, Cornelia joined Francois at the hospital, waiting for Bernie to be examined and diagnosed. The verdict: Bernie was anemic, and, if she would not stay off her feet for at least a week, she could lose the baby. The doctor asked whether she was overworked.

"You can say that," Cornelia replied. "She has been doing for a big household with four lively children, all on her own."

When Francois explained that Madame Bartok was the opera star who had been shot on stage in January, the physician remembered: "Dr. Sevignard gave an in-service on the serious injury that the shot had caused. I remember clearly, the bullet had entered the right, middle lobe of her lung, and you suffered from extreme blood loss." As Cornelia nodded, he continued, "So the young lady I have just examined is your back-up person, do I understand correctly?"

"Yes, she has shouldered all my household responsibilities and has done admirably well. It now seems, in the process, she has neglected to take care of herself," Cornelia agreed.

Here Francois entered into the conversation, "My wife is the long-time governess to the Bartok twins, and, since last year, we adopted two Jewish children whose parents were murdered in Poland. During the last months, she has faithfully taken the place of all the missing adults in our household. No wonder she herself is in need of some nurturing. I will try to help her more, and see to it that she gets a long-deserved break, now that Madame Bartok can again handle some of the responsibilities of our large family."

"I know that being with the children, there are constant needs to be met. The best thing to do would be to remove Bernie from the scene for a while and allow her to recuperate with good food, iron tablets, and lots of liver especially! Also, she would not have to be up at dawn and go to bed late," said Cornelia. Then she added, "And I know the right place for her to do that."

"Sounds like a good plan to me," the doctor agreed. "I would like to make an appointment to see her four weeks from today, take blood samples again, and find out whether there is any improvement. Can we do that?" He looked at Francois questioningly.

They were then allowed to see Bernie, who sat in an armchair in the cubicle where the doctor had examined her. She was crying. Francois went to her, put his arms around her, and pulled her up. She thanked him with one of her bright smiles. To Cornelia she said, "I feel like a wimp, not being able to help, when you've just returned, not fully well yourself."

"If you promise not to object and worry, my dearest Bernie," Cornelia said, "I have already a plan that might work for all of us. Let us discuss it on the way home." With that she helped Bernie put on her street clothes and helped her out, with Francois on the other side.

Back in the car, she said, "I think Frederic will approve of my plan, but we'll have to contact our back-up helper first. I am thinking of Rachel, who right now is on semester break from school. She might be willing to help us out for a few weeks while Bernie takes a vacation in the country, right where I come from. The Martys offered us the cabin whenever we want it, so let's call and make a reservation for tomorrow, if you are all with me."

"My darling Girl, we would not abandon you," added Francois. "But being separated from all the cooking, the laundry, and the cleaning just might rescue you and the new life you are carrying. I am willing to help out as soon as I know that you are in a safe, comfortable place."

"And on weekends, we could all show up, have dinner from the Martys, tell you about our week, and hear what you have experienced," Cornelia added.

Bernie smiled when she heard these plans. She offered, "It would be best if we first found out how such plans sit with Frederic, and, of course, the children. In fact, wouldn't this be a good time to share with them our baby expectation and assure them, especially Hannah and Max, that the new baby will in no way distract us from loving them?"

"May I offer my humble opinion?" said Francois, and, as both women listened, he said, "I don't think we want to blame the baby for Bernie's not being well. Perhaps we can mention the baby when she has been away for some time, and we come to visit her."

"Yes, dear Husband; that is a good point. Let's wait a little longer to tell them," said Bernie.

Cornelia concurred, "Wisely spoken, Francois. The children should know that Bernie has overdone and needs some rest, which will also teach them that none of us is indestructible."

Back home they bedded Bernie down on the sofa in the living room. Francois made breakfast, and a short while later Frederic joined them. They had prayer for Bernie and asked for guidance regarding this time of recuperation before her. Then Cornelia made the call to the Martys.

They heard her say, "Madame Marty, I am safely home, but we want to appeal to you for another member of our family who desperately needs rest. Would you have an opening, of at least a week's time, for Bernie to stay with you; she is supposed to stay off her feet for awhile?" Next they heard, "Sure, I think she would love that. When would it be convenient for her husband to bring her?" After a pause Cornelia ended with, "*Au revoir, Madame,* and *merci beaucoup!*"

"Madame suggested something even better!" Cornelia explained. "They have kept their daughter's room, across the hall from their own bedroom, made up all these years. She said it has its own bathroom and is very private. She thought that if Bernie were alone in the cabin and had to clean up and walk around, that it might be too strenuous for her. Perhaps a week later, she might consider moving to the cabin. Besides, she offered Francois to stay with her any time he wants to; the bed is humongous!"

They all laughed, and Frederic asked, "How soon would she be welcome?" He secretly felt guilty that Bernie had had to assume all of the household responsibilities and take care of the children after the attack on Cornelia's life at the Opera House. They had not only used her as a governess, but as maid, cook, and laundress. This had not been her job description to begin with.

"All she said was, 'bring her over whenever you want to,' so I suppose that would be today or tomorrow." They agreed that the children had to be picked up, dinner had to be cooked, errands had to be run, and food had to be bought for Sunday, as all the stores would be closed then. Therefore, tomorrow, Sunday, would be a better time to take Bernie to the Martys. While they were talking, Bernie had gone to sleep. So her husband carried her to their bed and saw to it that all the blinds were drawn, and that she was comfortable. He knelt for a moment, asking His Heavenly Father to preserve his lovely wife and the new life growing within her. Then he thanked Him for His grace toward their family and himself.

CHAPTER THIRTY-FIVE

NEW HOPE—NEW GOALS

Sunday morning the family had enjoyed a leisurely breakfast, during which the children reported on their school week. Afterwards, they gathered in a circle while Frederic shared from the Torah, and Bernie stayed on the sofa. Next they had prayer. For the children, seeing Bernie so passive and weak was an eye opener. In their world, the adults had been steadfast and able to cope with all situations; now suddenly they, too, had needs and were vulnerable as well. They all included Bernie in their prayers.

When they heard that Bernie was going to *"Jardins de Marty,"* Hannah was shaken and wondered whether she had not helped enough. As she quietly sobbed in a corner, Francois led her to Bernie and said, "Bernie, explain to Hannah that this has nothing to do with her not helping you; it is strictly that your body needs a little extra rest right now."

When Cornelia announced that Rachel was on the way to help out, the children had a new focus. Then Frederic added, "Not only will she join our household for the next weeks and be Bernie's temporary replacement, but she'll also bring along a surprise."

"Papa, what kind of surprise are you talking about?" asked Romi. "Is it small or big; does it bark or meow?" Everyone knew that Romi wanted a pet very badly, but because of the size of the apartment and living upstairs in the city, she had been told not to expect a pet at this time.

"Perhaps she brings us some patisseries from the Paris bakery around the corner," guessed Max.

"Not a bad idea, Max," said Francois, "but remember, she has to travel at least five hours, and such treats might spoil."

"How is she coming?" asked Hannah. "Will she come by plane, train, or car?"

"You all are a curious lot," said Frederic. "I actually wanted to wait with the big announcement, but Hannah has asked a good question. "Imagine—Rachel will drive down by herself."

Here Max chirped, "Don't you remember? Her Dad just bought her a brand-new Renault. It would be nice to have a second car around. She was always so friendly; she probably won't mind giving us a ride sometimes."

"Max hit it on the head!" Frederic exclaimed. "She has promised to share her new car with us. In fact, she wants to leave it here because she is afraid that it's not safe in Paris. I have promised to contribute a few thousand francs to the purchase price of the vehicle, and she is glad to have us share her car." Looking at Francois, he continued, "Therefore, my dear Francois, you need not worry about taking your wife in our 'only' car to the Martys. By this afternoon, we will have another car at our disposal, and Rachel will be here to help out, God willing!"

"That's another 'God-sent' isn't it?" smiled Bernie from her perch on the sofa.

Francois had packed Bernie's belongings, some books and magazines, and soon was accompanying his fragile charge down the steps. The good-byes had been said, and there was no commotion to indicate to the neighbors that the family again was making adjustments.

Three days later, Cornelia was seated in the well-appointed office of Monsieur Armande Ballon, the artistic director of the Lyons Opera. He was not in yet, so she looked around, appreciating the beauty of the room. There were beige, leather chairs in front of a large, impressive-looking walnut desk. Photographs of well-known singers hung in gold-frames on the walls, from which also gleamed two oval mirrors. There were brightly patterned love seats to her right which faced a shiny, round, alabaster-topped table. Everything exuded elegance and good taste.

Cornelia herself felt nearly normal again. She wore a pale-green suit with a cream-colored blouse. A small green hat kept her black curls covered. She wore black gloves and black pumps; a small leather purse completed her outfit.

She was looking at a picture of a well-known English diva, when Monsieur Ballon entered. "Do you like my collection of professional photos?" he asked. Then extending his hand, he smiled warmly and bid her sit on one of the love seats, while he settled into the other.

"Madame, I am so very glad to see you active and, apparently, much better than when I saw you the last time!" As Cornelia smiled and nodded graciously, he continued, "I hope you are planning to return to us and charm our audiences again, as you have done so beautifully in the past."

"My doctor has not yet declared me fit to sing professionally and on a regular basis, but I am preparing for the continuation of my singing career by planning a benefit concert. Our children will participate in a few numbers, so I will not have to bear the entire brunt of the performance myself."

"I had no idea that you also had talented offspring!" said Monsieur Ballon.

"During my enforced rest, I had time to work with our four children, and we have developed a few numbers that might have audience appeal. At least, my artistic adviser, Andre Girardeau, whom you met during my recitals last season, thinks so."

"I was only aware of you having twin daughters, where do the other two children come from?" he asked.

"When my husband left Czechoslovakia, he was entrusted to escort the two children of murdered Rabbi Englestein and his wife out of the country. They had been threatened to be put into one of those dreadful concentration camps the Germans have developed for doing away with Jewish citizens. These two children joined our family and were adopted by our closest friends, the Leclerqs, with whom we have formed a family relationship. Madame Leclerq is the long-time governess of our twins."

"Are these children musically gifted?

"I think to answer that question we will have to invite you to one of our rehearsals, Monsieur. As of now, we have no appropriate rehearsal facility, but as soon as we have that, we will let you have a preview of what we intend to do."

"If you need rehearsal space, perhaps a room with a piano and good acoustics, we can arrange that," Monsieur Ballon suggested. "In fact, I would hope that you will make your comeback here in the Opera House."

"Do you mean that, Monsieur? I imagine that your schedule probably keeps the opera stage busy until the end of May."

"I have that in mind; however, the entire ensemble will travel to Monaco on Ascension Day, by special invitation of the Prince. So we'll have a vacancy here for two days. That's how we can easily fit in a performance. Of course, it must meet our standards, you understand that, Madame?" he asked.

"Would that be toward the end of May?" and, as Monsieur Ballon nodded, she said, "Perhaps we can plan for that, prepare a show, and see whether we can fill up the house. I am convinced that our program will be an audience-pleaser, and could easily sell out two performances. I hope this to be entertainment of a lighter nature."

"Madame Bartok, let me show you what I have in mind for a rehearsal facility for you. It is on the top floor. It is well insulated, and you can't be heard downstairs. We have not used it recently because our personnel do not like to climb the stairs to the last floor. But formerly, it has been used both by the ballet and the chorus of the opera. It could be made available to you every afternoon after four o'clock. That's when our main rehearsals are over on the lower floors."

With that he led her to the elevator that went to the fourth floor. From there they used a staircase to the top floor, where he ushered her into the rehearsal room. What a delight! There was a baby grand in one corner, and ballet bars around three sides of the square room. A few chairs sat along the walls. These were the only furnishings, besides the piano bench.

"This would ideally meet our needs," she said and sat down at the baby grand, improvising a few chords that led into the "Emperor Waltz." The acoustics in the room sounded just right, and Monsieur Ballon smiled, seeing this talented woman again in action. "Until Monsieur Girardeau will be able to be with us, I will accompany the rehearsals," she said and added," If we can use the hall three times a week, we'll have our program under way in no time." They were heading back down, when she inquired, "How soon could we start, Monsieur?"

"You can start next week, Madame. Just let us know which days are convenient for you. And remember, I need to see what you have planned to present." She agreed to his request readily.

That's how they started coming to the Opera House to rehearse on Mondays, Wednesdays, and Fridays. Cornelia would lead the children through some warm-up exercises, and then have them learn the three numbers she had planned for them. The "Echo Song," which she taught Max, was no problem, although it depended on perfect timing for her to sing the theme and Max echoing with his high soprano voice from behind the curtain. On the last two verses, he would join her up front in a chorister's outfit which made him look like a young Lord Fauntleroy.

Secondly, they perfected the "*Quartet d'Oiseaux*," including a solo for each of the four birds. Mademoiselle Celeste was invited to the second rehearsal. Cornelia asked her whether she could produce costumes for the four youngsters that resembled feathered birds. She was intrigued by this challenge and promised to work on it. The third number was to be a children's dance song they had learned in Czechoslovakia.

Although the four children could sing the tune and knew the words, the movements for the dance were hard for them to learn until Hannah had an idea. "Why don't we take turns coming in, perhaps Irmi starting, then Romi joining her, picking up the same steps, then Max skipping in and picking up the steps, until the end? Then I'll come in, and we'll all join in a circle, repeating the steps at a faster pace, and that will make it look different." That seemed to be the key. After that, the number flowed in a happy rhythm.

They wanted Czech national costumes for the dance, but Mademoiselle suggested making do with what they had, as the audience most likely could not identify the authenticity anyway. So it was decided to make use of their Swiss dirndls and Max's lederhosen. The girls would add *babushkas* (headscarves), and a small hat with a feather was found for Max.

Meanwhile, Cornelia practiced her violin daily, also the harp, and reviewed pieces from the operettas she had in her repertoire. She wanted to make it lighter entertainment, as the summer was approaching. She also did not intend to tax her voice with arias that required more voice effort. As they came to this point, they invited Monsieur Ballon to view their work. He was delayed, however, which gave them another week of practice. During this time, Cornelia kept thinking that something was missing that would make the show more appealing.

Then one night, while she was lying awake, going over each number, she thought about how a frame might be of help, and she remembered Francois' talent as clown. It seemed daring, but she thought, why not? Francois was a seasoned and funny performer, perhaps he could polish up some of his routines, and they could present a light-hearted show with a circus flavor. That might add to the audience appeal. She thought she would ask. He could introduce the numbers and add to the performance's connectedness.

It was the last week of April, and time was getting short to prepare for a sold-out performance. Andre was not able to join them until the middle of the next week. When Cornelia asked Francois at the breakfast table, would he consider such an assignment, he thought a moment, and then asked the children, "What do my young family members think? Would a clown as introducer of each number add or distract from the show?"

"Abba Francois, you could actually help us by being there with us," Hannah said. "I am a little scared to sing in front of all those people. But knowing you are around would help."

"Yes," Romi exclaimed. "Hannah is right; we know you would help us and the show!"

"And if we forget a line or don't know what to do, you could be our prompter. We would be so happy, if you joined us," confirmed Irmi. "Besides, don't you remember, Romi's and my birthday is coming up. So you could give us this birthday present, to be with us."

Max just sat there with starry eyes, then he said, "Abba Francois, you can do everything well. Madame Cornelia would not have asked you unless she knew that you could help us out."

And so it was decided. He came along for their next rehearsal, bringing his outfit, saying, "I need to dress up; I'm not able to get into the character in street clothes."

They had two rehearsals of the entire program before Andre joined them, taking over the accompaniment. He was happy that he would not have to be the announcer between numbers. It was agreed that he would only give the opening statements, and then allow the other numbers to roll off as Francois introduced them.

In the first week of May, Monsieur Ballon made his appearance. He brought his assistant, a young lady by the name of Mademoiselle Broudeau. They both sat in stunned attention as the lively show ran by them. There were a few glitches, which involved costume changes and timing, but overall, it was very appealing. The children proved well-trained and delightful to watch. Cornelia's lovely singing voice, her violin solo, and the harp medley were as professional and charming as ever. Together with the clown's well-timed appearances, the performance proved an entertaining, versatile event that brought happy smiles to members of the audience.

"We'd better start the publicity machine rolling and get the tickets printed," Monsieur Ballon exclaimed. "I see we have only three weeks to get this show on the road. But with God's help, it will be done!"

The moment the announcements were made, and the public heard that the beloved Cornelia Kahn Bartok was to give a concert, there was a rush for tickets. Within days, the two performances were completely sold-out. The management added a matinee to meet the demand for more seats.

Nobody was disappointed. The show was a total success. Francois was at his clown's best. Andre proved himself again as the announcer who introduced the show and accompanied with the aplomb of long experience. The children were a delight and pleased the audience, especially little Max, who, though small in stature, had the silvery soprano of a perfect musician.

And then there was Cornelia! Her voice had again attained its velvety timbre. She acted out the light-hearted songs from Franz Lehar's *The Merry Widow,* and Johann Strauss' *Die Fledermaus.* Her audience was fully satisfied and pleaded for encores after each of her numbers. Besides, her violin performance of Vivaldi's concerto "Alla Rustica" was without flaw, and the harp medley of sacred music, superb. The performance was of such variety that even people who just came to see how the injured singer was doing, were enchanted.

241

Before school vacation started, they gave an abbreviated performance at the children's school. They also had made visits to Bernie in the country, in between rehearsals, while Rachel kept the home front, from collapsing into chaos. Their meals were on time, the homework got done, and when Bernie returned after several weeks with the Martys, they all rejoiced in hearing about the expected baby. When Bernie was able to pick up her duties as before, she had loving assistance from the whole household.

With the performances a golden memory, and both school and theatre vacations upon them, a new conflict arose. Cornelia received a contract from the Lyons Opera Theatre. Would she be willing to resume her schedule as before the "unhappy accident"? They offered her steady employment at a very decent salary, but for her, it involved great restrictions. Was she willing to put family second and continue the lifestyle of a prima donna, having to focus on her commitment to the Theatre first? Was she again ready to be in view of the public at all times and lack for privacy?

As Bernie's due-date was approaching in August, Cornelia wanted to be available for her dear friend. She had long discussions with Frederic, who was pursuing the acquisition of the bank in Tel Aviv with renewed energy. The signs of the times indicated that Hitler in Germany was not idle. Secret reports were received that the concentration camps in and to the east of Germany were being filled with Jewish people and political prisoners. What happened to them there was hard to believe. Frederic wanted to prevent his family being drawn into that spider web of evil and destruction.

His advice was to not commit to another contract. Could she perhaps aim for a guest performance agreement, where she would be available only for certain performances, on certain days, not to exceed three performances per month?

When she suggested this proposition to the administration of the Opera, the response was positive. They wanted her back under any condition. The agreement was made; she would rehearse and sing only if both the Theatre and she agreed on certain performances. This alleviated pressure and allowed her to plan on singing the operas and operettas of her own choosing.

CHAPTER THIRTY-SIX

THE WAR STARTS

The news was grave on September 1, 1939. Germany had started a *Blitzkrieg* against Poland. Germany's aircraft, then troops and artillery, attacked an unprepared Poland. The newspapers and radio messages told of an advance of the German war machine that no one had anticipated. "German troops enter Polish territory without declaration of war. Major German troop accumulations thrown against a mostly defenseless Poland. Polish cavalry impotent against German motorized units and artillery strength," the newspapers reported.

Two days later, on September 3rd, both Great Britain and France declared war on Germany. France mobilized more than a hundred divisions, but logistics were muddled, and efficiency was lacking. Although Germany's western borders were not fully staffed, there appeared to be no sudden threat to their defenses. In France, troop trains had priority over civilian transportation. The populace was excited and uncertain about their future.

The Bartok and Leclerq families had been following the news around the clock, while Francois served in his capacity as courier for the "Underground" on three different occasions since September 1st. When he returned from his last assignment, which had led him north to a suburb of Paris, he found a letter addressed to him in the mailbox of the apartment. The sender was anonymous. He read the contents to Bernie and Cornelia: "In case you think your activities have gone unnoticed, you are wrong. We are aware of your assistance to the

Underground. German occupation is now a foreseen conclusion. You will be denounced and held responsible for your actions. This is your only warning."

"Oh, my dear Husband, who could have betrayed you?" exclaimed Bernie, who was in her last month of pregnancy and walked with difficulty because she had a type of toxemia that caused edema in her lower extremities. She was to stay off her feet again.

"Francois, this has to be dealt with immediately!" said Cornelia. "I will call Frederic, and let's pray for wisdom as to what we should do." She reached for the telephone and dialed the Cohen house. She knew her husband would be at their home, as it was late at night.

Davide answered, saying, "Frederic sits with me here in the library. He will speak with you right away."

"This is a special surprise, my Dearest. You must have something urgent on your mind to call me so late."

"Right you are, Frederic. I don't want to upset you and Davide, but we need a word of wisdom from you. Francois just returned from another courier mission that took him up north. On his return, he found a threatening letter, warning him that he would be denounced and held responsible for his actions in support of the Underground. We don't know what to do, but we all need to pray that we will see the Lord's hand in all this."

"Do not fret, my Dearest, we know from the Word of God that 'all things work for good to them that love God, who are the called according to His purpose,' don't we? So this requires us to wait on the mighty God of the Universe for our next steps. I tell you what, you pray there, and Davide and I will pray here. I will call back in about twenty minutes. Meanwhile, feed Francois a good meal. Start trusting God, and don't fear evil!"

With that he hung up, and Cornelia related to the others what Frederic had said. Then she asked, "What do you want to do next, Francois? Are you starving? We have a dinner waiting for you, or should we pray first?"

Francois had gone to Bernie, and was holding her hand. He said, "We must pray first. I don't want to bring danger upon my family because of me, and only God the Almighty can shield and protect us. This we believe!"

Francois knelt by the sofa, and Cornelia joined him and Bernie there, glad that the children were tucked into bed. Then Francois prayed, "Almighty Triune God, we need your help and guidance. You know my motives, why I wanted to help out with the Underground; if I have displeased you by my actions, please forgive me! I commend our Bartok-Leclerq family into your hand. Show us clearly what our next steps ought to be. We know that you have complete authority in heaven and on earth. So we look to you for protection and wisdom!" He looked up and added, "I pray this in the Name of our Messiah Yeshua."

A very similar prayer went up in Paris. When Davide and Frederic finished, it was Davide who said, "The Lord seems to show me that Francois must leave the country and take his little family with him. Yes, I realize Bernie is about to give birth, but she can have this baby in Israel as well. The question is: how do we get them there safely and expediently? You know, Francois can be of great assistance keeping the wheels rolling on our transactions with Monsieur Levi. The latter can help their little family to get settled, and then he can depart for New York, as he has planned for so long."

"Sounds to me like a good plan," agreed Frederic. "We need a safe way for them to travel to Marseilles, and then we can book them passage on one of the freighters that goes to Tel Aviv. Could your son help with that?"

"Of course, Nathan should have a good idea on that. Let's get him out of bed and ask him," replied Davide.

Calling at this hour was advantageous; during daytime hours circuits were constantly overworked because of the threat of war over all of France. They reached Nathan on the first try, and he understood the situation and responded with, "I have two ships leaving within the next 48 hours. Each of them has limited cabin space, but could accommodate a family of four if they can get here by tomorrow. Is there any way that can happen?"

"Dear Son," Davide said, "we will try very hard to make the connection. Just reserve four places for two adults and two children, aged nine and six. God willing, they will arrive tomorrow. Adieu!"

Before they could call Lyons, the phone rang, and there was Francois on the line, saying, "It seems we are getting the message from our Commander in Heaven that we are to move on again. Both Cornelia and Bernie agree that we should leave here imminently. Of course, I hate to make my dear wife go on this trip now, but then we remembered what happened to Yeshua, how his parents had to travel to Bethlehem at the same stage of pregnancy, and they only had a donkey, didn't they?"

"You put that right, Francois. We actually got a confirmation as well. We think you should leave early in the morning, perhaps 6 a.m. Drive yourself, Bernie, and the children. Cornelia will have to go by streetcar with the twins to take them to school. We have Davide's son's address in Marseilles. His name is Nathan. You will have to see the British consul before you meet Nathan in order to get a visa for the British Mandate. Then contact him at the docks; he will see to it that you get on the right ship. He will also drive the car back to Lyons. God willing, once you are safely in Tel Aviv, go see Monsieur Levi. I will give him this information by international night letter, and you can act as our advocate there. That will be a great help for when we arrive later."

"God bless you, Francois. Be assured, we will be praying for you all. Before we hang up, let me talk to my wife for a minute. And do travel light, as if you are going on a short trip. We will see to it that packages with your belongings follow you later." Francois handed the receiver to Cornelia who had a short conversation with her husband, happy to hear that the answer to their prayers seemed to agree. She noted Nathan's address and handed it to Francois. Then they got out a piece of luggage for each of them. Francois did all the packing, then Bernie served him the much-delayed meal.

Cornelia packed some provisions in a small rucksack for Max to carry. Then tiptoeing down the stairs, Francois carried everything to the car. In the morning they would not stop to eat, but see to the children's dressing and leave. Hopefully, the twins would not wake up and be needlessly upset.

It was early dawn when Bernie awakened Hannah, while Francois took care of Max. The children quickly understood that they had to leave and made no scene. They left town before the traffic rush started and were already at Vienne, south of Lyons, at 7 a.m.

Once in the car and out of the city, Francois explained as simply as he could, their reason for leaving so suddenly. Bernie told them how they had all prayed after receiving the threatening letter, and how the Lord had worked on both ends, namely showing Frederic and Davide Cohen in Paris, as well as them in Lyons, that they were to leave right away.

"I would only have liked to say 'goodbye' to Romi and Irmi," said Hannah, wiping a tear off her cheek.

"What will they think if we don't go to school with them today?" asked Max. "The teachers will ask questions, won't they?"

"I am sure that Cornelia will explain, as best as she can, why we had to leave so abruptly. Our excuse is that we have business to conduct in Tel Aviv. Abba Francois is to start the arrangements for the others to follow soon." Then Bernie added, "Because of the threat on Abba Francois' life, we have decided to say as little as possible so that the Bartoks will not have difficulties because of us."

Then they all had a bit of breakfast from the provisions that Cornelia had packed. After that the children went to sleep, Bernie and Francois shared with each other their hopes for the future. Going south seemed to be less troublesome then heading the other way. The northbound traffic was stopped in many places. It took them close to four hours to reach the outskirts of Marseilles, as the weather changed from a steady drizzle to dismal rain.

At the consul's office, long lines had formed. So they had to queue up with the rest of the people. While his family was waiting, Francois found a phone to call Nathan, whom they had never met, but of whom both Rachel and her Dad had frequently spoken. He agreed to meet them at the consul's office and showed up half an hour later, just when they were given their application papers.

Nathan was a good-looking, dark-haired young man dressed in black slacks, a windbreaker, and a sailor's hat. He seemed to be friendly and outgoing. Fortunately for them, Nathan knew a young lady who worked as a secretary in the consul's office. He explained that his party had to catch a freighter leaving this afternoon for Tel Aviv. She was helpful in pushing their papers through. By early afternoon, they had the necessary visas and promised to be back within six weeks. This false promise had to be made in order to receive their exit visas. The young lady explained that they could change their minds and remain in the British Mandate if they later desired to do that.

Meanwhile in Lyons, when the twins woke up, there was great excitement when they heard that their friends had left. "Oh, we will miss Hannah and Max so very much!" exclaimed Romi. "They are such good friends! Will we see them again, Mama?"

"That is the idea," said Cornelia. "They had to leave before us, to get ready for our coming. They have to find a place for all of us to live, and Francois is helping to set up the bank business for Papa and Monsieur Cohen."

"But what will happen if Bernie has the baby very soon? Do they have hospitals in the British Mandate?" asked Irmi. "She looks so big, as if she'll have the baby tomorrow, and we will miss this important event," she said mournfully.

"About baby arrivals, nobody knows but God, and He will let it happen at the right time," Cornelia said. "Francois reminded us all last night that the baby Yeshua had to be born while his parents were on the way to Bethlehem, where they could not even find a room in the inn."

"What do we say when they ask at school why Hannah and Max couldn't come today?" Romi asked.

"It is best to say as little as possible, because we don't want to get in trouble here," explained Cornelia. "All we know is that Francois had to take his family to the British Mandate to help out with a business he is setting up there. We don't know whether they are coming back or not, period."

"That will be easy," observed Irmi. "We can just say that we weren't told why they left so quickly and just hope they will be back very soon." Looking at Cornelia, she said, "Would that be alright?"

"Just stick to that and say nothing else. By the way, we have to speed things up this morning, because the streetcar takes longer than if Francois is driving you."

A little while later, after they had eaten breakfast, they waited at the streetcar stop with a whole group of people. They were glad they had brought their umbrellas because a windy rain was blowing around them. When the streetcar finally arrived, they quickly mounted the steps and found seats. Cornelia sat between the twins, and they whispered to her about how they missed Hannah and Max.

"At least, we will not lose them forever," she said. "Actually, they have the harder part. They have to miss school and won't know anybody at the new place. We should pray for them, don't you think?" And that's what they did. By then they had reached the school, and Cornelia dropped them off. She had a quick word with Monsieur Germaine and explained their situation. She trusted him fully. He said he understood, and would let the teachers know, so no big fuss would be made about the children's absence.

Soon after her arrival home, Cornelia received a call from Frederic, who wanted to know whether the departure of the Leclerq family had gone smoothly. He told her not to worry, but they, too, would probably have to leave soon. He promised her that he would be in Lyons in two days, for the weekend, when they could discuss all the details. He told her how much he loved her and assured her that God loved them even more than that. Then they bid each other good-bye.

Cornelia walked through the empty apartment, made the beds, washed the dishes, and then had a call from the theatre. They wanted to know if she would be available to sing a performance on Sunday. Knowing that Frederick would come, she agreed, wanting to keep up appearances. She sat at the piano for a while, playing the parts she would have to sing in three days. Then she laid down for a much deserved rest, before having to pick up her children. She already missed Francois' faithful service, who had always been at her beck and call, with Bernie seeing to the meals and the homework.

CHAPTER THIRTY-SEVEN

TO THE PROMISED LAND

After saying their farewells to Nathan and transferring the car keys, Francois and family found themselves onboard a rather old freighter, the *Morning Dove*. It sported only two cabins besides the captain's and sailors' quarters. They were assigned a small cabin with two sets of bunk beds, a table, and two chairs. There were a few hooks along the walls to hang up clothes—no closets or bathroom. Everybody shared a bathroom a few doors down the corridor. A round porthole seemed to be their only source of light, until Max found a small lamp above each of the bottom bunks. This would enable the person in the lower bunk to read, at least, after dark.

They had been told their voyage would last between seven and ten days. They would have stopovers both in Tunis and Alexandria. Not long after boarding, the gangplank was pulled up, a foghorn sounded through the grey afternoon, and slowly the ship chugged out of the harbor into the choppy Mediterranean. While Bernie stretched out on one of the lower bunks, Francois took the children up to see Marseille slip out of sight. They leaned against the railing and saw the busy harbor scene disappear slowly.

"We have to find something interesting to do while we spend time on this tub, hoping it makes its slow trip safely from port to port," Francois said.

"I think I know what we need," Hannah said. "Don't they speak English in the Mandate?"

"As far as I know, English is the language of government and commerce in the British Mandate," Francois agreed. "And yes, we all ought to study it, but we don't have a teacher."

Just then a middle-aged couple who shared passenger privileges with them walked by, and the lady overheard that an English teacher was needed. She turned to Francois, saying, "If my husband and I can help, we would be honored. We are returning to Tel Aviv in order to take up our careers. My husband is a physician and works for the British government; I am a nurse at Hadassah Hospital on Mt. Scopus in Jerusalem. We spent our summer in England, but left when war was declared on September 3rd. We are committed to work, starting September 15th." She looked questioningly at Francois, "Didn't I see your wife with you earlier? She seemed to be close to giving birth. Is she well?"

"We had a hard time, leaving in a hurry, and the baby is due within two weeks, we think. So I asked her to lie down in our cabin for a while," responded Francois. Then he continued, "We really are not able to converse in English very well, our main language now is French. We originally spoke Czech. We left Prague last year, just before the German dictator usurped our country and added it to his great German Reich. If it would not be too much of an imposition, we would be grateful if you would teach us English while we are en route."

"Let's talk about it some more when we take supper together at the captain's table. And by the way, my name is Roberta McIntosch, and my husband's name is Michael."

Francois introduced himself, as well as Hannah and Max, and mentioned that he was going to Tel Aviv as representative of a bank. He hoped to establish a base so that his business associates could follow soon. He did not mention his or the children's Jewish roots, but he knew both Hannah and Max looked very much like Jewish children.

For supper Bernie appeared, looking rested and radiant. When she met the McIntoshes, Roberta said, "By the looks of you, Madame Leclerq, you carry a little boy. Among us nurses, we always say, mothers who look upbeat and radiant can be trusted to deliver little boys. Young girls are usually delivered by moms who manifest strain and whose facial features appear emaciated. It may sound like superstition, but it has proven true many times."

"As we already have one of each, it really does not matter what kind of baby our Lord gives us. My husband and I take the child we are given, don't we, Francois?" She smiled at him. They were now seated in the largest cabin of the freighter, the captain's quarters, which had additional space for dining. The captain took the seat at the head of the table, and asked all six passengers to make themselves at home.

"You may have heard of fancy captain's tables on big luxury liners," he said in French. "We try here to put decent food on the table, but are not able to present it in gourmet fashion. I hope you will enjoy it, regardless." He was a ruddy-faced, muscular individual with a kindly smile. He had taken off his captain's cap, showing a mane of dark, unruly hair. He was dressed in a blue uniform jacket with bright polished gold buttons, which fascinated Max.

The cabin itself was filled nearly from side to side by the massive table that was screwed on to the floor, thereby preventing it from sliding during stormy seas. The chairs around it were taken up by the passengers, leaving only one seat open. The captain explained, this is for Officer Benjamin. We take turns; when one of us eats, the other stands watch. Tomorrow you might have the pleasure of his company, barring unforeseen events.

Two young cabin boys brought the food in. There were two large bowls of lamb stew, green beans, and heaps of mashed potatoes. A green salad was served in small individual bowls, and a large spice cake with chocolate frosting appeared on a side table.

"Captain Porter, we are pleased to have been accepted by you on this trip," Dr. McIntosh said. "We feared that our desire to return earlier than we had originally planned would make us miss our chance to travel with you, but it seems that you have accommodated us anyhow, and we are thankful."

"We are glad to have you again, Dr. and Mrs. McIntosh! How many times have we traveled this route together now? I seem to remember five or six times. And as I recall, the two last times we had pretty stormy seas, didn't we?"

"I remember clearly, two years ago, how you had to navigate around the weather that seemed to pursue us," the doctor said. "But by God's grace, we made it, although the leg to Tunis took double the time we had expected."

"How long is it usually to Tunis?" Francois asked.

"Anywhere of three to four sailing days," the captain replied.

This understood, Francois asked, "Would it be alright with you, if we offered a table prayer?" And as everybody nodded, Francois proceeded to offer thanks for the food, the hands that prepared it, and a blessing on all who partook it with them. That set the right mood.

"Both my husband and I, as well as the children, are in great need of learning the English language. Only our daughter Hannah has had some basic instructions, but the rest of us need help!" Bernie said. "We had intended to start learning English, but there were many unforeseen circumstances that prevented us, and now we need to catch up. I hope that some people along the way will understand French," Bernie stated.

"You will have no problem in Tunis, our first stop, Madame," said the captain. "Also, in Alexandria, where we lay to next, you should have no problem, but coming into the "Mandate," it will be another story. There everybody is to know how to converse in English, or for another matter, in Arabic."

"I am willing to spend every morning after breakfast with the children and Monsieur and Madame Leclerq. We can go through some routine phrases and build vocabulary, if you think that might help. My husband is studying to be recertified as physician. Therefore he will be preoccupied. He is supposed to brush up on his medical skills," she explained.

Her husband smiled and said, "One gets mighty rusty in a hurry, when one doesn't practice one's business daily."

"Because of our early departure, necessitated by the declaration of war by our country on Germany, I left all my English reading matter back in England," Mrs. McIntosh said. "I wonder whether Captain Porter might have any books or booklets in the English language onboard." Looking at the captain, she cleaned up her plate with a slice of white French bread.

"Actually, I don't," Captain Porter replied, "but I have an inkling that Tom, our navigational officer, might have something. He is preparing for a job in the Mandate and has booklets of all sorts, as well as study cards to help him memorize concepts he might be examined on." After a pause he added, "You will want to approach him when he is not busy with his charts and graphs. He is tops in navigation and keeps track of our progress as we head across the Mediterranean, and then also as we stay close to the shoreline of North Africa."

"What is the tonnage of this freighter?" Max asked in French.

"What does a young man of your age know about tonnage?" Captain Porter asked in return, looking kindly at the dark-haired 6 year-old.

"Forgive my son, Monsieur Captain," Francois offered, "Max is very interested in motors, tonnage, and mathematics. He understands sometimes more than I do and remembers everything he learns."

"Do we have a young prodigy onboard?" the captain asked. "But to answer your question, this freighter has a tonnage of 2,350 tons. It is 267 feet long, and, you may have noticed, we have three decks."

"What type of cargo do you carry?" asked Francois.

"This may be our last peacetime cargo. We carry foodstuffs and building supplies to Tunis and Alexandria. For the British Mandate, we carry medical supplies. But we have already been warned that our next shipping manifest might include armaments and ammunition. Not a thing I look forward to, especially, if somebody stops and searches us . . ." here his voice trailed off. Then he smiled and said, "Most likely, I would not give you such information so willingly either."

By now their hearty dinner had been consumed, including the very delicious spice cake. Captain Porter wished them a good night, and, after agreeing to meet for the start of their English classes the following morning, they walked on the upper deck for a while through a steadily falling rain. Back in their cabin's limited space, Francois suggested he read to them until they were all tired enough to settle down for the night. So while the ship steamed through the dark waters of the Mediterranean, Francois read from Alexandre Dumas, the Elder's "The Three Musketeers," a book from the small collection the captain had onboard.

On Saturday, while Frederic was speeding south towards Lyons in the express train, Nathan Cohen had left early to return the family car to the Bartoks. He got caught in the war preparations of his native land. After struggling with delays, due to the overwhelming accumulation of supplies ordered to the eastern front, he decided to try side roads, by which he made more rapid progress northward toward Lyons. He arrived at his destination around noon, just as Cornelia was welcoming home Frederic, who arrived by taxi from the train station.

After introductions all around, Frederic said, "It's about time that we get to know the son of our esteemed friend Davide." Shaking Nathan's hand heartily, he added, "You have been so helpful in expediting Francois' and Bernie's departure from French soil. Thank you, dear Friend!"

"And now you are bringing back our car—how grateful we are. Can you stay at least overnight, Nathan? Or do you have to make it back to Marseille by a certain time?" queried Cornelia.

"I was hoping to catch the early morning train to Marseille. Ordinarily, on Sundays, there is less crowding on public transportation, at least that is my understanding." With that he greeted Romi and Irmi, of whom he had heard much about from his sister Rachel. Then they all sat around a well-appointed lunch table and shared their present anxieties and their hopes for the future.

"Nathan, you are involved in exports and imports into and out of Marseille; do you see a dramatic change coming due to the state of war France finds itself in?" Frederic asked after their meal.

"Changes are coming," the young man conceded, "however, how soon, only the next events will show. Hearing from friends in other parts of the country, I know, we Jewish people must have an exit plan. Once Germany is in control in our land, and it seems it will be, sooner or later, we'd better not hang around to find out what they devise against us, don't you think, Monsieur Bartok?"

"Exactly my thought, young Friend! Your father and I have foreseen this taking place for some time. We are in the process of turning over the bank to a responsible party and were going to wait for Francois to give us an idea of how soon we should depart. But, of course, he and his family are en route and are expecting a little one, besides. So we cannot depend on them at the moment. We will, therefore, have to make our decision, guided by our Master in Heaven, and the sooner the better."

Here Cornelia interjected, "Of course, our twins are enrolled in a very nice school from which we hate to disassociate them. And another minor matter—I am to sing *La Boheme* tomorrow."

"Doesn't the Lyons Opera Company want you to be available throughout the winter?" her husband asked. Then he added, "But our enemies are not idle, and, the way I see it, we mustn't give them a chance to attack us before it is too late."

"How could they attack us, Papa?" Romi asked, whose 7 year-old mind did not quite understand the danger they were in.

Nathan answered her, "We hear of Jewish families being treated badly all over, even by people in their own neighborhoods who they had thought were their friends. So your Dad is right by planning to leave and to join your friends in the British Mandate as soon as possible. I will be waiting for your arrival, Monsieur and Madame Bartok.

As of now, there are still a number of ships scheduled to run out of Marseille. Of course, if you could obtain flight tickets from here to North Africa and then on to the British Mandate, that might even be better, I think."

"What are your personal plans? Would you also head for the British Mandate?" Cornelia asked.

"Actually, I have business associates in South America and in the United States of America. From both I have received invitations and job offers. As I have no family yet, I am free to go. In fact, I was hoping Rachel might want to join me."

Here Frederic stepped in, "Your dear Dad, my friend and associate in the banking business, might not be very happy to hear about these plans. In all his planning, he has been counting on providing a solid inheritance for you and Rachel. Especially, as he is getting on in age and would like to have you both near him."

"I know, I know," Nathan replied, "it will take persuasion to change my Dad's mind, but he could head with me to Argentina, or to the USA, and would experience opportunities he has not even dreamed of yet."

The *Morning Dove* made its way to Alexandria after a day in Tunis, under the bright North African sun. By now the Leclerqs and the McIntoshes had become better acquainted, and the English classes were going well. Besides, the sailors under Captain Porter and Officer Benjamin were seeing to their well-being with many acts of kindness.

Two days out of Tunis, with their English class done for the day, everybody was on their way to lunch in the captain's quarters. They sat in their regular seats and had just settled down to eat. Two young cook's helpers brought in tureens of fish gumbo, bread and butter, and a luscious dessert of apple crumb, when Bernie excused herself. She rushed to the bathroom on the deck below. When she didn't return for fifteen minutes, Roberta looked questioningly at Francois. She left, knowing that he wouldn't go into the bathroom when a lady was using it.

She found Bernie in a pool of water, looking helplessly around her, crying, "Oh, Roberta, thank you for coming! I didn't dare to go back. I have to clean up, and I don't know whether more is coming."

"My dear Friend, I think your water has broken," said Roberta, throwing towels onto the pool on the floor. "This is a part of every birth. And, actually, is the signal for the labor to start big-time. Do you have any pains yet?"

"I have had some stomach cramps," Bernie admitted, "but I thought they came from eating too fast at breakfast." Roberta was helping her to her cabin now and prepared the lower bunk for her to lie down on. Suddenly Bernie cried out, "My abdomen, it feels as if it will tear apart. Is this the pain you asked about, Roberta?"

"Yes, my Dear, that's how it starts, and it will repeat a number of times before the little one makes its entrance. It helps to take deep breaths in between the pains, which are called contractions. Then we will check how soon these contraction pains follow one another. That gives us a clue as to how soon the baby might arrive."

"I had hoped so much that the little one would wait until we were on Israeli soil. But here comes that tearing pain again! Oh, Roberta!" Roberta helped Bernie into a comfortable shift, then assisted her to lie down.

"Perhaps I should go and tell the others that your labor has started, what do you think? I also need to clean up the bathroom floor. Come to think of it, I know Captain Porter maintains a small First Aid room on the lower deck. There is a bed, clean sheets, and all kinds of antiseptics. Perhaps he would let us use it during your time of labor, because here you will end up banging your head each time you try to get up suddenly. The upper bunk is so close."

"That is a good solution, so the children won't have to participate in my agonies," Bernie said. Then the next contraction hit, and she cried, "These pains are not letting up. I need to control my breathing!"

"If you don't mind, I'll bring Michael in after lunch. He will be able to tell better than me. I wasn't trained to be a labor and delivery nurse. My specialty is orthopedics. For now, just take extra deep breaths when the pain comes on and also in between. The Lord will sustain you." With this she disappeared, while Bernie looked for handholds to use when another wave of pain hit.

On her way back, Roberta cleaned up the bathroom and handed a bunch of dirty towels to a sailor, saying, "We are close to have a newborn on the *Morning Dove*! Madame Leclerq has gone into labor."

"You don't say," the startled sailor replied. "Shall I ask the mate whether we should get the First Aid room ready?" As she nodded, he headed down the steps to the lower deck.

Roberta stopped by her cabin to clean up, then returned to the captain's quarters. Francois rose and motioned her to sit down to have her meal. Then he asked, "How is my wife?"

"She is over the first hurdle. Labor has started, but she has a while to go. I came to appeal to Captain Powers to allow us to use the First Aid room for Madame Leclerq until the little one shows up. She would have more privacy there." As she seated herself, she added, "When you've all finished your meals, then Michael should come with me to check Madame Bernie and help us get her set up in the First Aid room."

"That is the perfect solution, I think," said Captain Powers. "You go ahead and use it until we need it for another mishap. Forgive me, I don't mean to say giving birth is a mishap. It is a very happy, positive event, and I am happy to have it happen on my watch on the *Morning Dove*. Later he said, "How would it be if I invited Mademoiselle Hannah and Monsieur Max to visit me on the bridge after lunch? I've wanted to show them all along how we steer the ship."

"Thank you, Sir!" Francois said, then left to be with his wife. He could hear Bernie heaving and praying when he opened their cabin door. She was trying to suppress the pain of another contraction. He quickly knelt by her side, holding her hand, then moved her blond curls away from her perspiring brow.

She looked at him with a grateful smile, saying, "Dear Francois, I'm a mess, and I can't control the pain. Please pray for me!" She relaxed when he laid his hand on her abdomen and offered a prayer for her and the baby's well-being.

"Dearest Bernie, you will make it through this hard time. The baby will get here sooner or later. You have us all supporting you in prayer, but only you can bring forth the little one, so be brave, my Treasure."

Then Francois added, "The captain has given the go-ahead for using the room downstairs, a place where they usually treat minor accidents. I think they are getting the bed ready for you now. This way, Hannah and Max don't have to participate in all that transpires. Right now the captain is taking them up to the bridge in order to distract them. They both are very concerned about you, as you know."

"I see God's mighty hand in this too," Bernie acknowledged. Then she felt a new wave of pain coming on. At the same time there was a knock at the door, and Dr. McIntosh stepped in.

"Madame Bernie, are you able to walk? I want to help you and your husband to go downstairs. I am afraid we all bang up our heads here in these tight quarters."

With Francois in front, and Dr. McIntosh behind her, they made their way down the narrow row of steps to the small, clean First Aid facility. The bed linen was crisp and fresh, the light was on, and the sailor in charge of medical treatments stood by. He said, "Usually, we treat accidents in here, but having a baby arrive is a first!"

"If you will wait with Monsieur Leclerq outside the door, I will examine Madame and let you know how things stand." Dr. McIntosh was all professional now, he checked her abdomen, listened to fetal heart sounds with his stethoscope, and checked whether the baby's head was crowning.

"It seems we are still in need of patience," he concluded. "Let us just pray that the little one will make its entrance into the world normally!" Then he patted her tummy and went to report to the men waiting outside.

Meanwhile, Hannah and Max had a visit to the bridge and stayed with Captain Porter while he steered along the northern coast of Africa. He allowed first Hannah, then Max, to steer for a little while, which made them feel very important. He explained the instruments and controls in the bridge cabin to them. Then Francois came to pick up the children. "We are still waiting and praying," he said. "But my wife is brave and will soon help to get the little one here."

"The *Morning Dove* has ploughed these waters many times between Marseille and Tel Aviv, but to have a little one born on it, that is a first for all of us!" the captain said.

Around five in the afternoon, Roberta invited the children to visit Bernie for a short while. She knew that both were anxious about their Mama's well-being. So Hannah and Max came downstairs. Following Francois, they entered the little First Aid station.

Bernie was sitting on the exam table, smiling. She hugged Hannah and Max and said, "Whoever our Lord is sending to join our little family is a reluctant one to get here. Please pray to the Lord, that He will push the baby out; we want to see it, don't we?" Then came a new contraction, and she said, "Perhaps you had better go now with Abba Francois. I have to fight this battle until it is done!"

"Are all babies so hard to get here?" asked Max.

"I will pray hard for my Imma to soon have this baby in her arms!" Hannah added.

Just then they heard an ear-piercing scream, and both Dr. McIntosh and Roberta came running. Perhaps the waiting is over," the good doctor said. Inside the room, they heard him say, "Push, Madame, push as hard as you can, we'll get this baby out now."

Then they heard Roberta, "I can see its little head, lots of hair! Here it comes . . . . It is a beautiful little boy! Thanks be to God!"

Outside the door, Francois held both Hannah and Max close. He couldn't believe that this miracle had been accomplished, and he was a real father. They hadn't noticed, but several sailors who were not on duty had joined them and stood nearby. When the door finally opened, Dr. McIntosh was carrying the little one in the crook of his arm and smilingly showed the little boy around. Everyone broke out in a round of applause. They had heard the baby's first cry, but now he seemed content, and his red, wrinkled face was at peace, his eyes tightly closed.

"May I hold him a moment, Dr. McIntosh?" said Francois. "Then I will return him to his mother." With that Francois reached for his young son, showing him to Hannah and Max and to the sailors again. Then he stepped through the door, where a smiling, exhausted Bernie greeted him.

"Dr. McIntosh asked, "Do we have a name yet? I'm supposed to fill out this form. If you don't have a name, I'll just say 'newborn.'"

"Actually, we have picked a name, haven't we, Francois?" said Bernie.

"He will be Joseph Nathan Leclerq," the proud dad pronounced.

Then Bernie spoke up, "Dear Hannah, would you be so good and get the small satchel with the baby clothes from out of my suitcase? Let's hope they fit."

CHAPTER THIRTY-EIGHT

UNITED IN THE HOLY LAND

That Sunday evening, after Cornelia had sung an admirable *La Boheme*, they were sitting around the dining table late into the night. Nathan had stayed when he heard that Cornelia might not sing another performance for the Lyons Opera. He was a knowledgeable opera fan, having been brought up by a mother who had subscribed to the Paris Opera for many seasons. He was impressed by Cornelia's lovely voice and stage presence and assured her that she must continue to sing wherever she would be led to live.

During their time of musing and considering which steps they should take next, Davide Cohen called from Paris, advising Frederic that he was ready to enter a contract of sale with the man they had conferred with. He was an American who wanted a financial base in Paris, regardless of the political developments.

"Frederic, once this is done, and I need your signature as well, we are ready to head where our Lord is leading us. Are you able to return on the morning express?" he asked.

"I would have been on the train tonight, but I promised to stay with the twins while Cornelia fulfilled her obligation at the Opera House," Frederic replied. Then he added, "You won't believe who is sitting across the table from me?"

"It wouldn't be my beloved son, would it? I had an inkling he might bring your car back this weekend."

Here Nathan reached for the telephone, saying, "Abba, perhaps I'll bring Monsieur Bartok back to Paris. If we leave by 6 am, we could make it to you by noon, at the latest. We must discuss some things, also the car needs to go north, I think."

"That would be a delight for both Rachel and me. We will be looking forward to your visit!"

The operator cut them off with the usual comment, "Long distance calls can't exceed eight minutes."

"When did you decide to drive with me, Nathan?"

"I just realized that my father might be out of the country within days after signing over the bank and that this was my last opportunity to reason with him regarding our family future. By the way, my boss in Marseille will understand. I haven't taken a vacation for the longest time."

"Nathan, you could bed down in Francois and Bernie's room, while Cornelia and I clean up and talk another minute," Frederic suggested.

"Let us lay our plans before our Messiah Yeshua. We need His will and timing in our upcoming plans," Cornelia said. So after they heard Nathan settle down, and the apartment was still, they had a prayer session, then went to bed knowing that God's guidance would lead them.

Cornelia rose with the first light, prepared a warm breakfast, then woke Frederic and Nathan. They spent the shortest time dressing and eating and were out of the house at six o'clock. An hour later, Cornelia awakened her children, helped them to get ready for school, and, after feeding them, sat with them in the streetcar on their way to school. She wanted to maintain a routine as long as possible, not knowing when the twins would have a structured life again after leaving Lyons.

When she returned home, she was extremely fatigued. After cleaning up the breakfast dishes, she laid down for a necessary rest. Her trust in her loving Messiah was such that she fully surrendered her and her family's future plans to Him. The telephone awakened her two hours later. Monsieur Ballon wanted to know whether she would sing the following Sunday again. "Would she consider *Aida*?" he asked.

Knowing she could not commit herself to an engagement even a week away, she tried to hedge by saying, "My husband has plans for the family. You know, he comes down from Paris on weekends, so I must confer with him first before I could agree, Monsieur." Secretly she knew within her heart that last night's performance had been her finale in Lyons.

She took the streetcar again in the afternoon, picking up Romi and Irmi. In order to give them another focus, she suggested visiting *"Tete d'Or"* and walking through the park, watching the animals, and enjoying this lovely fall day. They immediately agreed and had a delightful time among brilliant autumnal colors, visiting their favorites, the bears, the tigers, the monkeys, also the Aviary, with its hundreds of birds. They met fans of Cornelia's who beset her with requests for autographs. When dusk fell, Cornelia led her charges to a nice restaurant where they enjoyed great Italian food.

Meanwhile in Paris, there was a happy reunion for the Cohens. Rachel had stayed home, aware that her brother wanted to discuss family matters with their father and her. They signed the contract in the afternoon, giving the American businessman full responsibility for the bank. Davide had arranged for two days to transfer all transactions in order for them to sever ties. The funds invested by telegraph to Monsieur Levi in Tel Aviv were confirmed by return telegram.

In the evening, all of the Cohens gathered in Davide's library, and Frederic could hear lively discussions as Nathan presented his case. He had shared with Frederic on their long drive that he thought his father, along with Rachel, could be persuaded to join him in Buenos Aires where he was preparing to become a partner in an import-export business. A man of financial know-how was needed to head the accounting department. He believed that his father was cut out for this role. For Rachel, he was hoping that she would manage their household besides teaching on a part-time basis.

Frederic was wondering how all this would fit into Davide's and his plan to run the bank in Tel Aviv together. He had enjoyed their collaboration in Paris, as they both were gifted in different ways: Davide the banker, and Frederic the businessman with banking experience. He was interrupted in his musings by a startling phone call from England.

A voice he did not recognize explained that he called on behalf of "Mr. B" who had taken a personal interest in the Bartok family because he also was from Czechoslovakia. He had been informed that Frederic was planning to change places of employment and wanted to make him a special offer. Could he come to London within 48 hours and bring his family also? If it was agreeable, flight tickets for all four of them would be provided.

"Is this a proposal I can trust?" Frederic asked. "I am not familiar with a 'Mr. B.' My plan is to fly to Tel Aviv in the near future to begin a new banking business there."

"Would it be of help if you knew that Joseph Novak had recommended you? Are you familiar with this man?" the voice asked. "Once in England, there are new avenues to see to your family's welfare. This is all I can say at the moment. If you agree, we make arrangements for your visit."

Frederic usually did not make snap decisions, but he believed this was a legitimate offer, and he agreed, saying, "Because you mentioned Mr. Novak, my family and I will try to meet you at the appointed time." Before hanging up, he asked, "Will I hear from you regarding the tickets?"

"Certainly," the voice assured him, "we'll arrange for your wife to fly from Lyons with your children in order to meet you in London on Thursday. We hope this gives you enough time to make arrangements."

Frederic heard the phone click off. He replayed this conversation a number of times in his mind and tried to write it down verbatim so he would not forget its contents. He concluded that this was an invitation to break off all ties in France and trustingly come to England for further instructions. He jotted down what all had to be taken care of before such a departure, which left little time for slow, thoughtful actions.

He heard Nathan's insistent voice downstairs, as he dialed his wife's number in Lyons. He hoped that the twins were in bed so he could confer with Cornelia without interruption. After the phone chimed several times, Romi answered, saying, "Mommy is in the bathroom giving Irmi her bath. Should I give her a message or call her to the phone, Papa?"

"I need to talk to Mama later, please have her call me when you both are in bed, and have her bring a notepad and a pencil so she can write down what she needs to know. Have a good, restful night, my Darling, and say 'Hello' to Irmi. I love you both very much!"

"*Au revoir*, Papa!" was all she could say, then they were cut off again.

Forty-five minutes later, Cornelia was on the line, asking, "Do you have very important news for me, Dearest? Romi was quite insistent, saying I must come to the phone with a writing pad, ready for your instructions."

"Cornelia, you have to trust me. Write down exactly what I tell you." Then he continued in Czech, and she realized that he didn't want anyone to overhear them. "First of all, the girls can only go to school for two more days. You will receive tickets to fly from Bron aerodrome to London on Thursday. Be prepared to leave everything you cannot pack in the next two days. I suggest hiring Mademoiselle Celeste and her brother to help you pack and clear out the apartment. Arrange only for the grand and the harp to be taken. All other furniture must remain behind. Sell it or give it away. Perhaps Celeste and her brother can take care of that for you, be sure to be generous with them. We need their help."

"All moveable objects should be packed in small boxes and sent to Nathan's address. He will see to it they follow us to Tel Aviv. Please pack Francois' and his family's things as well and send them on. You must travel light. Do not tell anyone about your leaving. The authorities could detain you if they hear about your departure. We will send telegrams to people once we are in England. If anyone asks, you have agreed to meet me in England on special business; say no more. I love you. Please trust God and these arrangements."

The operator cut them off. She sat for a moment, totally stunned. To England? What would await them there? She decided that she had to move in faith. While her twins slept the innocent sleep of children, she began to gather all available boxes, satchels and suitcases. She started with the transportable belongings of the Leclerqs and had everything of theirs packed, that was ready to go; then she fell into bed, exhausted.

The girls noticed the packed items and wanted to know what she was planning to do. Cornelia explained that their Papa had given her instructions to pack things. Also, nobody was to know about their plans.

On the way to school, they sat quietly, trying to digest that their stay in Lyons was limited now.

Cornelia wrote herself lists so that she could proceed in an orderly manner with all that had to be done in the shortest of time. She prayed about calling Mademoiselle Celeste and found her home, willing to come over and help. Her brother was not available today. The next call was to a moving company to arrange for the grand piano and the harp to be sent to Tel Aviv via ship. A big expense, but necessary, she concluded.

When Celeste arrived, Cornelia offered her a cup of coffee and swore her to secrecy, sharing with Celeste her intent to join her husband in England. Celeste agreed that the theatre didn't need to know about Madame's plans until later. Then they went to work. Cornelia threw all portable objects on to her bed and Celeste took them from there and packed them. By the time noon rolled around, they needed more boxes. They remembered that the moving company could provide these as well, and they had a dozen delivered, agreeing to send them off the following day.

After the twins came home, Mademoiselle Celeste had to leave, as she was continuing in her position at the theatre. She promised to return in the morning. Cornelia enlisted the help of the twins. For their trip to England, they would each carry only one piece of luggage. Cornelia instructed Romi and Irmi to put their most necessary items on their beds, from where they packed them in the most efficient manner. She explained again how important it was not to reveal to anybody even the slightest hint about their upcoming plans.

"If anyone finds out we are leaving, they could decide to hold me here and have me continue with the Opera. We don't want to get into such trouble, do we?"

Both girls assured her that she could trust them. Then their Papa called, asking whether they had received the tickets yet. The girls spoke with their Papa in Czech and were delighted to trick the always intruding operators that way.

When they sat at supper, the doorbell rang. An express letter, for which Cornelia had to sign, was handed to her. Back inside, both girls waited with anxious eyes for their Mommy to open the letter. Three tickets fell out, showing a Thursday morning departure time from Bron aerodrome.

They kept busy trying to decide which items would be necessary to take on this trip. The next day flew by with the girls going to school for the last time at *"L'Ecole Germaine."* They said that not being able to say good-bye to their friends made them feel bad. While the twins were at school, Celeste and Cornelia emptied all the remaining closets, cupboards, and shelves. They talked about the future. In fact, Cornelia asked, whether Celeste would ever consider working for her in another country. She had grown to rely on and trust this faithful woman. Celeste realized that her country was on the verge of major changes because of the war, and didn't have to think long before replying. She said she was open to such a proposition.

The moving company showed up late that afternoon and hauled away the grand piano, the harp, and all the boxes. The remaining furniture Cornelia bequeathed to Mademoiselle Celeste to do with as she pleased. She also paid her well for her tireless work on behalf of their family. Then they parted with hugs and promises to see each other again.

In the morning, Cornelia and her children took a taxi to Bron. The children carried small bags—Cornelia, one suitcase and her violin. There were no long lines when they boarded their plane for London. Two and a half hours later they landed on Gatwick airfield, outside the capital of Great Britain. After they checked into customs and were given entrance visas, they had to go into an embarkation hall.

Frederic and a gentleman in a black business suit were waiting for them. The man in black explained to them that President Benes, who had been familiar with the prosperous bank of Frederic Bartok in Prague, had suggested Frederic's name to a leading administrator in the British Mandate, after hearing of Frederic's plans to emigrate to Israel.

The officials in charge of the administration in the British Mandate needed a reliable banker who, also, by being a Jew, would strengthen their Jewish-British relations. They offered to fly him and his family to Israel with one of their regular supply flights. "We believe, by offering you our means of transportation, you are being spared a long, dangerous sea voyage. We have information that boats are being intercepted by hostile powers. We would also like to have a friendly banking institution up and running soon."

The gentleman continued, "Knowing that you had to make hurried preparations to come our way, we took the initiative and booked you into one of our guesthouses. There you will be housed until the next flight is scheduled for the Mideast. We hope these arrangements will be acceptable to you." They had been slowly walking through the huge embarkation hall and arrived now at the curb outside, where a fancy black limousine awaited them.

On their drive through London, the gentleman, whose name was Mr. Green, showed them many landmarks. They passed Trafalgar Square, where they saw the statue of Horatio Nelson, the British naval hero. They passed Kensington Gardens, where Mr. Green pointed out another well-known statue: Peter Pan near the famous Round Pond.

"Oh, Mama, we can't see anything when we pass through this town so fast, would it be possible to walk for a little while and see some of these sights close-up?" asked Irmi.

"Yes, it all blends together," said Romi. "Maybe, once we have settled into a place, we could take a sightseeing trip, could we?"

"It all depends on how long we are supposed to stay here and wait for a flight to the Promised Land," Frederic said. "If we have a few days, perhaps we even can contact Uncle Raoul, who would probably love to show us around."

"Are you talking about the famous basso, Raoul Norok?" Mr. Green inquired.

"Yes, Sir, he is a dear friend and former colleague of mine. We worked together at the Prague Opera for a number of years," said Cornelia.

"Madame, forgive me, "Mr. Green stated. "Of course, I was told that you are a well-known singer and had a very successful career until you were attacked on stage, isn't that so? With all the arrangements to get you here safely and coordinate your arrival time, this important fact had slipped my mind. Of course, we can arrange for you to met Mr. Raoul Norok, if you desire."

"Not a bad idea," conceded Frederic, "being in a strange city, my wife and children might enjoy meeting a friendly soul. And Mr. Norok truly is a good friend of ours."

"I suggest that we first find your accommodations, then you can use the phone to make your desired connections."

They were driving through a beautiful neighborhood; the trees bordering the wide avenue stood in full fall colors. Many dahlias and asters beckoned over low garden walls. Finally, Mr. Green turned into a driveway and pulled up to a friendly-looking, semi-detached house which sported hydrangeas alongside the entrance. He produced a key and led them into a spacious foyer, from which doors opened on both sides, and a staircase led up to the second story. He said, "We thought you might enjoy your stay here for a few days. By the beginning of next week, we surely will have a supply flight going to Tel Aviv, and we hope that you will be on it."

"This is a lovely place," Cornelia observed. "Does anybody else share it with us?"

"No, Madame, this is entirely at your disposal. Make yourselves comfortable, and let us know whether you need any other conveniences. We understand that you could only bring the most essential items with you."

Romi and Irmi were looking curiously into the rooms off the foyer, when Romi called, "Mama, here is even a baby grand piano for you!"

"And the kitchen is so much nicer than our dreary one in Lyons," Irmi added.

"There is a delicatessen not far from here, should you desire to purchase some groceries. We stocked the fridge with some basic items: milk, butter, and eggs. Also, there are canned soups in the pantry and a loaf of bread. But we didn't buy fruits or veggies because we didn't know for sure whether you would make it in time," Mr. Green said. Then he asked, "Mr. Bartok were you able to exchange some of your money into English currency?"

"Yes, we brought sufficient funds with us," Frederic replied.

"I had no idea!" whispered Cornelia in Czech into her husband's ear. "We will be in need of transportation," she said out loud, "is there a bus stop or tram nearby?"

"Yes, Madame, around the corner is the stop, not even a five-minute walk away." Then Mr. Green bid them farewell, closed the door, and left them to their own devices. Romi came skipping down the steps, saying, "There are three bedrooms upstairs, and they are really lovely. There is one for you, Papa and Mama, one for Irmi and me with twin beds, and even one to spare, with a very nice bathroom besides. I really like this house, don't you?"

"We need to freshen up and get settled before we go out; but I suggest that we try to reach Raoul. Perhaps he is free and could visit for a little while," said Frederic.

"There is only one bit of news I need to ask you about, dear Frederic. Here we are with plans to leave Europe for good, but what about the dear Cohens? Are they coming soon too?" asked Cornelia.

"Dearest, their plans have changed. It seems that Davide listened to Nathan, who plans on immigrating to Argentina. Nathan persuaded his dad to go with him, because he thinks that Jews will be assimilated in a much better way in Argentina than in Israel, where he thinks many troubles lie ahead. Nathan has enough funds to support his Dad, his sister, and himself. So the agreement for now is that Davide will be co-owner of the bank in Tel Aviv. I will share profits with him, and, in due time, he will either be paid off, or come and join us in the Promised Land. All of this is due to our God's leading."

"This is an unexpected turn of events!" Cornelia conceded. "And I know we all will miss the Cohens. "We must pray that their lives and ours will be in God's perfect will!"

When they tried to reach Raoul sometime later, he was home, and yes, he wasn't singing tonight. He was delighted to hear that the Bartoks were in town. Two hours later he joined them. There was much to share before he invited them to go for a drive around the old, historic town they had come to visit. "I really have gotten to like old London," said Raoul, as he chauffeured them around in his Rolls Royce, going first by Buckingham Palace and the British Museum, and ending at Covent Garden.

"You have to see where I spend my evenings," Raoul said. "And come to think of it, Frederic, you actually have been the catalyst that made me apply here, at the Royal Opera House. If it hadn't be for your warning when I came to visit you in Prague that long ago day, I would have never left Vienna. And only five years later, the despot from Germany snatched up that small country, then Czechoslovakia, and now Poland, and it has not been bloodless!"

He had parked the car in front of Covent Garden and led them through a stage entrance into that famous theatre. As it was afternoon, there were not many people around. Although Raoul was not performing this particular evening, the Royal Sadler Wells Ballet would be appearing on the big stage in Tchaikovsky's *Swan Lake* this very night.

They opened a side door and found themselves behind the voluminous curtain on the main stage. Raoul intoned, just for fun, "Summertime" from *Porgy and Bess*, Gershwin's musical. On the spur of the moment, Cornelia circled the stage, singing her solo. They joined in this improvised duet, while Frederic and the children watched the proceedings. But they were not alone, the conductor for the evening's performance had arrived early, and hearing these two magnificent voices, stopped and listened as well. It was a spellbinding scene, and he did not interrupt. When later he stepped forward, and Raoul introduced him, he couldn't believe that the well-known Cornelia Kahn was present.

"Madame," he said, "I have known of your artistry and your giftedness, but hearing you in person surpasses all of that. If it was up to me, I would beg you sincerely to consider remaining with us to brighten our stage with your talented presence." Then turning to Raoul, he asked, "Sir, could you persuade Madame Kahn to sing for us in the benefit next week. You heard that Elisabeth Rethberg, who was to come from the Met in New York, has cancelled due to ill health."

"But my dear friend Cornelia is just passing through," Raoul remonstrated. "She is to fly to Tel Aviv with her husband and children next week."

"Nevertheless, we don't know whether London audiences would ever have the chance to hear the Nightingale from Prague, if she leaves the European continent." And addressing Cornelia, who had returned to her husband and children, he asked, "Madame, may I introduce myself. I am Constant Lambert, presently on the podium for all ballet performances. Did you follow Raoul's and my conversation? We have a benefit planned in which Raoul graciously consented to participate, as it benefits the refugees. But the famous Rethberg, who had agreed to come, has backed out due to illness. So we are minus one of our biggest drawing cards."

Then turning to Frederic he added, "Sir, I understand you are just passing through on your way to the Middle East. What would you say if your wife was willing to help us out?"

Here Irmi broke in, saying, "Mama, you have done so many benefits. Perhaps God Almighty will reward you if you help poor people by singing."

Cornelia, hearing these pleas, looked at her husband questioningly. Her black eyes were luminous.

Frederic said, "This is entirely my wife's decision and probably dependent on when the arrangements for our flight to Israel have been completed. If she decides to do it, we will surely not stand in the way. She has my full support either way."

"Madame, if you give me permission, I will inquire whether we could submit your name for our program. Would you have perhaps three numbers available that would not require excessive rehearsal time?"

"Knowing my friend Cornelia, "Raoul interjected," she has not only three lovely solos, but also a violin concerto ready to perform, don't you, Dear?" As she nodded in reply, he added, "We went to school together, and Cornelia always had her assignments ready and memorized before the rest of the class. I know the scope of her repertoire, and she still excels in that.

"We had better inquire of Mr. Green, whether he sees such a performance as a possibility. Of course, we must know date, time, and place before we do this," Frederic suggested. That same afternoon they were notified that their flight to Tel Aviv/Yaffa had been arranged. Because bomb attacks were feared on London in the near future, they would fly out the coming Monday at 6 am. That ended the short hope for Cornelia to be part of the benefit performance.

Raoul assured them that other artists had promised their contributions, especially as this was to benefit the refugees that were steadily coming into England from points east. Constant Lambert, the conductor, was chagrined that he was not able to conduct music for the famous prima donna from Czechoslovakia, but he understood that the flight to Israel had to be undertaken before greater restrictions were enforced.

Monday found the Bartok family overflying France, Italy, and the blue Mediterranean. The British cargo plane, which sported only compartment-like seating arrangements for civilians, was filled with returning troops and civilians. There was not a seat to spare. When they landed on Israeli soil, the Bartok family expected nobody to herald their coming; but at the customs gate, when the dust had cleared and their fellow passengers had disbursed, there were Francois, Hannah and Max. What a wonderful surprise!

Cornelia, after greeting Francois and the children, knelt down on the dusty Tel Aviv harbor road and said, "This moment must not pass. I have longed to set my feet on the ground of this special piece of real estate, God's own land, for so long. Let me kiss this precious soil as my first act of showing that I want to serve my Lord here with all my heart." And while the family looked on, Frederic joined her, and they both kissed the ground of their new homeland.

Francois was driving Mr. Levi's car, an aged Rolls Royce. He quickly loaded their few pieces of luggage and had them sit in the spacious car. He drove directly to the home that Mr. Levi had procured for them on a rental basis. It was a spacious, white, sandstone building, surrounded by a high wall. When they stopped in front of a tall, wrought iron gate, Max jumped out and opened it, allowing the car to drive in.

The first thing they saw was Bernie, standing in front of their new home, dressed in a light-green frock, her blond hair in a French twist, holding a white-clad bundle. She was joyous, seeing her friends and former employers, the Bartoks and their dear twin daughters. They in turn exclaimed, "The baby is here!"

"We had not heard."

"Francois told us nothing!"

"What a beautiful surprise."

Hannah said, "Our Imma Bernie had the baby on the boat! He is now two weeks old!"

"So it is a little boy," Cornelia said, "Congratulations to the whole Leclerq Family!"

"Yes," Hannah said, "his name is Joseph Nathan Leclerq. And both Max and I are permitted to hold him sometimes."

Warm hugs and kisses were exchanged, and the beautiful baby boy was handed around. It was a very joyful reunion.

Mr. Levi had been of great help during the past few days. He had found and rented this suitable house, which had five bedrooms, three baths, and beautiful, airy living quarters. It was an answer to their prayers. Francois had been able to assist in furnishing the bedrooms and had persuaded the owner to leave some of the needed living room and entrance hall furnishings.

When they all sat down for supper, prepared by Francois and the children, they joined in a prayer of thanksgiving. Then while the dishes were handed around the large table, there was an exchange of all the latest happenings in both families. All were aware that their Odyssey had ended.

CPSIA information can be obtained
at www.ICGtesting.com
Printed in the USA
FSOW01n1747160215
5254FS

9 781490 801131